R. K. NARAYAN

A Tiger for Malgudi
and
The Man-eater of Malgudi

Introduction by PICO IYER

PENGUIN BOOKS

PENGUIN BOOKS
Published by the Penguin Group
Penguin Group (USA) Inc., 375 Hudson Street, New York, New York 10014, U.S.A. • Penguin Group
(Canada), 90 Eglinton Avenue East, Suite 700, Toronto, Ontario, Canada M4P 2Y3 (a division of Pearson
Penguin Canada Inc.) • Penguin Books Ltd, 80 Strand, London WC2R 0RL, England • Penguin Ireland,
25 St Stephen's Green, Dublin 2, Ireland (a division of Penguin Books Ltd) • Penguin Group (Australia),
250 Camberwell Road, Camberwell, Victoria 3124, Australia (a division of Pearson Australia Group
Pty Ltd) • Penguin Books India Pvt Ltd, 11 Community Centre, Panchsheel Park, New Delhi – 110 017,
India • Penguin Group (NZ), 67 Apollo Drive, Rosedale, North Shore 0632, New Zealand (a division of
Pearson New Zealand Ltd) • Penguin Books (South Africa) (Pty) Ltd, 24 Sturdee Avenue, Rosebank,
Johannesburg 2196, South Africa

Penguin Books Ltd, Registered Offices:
80 Strand, London WC2R 0RL, England

This volume first published in Penguin Books (USA) 2009

1 3 5 7 9 10 8 6 4 2

The Man-Eater of Malgudi first published in the United States of America by The Viking Press 1961
First published in Great Britain by William Heinemann Ltd 1961
Published in Penguin Books (UK) 1983
Published in Penguin Books (USA) 1983
Copyright © R. K. Narayan, 1961
Copyright renewed R. K. Narayan, 1989
All rights reserved

A Tiger for Malgudi first published in Great Britain by William Heinemann Ltd 1983
First published in the United States of America by The Viking Press 1983
Published in Penguin Books (UK) 1984
Published in Penguin Books (USA) 1984
Copyright © R. K. Narayan, 1982, 1983
All rights reserved

The introduction to *A Tiger for Malgudi* originally appeared in *Vassar Quarterly*. In the United States a
selection from *A Tiger for Malgudi* first appeared in *The Missouri Review*.

Introduction copyright © Pico Iyer, 2009
All rights reserved

Publisher's Note
This is a work of fiction. Names, characters, places, and incidents either are the product of the author's
imagination or are used fictitiously, and any resemblance to actual persons, living or dead, business
establishments, events, or locales is entirely coincidental.

LIBRARY OF CONGRESS CATALOGING IN PUBLICATION DATA
Narayan, R. K., 1906–2001.
A tiger for Malgudi ; and, The man-eater of Malgudi / R.K. Narayan ; introduction by Pico Iyer.
p. cm.—(Penguin classics)
ISBN 978-0-14-310580-0
1. Malgudi (India : Imaginary place) —Fiction. 2. Tigers—Fiction. I. Narayan, R. K., 1906–2001.
Man-eater of Malgudi. II. Title. III. Title: Man-eater of Malgudi.
PR9499.3.N3A6 2009
823'.912—dc22   2009014280

Printed in the United States of America • Set in Adobe Sabon

Contents

Introduction:
The Conjuror of Lives

A few years ago, in a small town in northern India, I met a man who lived in a tiny guesthouse. He was small, nut-brown, and had a high forehead that accentuated his air of eager intensity. Every evening he stood on the rooftop of the Kalsang guesthouse and offered yoga lessons to anyone ready to pay two dollars or so. Every morning, too. It was a town full of foreigners, so he was never short of students and when I followed his handwritten flyer up to the roof, one sunset in spring, it was to find him turning himself into a human pretzel, while a large-boned boy from Iowa in front of him tried to do the same.

Gobi worked every winter in Goa, on the beach, he told me; he came to Dharamsala, in the foothills of the Himalayas, in the spring. "I am honest man, sir," he said disarmingly. "Good teacher also. Ask him."

"Sure," said the kid from Dubuque, waking up. "He helped my girlfriend lose five pounds in a month. You should try it."

Gobi had no wife or children, he volunteered; no moorings. He traveled from run-down guesthouse to guesthouse, in towns full of backpackers, offering his services for less than half what others charged and living like something of an ascetic. The more I saw of him in the month that followed, the more I was startled: He seemed to have no criminal intent whatsoever, only good nature, plenty of philosophical maxims, and a kind of pious innocence.

When I returned the following spring to Dharamsala, however, there was no sign of my new friend at all. On almost my last night in town, though, on Temple Road, suddenly I felt a hand on my arm, and there was a familiar face by my side, saying, "Sir, sir, I am waiting to talk to you. I have so many things to ask you, sir."

"Really?"

"Really, sir. I want to ask you so many questions."

I invited him to a nearby tea stall and Gobi told me how he had been pushed out of town, through some unexpected turn of events, how he was staying in an even tinier room in the town below, how he was living with almost nothing, pursued by what sounded like enemies and upholders of the law at once. This strikingly sweet and generous soul seemed to be living as a fugitive (and no questions emerged from him at all, only a torrent of answers).

I didn't know what exactly to make of the man, so shifting a mixture of unexpected kindness and shady circumstances, until I remembered that I had met him before, a hundred times over, in the pages of the first Indian writer who had ever made his town my own, R. K. Narayan. Not just Gobi, of course: I had met my mother's tailor there, my uncles' neighbors, the South Indian priest who wrote to me once (after I wrote an essay in *Time* magazine on affirmative action), asking for "*Playboy*-style pictures of yourself." Long before Indian writers were everywhere in London and New York, decades before call centers and yoga teachers and sandaled pilgrims were a familiar part of the West's story of itself, Narayan had been giving us a small town, Malgudi, where gods and everyday layabouts were mingling as feuding friends and where their daily dramas of hope and frustration might have been taking place down any street.

The two novels you will find in this volume are separated by more than twenty years in Narayan's career: *The Man-eater of Malgudi,* published in 1961, when he was fifty-four, is classic, vintage Narayan, of a piece with nearly all his work, where *A Tiger for Malgudi,* from 1983, when he was in his mid-seventies, is very much a late work, placing a frame around all that has come before. But for all the shift in perspective, both are really just pieces, all but interchangeable, in a vast canvas that Narayan spent his life filling in, a human cosmology of sorts, a *Ramayana* for mortals. Time was largely suspended in his world—

there are no clocks—and very little changes, even as sudden events shake the lives of his characters, and so our own, on every page. It's possible, in fact, to say that Narayan was not just a world-class novelist, constantly mentioned for the Nobel, but also a kind of village storyteller, an archivist for the small town that you will find in Chinua Achebe's West Africa as much as in Gabriel García Márquez's Colombia. Part of his special art was to suggest that all he was doing was enjoying his daily stroll—from the bookseller's to the stationer's to the printer's, for three or four hours every morning—and simply recording the stories, the dramas and questions that came to him en route.

Born in Madras in 1906, Rasipuram Krishnaswami Narayanaswami Iyer, as he was sonorously called, was shipped off before he was three to live with a grandmother and an uncle—and, as he later remembered it, a peacock and a monkey, who, he claimed, were his closest friends (he chattered to the monkey every day when he came back from school, he said—and the monkey chattered back). Like the friendly and feckless characters in so many of his stories, he failed his high-school English exams—not a good augury for the son of a schoolmaster—and later, having somehow completed his studies at the Maharaja of Mysore's College, gave up his inherited career of teaching after all of three days.

Having announced, to the consternation of all, that he was going to take up writing—licensed dreaming, in effect—he bought an exercise book on a day chosen by his grandmother for its auspiciousness and commenced. His first book, *Swami and Friends,* was rejected everywhere in London, however, and he instructed an Indian friend at Oxford to cast it into the Thames. Much as in an R. K. Narayan story, the friend gave it instead to Graham Greene, then in the early stages of his own novel-writing career, and the delighted English novelist not only sold it to a publisher, but also became Narayan's lifelong champion and adviser.

It is the mark of a Narayan story, though, that the sunshine is never unqualified. In 1939 the novelist's beloved wife of four years, Rajam, died of typhoid, leaving Narayan to raise a small daughter, Hema, alone. For a while the writer was so distraught he could not put pen to paper; it was even feared that he might try to throw himself onto his wife's funeral pyre. In time, though—and again his life seems to be walking side by side with his art—he found a medium, who put him in touch with his departed partner, and the words began to flow again.

For more than a half century, the flow seldom abated, as the single man serenely went about his daily routine, writing for only an hour or two every afternoon, and giving his barely legible scrawls to a six-foot-tall local giant to type up. With success, he was constantly being invited to travel, to teach, to come and be feted in the West—Greta Garbo asked him to show her how to meditate—but Narayan preferred to stay close to home, turning the adventures of his friends and neighbors into more than a dozen novels, as well as stories, a memoir (*My Days*), and retellings of classical tales. Like his younger brother, R. K. Laxman—long India's most celebrated cartoonist—he appeared to realize that he could not function without his constantly amusing and surprising community any more than it could function without him. He died, not far from where he was born, in 2001, at the age of ninety-four.

When you pick up, let's say, *The Man-eater of Malgudi*—or any of Narayan's work—you quickly see that *Homo Narayanus,* as the life story suggests, is an "in-between type," a man (nearly always) not notably rich or desperately poor, living in a small town with modest goals and mostly modest gifts. His only wish, here as always, is to get by, with as little fuss and pressure as possible—Narayan figures like to chat and idle more than to join in the push and thrust of life—but, such is the nature of the complex universe, just getting by involves slipping a coin to the *jutka* driver or outwitting the wife or mother who has designs upon his peace. She, too, after all—and the journalist, the headmaster, the dog called Attila—are also trying to get by and it is the nature of their small community (and, in fact, of the Hindu worldview) that all their destinies are intertwined.

As soon as one creature moves, in short, everything else is

shaken, with the result that life can never be as peaceable as most of these characters (like Nataraj in *The Man-eater*) would like. And the smallest attempt to change one's circumstances can have cacophonous repercussions in a world order where everything has its place. Narayan's creatures make daily offerings to the gods and observe most of the ritual pieties of their Hindu universe—*The Man-eater* carefully begins with this—but every hope or plan or shortcut they conceive threatens to upset a framework that has been set there by gods who seem as capricious (or sometimes merely as confounding and erratic) as themselves. Malfunctioning Municipality Offices and quid pro quos may be the official makers of chaos in Malgudi—the wish to change the town's street names in the wake of Indian independence means that everyone gets lost—but the real carriers of mayhem are the local versions of Jupiter and Mars.

The result is a tangle of ironies and unintended consequences that can drive even the mildest-mannered, most law-abiding man (like Nataraj) mad. An office worker, in one typical Narayan story, promises to take his little girl to the cinema, but then he suddenly gets a raise, as he's about to threaten to resign, and the upshot of his good fortune is that he cannot return home to fulfill his promise, and the child waits and waits, brokenhearted, in her best dress. An archetypal Narayan character who can never pass his exams, and is the butt of every local joke, can finally take it no more and pens a suicide note—though on this occasion, inexplicably, he has passed at last. A thief picks pockets just to give sweets and books to his children—and to offer some coins to a beggar—and it is only when, in a sudden spasm of conscience, he tries to *return* the money he has taken that he gets apprehended and taken to prison.

At some level, all these Everymen are living (in ways literal and metaphorical) in a small, half-lit settlement encircled by forest. And the gods who seem to be placing traps and barbed-wire fences on every side—as in ancient Greece or Shakespeare's England—only compound this sense of an unexpectedly crowded universe in which the simplest and most tranquil of worlds (as at the beginning of *The Man-eater*) soon comes to seem almost impossibly congested. By circumstance and by nature Narayan's characters are hostage to children, to neighbors, to parents and friends (a conundrum that Graham Greene would have recognized), and if ever they try to break free of them, they are reminded that they can no more escape the iron laws of karma than you can munch on apples in Eden. It is a feature of Narayan's universe—as of Graham Greene's—that it turns much more upon male friendship than upon romance, and the fact that nearly all the figures we see on Abu Road, or chatting at the Boardless Hotel, come from the same small Hindu system means that it is a compact model of a world.

The key word in all the work might be "limitation": Narayan is a poet of circumscription. His people seldom travel or even glance beyond the small, not unpleasant bounds of their community. The outside world seldom impinges on them—past and future are mostly a matter of local stories and astrologers—so they are bounded in time, as well. The tales themselves have a wonderful roundedness and sense of control, in which they simply proceed from beginning to middle to end, with few digressions or moments of introspection or signs of authorial strain. We lazily call Hinduism a doctrine of fatalism, but in Narayan's world at least it is really one where people don't know, or refuse to accept, their fates and so, in their innocence, make plans that are at variance with whatever destinies have been marked out for them.

You don't have to be a Hindu to appreciate any of these universal tangles, but Hinduism seems to have given Narayan the fixed and clearly bordered field in which his art could make merry. And the faithful, orthodox vision underlying the work gives it a strength that his many more sophisticated imitators cannot match. When V. S. Naipaul began writing—as he has often, and generously, said—he could find few precedents for English-language fiction from those of Indian ancestry other than that of Narayan (Narayan was a "comfort and example," he later wrote; "he always appeared to be writing from within his culture. . . . He truly possessed his world. It was complete and always there, waiting for him"). Yet Naipaul did not believe in gods, and so his tales of small-town shopkeepers and dreamers quickly turn into much more brittle stories of ambition and humiliation. The self-made man has a ruthlessness and cynicism in Naipaul that cannot exist in Narayan's more peaceful order, and Naipaul's characters are always competing, fiercely, against themselves and others, where in Narayan's world, larger forces, felt if rarely seen, keep everyone and everything in place.

Naipaul, too, even in his fond and humorous early work, has a much more wide-ranging sense of disenchantment; part of the beauty, the particular power, of Narayan's vision is that he is wryly unillusioned about men, but seems imperturbably accepting of the order in which they find themselves. In later years, Naipaul would criticize his first mentor for creating a static, almost mythic world that took no note of the historical convulsions and postcolonial flux that became Naipaul's great subject. But that is akin to saying that *The Odyssey* is not topical enough. Narayan's intention is not political, but human, which is to say, religious; his concern is always less with circumstances, which change, than with patterns of behavior, which don't. It's intrinsic to the instantly familiar world he creates, in fact, that it take place not in Mysore (which might be known to most English-language readers), but in make-believe Malgudi (which is not); as Graham Greene surely recognized, Narayan writes to us from a place that is less likely to be found on any Rand McNally map than somewhere inside every reader.

The Man-eater of Malgudi is for me one of the clearest and most engaging illustrations of how Narayan polished his daily observations into art. Although his native language was Tamil (as was his characters'), he writes in an English that puts you instantly within the rickety stalls and aromatic streets of almost anywhere in India today. This is a world of "semi-VIPs" and "nondescripts"—each of the phrases sums up a world—in which the smallest phrase ("edibles" or "domestic felicity") reminds you of how India's great talkers and lovers of literature, often with a copy of Max Muller or Plato on their desks, have always managed to remake the English language to their advantage. "Government office is not your nuptial chamber, for you to demand things," one character says (in *A Tiger for Malgudi*), and somehow the smell of strong tea, the wooden desks, the peeling posters of an Indian office are instantly all around you.

Writing in English, perhaps, allowed Narayan to step just an inch outside his territory, and to give us the larger perspective that puts all his *tonga*-drivers' deeds in place. The other thing that strikes you, within three pages of the beginning of *The Man-eater,* is how you can hear the jingling ox bells, smell the spices, see the humble scene with "appetizing eatable on a banana leaf and coffee in a little brass cup." You can feel the scratch of a character's "blue bush shirt and dhoti," imagine a boy being taught to buy sugar every morning to feed ants, hear the kind of well-meaning dreamer who says, sorrowfully, "I could never be a successful enemy to anyone."

"A lorry was passing down the road," Narayan writes, in a typically brushstroked moment of scene-setting, "raising a blanket of cloud; a couple of *jutkas* were rattling along on their wooden wheels; two vagrants had stretched themselves on the parapet of the fountain, enjoying a siesta; a little boy was watching his lamb graze on the lawn which the municipality was struggling to cultivate by the margin of the fountain; a crow sat on top of the fountain, hopefully looking for a drop of water. It was an ideal hour for a transaction in junk."

There are snake-charmers and swamis and elephant-doctors here, but none of them are seen as more unusual than a knife-sharpener or a seller of "coloured drinks"; everything is regarded with the imperturbable good nature of a man just looking in on his neighbors. In that way, the exoticism of India is never Narayan's selling point or his interest; he writes of—and seemingly for—his associates as you or I might write of the Lower East Side or the area where I live in Japan. Again, I can hear my South Indian uncles speaking fondly of their wives as "The President of the Union" (or "The Speaker of the House") and catch all that is engaging and heartfelt in India when I read of the tough guy devouring a hundred almonds every day to train to become a taxidermist, the poet trying to write the entire life of Krishna (the completion of even a part of which causes mayhem), the forestry officer making up a collection of "Golden Thoughts," arranged alphabetically. The textures and flavors and cadences are as Indian as palaver or hugger-mugger; the dramas and hopes and vexations belong to us all.

Reading Narayan, *The Man-eater* reminds you, is a little like sitting on a rocking chair in a steadily churning train; the story is always pushing forward, with not a wasted sentence or detail, and yet its theme and often its characters are all about going nowhere and getting nothing done. There is a kind of ambling inevitability to the rhythm of a Narayan story, sleepy but intensifying, that at once evokes a leisurely and mischievous master plotter and puts you inside the frenzied, but changeless, world of India today. The fortune-tellers and astrologers who are such a staple of this world are always figures of gentle fun because no one can begin to predict what's going to happen next. People learn to rue their acts of kindness and are constantly urged, for the good of all, to be cruel. No good deed goes uncomplicated and no sin is ever overlooked.

You can see very soon how and why Graham Greene, patron saint of the honest thief and the likeable layabout, whose characters long to believe in the mercy and logic of a benign God, but are hard-pressed to do so in the midst of an unraveling world, would have found his Indian brother in the creator of Malgudi. The son of a headmaster himself, always preoccupied with waywardness, unable to turn away from his lost sinners and schemers because he so keenly feels their vulnerability, Greene became Narayan's great supporter and friend for more than fifty years, though they did not meet for more than twenty. When the Tiger from Malgudi's Master says, "People only follow their inclinations, and sooner or later find their reward or retribution. That's the natural law of life, as inevitable as the ripening of a mango in its season or the fall of a withered leaf," he might be offering us Greene's central sacrament; and when the English novelist told an interviewer once, "My own wish always is to produce a central figure who represents some idea of reasonable simplicity—a mythical figure, if you like," he might have been speaking for Narayan.

Narayan, like his British friend, refuses to push his people into boxes or make of them cartoons; when a priest is encountered, he is never seen as a straight con man, and rarely regarded as a true sage, but, much more interestingly, depicted as both at once. There is an uncle's shrewd compassion underlying the work of both writers that begins to explain why both of them so often show us muddled men trying to protect their daughters, and why nothing is seen as evil except those grand abstractions—the far-off government, the Controller, Providence itself—that sometimes treat human beings as abstractions.

Narayan's world isn't, after all, about people immune from time, but rather about people seen in their relation to something more than time; the writer registered the changes that come into Malgudi—we see in *A Tiger* a hunter who's lived in America, a "Cine-Director" whose visiting card gives off a sandalwood perfume, even an allusion, startling, to Roman Polanski—but looked for those qualities and dramas that endure (the week I read his account of a stampede at a religious festival, the newspapers brought me reports of a stampede that had just killed 145 at a religious festival in India). Often, in fact, he points out how his ageless figures, going about their immemorial rounds, are suddenly co-opted by the noncyclical, forward-rushing designs of governments—and the saddest, most shocking Narayan story I know is of a knife-sharpener committed in his innocence to forced sterilization.

We smile, inevitably, at the antic piety when a man vows in his devotion to a goddess. But then we recall that the promise arises from the fact that the poor man has seen six children die before their first birthday.

When Naipaul called Narayan a "natural writer," one thing he might have been thinking of was his economy. Within a few paragraphs of the beginning of *The Man-eater* we know everything we need to know about most of the characters and they are ready to walk off the page and back into their lives. And when, in a story, Narayan writes, calmly, "The compartment built to 'seat 8 passengers; 4 British Troops, or 6 Indian Troops' now carried only nine," I'm not sure whether I admire more the "only" or the way he's captured colonialism in one quiet phrase. Part of the poignancy of his "bullock cart drivers and cobblers and ragamuffins" is that they are nearly always the victims not of evil, but of their own foibles or good nature, and though Narayan wrote many short stories, he seemed to need the larger space of the novel to catch the particular logic of India's cheerful complication, whereby the printer has to fob off the fruit-juice man so that he can tend to the poet who needs his "little exercise books stitched by himself and wrapped in brown paper" taken care of.

The way he braids together the innocence, the aspirations, the vexations, and the friendships of these guileless rogues, with such seeming ease, may begin to explain how and why Narayan has influenced later writers in ways much more dramatic and lasting than his modest habits and ambitions would suggest. Kiran Desai, who would win the Man Booker Prize with her second novel, *The Inheritance of Loss,* writes very much in the shadow of Narayan, and of his most famous novel, *The Guide,* in her debut, *Hullabaloo in the Guava Orchard;* Hanif Kureishi seems to be working from the same model—and bringing it to his own distinctively swarming, multicultural London—in his most striking novel, *The Buddha of Suburbia.* Yann Martel's popular Booker Prize winner, *The Life of Pi,* turns upon the very Malgudi-ish figures of a tiger and a human sharing a lifeboat, and Alexander McCall Smith's stories of southern Africa are hard to imagine, in their tender dailiness, without Narayan on his desk.

When Narayan's books first began to appear, there wasn't even an appropriate place for them on the shelves; in my local research library in California, he is placed next to Middleton Murray and Saki—not far from Maugham—in the regular patch reserved for "English literature," because when he arrived, there was no "postcolonial" or "Commonwealth writing" section set aside for people called Rushdie or Seth or Roy. Yet when I read Rohinton Mistry's deeply affecting stories of cobblers, trying to get by in a corrupt and overwhelming India, I can't fail to see the shadow of Malgudi coming to modern Bombay, and Narayan's shade is there, too, hovering behind at least one story—of a tour guide—in Jhumpa Lahiri's Pulitzer Prize–winning first collection of tales. V. S. Naipaul's first book, *The Mystic Masseur,* seems almost a West Indian transcription of Narayan, with its drifting small-town characters, its local feuds, its main figure suddenly taken for a miracle worker. Though Naipaul later, in a gracious obituary for *Time* magazine, called his first mentor the "Gandhi of modern Indian literature," his first book, as clear and direct in its storytelling as Narayan, actually creates a far-off character called "Narayan," the editor of a local magazine called *The Hindu* and a rival who is rattled by the rise of an upstart writer who sounds quite a bit like Naipaul himself.

For me, the great crowning achievement of this lifelong project— the final piece in the collective portrait of Malgudi—is *A Tiger for Malgudi,* not just because it has an old man's valedictory air to it, a sense of summation, but, even more, because it is the rare work by Narayan that rises a little bit above Malgudi to place the small town and its surroundings in a larger, almost cosmic perspective. The circus at the center of it becomes the perfect distillation of Malgudi, its animals observing their own hierarchy as scrupulously as the postman, the exorcist, and the ribbon-seller might, and a difficult-to-please Captain making the main character jump through hoops or sit in place, for no good reason, just as the gods seem to do with mortals. The poor tiger is more than ready to take instruction without being hit, but, like every Malgudi-ite, he cannot find a way to convey this to his bosses.

Throughout Narayan's work, the lines between animals and people are completely porous, and we see that the hyena, the snake, and the monkey are as much a part of the latticework of living things as are all the other beings with two paws. "Most animals and men are alike," as an animal doctor calmly notes in *The Man-eater,* "only the dosage of a medicine differs." In that regard, it may not be surprising to find a "chimp in tuxedo and wearing spectacles" lecturing a tiger on the virtues of vegetarianism and nonviolence.

Part of the beauty of the story, I think, comes from the way Narayan so easily offers us the tiger's heart and voice that Raja the "miracle tiger" very quickly comes to seem almost identical to the two-legged Rajus and Ramus and Ramas and Raos at the center of all the other stories. "I know only my corner and whatever passes before me," the great cat says on the first page, and we hear the voice of the printer in the earlier novel, or any of the other shopkeepers on Market Road (perhaps even of the writer himself). The zoo in which the tiger finds himself is not so different from the confinements they find themselves in, and as always Narayan lavishes so much human fondness on every creature that it's hard to remember whether Kumar is an elephant or a vendor of sweets (he's an elephant, as it happens), or whether a man or a dog is the poor creature being thrown out of a house (a man, very often).

This is, again, part of the worldview of Hinduism, and one reason why Narayan, a good orthodox Hindu, was a vegetarian; all "sentient beings" are linked together, part of the same community, and it doesn't seem improbable to anyone in Malgudi that in a past life a tiger might be the brother of a sage (or that it's worth remaining on the right side of a dog, because he might be your cousin in the next). Somewhat like the tales of Aesop—or, for that matter, the *Jataka Tales* of Buddhism—the stories of Narayan's India assume that animals can play out fables of longing and duty as much as humans do; in the great Hindu epic, say, *The Ramayana,* which Narayan retold in one book, the assistant of the god Rama is the monkey-god Hanuman. In California, where I write this, I was told only this morning how to act if I met a mountain lion along the road on my daily walk, and a few days ago was ushered into a little dining room that had a bear's fresh paw marks all over its door.

It doesn't take long, in the volume you now carry, to notice that the "man-eater" of one title proves, in fact, to be a human, while the tiger of the other is in fact as endearing as any other Panza or Quixote here, an everyday shopkeeper in disguise. To the tiger, of course, men are as scary and disruptive as to the people in the streets of Malgudi the tiger is a "devil" with wings, a terrifying intruder. Narayan's central character in *A Tiger for Malgudi* muses on how human beings are always pontificating, in their ignorance (or innocence), of tigers' ways, of which they know nothing, and in the process suggests that he is guilty of the same tendency.

The lovely surprise of this late work is that even a tiger, in

Narayan's benign universe (as settled, at times, and even as un-
fallen as that of P. G. Wodehouse, though its dramas carry
much larger stakes than those of Bertie Wooster), seems a good-
natured, if frightened, soul, just trying to find his right place in
the world. And in the Master that he follows—all the way to
vegetarianism and Gandhian nonviolence—he brings us toward
a conclusion that all Narayan's work has been leading up to. In
most Malgudi stories, the very appearance of capital letters—as
in the Chairman of the Municipal Council or the District Superintendent of Police, not to mention the Department of Animal Welfare, World Q.R.L. (World Quadruped Relief League,
Calif.)—spells trouble. But the Master is someone who seems
to have earned the honor, having completed the "householder"
stage of life, as Hinduism recommends, and then gone off to
become a wise man.

This being Narayan, even a meditating ascetic comes with a
pleading wife, a quick tongue for flunkies, and a clutch of obli-
gations that he seems to be neglecting. But his sharp reminders
to everyone that you cannot write even a tiger off as a "brute"
or a "beast" and the laws he lays down, amidst his verses from
The Bhagavad-Gita, all suggest an open sincerity in Narayan
as he neared the end of his days. The Master is the rare figure
in Malgudi who is not an everyday bungler and who lives apart
from the vagaries of the town around him; indeed, he is the
rare character who seems irked by the respect and adoration of
others (a little as his maker was).

In some writers the sage philosophizing of the Master might
seem like speechifying, or a heavy-handed imposition of a
moral, a message, on a story that ought to have a life of its
own. And to some readers the Master's advice to his new, furry
disciple—that the imprisonment of the zoo is a kind of protection, and that it is wiser to accept the boundaries around us
than to choose the hazards of the open road—might sound con-
servative, old-fashioned. And yet it is the very enclosedness of
Narayan's world, its sense of firm laws governing everything
and a larger cycle of reward and retribution playing through
things that accounts in part for its charm, its serenity, the comfort it offers. There is an odd sense of protectedness at play

here that makes us feel that a hidden logic is working itself out and everything will end up half okay.

V. S. Naipaul would find rootlessness and flux to be his great theme—his home—and his books draw for their strength on their anguish and their passion. Narayan, by comparison, admits us to a more settled order under the jurisdiction of forces we can't understand, but still can't cross. I think of Gobi, my disarming new friend in Dharamsala, and remember how, every time I saw him—with no firm prospects or family to support him—he always seemed to be walking toward Temple Road, or away from it, with a smile.

PICO IYER

A TIGER FOR MALGUDI

To Charles Pick,
who, to my great joy,
brought me to the windmill again

Introduction

During the Kumbh Mela festival, which recurs every twelve years at the confluence of the three rivers Ganga, Yamuna, and Saraswati in Allahabad, a vast crowd gathers for a holy bath in the rivers. Amidst that ocean of humanity also arrives a hermit with his companion, a tiger. He does not hold the animal on a leash since he claims they were brothers in previous lives. The tiger freely moves about without hurting or scaring anyone.

Such a combination seemed incredible when I read reports of it and saw the photographs. But as I got used to the idea, I began to speculate on its possibilities for a novel. Also I came across a few other instances of enduring friendship between tigers and human beings. This theme was on my mind in a general way, but it narrowed down to a specific issue about a year ago, when I came upon a bookmark, a four-inch-long strip of cardboard with the picture of a young tiger pleading, "I'd love to get into a good book." That sounded like a hint from the Muses (if they care for novelists too). I said to the young tiger, "Surely you will get into my book, but the goodness of the book itself I can't guarantee."

It also occurred to me that with a few exceptions here and there, humans have monopolized the attention of fiction writers. Man in his smugness never imagines for a moment that other creatures may also possess ego, values, outlook, and the ability to communicate, though they may be incapable of audible speech. Man assumes he is all-important, that all else in creation exists only for his sport, amusement, comfort, or nourishment. Valmiki, the greatest of poets, who composed *The Ramayana*, cried out when he noticed the agony of a bird whose mate was shot down by a hunter, "Man, the destroyer, who'll not let innocent creatures mate in peace . . ." I wished to examine what the result would be if I made a tiger the central character in a novel.

"Why tiger? Why not a mouse?" asked a smart journalist who had come to interview me, when I mentioned the subject of my novel. I could only reply, "So that the chief character may not be trampled upon or lost sight of in a hole."

My story begins with an aged tiger lying in its cage ruminating on its past, beginning with its cubhood and wild days in the jungle, and later life in captivity as a circus star. It attains freedom when it breaks loose from a film-shooting camp and wanders into the town. The terror-stricken public attempts to get it shot but an ascetic who appears on the scene protects and adopts it as a companion.

"Who is he? Where is he from?" are naturally the questions that occur to everyone. But whenever he is asked "Who are you?" he just says, "What I am trying to find out." This sounds like a mere metaphysical quibble, but it is a plain, literal answer to the question. When one is seized with a passion to understand one's self, one has to leave behind all normal life and habitual modes of thought. One becomes an ascetic; the terms *sannyasi, sadhu, yogi,* or *swamiji* indicate more or less the same state.

A *sannyasi* is one who renounces everything and undergoes a complete change of personality. Why one would become a *sannyasi* is not easily answered—a personal tragedy or frustration, a deeply compelling philosophy of life, or a flash of illumination may drive one to seek a change. Whatever the cause, when one becomes a *sannyasi,* one obliterates one's past. A *sannyasi* is to be taken as he is at the moment. You can never ask a *sannyasi* about his earlier life. He will never refer to it. It would be a crass, inconsiderate act even to ask a *sannyasi* his name. He assumes a new name, bearing no mark of his ancestry or class, but indicative of some general beatitude. He has freed himself from all possessions and human ties. Among certain sects, the man will even perform his own funeral ritualistically before becoming a *sannyasi*. A *sannyasi* is a wanderer living on alms, never rooted to any place except when he seeks the seclusion of a cave or forest at some stage for prolonged meditation.

Apart from the genuine types, there are also fakes who adopt this life for its sheer vagrancy, or to exploit the public in the garb of holy men. During certain yogic practices, eight kinds of supernatural powers may be roused; one could become invisible, levitate, transmute metals, travel in space, control animals and men, live on air, and so on and so forth. But such magical powers are considered to be stages in one's evolution, incidental powers acquired on the way, to be ignored and not exercised for profit or self-promotion, except to mitigate pain or suffering in others.

Now, in my story the "Tiger Hermit" employs his powers to save the tiger and transform it inwardly—working on the basis that, deep within, the core of personality is the same in spite of differing appearances and categories, and with the right approach you could expect the same response from a tiger as from any normal human being.

R. K. N.
October 1982

I have no idea of the extent of this zoo. I know only my corner and whatever passes before me. On the day I was wheeled in, I only noticed two gates opening to admit me. When I stood up I caught a glimpse of some cages ahead and also heard the voice of a lion. The man who had transferred me from the forest stepped out of his jeep and said, after a glance in my direction, "He is all right. Now run up and see if the end cage is ready. This animal is used to human company and a lot of free movement. We must keep him where people will be passing. The open-air enclosure must also be available to him, when the wild ones are not let out. See to it."

They have shown me special consideration, by the grace of my Master, whom I may not see again. All the same, lying here on the cool floor, I madly hope that my Master might suddenly appear out of a crowd, open the door of my cage, and command, "Come out, let us go." Such is my dream. I keep scrutinizing faces, but all faces look dull and monotonous, none radiant like my Master's. Men, women, and children peer through the bars, and sometimes cry aloud, "Ah, see this tiger. What a ferocious beast!" and make crude noises to rouse me, fling a stone if the keeper is not looking, and move on to appreciate similarly the occupant of the next cage. You are not likely to understand that I am different from the tiger next door, that I possess a soul within this forbidding exterior. I can think, analyse, judge, remember and do everything that you can do, perhaps with greater subtlety and sense. I lack only the faculty of speech.

But if you could read my thoughts, you would be welcome to

come in and listen to the story of my life. At least, you could slip your arm through the bars and touch me and I will hold out my forepaw to greet you, after retracting my claws, of course. You are carried away by appearances—my claws and fangs and the glowing eyes frighten you no doubt. I don't blame you. I don't know why God has chosen to give us this fierce make-up, the same God who has created the parrot, the peacock, and the deer, which inspire poets and painters. I would not blame you for keeping your distance—I myself shuddered at my own reflection on the still surface of a pond while crouching for a drink of water, not when I was really a wild beast, but after I came under the influence of my Master and learnt to question, "Who am I?" Don't laugh within yourself to hear me speak thus. I'll tell you about my Master presently.

I recollect my early days as a cave-dweller and jungle beast (however much my Master might have disliked the term) with a mixture of pleasure and shame. At the far end of Mempi range, which trails off into the plains, I lived in my cave on the edge of a little rivulet, which swelled and roared along when it rained in the hills but was fordable in dry season, with the jungle stretching away on the other side. I remember my cubhood when I frolicked on the sandy bank and in the cool stream, protected and fed by a mother. I had no doubt whatever that she would live for ever to look after me: a natural delusion which afflicts all creatures, including human beings. However, she just vanished from my world one evening. I was seized with panic and hid myself in the cave. When I ventured out, I was chased, knocked down and hurt by bigger animals and menaced by lesser ones. I starved except when I could catch miserable creatures such as rabbits, foxcubs and squirrels, and survived somehow. Not only survived, but in course of time considered myself the Supreme Lord of the Jungle, afraid of no one, striking terror in others. It was, naturally, a time of utter wildness, violence, and unthinking cruelty inflicted on weaker creatures. Everyone I encountered proved weaker and submissive, but that submissiveness did not count—I delivered the fatal blow in any case when I wished and strode about as the King of the

Forest. By the way, who crowned the lion King of the Forest? Probably a fable writer, carried away by the pompous mane and beard, I suppose! A more slothful creature was never created. All his energy is conserved for hunting food, and once that is accomplished he lies down for days on end, so reluctant to move a muscle that he could be used by any other jungle creature as a mattress; it would make no difference to him if birds nested in his beard and laid eggs. As for his supreme strength I had a chance to test it in the circus ring once, when we were let out to fight and he fled into a waiting cage thanking the Creator for the damage of only one ear, which came off when I tried to comb his royal mane. I got a pat on my back from the ringmaster himself.

Every creature in the jungle trembled when it sensed my approach. "Let them tremble and understand who is the Master, Lord of this world," I thought with pride. When I strode out from the cave, the scent went ahead, and except monkeys and birds on trees all other creatures shrank out of sight. While I prowled through, half-sunk in jungle grass, I expected the deferential withdrawal from my path of other creatures. We the denizens of the jungle can communicate, without words, exactly as human beings do—we are capable of expressing to each other sympathy, warning, abuse, irony, insult, love and hatred exactly in the manner of human beings, but only when necessary, unlike human beings who talk all their waking hours, and even in sleep. When I passed by, rabbits scurried off, and if a jackal happened to be in my path, he put his ears back, lowered his tail, rolled his eyes in humility, and cried softly: "Here comes our Lord and Master. Keep his path clear . . ." Such attention pleased me, and seemed to add to my stature. Occasionally I came across a recalcitrant member of our society who probably thought highly of himself and I always noted, through a corner of my eye, how he pretended not to have seen me, looking the other way or asleep behind a thorny bush out of my reach. I made a mental note of such lapses of courtesy and never failed to punish him when a chance occurred. It might not be more than a scratch or a bite while passing him the next time, but that would take days to heal, and he would lose an

eye or a tooth or earn a cut on his lips making it impossible for
him to eat his food, all of which I counted as a trophy. Whenever I saw the creature again, you may be sure he never displayed any arrogance. Among our jungle community, we had
an understanding, which was an acknowledgement of my superiority, unquestioned, undisputed. My Master, when I mentioned it, explained that it was also true of human beings in
various degrees and versions.

While all living creatures avoided me, there was one which I
took great care to avoid—the porcupine, after an early experience. Out of a sort of recklessness I once tried to toss him
about, and received such a stab of quills over my nose, jaws,
and paws that I retreated to my cave and collapsed. I lay there
starving for several days; I expected I would soon be dead. A
long-tailed, black-faced langur, perched at a safe distance on
the branch of a fig tree, munching fruits as the monkey tribe always do, simpered, leered, and said, "Served you right. No one
in his right mind would ever go near a porcupine. Ignorant
fool. Should you run after every kind of flesh indiscriminately?
You think no end of your prowess!" I looked up and growled,
wishing I could reach him. (He then went out and spread the
news far and wide, making it the joke of the season in the jungle.) "Shut up," I cried, and the long-tailed one said, "Yes, after
I have said this, you despot, now listen carefully. If you can
move yourself across the stream, not far off there is a yellow
shrub with bristles. Brush against it; milk from its leaves will
loosen the quills and heal your sores. You see that hollow over
there, go, drop yourself in it, sink down in it, roll in it; it is full
of those plants . . ."

Forgive me, if you find me running into the past. Whenever I
recollect my forest life, I am likely to lose all restraint. I have
often felt guilty at reminiscing, but my Master, who reads my
mind, has said that there is nothing wrong in it, and advises me
not to curb it—it being also a part of my own life, indispensable
and unshakable although I have come a long way from it . . .

I only worried about monkeys—they lived at a height and
moved and ran about as they pleased, and thought they were
above the normal rules and laws of the jungle, a mischievous

tribe. I was aware of how they hopped from place to place, hiding amidst foliage, bearing malicious rumours and trying to damage my authority. Their allies were birds which lived at a height and enjoyed greater facility than monkeys in that they could fly away at my approach. How I longed sometimes to be able to climb or fly even a short distance. Then I would have eliminated this whole contemptible clan; I particularly wished to get at the owl, the wise one with his round eyes always looking down his hook nose, a self-appointed adviser to all those despicable creatures who secretly wished my downfall. (I'm only expressing my mentality in those days in the idiom of those times.) Every time I passed below a tree, I would hear a cynical cackle and hoot and if I looked up I'd see the loving couple, the owl and her mate. One would say to the other, "When the King passes, what should one do?" There would be some answer to that.

"If you don't?"

"Then he will nip off your head."

"Yes—only if he could carry his mighty bulk up a tree trunk . . ."

The crow was particularly treacherous, always following my movements and creating enough din to reveal where I had the kill, making it impossible for me to eat in peace, sneaking up to peck at my food and retreating when I turned, again and again. Worse than the crow were kites, vultures, eagles and such, which circled loftily in the high heaven, but to no greater purpose than to spot out carrion, glide down and clean it up to the bone. Mean creatures, ever on the watch for someone else's kill.

Another creature that I had my eyes on was the leopard. I don't know how many members of that odious family existed in my forest—they didn't seem to breed or multiply too openly. The leopard was so secretive that you never noticed more than one at a time and hardly ever a family. It has always been a mystery. When I passed by he would climb a tree pointedly to emphasize the fact that he was higher than myself. I tried to ignore this creature, since he possessed great agility and could get beyond anyone's reach, but he was mean, and always made it clear that he was there and didn't care for me. He made all kinds of noises while I passed, and purred and growled and sneered. When he was with his mate it was worse. They made audible remarks most insulting to a tiger, and talked among themselves about the superiority of spots over stripes.

There was a jungle superstition about how the tiger came to have stripes. The first tiger in creation was very much like a lion, endowed with a tawny, shining coat of pure gold. Imagine! But he offended some forest spirit, which branded his back with hot coal. Thus goes the fable, which I didn't believe in, a canard started by some jealous creature like the leopard who felt inferior owing to his spots, but made a virtue of it. The leopard couple sang this fable every time I passed by, a monotonous silly song; I would have put an end to their song if I could have seen where they were—they were mostly unseen, and just streaked away like lightning when glimpsed. I was helpless with this truant. It hurt my pride as a ruler of the jungle, while all other creatures respected my status, bowed to it and kept out of my way. Night and day I spent in planning and thinking how best to humble the leopard or exterminate him. Sometimes I set out to track him down in his lair, in a deep hollow or inside a cave. When I went in quest, he would invariably anticipate my arrival and sneak away, and then sit atop a steep, slippery rock, and eye me with contempt or go up a banyan tree with the ease of a squirrel . . . I realized soon that I had to tolerate his existence and bide my time. This was a great worry for me. He disturbed and scared off my game and was ahead of me in hunting.

The leopard was not the last of my worries. I could ignore him and go my way. Not so a female of our species, whom I encountered beyond those mango groves—a creature as large as myself, I suppose. I smelt her presence a long way off. I hesitated whether to turn back or advance. I was out to hunt for the evening, and if I had not been hungry I would have withdrawn and gone my way in a different direction. But I was proceeding to the meadow beyond the valley where I knew a herd of deer always grazed. I noticed her sitting erect in the middle of the road blocking my passage. I'd never seen her before;

probably from an adjoining forest. Normally we respected each other's territories and never intruded. My temper rose at the sight of her. "Get out of my way and go back where you belong," I roared. She just took it as a joke and showed no response except a slight wave of her tail. This was complete insolence and not to be tolerated. With her back to me she was watching the herd in the meadow. I was furious and jumped on her back and tried to throttle her, with the sort of hold that would make a wild buffalo limp in a second. But this lady surprised me by throwing me off her back with a jerk. My claws were buried in her skin, but that did not make any difference to her as she turned round and gashed my eyes and bit my throat. Fortunately I had shut my eyes, but my brow was torn and blood trickled down my eyes. The jackal, as always attracted by the smell of blood, was there as if summoned, hiding behind a thicket of thorns; he made his presence felt, and mumbled some advice, which was lost in the uproar the lady was creating as she returned for the attack and knocked me off my feet by ramming into me. I have never encountered anyone so strong. Now the safest course for me would be to retreat gracefully to my cave and get away from this monster quickly. But my dignity would be lost—especially with the jackal there watching my humiliation. I should fight it out, even if one of us were to die in the process. We butted into each other, scratched, clawed, wrestled, grappled, gashing, biting, tearing each other, and I also stood up and threw my weight on her and struck, but it was like beating a rock—she was no normal animal: there is a limit to physical endurance; and I could stand it no longer; I collapsed on the ground bleeding from every pore; I had no strength even to run away, which I wished I had done earlier instead of bothering about prestige before the damned jackal. If I had seized and choked the jackal, I could have saved my blood.

In a few places my skin hung down in ribbons. My satisfaction was that the monster, my adversary, seemed to have fared no better. She had also collapsed in a ditch, no less bloody, with her flesh torn up and exposed. I noticed also that while I could open my eyes with blood dripping, she lay with her eyes swollen and sealed. I remembered aiming at her eyes just as she was trying to gouge out mine, but I seemed to have had better luck. It was her inability to open her eyes, more than physical collapse, which forced her to withdraw.

While both of us lay panting, the jackal came out of his shelter and, standing at a safe distance, raised his voice so that both of us could hear him. He knew that neither of us was in a state to go for him if we did not like his words; all the same he kept his distance and a possible retreat open. The jackal asked with an air of great humility, "May I know why you have been fighting and brought on yourselves this misery? If you can show even half of half a reason, I shall be satisfied." Neither of us could answer, but only moan and growl. For the condition I was in, the jackal could have patted my cheeks or pulled my whiskers and got away with it. I could at least see the world around but the tigress was blinded for the time being. The jackal continued ingratiatingly, "If you cannot discover a reason to be enemies, why don't you consider being friends? How grand you could make it if you joined forces—you could become supreme in this jungle and the next and the next; no one will ever try to stand up to you, except a crazy tusker, whom you could toss about between you two . . . If you combined you could make all the jungle shake."

His words sounded agreeable. I felt a sudden compassion for my adversary and also gratitude for being spared my life. I struggled to get up on my feet and, mistaking my action, the jackal swiftly withdrew and disappeared before I could say, "You have advised us well." I limped along to the tigress very cautiously and expressed my contrition and desire to make amends. She was in no condition to rise or see me. I cleaned up the bloody mess covering her eyes and sat beside her huge body, paying all attention and performing many acts of tenderness— till she was able to open one eye slightly and stir, and it filled me with dread lest she should kill me instantly. She could have easily done it, if she was so disposed. But a change had come over her too. My ministrations seemed to have helped her to recover her breath, vision, and the use of her limbs. She followed me quietly, although both of us were limping, to an ad-

jacent pond and we splashed about in the water till we were
cleansed of blood and felt revived.

We have no reckoning of time in the manner of human beings.
But by the time the scars on our backs were dry, a litter of four
was added to our family, climbing and jumping over us all the
time in the cave.

It was all very well as long as they were sucklings. At that stage
they never moved away, their horizon being their mother's belly.
The little ones were happy, continuously suckling, or when
fully fed, climbing and jumping over their mother's immense
sides as she stretched herself across the floor of our home. It left
me free to roam in the jungle and rest, away from the family.
Usually I found the shade of a bamboo cluster very pleasant—I
merged in its speckled shade so completely that some little buck
or minor game would stray near me, and I'd only have to turn
and grab in order to provide food for the cubs.

When they grew up and discovered the use of their limbs, they
ran about in different directions. They were now at an unsafe
stage. Any bear or bison could trample them out of existence: no
reason why such a thing should happen—except that the jungle
was a devilish place, where the weak or the young received no
consideration for their helpless state. We had to guard them all
the time. One would run in the direction of the stream, another
wade through, and the third would have climbed a rock, where
a colony of giant eagles nested, which might swoop down and
carry him off, leaving his bones to bleach in the sun. Equally
dangerous were the pythons who just swallowed whole whatever came their way. Also there was the danger of the cubs slipping and rolling down into the ravine. We had to save them
from destruction every other minute. They were now too large
to be carried by the scruff, and we caught and pummelled them
along back into the cave, and one of us would lie across the entrance to prevent their going out again. This could be no permanent solution.

A time came when the obstacle at the cave-mouth made no
difference to them. When the sentry parent was fallen into a
doze, they could easily hop over him and explore the world.

Though we enjoyed the spectacle of our cubs' activities, it was becoming a sore trial. It was my turn one evening to guard the cubs. Their mother had gone out in search of prey. I saw her go down the sandy slope across the river and climb the other bank. I had supposed the cubs were playing inside at the back wall of the cave. But at some moment when I was not alert enough, they must have vaulted over me and escaped. When I woke up I saw them wading across the river, their little heads bobbing above the water. I watched them go, feeling too lazy to run after them. Evidently they were following their mother's scent. No harm. I could see them go up the opposite bank; they could reach their mother and come back later. After all they had to gain experience: it'd do them good to watch their mother hunt and share a fresh kill.

The air blowing in our direction brought some strange unfamiliar noises, and crackling sounds like twigs breaking. I felt disturbed and bewildered. No sign of the cubs or the mother. I let out a roar that should ring through the forest, valleys and mountains, and summon back my family. Normally when I called there would be an answer, but today there was none—only the twittering of birds waking at dawn. I ventured out, down the sand and across the river, following the course I had watched the cubs take; the scent led me on and on to the ridge, and then down a valley to the plains which had a path leading to human habitations beyond the jungle. I cried in anguish and desperation—but silenced myself and crouched unobtrusively when I noticed far off in the valley down below a line of men passing, pulling and pushing an open cart on which were laid out the cubs and their mother. The men were singing and shouting vociferously, and did not hear my cry. I had thought till now that our jungle home was impregnable, and unapproachable for human beings. In fact, I had hardly seen any specimen till this moment. Now human feet had strayed in and touched our ground, and that brought to my mind strange forebodings. I watched the revellers wend their way. They were too intoxicated to notice me, since I lay concealed behind the boulders. As the procession wound along, I hopped on to another rock and stalked them. As the sun came up my eyes were dazzled, and the procession melted into thin air. I edged to the shade of an overhanging cliff and stayed there.

I slept till dusk. I got up and moved in the direction the procession had gone. I took care not to be noticed by any jungle creature—particularly the owl or the jackal who always spied on my movements. I moved away from the trees on which the owl generally was perched and the bushes where the jackal would be sneaking around. I kept my movements along the rocks on the hill at a safe height. When I arrived at a village, I found most of the inhabitants asleep. Noiselessly I went up and lay beside a well until everything was quiet.

The cart in which the cubs and their mother were laid out was left to one side in the village street. I could see it all clearly from my hiding place. The sight of my family stretched out there filled me with fury. In those days I was still a tiger, an unmitigated animal, and the only feeling that was aroused in me was fury, rather than grief, which I understand now. A blind, impossible anger stirred within me: I just wanted to dash up, pounce upon every creature, bite and claw and destroy. I wanted to spring forward, pick up the cubs and carry them away.

Just as I was getting ready to dash up, a set of human beings arrived in a strange vehicle, which I now understand to be a jeep. They shouted and summoned the villagers. The village was astir and a crowd gathered around the cart, and there was much jabbering, arguments and shouting. I held myself back although I felt a great drive within to pounce on that whole lot and tear their entrails. But I held myself back. No one knew that I was there. I lay low, watched them transfer the carcasses to the back of their jeep, and drive off. The villagers went back to their homes; silence and darkness fell on the village. I came out of my hiding place behind the well and prowled around. Some of the street dogs started barking and woke up the villagers again. Before they could notice me, I withdrew and went back to my hiding place beside the well. Even there I could not stay too long. Women started approaching the well carrying pots and buckets and chattering among themselves; I slipped back and hid myself on the hill behind *lantana* bushes.

Another day's sun came up, and I dozed off till the evening. When the sun went down again and dusk fell, I watched the villagers returning from their fields, carrying bundles of firewood on their heads, driving their flocks home. I slipped through the *lantana* shrub and lay in wait by their path, well concealed behind a boulder, and pounced upon the last animal in a column, seized its throat, and made off with it. My hunger was appeased for at least two days. I could not repeat this strategy. Later when the villager realized that he had lost an animal and followed the bloodstains, I had to change my tactics, as well as my abode. I eluded the villagers again and again.

They must have begun to wonder about the shape of the predator in their midst. "Can't be a tiger," they must have thought, "the hunters have taken away the entire family, by this time they'll have sold the skin of the adult, and stuffed the cubs as trophies."

"But it was a tigress; the father must still be at large."

"Oh, no," the local animal expert must have explained, "you must understand that a male tiger hardly ever lives with the family . . . Must be a visitor from another forest. Tigers are not family-bound like monkeys and other creatures. Monkeys belong to a more advanced group . . ." Human beings have their own theories, and it is always amusing to hear them talk about us. Such ignorance and self-assurance!

Presently they must have concluded: "It could not have been a tiger at all, but a cheetah, or even a hyena, which steals up and attacks. A tiger would not be satisfied with a sheep, but always attacks larger cattle . . ."

Nowadays I chose a smaller animal from the herd, since I could manage it without leaving a trail, and eat afresh a whole thing. With a larger animal, I had to keep the kill for a second meal, and that always betrayed my presence, since it attracts the wretches who trailed me for scraps and leavings. I kept my abode constantly changing. It was safer and advantageous too to move along the mountain range. It gave me a very wide area of cover. I moved from place to place, and discovered that below the mountain range in the valleys and plains there were human habitations, to which the cattle were driven back in the evenings. I could repeat my tactics everywhere: lie in wait and seize the last one in the herd and vanish. Among those scattered villages, news spread very slowly, and that was to my advantage. I preferred my present method of seeking food—it spared me all the fatigue and uncertainty of hunting in the jungle. Jungle creatures are more alert and elusive than the village cattle, stupid creatures which could never anticipate danger even when passing under my chin while I crouched on a rock.

Village folk soon realized that they were losing their animals regularly. Some thought a devil was around, and were preparing to perform propitiatory ceremonies in their villages. Also they took care to drive their flocks back home while there was still sunlight, and had more men to guard them. This affected me adversely, but only for a short time. I began to scout around the villages at night, when the men put out the lamps and retired for the day.

Once, along a ditch running down a village street, I moved on soft foot; nothing stirred except bandicoots, scampering away. The village mongrels curled in the street dust were unaware, so silently did I move. Otherwise they would have howled and brought the entire village on me. At the centre of the village, I noticed an enclosure made of bamboo and all kinds of brambles and thorn, with a little door of the same kind. The door could not be pushed open by the stupid sheep penned within the stockade, but I could get through it without any effort. I seized the nearest creature, but before I could turn round and get out, the cry of the lamb I had caught set the whole flock bleating, crying, howling in panic, enough noise to wake up the villagers peacefully slumbering in their homes. In a moment they were out, screaming and shouting obscenities at the enemy invading their sanctum. "Ah! Now we know! We have him. He must not escape . . ."

They came rushing down in great force holding up flaming torches, hatchers, crowbars, and staves. I was about to dash out with my prize, but in the confusion that ensued, I lost sight of the door. I had never seen humans in such a frenzy of shouting. I never knew that humans beings could be so devilish. They were all armed, aimed spears at me and hit me with arrows while I was desperately trying to find a way out. More than their weapons, the sight of their flaming torches, red-coloured and smoking viciously, was completely unnerving. I dropped the lamb, my only ambition now being to escape with my skin intact. I had never been so close to fire: sometimes in summer, we noticed forest fires far off, but they would not be frightening, and we kept our distance from them. But now the fire was choking, blinding and scorching: one fellow flung his torch at me, which singed my skin, another threw a spear which gashed my side; I ran round and round madly; I could not fall upon my pursuers as I could not see them clearly. The crowd was intent on murdering me. They were heaving huge rocks at me. Men in their frenzy seemed to have lost all fear, and boys of all ages were cursing and chasing me round and round—I could have fallen on any of them and scattered them but for the fire in their hands. It was unbearable. I was bleeding from the cuts on my face and limbs and I wished I were dead. I would have welcomed death in preference to the torture I was facing now.

Penned in the stockade, I felt hopeless and exhausted. The monsters chased and tormented me. Luckily for me a mishap occurred at this desperate moment. A boy who was capering with a torch at the end of a bamboo pole, while attempting to poke me, held his flame too close to the fence, which caught fire. Their attention was now diverted to saving the sheep. They demolished the stockade and opened a way out. Wedged between bleating sheep, which received the blows meant for me, I ran out and escaped into the night.

Looking back, I feel that I should not have chosen the easy path—of raiding villages. Stepping into human society was a thoughtless act. Instead of living the rest of my life majestically as an honest-to-god tiger going in and out of his cave, eating and sleeping, performing no act except what he wished, Lord of the Jungle, before whom other creatures from a squirrel to a bear quaked in fear, I had let myself in for ultimate slavery. I had thought that there could never be any creature stronger than a tiger. I was mistaken. A human being may look small, without prominent teeth or claws, but he is endowed with some strange power, which can manoeuvre a tiger or an elephant as if they were toys.

After my attack on the village, people there not only began to guard their cattle better, but also approached the authorities for help. They sent their spokesmen to the town to meet the Collector and demand his help. They were vociferous and gave sensational and exaggerated reports of how a tiger was terrorizing the countryside, invading the villages and carrying away cattle, and mauling and maiming people going into the forests to gather firewood: they gave a list of names of persons who were killed. They were building a case against me and were inventing stories. I had always tried to avoid encounters with human beings, and if I had wanted, could have mangled and messed up the human creatures that had entered the stockade that night in the village. But I didn't, I didn't want to. If I had been present at that meeting with the Collector I would have proved that the villagers were lying. But I came to know of it only later in my life.

The Collector, being a man used to such representations, just said: "I'll look into your case. I can't promise anything. How do you know that there is a tiger around?"

"We saw it."

"How many of you saw it?"

"All of us . . ." said the deputation.

"How many persons live in your village?"

They looked at each other in consternation, being unfamiliar with numbers. "More than a hundred, sir," ventured an elder.

"Have all the hundred seen the tiger?" asked the Collector.

"Yes," they chorused.

The Collector fixed his gaze on someone arbitrarily and asked, "How big was the tiger?"

The man blinked for a minute and then indicated with his hands some size, whereupon another man pushed himself forward and said, "He is wrong. The tiger was this big . . ."

A heated argument started, many others joined for and

against, until the Collector said, "Silence, are you both talking of the same tiger or two different ones? Was there one tiger or two or three?"

Someone said, "Five in all, sir. Four cubs and a tigress, which were shot."

"Who shot them?" asked the Collector.

"Some *shikari* from the town . . ."

"Which town?"

"We can't say, sir, we don't know."

"Did they have a licence to shoot? Who gave them licence?"

The petitioners, feeling they were being dragged beyond their depths, became tongue-tied.

The Collector observed them for a moment and said, "Have you brought your petition in writing?" They looked terrified, having no notion of the world of letters. The Collector felt compassionate and said, "I can't take action unless there is a written petition. Go to a petition-writer . . . you'll find one in the veranda of the law court or at the market gate. Get the petition engrossed on a stamp-paper of one rupee and fifty paise, and leave it with my clerk at the office. Then I'll fix a date for inspection and take action . . . For all I know there may be no tiger whatever. You may be imagining! One mentions one tiger and another says five!" And he permitted himself a dignified grin at the joke. "However, it is my duty to look into it, if you have a grievance."

The deputation of villagers had to visit the Collector almost once a week, spending time and money to no purpose. From within the jungle where their villages were situated, they had to trudge ten miles to the highway and wait endlessly for a chance lift in a passing bus or lorry. At the Collector's office they could see, after much waiting, only the Collector's clerk, who took their petitions and then directed them to satisfy further official formalities. At the end of the day they returned to their villages, dreading lest the tiger should waylay them.

I had perfected my system of snatching cattle at night. I became quite familiar with their movements and timings and the weak points in the enclosures that the creatures were penned

in. The villages were all alike and the villagers had similar habits in tending their sheep or cattle. They could never anticipate
where I'd strike next. I covered a large perimeter. If I took a
sheep from this village today, my next target would be elsewhere, in your terms, several days later. In between, they'd not
know where to look for me. Some parts of Mempi hills had
deep ravines, quite inaccessible to human beings. I hid myself
in them and planned to attack with considerable calculation,
taking care not to be seen in the same area again. I had perfected the art—no village was too far out, and no fencing was
impregnable. I walked in and out of places, hardly aware at
that time how very desperate the villagers were beginning to
feel. They began to adopt defensive measures, such as keeping
up a bonfire all night, and posting vigilant guards, armed with
sharp weapons, and in one or two places they had even scattered poisoned meat for me; but I'd not touch such things—
only some wildcat or mongrel nosing around ended its career
then and there.

When he announced his name as Captain, they always asked,
"Of what?" He would always reply, "Just Captain. Mister
Captain, if you like."

"Oh, we thought it was an army or football captain." He was
used to such quips wherever he went, but he could not afford
to mind it and treated it good-humouredly. A man about town,
he had to be seeing people constantly on business—running his
circus, which had its origin in a certain "Grand Irish Circus."
When questioned on the Irish origin or contents of his circus,
he generally explained, "When I was down and out at Poona, I
met a chap, a down-and-out Irishman, who owned a half-
starved pony, a yellow monkey, and a parrot which could pick
up numbers and alphabets from a stack of cards. He took them
about and displayed them here and there in the city. He dispensed with his pony, selling it off to a tonga owner, and managed with the parrot and the monkey, which became his sole
assets; he could maintain them inexpensively with a handful of
nuts for the monkey and a guava fruit for the parrot. He had a
portable signboard painted, GRAND IRISH CIRCUS, and set it

up in the town hall compound, street pavements, or market square and attracted a crowd. He called himself O'Brien though he had a brown skin and never uttered a word of English or Irish but spoke only 'The Native Language' in order to establish rapport with his public, as he always took the trouble to explain." Captain always wondered what sort of an Irishman he was, but said to himself, "If I could call myself Captain, by the same logic he could be O'Brien." At some point in their association O'Brien took up some other business and sold his good will and the circus to Captain for fifty rupees. Captain used the signboard, monkey, and parrot to make a living following O'Brien's tradition. Feeling that he should do better, he approached one Dadhaji, owner of "Dadhaji Grand Circus."

The grand old man was reclining in an easy chair in his special tent. Young Captain approached him with all humility with the monkey on his shoulder and holding the parrot cage in his hand. Dadhaji watched the visitor for some time and asked, "What do you want?"

"I want to work here, sir."

"What do you know of animals?" Captain was afraid to give an answer. After waiting for a moment the man thundered, "Have you no answer? Be frank. I would appreciate it. I like people young or old to be frank."

Captain felt like turning round and fleeing. But he was standing too close to the great man to run away. His aides, standing at different points, were watching him with contempt. The only animal Captain had known was an alley cat and its mates in his boyhood in Abu Lane. And a mongrel he was fond of, which used to curl up in the street dust. The several attempts he made to shelter it in his room were frustrated by his father who was strictly anti-canine. Even after his death, Captain could not realize his ambition, since their creditors took over their property, which resulted in the scattering of the family. Captain, with his little savings in hand, set out to seek his fortune and ended up in Poona. These flashes of memory were not worth recounting, and he helplessly wished that his retreat were not blocked by all those terrible aides in grey uniform with their pockets embroidered in yellow thread: "Dadhaji Grand Circus." Frightening. The old man was evidently enjoying the young fellow's discomfiture. Captain felt suddenly challenged and said, "Born and bred in Abu Lane of Malgudi town, sir, no chance, sir, of encountering animals, sir . . . The very reason why I have come to you, sir, is to learn about animals and their training." He had found his tongue, which pleased the old gentleman.

"Ah, that's better. You should talk, otherwise you will be left out. A young chap who comes out to learn and earn must be alert. I know where we stand now. I seem to know the monkey on your shoulder and the parrot, they were once with the worthless fellow who called himself O'Connor or some such thing. Don't know where he got the idea that he was Irish—a bastard possibly out of our own slums. I am not going to waste my time asking how and where you met him and all that. It's your business. Keep that monkey, if you like, or drive it back to its treetop, so also the parrot. If you hoped that you could add them to my show, you were mistaken. They are too insignificant for my circus. When I say 'show' I mean acts of large quadrupeds and bipeds, whose movements would be visible from any part of the auditorium. Otherwise it is no show. What you carry is fit for street corners; I have no use for them. Now you may go if you choose—or stay if you are willing to work here."

Captain was fascinated by the old man's alternating moods of aggression and tenderness. "Let me stay here, sir," he said, "and learn to work."

The old man said, "I have around one hundred and fifty animals in this camp. Are you prepared to start with the horses? You will have to clean their stables first and also groom them. And then I'll tell you what you can do. Ultimately, if you prove your worth, you will be in charge of the cages of tigers and lions. That is all for the present. You will be fed and sheltered and given pocket money. Think over this offer and give me your answer tomorrow . . ."

Captain said, "Not tomorrow, sir. I'll stay here."

"When I say tomorrow, I mean it. Take twenty-four hours to think it over."

That was how Captain started his career when he was hardly

twenty. Dadhaji imparted to him unreservedly all his knowledge and skill in the training of animals as well as his business
methods. Dadhaji often explained his philosophy: "There is no
such thing as a wild animal—any creature on four legs can be
educated if you apply the right method. For over fifty years I
have lived with animals—over a hundred at a time—and I know
what I am saying."

Dadhaji began to depend on Captain more and more. When
he became too old to manage things, he made him his working
partner. At his death the entire circus with all its property and
assets and animals were bequeathed to Captain. The transition
was unnoticed since Captain had virtually been running the
show for years, only presenting periodical reports to Dadhaji
while he rested in his tent.

After Dadhaji's death, Captain shifted his circus to Malgudi. It
was a mighty undertaking. He sold the ground at Poona, taking permission from the purchaser of the land to keep his animals there till he was able to move his business to Malgudi. He
had enough money to negotiate for the wasteland beyond the
level-crossing. Within three months the land was transformed
and in big letters loomed the sign GRAND MALGUDI CIRCUS.
He had originally intended to name it after the Irishman or
Dadhaji, but the municipal chairman and members showed
some reluctance in their attitude until he assured them that he
was putting Malgudi on the world map by naming it Grand
Malgudi Circus. "Just to show my roots are here, although I
must confess that I had thought of perpetuating my benefac-
tors' names originally. Hereafter Malgudi will be the home for
hundreds of animals and scores of acrobats and performers of
all kinds. You will be proud of it . . ." His talk was captivating.
He liberally dispensed money to smooth out the passage of all
kinds of transactions and favours, and in a short while Malgudi became more famous for its circus than for its mountains
and river, and Captain was viewed as the wonder man who had
transformed the town.

It was the result of hard work. Captain rose at five in the
morning and went on a tour of inspection. Elephants and cam-

els and giraffes were at the eastern end of the camp. He went up there first with his chief executive Anand, who had been with him since his Poona days. He started with the camels at one end, keeping in mind Dadhaji's injunction, "You must watch the condition of every animal and anticipate how long it will last, and get an immediate replacement if one dies. Keep an eye on the sources, if you are not to face embarrassment in public. The show never halts because of one animal." He could judge their health and welfare by observing their stance and attitude at five in the morning. Animals, in his view, looked their brightest at that hour if they were in good health. The animals stirred and gave some indication of recognizing his presence when he approached, and that pleased him. He passed on from animal to animal, checking their welfare; if they were sick, he sent Anand to wake up the veterinarian immediately. Starting with camels, he passed on to elephants, horses and lastly to the minor performing creatures, and by the time he reached his office he would have understood the condition of every creature under his control. He sat at his desk and noted down his observations and suggestions or criticized the state of cleanliness of cages or surroundings and indicated punishments for erring assistants. When he finished his job at the table, his wife would ring the bell for breakfast.

"All our animals from the performing mongoose to the tusker are in excellent condition," he boasted at breakfast.

"Yes," said his wife, "they are tended better than your family."

"You must say something unpleasant—otherwise you are never happy."

"Your beloved animals may also have something to say if they could speak . . ."

"What really is your grouse? I never understand. You demanded that the boys should be sent to Lovedale School; that I have done, swallowing my own ideas at such a cost!"

"Good thing too—otherwise you would have made lion-tamers of them as well."

"I don't know why you say such things, knowing full well where the money comes from, so much needed for you and your damned family at Madras—all hangers-on, none of them will do anything except sit back and wait for my cheque every month . . . If you wish to see them get on, why don't you ask one of your brothers to come and type my correspondence at least?"

"Isn't enough that I slave for you? You want the entire 'damned' family at your beck and call? I am tired of everything, my boy. As soon as you get someone to lead your trapeze team, I'll retire and go back to Madras. I'm tired of jumping and swinging and the perpetual tent-living." When she became too trying, Captain would abruptly leave the table. When she saw him rise, she felt uneasy and said as if nothing had happened, "Your coffee. Want more milk, sugar?" He never answered, but just emptied the cup at one gulp and walked out of the tent. She kept looking after him and muttered, "He has lost all sense of humour, the slightest upset and he flounces out, let him . . . I don't care. Only animals seem to be fit for his company."

He told himself, "Women are impossible. Worse than twenty untamed jungle creatures on one's hands at a time . . ."

Captain had gone to the Collector's office to renew some petty licence. He pricked up his ears when he heard the word "tiger." He was about to leave but halted his steps, remembering another of Dadhaji's injunctions. "If you hear the word 'tiger,' don't leave. Stay back and find out." And he was hearing the word "tiger" not once but several times through the babble of four villagers. "This is our twentieth visit and you always keep saying, 'Come tomorrow' . . . Are you playing with us? You are waiting to see us and our cattle eaten by the tiger and digested before you can think of saving us."

"Every time we have to walk from our homes ten miles for a bus to reach here," said another.

The clerk was irritated and said, "No one has invited you."

"Then why did the officer promise help?"

"Ask him. Why should I answer that question?"

"Yes, if we see him. As it is, we meet only the *Pujari*, not the God in the sanctum, and the *Pujari* denies what the God promises." And they laughed at their own quip.

"This is not his only business, he has more important work than listening to your stories."

"Ah, stories, you think! Come and spend a night in our village and you will know."

"My boss will inspect your village . . ."

"When? After the tiger has had his fill?"

"There is no tiger and he will not eat you," said the clerk. "The officer will come on inspection next month . . ."

"Next month! Next month! You have been saying it for months while the tiger is fattening himself on our cattle."

"You get out of my office! Have you no eyes to see that I am busy now?" He beat his brow in despair. "This is a cursed seat. No peace. I'm not allowed to clear these papers. Tomorrow when the boss comes, he will bawl his head off." He lost his temper suddenly. "What do you take me for? Government office is not your nuptial chamber, for you to demand things. I'll call the police if you are going to be riotous. Mind your manners. The officer will come on inspection to your village and then take necessary steps. Till then you must wait."

Captain watched them as they left the place grumbling, but afraid to curse openly. The clerk got absorbed in his files once again, muttering, "The officer is always on tour, what can I do if everyone comes and bothers me? Am I the officer drawing a fat salary?" This was addressed to the Captain, who was at the door, and he just said, soothingly, "Of course, you are not," and followed the villagers out.

He followed them a little distance, and threw out a general question in order to attract their attention, "Are you the headman of the village?" At which they turned round and stopped.

"How did you know us, sir?"

He introduced himself. "You see that circus there—that's mine and I often come to this office on business. Not bad fellows at this office but they delay. That poor fellow, he can't help it. Only his master has to do things . . ."

"Every time we come, we bring him some offering—cucumbers or sugar cane, pumpkin, melon, or anything. Never see him barehanded, and yet he is unhelpful."

Captain made himself agreeable by listening to them patiently. All that they seemed to want was a hearing. They did not know who he was, but his dress—trousers, bush shirt and the sun-hat—impressed them, and he spoke to them in Tamil, which endeared him to them. He treated them to coloured drinks from a wayside stall, while eliciting information about the tiger. He invited them to come up and see his circus. "I have work to do, next two days, and then I'll come to your village. If you help me I'll catch the tiger. You will have to show me where he lives."

"We don't know, sir. We can't say. He is here, there and everywhere. We think he is a devil and has wings and not an ordinary creature. We saw him only once . . . We would have burnt him with the torches and cooked him alive but he escaped. He slips in and out, and can never be caught or killed . . . He is no ordinary creature. Before we can notice, he snatches away even the biggest buffalo, and vanishes."

"He is an ordinary tiger, black and yellow, with four legs and only one tail and no extraordinary creature. I'll deal with him, don't worry. I'll see you on Thursday next . . ."

He took directions from them to reach the village, and was with them on the appointed day. The village was set far into the jungle, a single street and about thirty homes of bricks or just thatched huts, and a lot of cattle and sheep—mostly a pastoral community. He had gone in a small car, but he had to leave it on the main highway and walk down to the village, which was full of excitement. Women and children stood around him. Most of the men were out working in the fields. Seeing Captain's grey uniform, the boys cried, "The police have come," and ran around to fetch the men, who recognized him and cried, "Oh, it's our hunter, who is going to kill the tiger."

Captain corrected them. "I'm not going to kill, but take him away . . ." Some rushed into their homes and brought out ancient stools and benches and offered him seats. Some brought him tender coconut and chipped off the top and offered him a drink. Others brought him papaya and banana. Captain felt overwhelmed by their hospitality and promised, "I will see that you are not bothered by the tiger. But you must all help me. I must know where he is and how he comes and goes and where he keeps himself during the day."

"Oh, that's difficult, sir. If we follow him, he may turn round and attack."

"If you don't tell me where the tiger is, how can I catch him? I may also begin to think, like those officials, that you are all fancying the tiger."

At this they protested. "Even two days ago, two fellows who were out to cut wood were mutilated—one fellow lost an arm."

"Will you take me to him?"

"Not in our village, but there on the other side of the hill-ock . . ."

"Will you come with me and show me the man and where he was attacked, so that I may find out the tiger's movements?" Strangely they seemed to be averse to this procedure. The victims of the tiger seemed as elusive as the tiger itself. They would complain and pour forth their grievances, but somehow at the same time show reluctance to help him directly. They would not be explicit about the attacks. But Captain would not give up. He changed his tactics. He contacted the forest guards, offered a fee for information about the tiger, followed their tips. Leaving much of his circus work to his chief executive, he unrelentingly pursued the tiger, and finally arrived at the rivulet beyond which was the cave at the tail end of the Mempi range. Captain had taken special precautions to camouflage himself with certain types of foliage. He hoisted himself onto the branch of a tree and stayed there all night in the company of the forest guards, and finally had a glimpse of the tiger returning to his cave.

Although I was cautious and avoided all the traps laid for me, ultimately I yielded to a temptation, and that proved to be the end. After trying many hideouts, I had come back to my original home. As I emerged from my lair late one evening, passing through the long grass, I heard a bleating and, following the sound, saw a well-fed goat in front of me. I hesitated only for a moment, looked about, took a leap and landed on its back. At the same time I heard a strange, unfamiliar clattering noise—an iron door came down and shut me in. I was trapped. I was at once surrounded by unfamiliar figures and heard strange voices. A flashlight was pointed at me and a man was saying, "Just what I was looking for. A magnificent fellow."

"Mr. Captain, isn't he rather big for our purpose?"

"No, he is just right. Only we may have to starve him for a while."

"Will you be able to make him obedient?"

"Of course," said the other. "You will see, I'll make him a star."

"It seems to me he is too heavy for our purpose."

"He is all right. He'll become slim and agile. Leave it to me." Then he turned round and said to someone, "Pay off all the men who have helped us in trapping. Give them an extra tip, but make sure that their services are terminated. Keep the six men from our own staff, and they will take care of the business of wheeling this cage to the town. It may take four days, if drawn by bullocks. All along the way crowds will watch and follow; that will be an excellent advertisement for our circus."

My Master, later in my life, has mentioned hell, describing the conditions that would give one a feel of it. Now, recollecting the day of my trapping and the journey onward, I realize its meaning. The trap was narrow and I felt cribbed and cramped. I, who had lived a full and free life—stretching myself as I pleased, or burying myself in the jungle grass—now had to keep standing as the trap on wheels was drawn along. A pair of bullocks was yoked to it and the driver kept yelling and whipping them; the wheels rolled on rough ground, and I was jolted from side to side. I felt strangely uncomfortable to be moving without the use of my legs! First time experiencing locomotion. They had screened the trap with a lot of foliage, so that I might not see the bullocks or the driver; they had some irrational fear that if I saw them, I might want to eat them up. They forgot that the goat which was the bait was still in my company—although not alive.

Through many villages and towns they took me. My captors

walked along behind the cage. Now and then they stopped under a wayside tree and unyoked the bullocks to give them rest.
At such times the front portion of the carriage rested on the
ground, and the floor sloped forward and I kept sliding down,
with the remains of the goat flowing over me. It was uncomfortable, and I had to roar out my displeasure. The noise I made
scared the spectators surrounding my cage and sent them running. My guards broke into laughter and shouted at the crowd,
"If you are so scared of the tiger locked up in the cage, what'll
you do if we open the door and let it out?" This was their way
of joking. And then much talk, inevitable wherever human beings
are gathered. For one used to the grand silence of the jungle, the
noisy nature of humanity was distressing. In due course, I got
used to it. When I imbibed my Master's lessons, I realized that
deep within I was not different from human beings, and I got into
their habit myself and never had a moment's silence or stillness of
mind—I was either talking (in my own way, inaudibly) or listening, and thus became fully qualified to enter human society.

After days, how many I didn't know and could not reckon,
we came to a stop. The sides of the cage were still screened with
brambles and foliage and I had no idea where we were. I only
heard, as usual, a lot of talk and shouting and counter-shouting,
and much movement outside. Suddenly all the twigs and foliage screening the cage were torn away and I saw through the
bars a new world such as I could never have imagined in my
life—a stretch of land with no trees or rocks or long grass or
bamboo clusters or *lantana* bushes or other undergrowth, but
bare and clean ground as far as I could see, ending in what I
learnt was a big tent surrounded by smaller tents and shacks,
the whole ground swarming with bipeds. I had no notion that
the earth contained so many human creatures. Naturally they
stared and gaped and talked. I tried to head my way out by
pushing, and hurt myself in the attempt.

Now I saw a man with a long staff in hand standing close by,
saying, "Want to get out? All right, come on . . ." and he poked
with the staff and laughed when I protested. "Ah, what a beautiful voice. If you were a singer, you could enchant an audience

of thousands without a mike," and laughed at his own joke. Others laughed with him too. I learnt later that they were obliged to laugh at his jokes, being his subordinates. As I went along I learnt that he was the owner of the circus. He was the one who met me when I was trapped, and he was to be my commander for years to come. He now poked the staff through the bars and was greatly amused when I jumped about in pain and confusion. He said with a guffaw, "Ah, you are a promising dancer too!" He turned to his assistant and said, "Let us advertise—a tiger *Bharatnatyam,* something that no circus has ever attempted."

"Yes, sir, that's an excellent idea, sir," said Captain's "yes-man" who was always by his side agreeing with everything he said, his second-in-command.

"We will teach this fellow every accomplishment in due course," said Captain. "But our immediate job is to drive him into the other cage, which is going to be his new home." He prodded me with his staff and hit me to the accompaniment of stentorian commands; I was to hear the voice again and again in the years to come. Also he drew the staff along the cage's bars, creating a rat-tat noise which confused me. When I tried to understand what it meant, he withdrew the staff and jabbed my side with it. I was miserable and did not know where to keep myself. He gave me no rest, but drove me round and round with that staff in the narrow space till in sheer desperation, edging away from the probing stick, I dashed on and found myself in another cage, where the door immediately came down. This was my first act of obedience. Captain now withdrew his staff and said, "Ah, good. Stay there." He said to his yes-man, "Take the other cage for cleaning—awful mess, stinks to the high heavens."

As night fell, I could see more clearly. I heard a lion roar, and the voices of other jungle fellows; and over all that, of course, human talk in different keys. I saw only empty grounds before me and a glow of lights somewhere. I was bewildered and did not know why I was brought here, or what they were planning to do with me. Captain and his yes-man would come off and on, stand looking at me, say something between themselves, and then leave. It was irksome to stay in that cramped space all day and night—my only activity being lying down and getting up, and again lying down and getting up, stretching myself to the extent possible, and turning round and round, grumbling and whining. But no one cared. Being used to the vastness and freedom of jungle life, I found this an impossible condition of living. I could do nothing more than pace up and down in despair.

For three days I did not feel hungry. On the fourth day I felt a stab of hunger and did not know what to do about it: how was my hunger going to be appeased? This was hell, as defined by my Master, an endless state of torment with no promise of relief or escape. I still had no conception that food could come one's way without a chase. These were the stages of knowing attained through suffering. I can hardly describe that kind of suffering, an emptiness, a helplessness, and a hopelessness behind the bars. Now, of course, I have got used to it, after years of circus life and then the zoo. But at that time I just had no conception of that kind of life. Bars of iron, unbending and perpetually pressing against one's face. I had had no contact with any sort of metal in my life; now this combination of man and metal subdued me—metal which in various forms served the evil ends of man as prison bars, traps, and weapons. I desperately tried to smash the bars again and again and only made my head bloody. When Captain viewed me in this state, he only laughed and remarked to his aide, "All these stupid creatures are alike! They all expect the bars of the cage to be made of butter. No harm if he learns the facts of life in his own way!" And they left me alone.

I began to despair when they left. When Captain showed himself outside my cage, a hope always rose in me, however slight, that some improvement was likely in my lot. That was probably the way he worked, driving me on to look on him ultimately as my Saviour. He was considered to be an expert in animal training and deeply versed in their psychology. I began to look forward to his company. Pacing around that cage, I'd pause to press my nose close to the bars to watch the direction of his coming. He'd look at me and ask, "How are you, sir?

Learn to be a good boy and I'll make you happy . . ." I had no
idea how to become a good boy and attain happiness. He con-
tinued to make me suffer loneliness, immobility, and above all
hunger. For the last, I was hoping that he'd let me out now and
then to hunt for food. He didn't seem to think that way.

Later, when I explained this stage of my life to my Master, he
said, "You probably in a previous life enjoyed putting your
fellow-beings behind bars. One has to face the reaction of every
act, if not in the same life, at least in another life or series of
lives. There can be no escape from it. Now you have a chance
to realize how your prisoners must have felt in those days,
when you locked them in and watched them day by day to measure how far you had succeeded in breaking their spirits."

"Why should I have done that?"

"I can't answer it; people only follow their inclinations, and
sooner or later find their reward or retribution. That's the natural law of life, as inevitable as the ripening of a mango in its
season or the fall of a withered leaf."

For days they kept me without food and water. Only Captain
with his companion would come to observe me, and then comment, and leave. I lost all my strength and could hardly stand
up, much less pace around my cage. Even that little movement
was lost; I might be a carcass for all it mattered. In this state my
cage was moved one day and the door opened. I was let into a
larger enclosure. I jumped out gratefully, but I found that my
legs could not support me. But Captain was there at the centre
of the enclosure and would not let me lie down. He was uttering a command in a voice which could be audible in the next
jungle. He held a long whip in one hand and a chair in the
other. He lashed my face several times. My face smarted. I had
never experienced such pain before. When I tried to ward off
his attack, he wielded the chair as a shield. With my paws I
could only hit the chair, and he constantly poked my face with
it. He commanded, "Run, run," and kept repeating it with every
lashing.

To my shame and dismay, this was being watched by other
animals, beyond the enclosure. First time I was setting eyes on

those odd, unfamiliar creatures. I could not understand what species they belonged to. Some of them were tethered to a post, some were free, some in different types of cages. Among the birds I could recognize a parrot, but not some of the long-legged ones. A grotesque one was the camel. I was aghast at its height and humps. A majestic animal, to my surprise a grass-eater, I was told was a horse—there were many of them; a meaner version of the horse, not so handsome either, was also there, a donkey. Another one that took my breath away was a hippopotamus, which I mistook for a piece of ill-shaped moun-tain. Of course I could recognize the ape, which moved about freely—shaggy one with awkward swinging arms, which seemed to be well integrated in human society, able to move with hu-mans on equal terms . . . I had a glimpse of a bear, but no deer, which did not seem to have come to the notice of Captain. So far so good for them; only cursed creatures, weighed down with the *karma* of their previous lives, seemed to have come to his notice, who wielded his chair and whip like a maniac. I now understand that he had held me up as a lesson to other crea-tures, of what awaited them if they did not obey. At least they were fortunate in knowing how to show their obedience. They were all excellent performers; I was to become a colleague of theirs.

I was ignorant, bewildered, and in pain. It'd have been a re-lief to be able to pounce on that man and leave it to chance for one of us to survive. But that chair which he held made it im-possible for me to approach him, while his whip could reach me all over. He was crying out like a frenzied creature, "Run, run, come on!" While I stood paralysed and in great suffering, I heard one of those watching animals suggest to me in our lan-guage, which no tyrant could suspect or suppress as it would sound like merely a grunt or a sigh, "He wants you to run round and round as if stung by bees at your backside. Do it and he will stop beating you. Otherwise you have no chance." I couldn't guess where the message came from—could be the ele-phant placidly munching sugar cane, giving no suspicion of ever noticing my predicament, except through a corner of his eye. Ah, that was a great help.

I said to my well-wisher, "But I feel faint, can't stand on my feet, starving, not even a drink of water."

"Never mind. You will get everything—only run round as he commands. He is a madcap and we must learn to live with him. We are in his hands."

"Why do you tolerate him? Any one of us can stamp him out."

"Not so easily, he is really stronger than ten of us. Once all of us tried and were sorry for it . . ." Mutual communication was one privilege left for us animals: human beings could not interfere with our freedom of speech because they never suspect that we have our own codes, signals, and idioms. Fortunately they usually did not notice when we grunted, hissed or sighed, but when they did, they would talk among themselves anxiously: "Poor thing is making peculiar noises, I hope it is not going to be sick. Must tell the veterinarian to look over the beast: it must be in perfect form for the show tomorrow, for the specially advertised item, otherwise the public will smash the chairs and the gallery . . ."

The ape was the most light-hearted of all. He was the happiest animal in the circus, walking about freely in human company, fondly clinging to the finger of one or the other—even holding hands with Captain sometimes. He must be conceited, fancying himself to be a human being; smoking cigarettes, sitting in chairs and drinking tea from cups, wearing trousers and coat and cap and spectacles, and chattering merrily all the time. His acts in the ring were not different from what he did outside the ring—except a cycle ride combined with trapeze acts. He continuously chattered, grinned and grimaced—a happy soul. In my first glimpse of him, he also added a word of his own: "Hey tiger, run round and round as our boss demands. Let us hope and pray we'll see the day when he'll do the running and we shall hold the whip . . . Anyway, till that good day arrives, obey him and that simpleton will protect and feed us—we are at least spared the trouble of seeking food and preserving ourselves from enemies. He is doing all that for us. He is a damned fool, but doesn't know it; thinks that he is the Lord of the Universe."

"At one time, I had also thought so of myself," I said.

I ran round and round in circles in pursuit of nothing—and
that seemed a very foolish senseless act. At least a hare running
ahead would have provided a show of reason for running. But
that's how Captain seemed to want it; I held my breath, and
though my eyes were darkening with faintness, I ran and kept
running as long as he kept the whip cracking in the air without
touching my back—and that was some improvement indeed.
He went gyrating round and round following my movement. It
seemed as much hard work for him as for me. When the cracking of his whip ceased, I too stopped. It was not possible to run
any more. I was ready to fall into a faint and probably breathe my
last; breath coming and going so fast. When I came near my cage
I found the door open and leaped in and lay down—expecting
to be killed outright for my disobedience. But when I opened
my eyes, I saw Captain outside looking at me more kindly than
ever. "Well, that was a fine performance. I now have confidence
that we can use him." The whip and the chair were put away
and he was unarmed, and that itself seemed to me a good sign.
My cage was wheeled away to its original place, away from
other animals. I was sorry because I felt better watching others
and being in communion with them. Just as I was closing my
eyes, some warders poled and prodded me to move to another
cage. I was happy to find there pieces of meat and a trough of
water. My first piece of education.

I understood the business now and the routine to be followed. Every day at the same hour they would drive me into a
wheeled cage and draw it to the larger enclosure and let me
out, where Captain waited with chair and whip. The moment
the door was raised and the whip was flourished, I started running round and round. Then back to the cage, to be wheeled
off to my home, which I found cleaned and washed and with
food kept for me. That was very welcome. I'd have nothing
more to do for the rest of the day. Life was not so bad after all.
Captain was not such a monster after all. I began to respect
him for his capabilities. I began to admire him—a sort of wor-
shipful attitude was developing in me. I had thought in the jungle that I was supreme. Now that was gone. I was a defeated

king, and Captain was the unquestioned suzerain. After all, what he expected of me seemed so simple—instead of understanding it, I allowed myself to be beaten, and suffered through ignorance. And running around the enclosure was quite beneficial for one cooped up in a cage all day.

But soon I was to realize that that was not all. It was only a preparation. When I became an adept at running, I was ready for the next stage of education. The more difficult part was still to come.

I was let out into the enclosure as usual one day, Captain alert as ever with his chair and whip. At the crack of the whip, I started running as usual, but I found my passage obstructed by a strange object which I later knew as a stand, placed across my path. I checked my pace, at which he let out a cry, "Jump! Go on, jump!" and the whip came lashing on me. All the good name I had earned and the good feeling I had developed for Captain seemed to be lost. I felt infuriated at the lashing and felt like jumping on him; but he held that terrible chair. Now I know a chair is a worthless, harmless piece of furniture but at that time I dreaded the sight of it. It appeared to me a mighty engine of destruction. How Captain and men like him could ever have realized how a chair would look to a tiger is really a wonder. Now I have enough understanding of life to smash a chair if it is flourished before my eyes. But then a chair looked terrible. When I was lashed, once again all the old terror of not knowing what I should do came back to me. My friends who had advised me on the first day were not there. They had been taken away to some other part of the camp by their trainers; it was a vast world where many activities took place according to Captain's plans.

I stumbled on the obstacle and kicked it away and ran on my usual round. This enraged Captain, and he came dashing behind me shouting in a frenzy, "Jump! Jump!" and applying the whip liberally. I thought that this man was unsteady, alternating between occasional sanity and general madness. At the moment he was in the latter phase. What did he mean by bothering me like this, forcing me to do some obscure act? I ran hither and thither and tried to run back into the cage. That made him more angry. He came after me in a delirium and hit me as I crouched trembling in the cage. He shouted and ordered me out; I jumped out and started running round and came against the hurdle once again, knocked it down and ran hither and thither and went back into the cage. Red in the face and panting like an engine, Captain ordered, "Take the devil away. Off rations for three days, not even water, and he will come round, you will see . . ." He kept glaring at me.

Now I follow human speech, by the grace of my Master, but in those days I was dense and did not know what the word "jump" meant, and suffered untold misery. Today I would have immediately understood that Captain wished me to cross the hurdle in a jump and proceed to go round, come back to the hurdle and jump over it again and again until he was satisfied that I had mastered the art. Absolutely a pointless accomplishment, but Captain had set his heart on it. On the day I understood and performed it, he was beside himself with joy. He stroked my back with the whip handle as I gratefully rushed back to my cage and said, "Good. Keep it up; now you have earned your dinner . . ."

Every day I was put through this exercise. After a course of this, the next was only an elaboration of it. A few more obstacles were placed along the course of my run and they had to be cleared with the same smartness. My only aim now was to please Captain, and when I did that I got the reward, pieces of meat and water and undisturbed sleep in my cage. The hurdles were of different kinds, some labyrinth-like, some so twisted that I feared I might get permanently crooked. Into some I had to crawl on my belly and then out; some hurdles would lead me back to my starting point, and I had to clear them at the same speed, while he went gyrating like a spring doll, cracking his whip and commanding: "Come on, come on, don't waste your time." He held a watch in his hand and timed my run and movements, so that whatever perverse design he might have, I had to come through to the starting point at the same time. During the actual performance, he would announce: "Raja is now running at a speed of sixty miles an hour, the pace he generally maintains while chasing game in the jungle. From his starting point in the ring back to the same spot in two minutes five seconds. Whether he goes one round or several rounds he will maintain the same speed. After that you will see him go through several kinds of obstacles, hurdles and mazes . . . You will see, ladies and gentlemen, that whatever the hurdle, he clears it and finishes his round within the same time, adjusting his pace appropriately. He is uncanny in his timing. Anyone who wants to prove that he takes more time and I am wrong, is welcome to step in here and hold this stop-watch I have in hand. Anyone who can prove that he takes even one more second than what I have claimed will get a reward of five hundred rupees . . ." And he flourished five fresh one-hundred-rupee notes in the air. Quite a few in the audience came down but, finding that they were expected to stand within the enclosure to try their luck, withdrew.

Captain had a vast army working for him—trapeze artistes, clowns, trainers of monkeys and parrots and so on, horse riders, elephant and camel men. Each one handled a particular animal and had influence over it; there was one who could even make the hippo climb some height and occupy a stool. Every one of them had his peculiarities and problems and had to be kept in good humour as well as discipline. Captain's wife, Rita, was at the head of the trapeze team. He had many workers, who pulled, pushed, unrolled carpets and set up fences, furniture, and various other properties, and changed them quickly for the next item. As I became an established member of that circus, I was not isolated any more, but was allowed to stay around Captain in my cage. Thus I was able to watch him all day. And I also picked up a lot of information from other gossiping animals when we were kept near each other. The chimp was always bursting with news. Whenever we gathered together our main topic was the boss. He had other animals including a lion, which remained aloof but kept roaring incessantly, stimulating all other animals to make a noise. When Captain wanted quiet, he would go round cracking his whip and shout "Shut up!" in a thundering voice, overwhelming the lion's roar. At that time, I only knew that he had some concern for me, but I was not ripe enough to grasp the meaning of what was happening. Only in recollection now can I appreciate Captain's energy and power and the variety of tasks he was able to perform: to be successful and provide all that variety and quantity of food for us, also appear on stage, and do a great deal of off-stage work too, such as checking accounts, making payments, handling his men and so forth, activities that would go on far into the night. In the midst of all this he would also be thinking of new turns and tricks and novelties to announce to the public.

He called his a Creative Circus. After getting an idea he would shut himself in his tent, do some paper work, call up his chief executive, and say, "Here is a new idea, see how it can be worked out." It was not his habit to consult but only to issue orders. He would just state what he wanted done and then tell his staff to achieve it in practical terms. They were not to say yes or no but only proceed with it. Now Captain called his chief executive and said, "It's time to give a new twist to the trapeze items. It will be a sensation if the trapeze act also includes two somersaults in the air and then a passage through a ring of fire—I've thought out the details to some extent. I realize that a fireproof undervest for the artistes, which doesn't show, will be the first requisite . . . Here's a sketch I have made of the position of the ring in relation to the swings and the net below—you work out the mechanical details and modalities. Bring your report tomorrow morning."

The executive came up next day with the report, after working on it all night, but said, "Madam is not for any change." Captain brooded over it for a moment and said, "Put Lyla in Madam's place . . . the rehearsals must begin soon." Lyla was number two in the team.

This issue precipitated a domestic crisis. That night much shouting could be heard in their home tent. Madam threatened to quit the show once and for all. She said, "I'm not prepared to spare any of my girls or set fire to myself just to please your fancy. I'm not an orthodox wife preparing for *sati.*"

He retorted, "Look, don't talk like that. I'm not planning to set fire to you, you know that; I'm only thinking how we could give the public something new, some new thrills. Public must find it rather stale to see you and your girls in your satin tights swing up and down."

Here his speech was cut short by the lady saying, "You think our items are cheap and that easy? Have you any idea how every second one's life is being risked? You think whipping and bullying dumb beasts the only great act? Why don't you come up on the swing at least once and try, instead of talking theories?"

"You forget, my dear, that I did trapeze at one time, that's how I started, but I outgrew it . . ."

"Naturally, you had to give it up, otherwise the swings might have snapped or the roof itself might have come down."

"Since you fancy your figure has remained unchanged, I am suggesting you try and put it to some use so as to make people say 'This lady is capable of more than jumps and twists in the air, she can pass through fire rings so easily, being slim!' "

"Why don't you put your head down your lion's throat and sing a popular song?"

"You are not suggesting anything original . . . I'm planning it, maybe for the Jubilee Show."

"You are constantly talking of Jubilee. What sort of a Jubilee are you celebrating? May I know?" she asked cynically.

He ignored her remark and continued, "If you are not interested in the new trapeze act, keep off, that's all. The show will go on . . ."

Such a determined man that he planned, prepared, rehearsed this fiery act and presented it to the public later at what he called the Jubilee Show. Rita went through the act, unwilling to let Lyla take her place. The accuracy and timing with which the artistes performed their trapeze acts, somersaulted and shot through a flaming ring before coming to rest on the safety net below, was exciting and repeatedly applauded by the audience. But this happened at a later phase of my story. Let me go back to my training period.

———

After I had become an adept in racing over and through a variety of obstacles, I expected to be left alone. I was ignorant of the fact that it was only a preparation for another stage. What Captain had in mind could not be guessed by anyone. He always allowed an interval between stages of training so that I'd live in an illusion of having nothing more to do. But just as I was resting, my cage would be drawn to the training enclosure and there I'd find Captain waiting, whip in hand. When I saw him thus, I would wish we could talk it over and come to an understanding instead of going through the hard way to get a pat on my back for understanding his wishes.

Today he held a new terror for me. It was not enough that I ran around fast and also through the hurdles. At one point, while rounding a bend, I saw fire and shrank back. I thought, "Kill me now, but I won't go near the fire." I was reminded of the village fire when flaming torches nearly roasted me. I shrank back and naturally the whip came down and bruised me more than ever. He would not allow me to retreat from the fire, nor go round it or away from it. He blocked all my movement with his person, shielded only with the chair, while his whip could reach me from quite a distance: the state I was in, I could have easily destroyed him without a trace. Driven by desperation, panic and fury, I had to content myself with roaring out, "Leave me alone, you monster." But he overshouted me: "Raja, come on through that ring, in there, come on, come on . . ." The uproar and pandemonium we both created must have been heard all over the town. I snarled, showed my teeth, wrinkled my nose, opened my mouth and shut it, and growled as if the earth were rumbling. But he was unaffected and warded me off with his chair, and pushed me closer and closer to that fire. All my movement was restricted in such a way as to leave no room for me to move or turn except through the fire. First time my belly was singed but in course of time I could pass without touching the flames. And when I performed diligently I became Captain's favourite again; with meat and water back in my cage, I was once again left to laze and live in the delusion that my trials had ended and I was going to live a happy and free life hereafter.

The next piece of training was surprisingly mild. I was driven on round and round and then stopped where a stool had been placed. I had to sit on it dangling my tail on the floor. A saucer of milk was placed on a table. I was again and again forced to sit up in front of the saucer with Captain howling "Drink, drink, drink!" and holding his chair up; he bent down and put out his tongue over the saucer to indicate what I was expected to do. I watched completely baffled, but he was untiring in imitating the act of drinking off a saucer. "Lower, lower," he was howling. "Put head down and tongue out, tongue out," and he cracked the whip. When he did that I knew that the next would be on my back. I was quite desperate to understand him. Surely he was not expecting me to drink that white stuff in the saucer. It looked like poison to me. But there was no escape from it. He hit me so hard while I had my head down that I had to bend further down with my tongue out. No sooner had my tongue touched the saucer than I was seized with nausea and a fit of sneezing. What stuff was it, tasting so awful?

Later that day the chimp strolled along near my cage. How I envied his freedom! I wished I could also go about like him. But a tiger seemed to have a curse on it—no one can tolerate the sight of a tiger walking freely about, being burdened with size, might, and the fierce make-up that nature has given us. What a blessing to be the stature of an ape! Human beings approve of him because he approximates to their idea of what a creature should be in appearance and size. The ape was grinning as he clutched the bars of my cage and asked, "How did you like it?"

"What?" I asked.

"The milk in the saucer which you had to lick up."

"Terrible," I said. "Why should I drink it?"

"You will see for yourself soon. Why, don't you like it?"

"How can anyone like that terrible stuff?"

"Human kids are brought up on it right from birth. Men think no end of it."

"Do you drink it?"

"Yes, of course, I don't mind it, but I prefer banana and what they aptly call monkey-nuts."

"Why do you have to drink it?"

"Can't help it, when Captain thinks it is good for us, we have to take it."

"What is it made of?"

He answered, "It is made by the cow inside, and is squeezed out by men every day."

"Every day? But don't they have to kill it to get it?"

"It is drawn out without killing the cow—so that they are able to have it every day."

It seemed to me a strange world into which I was drawn. I said, "It is evil tasting. Surprising it should be found in the cow, which itself tastes so good. I won't drink that stuff whatever may happen!" Before I could ask for further explanations he hopped down and was off.

By the time I could get a pat of approval on my back from Captain, I had become resigned to the taste of milk. After that a new item cropped up. As I looked up from the saucer at a training session, I found seated opposite me across the table a goat—an extraordinary thing to happen. I thought I was being specially rewarded with fresh food for accepting the milk, though it made my head reel . . . A goat sitting up with a tiger as an equal—what a crazy situation! No goat would ever dare do such a thing. Anyway I'd accept the gift and get the milk taste out of my tongue. I gave a shout of joy and the usual victory cry before pouncing across the table. But when I stirred, I was whipped back to my seat and the goat was withdrawn. When I was back in my seat, another pan of milk appeared and the goat was back in his seat. I could not understand. This kind of jugglery was disturbing. Sitting on my haunches was irksome and painful: the sight of the pan of milk was offensive and the goat was appetizing. But what was happening was beyond my understanding. What perversity that I should consume what I hated and leave what I would relish! There seemed to be an eerie indestructibility about the goat and the pan of milk. Any other goat would have run away or vanished into my belly. This sort of dodging and reappearing—I didn't like it. It was confusing, maddening, I didn't like it at all. I went at it

again and again, and it disappeared and reappeared after I had
been whipped back to my seat. Ultimately I realized that it'd be
best to keep still, and take no notice of the goat. If it was not
meant for me, why were they offering it? The ways of Captain
were mysterious. Whatever he had in mind, he seemed to be
able to express it only through violence. How I wished that he
could speak my language or I his. There was no meeting ground
between us, but still we had so much to do with each other all
the time. That was the irony of fate. Captain was convinced
that if he bellowed deafeningly I'd understand, stupid fellow;
although I had to admire him for several reasons.

Ultimately by sheer doggedness he made me realize that I
was to ignore the goat. If I had realized it was only a dummy
for purposes of practice, it'd have been quite simple. But it was
so lifelike, I was deceived. I ignored it now. I sat peacefully,
hoping as usual that my trial was ended and that I could go
back to my home. But there could be no such thing as the end
in my life. The end of one trouble was but the beginning of another. Here I was disciplined enough not to move a muscle in
the presence of that supposed goat. I do not know at what
point they had substituted the real one. But it bleated and that
roused me. I involuntarily tensed, but Captain was too watchful and shouted, "Stay back, Raja," and that was enough warning for me. The stupid goat forgot its perils and became greedy
at the sight of the milk; it immediately put its head down and
lapped the saucer dry, and sat up to look at me as if to ask,
"What next?" Captain directed it with the slightest flourish of
his whip and without any display of the chair. He looked pleased
at the performance of the goat. With a smile on his face, he ordered for more milk, just as I was feeling relieved that the terrible drink was gone.

When another supply of milk came, he said, "Raja, now that
milk is for you. Lower your head and drink that milk." What
an impossible torture! I'd preferred to have that goat sitting
and blinking before me. I couldn't understand what he kept it
for. Milk indeed! I hesitated, noticed a slight movement of the
whip and bent down to the saucer, pretended to lick the milk,
and sat back, as well as I could. Next it was the goat's turn.

Captain ordered it with a slight wave of the whip, and the goat bent down and licked the plate dry. It was surprising how much milk that goat could consume. It looked as if it were Captain's intention to fill the goat to bursting point. He filled up the saucer again and again. It was merciful of him not to order me to drink the whole lot each time; he was satisfied if I dampened my nose or tongue, and then I could resume my seat. This went on all afternoon. The goat finished his portion first and then whatever remained in the plate after my show of drinking. Though I had by this time been forced to get used to the proximity of the goat, I began to hope that the goat might explode loudly with the quantities of the milk inside him and when that happened they would surely pass him on to me as they would have no further use for him. We had to be licking the milk alternately that whole day. I felt completely exhausted when I was allowed to return to my cage, and could hardly eat when my meat was brought in because of the lingering smell of milk. I just sank down and slept.

Next day I was put through a new set of exercises. I had to sit still until the goat had started lapping it up and then take my mouth to the saucer at the same time and pretend to enjoy the drink in his company. This was a trying moment as the proximity of the goat's head and its flavour was overpowering. I was perplexed at the way the whole thing was working out. I was amazed at the foolhardiness of the goat, which enjoyed its milk notwithstanding possible annihilation any moment. We had to rehearse this piece day by day until I was supposed to cultivate a taste for milk and an apparent distaste for the goat. When Captain was satisfied with the results, he made me rehearse the whole series, starting with running round through obstacles and fire, and coming to rest for a saucer of milk. (He set special value on this part and announced it with fanfare for the Jubilee Show, where it was to be presented as a Four-in-One Act.) Before the Jubilee he presented me in single-item acts, each once a week. He announced me to the public as "that miracle tiger Raja—the magnificent." I must have indeed looked grand and mighty with my yellow and black acquiring a special gloss, possibly through doses of milk imbibed each day. He explained that I was not an ordinary, commonplace tiger but an intelligent creature, almost human in understanding. (He was prophetic.) "He can read the time . . ." He always held up his stop-watch in my face before I started my round of runs, saying, "Mark the time, Raja, and keep up your speed."

Captain presented his shows six months in a year in Malgudi town. A team of men went round to the villages in the district clad in fancy costumes and with the beat of drums and a megaphone advertised the circus. They drove around village streets in a Model T Ford painted black and yellow to remind one of the tiger. They went up to Kommal, the farthest village, nearly fifty kilometres from Malgudi. On festivals and holidays the patrons arrived by bus, lorry, bullock-carts, and bicycles for the show; coming into the town for the circus was an exciting event for villagers, who turned up in family groups and camped in the town under the shade of trees, in the veranda of Albert Mission College, or in their wagons after unyoking the bullocks and leaving them to graze in the fields. At every show all seats in the galleries were taken as were the benches and wooden chairs and the squatting space on bare ground not far from the stage. Six cushioned seats were always kept in reserve for a hierarchy of local officials on whose goodwill depended Captain's survival.

When the monsoon set in, in October-November, the circus moved out of Malgudi to other centres in a long caravan, parading the animals, which made the circus known all along the way; the central office at Malgudi worked all through the year.

At every show, Captain made a speech, sometimes autobiographical and sometimes to boost a special act, such as mine. He delivered his message in at least three languages, as he explained: ". . . in Hindi since it is our national language and given to us by Mahatma Gandhi himself; also in English because as our beloved respected leader Nehru put it, it opens a window on the world. In Tamil, because it is, ah, our Mother Tongue, in which our greatest poets like Kamban and Valluvar composed; also the sublime inspiring patriotic songs of Bharathi, who can ever forget them?" Whatever the language, he spoke flamboyantly, always touching upon his personal life. "Ladies and gentlemen, friends, Romans, and countrymen, as Shakespeare said, I love my circus and the animals that have made my business a success; and I have pitched my tent here because I love Malgudi; I love Malgudi because I was born and grew up here. I was a back-woods boy—living and playing in the dust of Abu Lane. They sent me, hoping to make a scholar of me, to Albert Mission School, but fate willed it otherwise. I won't waste your time re-counting my adventures while you are all eager to see the perfor-mance begin. You will see my life history in book form (a shiny colourful brochure with his portrait on the cover) sold at the gate at cost price, so that young people may cultivate ambition and a spirit of adventure and bring our nation a great name . . . All that I wish to say is that the great circus master Dadhaji of Poona adopted me and trained me though I looked like a va-grant and was indeed one; and he employed me at first to clean the stables and then taught me how to educate animals. I cannot begin the show without bowing in homage and gratitude to the memory of that great master . . ."

Captain was considerate and helped us conserve our energies by regulating our rest periods. On off days he sent away all the herbivores to forage in the lower reaches of Mempi range—camels, horses, elephants, and zebra went out in a sort of pa-rade through the streets of Malgudi and returned in time for the next show. A set of animals always had at least two days' rest between performances. He did a lot of paperwork before-hand, scheduling each animal's duty and off-hours in a month. He studied the roster containing the names of animals (he had christened every one of the animals in his collection) and drew up a sort of chart for each one of them. The most strenuous part of their lives was during the training period. At that stage he was unsparing; and if they perished during the training, he took it as an inevitable risk of his trade. Once they were trained to perform, he viewed them as his assets to be protected, his own prosperity depending on their welfare.

He bestowed special attention to my part of the work. It al-ways came after the trapeze sequence, which was his wife's show. He never made any speech for introducing her—a matter which made her grumble from time to time. But he just waved her off: "Everyone knows what a grand team you lead, your girls are famous and need no introduction, also it'd sound odd to boost one's wife."

"While your wit and eloquence are reserved only for the tiger and the rest, I suppose."

"Yes, they need introduction, not you. Why are we always talking like this? Something wrong with our horoscopes . . ."

"Your horoscope and the tiger's seem to be better matched," she would say.

"Don't talk in that style. Someday you will be sorry that you have disturbed my mind. You don't realize that I need a calm mind and concentration in my work. My mood must not be spoilt . . ."

"As if I don't need a calm mind in my job! You think only of yourself and your tiger."

I don't know why she was measuring herself against me all the time. Fancy anyone being jealous of a tiger! Yet it was not really so. Given her chance, I don't think she would have poisoned me. She enjoyed being argumentative, that's all. They were a peculiar couple, devoted to each other but not betraying their feelings in speech. When I mentioned this subject to my Master, later in life, and sought his verdict as to whether they were to be considered friendly or inimical to each other, he just smiled and said, "Human ties cannot be defined in just black-and-white terms. There can be no such thing as unmitigated hatred or unmitigated love. Those who are deeply attached sometimes deliberately present a rough exterior to each other and that is also one way of enjoying the married state. Some wives in this world show their deepest love only by nagging, and the husbands also enjoy putting on an air of being victims. You must not forget that everyone is acting a part all the time, knowingly or unknowingly. But God who sees everything must be aware of their thoughts and the secret ecstasies of companionship of even that Captain and his wife . . . So don't make the mistake of thinking that they were not properly matched, judging merely from conversation overheard." Do you know, at the end, though his death was sudden, with the last flicker of consciousness he worried about his wife and how she was going to manage without him. Do you know what she did when she came over and saw him? She stood looking at the body without a word or a tear; and when others tried to comfort her said, "Leave me alone." After that she went back to the circus tent, climbed to the top where the swings were clamped, took out one, took a full swing up and down, and when the swing touched the ceiling, let go her hold . . .

"Jubilee" seemed to have become a self-explanatory word. When Captain started the publicity for his special Jubilee Show, no one questioned it, although his wife continued to taunt him. Announcements were made through colourful lithographed posters pasted on every wall in Malgudi. You could find the posters stuck side by side, starting from Albert Mission College compound wall, the first available wall when you turned town-ward from the circus grounds, on which was originally to be seen the bold stencilled warning, BILL STICKERS WILL BE PROSE-CUTED. Captain's men had come back to consult him about it, and Captain advised, "Stick the posters well over their warning and that will make it lawful . . . If we are questioned we shall send complimentary passes to the principal and professors." He had planned to put up a few more special ringside seats to take care of all possible objectors and obstructors, from the sanitary department to the jail superintendent, who could have created trouble for Captain at any stage; though law-abiding in a general sense, he had contempt for what he felt were silly objections. This was not the time for one to be finicky. He had to make use of the sprawling Central Jail walls, paint over them his Jubilee messages in giant lettering so that travellers journeying on the highway could not miss them. He had always felt that such walls were going to waste and should be utilized properly. He differed from those whom he considered a bunch of eccentrics, calling themselves Town Arts Council, who were opposed to every kind of announcement and hoarding, never realizing that they were thus cramping our economic life and ultimate prosperity.

When his plans were opposed, he had his own technique of

winning over opposition, a few complimentary tickets (not always for VIP seats; he had a few seats for semi-VIPs and non-
VIPs, accommodation in rattan chairs, wooden chairs, and
galleries, depending upon the status of those to be favoured).
When mere tickets would not work, he donated cash from a
fund he had earmarked as "Birthday Gifts" in his account
books, and Income Tax rarely questioned whose birthday. He
invaded every blank space in town to advertise the Jubilee.
Starting with Albert Mission College, as we have seen, to the
end of Abu Lane which splintered off from Ellamman Street,
the last outpost of Malgudi eastward, every kind of wall, of
shops, schools, houses, and hotels, proclaimed the Jubilee of
the Grand Malgudi Circus, displaying Rita in death-defying
trapeze acts, the chimp riding a motor cycle, the tusker carrying on its back the chimp dressed as a Maharaja with crown
and all, a giraffe doing something or the other, and clowns
tumbling. At every corner people stood staring at the wall.
Even those in a hurry to go to work paused to read the notice.
Not a single soul was left in doubt about the coming Jubilee
celebrations of the circus. In the same manner the countryside
was also informed by the usual team of clowns with extra noise
of drums.

As a result of this publicity, the box office presented an air of
a besiegement on the opening day. Every inch of the auditorium
was occupied for all the three shows each day—noon, evening
and night.

Captain reserved the tiger's act for the night show. It came
after Rita's trapeze act, somersaults, and dive through a fire
ring. When the tiger was wheeled in and the enclosure was
erected around the ring, Captain, dressed in satin breeches and
a glittering vest, holding the whip in hand, appeared before the
audience in a kind of light skipping movement, bowed to the
public deeply in all directions, and introduced, "Ladies and
gentlemen, you are about to see our Raja perform an act which
I have named 'Four-in-One,' which is actually a symphony in
movement as you will notice when the band plays. I have composed it with a lot of forethought. It's a sequence of precise
acts, timed properly, which sense of time is displayed uncannily

by Raja. He will go through the act with precision, and finish
the sequence as befits a country dedicated to non-violence, with
a sip of milk in the company of a goat. I'd now appeal to you
ladies and gentlemen to watch this act unwinkingly, keep your
eyes open and your nerves cool—never fear for a moment that
Raja will ever overstep the bounds in any manner."

After this speech, which created suspense and anticipation in
the audience, he let me out of the cage, opening the door with
his own hand. He carried nothing more than his whip; he had
put away even the chair. He wished to demonstrate that he was
absolutely confident of his authority over me and had nothing
to fear. He cracked his whip in the air twice to start me off. I
galloped around the ring, while he watched with a side glance
at his stop-watch, keeping himself deftly at a distance just a
foot beyond my pouncing range, but always close to an emergency exit. The audience watched in absolute silence without
stirring. I too caught the atmosphere and enjoyed showing off
my talent. When the rounds were completed, the hurdles and
mazes and labyrinths appeared at the appropriate places, and
then rings of flames at some points, followed by the item of the
goat and the milk. My mouth watered at the sight of the goat,
but Captain was very careful to crack his whip and drive me
back to the cage, unobtrusively, when he noticed it.

No one had witnessed such a composite and complex act before. When the applause subsided, Captain came forward and
said, "Sorry, gentlemen, no encore is practical for this particular act, nor am I in a position to ask Raja to take the bow personally. I'll have to do it on his behalf. But I also hope someday
I'll educate him in proper manners to respond to his adoring
public." And more applause . . .

The Four-in-One act and the fiery dive of the trapeze artistes
were very popular and brought Captain great fame. His box-
office collections soared, and apart from that his admirers
showered on him cash and presents of all kinds. He had done
something original and really creative in the annals of circus
and no one could repeat or imitate his programme; the success
was entirely due to Captain's genius. Jubilee, going on and on,
each week bringing in more crowds than ever. Captain looked

particularly happy and ordered an extra ration for all the animals every day. He was careful not to overfeed any animal that had, like myself, difficult acts to perform: "Keep Raja light, and feed him well at the end of his act, late at night. If he becomes heavy, he won't be fit to run through his acts so smartly"—with the result that they hardly fed me until midnight, when all my duty was done. This compulsory fasting the whole day kept me always hungry, and made it more and more difficult to accept the milk in the goat's company.

Thus it went on day after day, week after week, for a very long time. One evening I had just gone through all the turns preceding the milk—run with and without hurdles and through fire—and was sitting before the pan of milk. As a piece of courtesy to a weaker companion, the goat must be allowed to sip the milk first. He now had great confidence in me and took me for granted—rather a risky thing to do. I sat up watching him, assuming as benign a look as possible since the slightest frown on my face might bring the whip down, Captain being watchful as ever. As the goat bent down and stretched its neck to reach the milk in the pan, I felt a powerful impulse to seize that smooth white neck held out so temptingly—the agony of self-control was worse than the raging hunger. The gluttonous goat was lapping up the milk. How lovely it'd be to put one's teeth to it and go off to the bamboo bush to a leisurely meal. Forest memories overwhelmed me while that silly goat was relishing its milk, as if he had never tasted it before.

If only he had lifted his head, withdrawn even slightly, out of my reach, the world would have heard a different story. As it happened, the temptation stayed too long—holding myself back seemed impossible. Captain, reading my mind, was more alert than ever; he cracked his whip as a warning and commanded me to share the milk while the goat was still at it. But I hated that milk more than ever, and was delaying the unpleasant task. Normally when Captain fixed his look on me, I'd be nearly paralysed, and obey. But now, suddenly he had to look away, when he heard a commotion in the auditorium as someone fell off the top rung of a gallery. I chose this moment to shoot forward and nip off the goat's head. There were shouts and cries and confusion from a section nearby for a minute, and Captain whipped me hard, picked up his chair, hit me with it, and drove me back to my cage. The goat was finished, but of no use to me whatever, as it was snatched away out of sight at once and the place was cleaned and cleared as if nothing unusual had happened. Among the several thousands in the hall, a handful in the front row had noticed the end of the goat, but they were dignified VIPs who would not normally scream even if they noticed a fire or murder. Before the general spectators in the hall could know what was happening, I was back in my cage. The men had cleared the place very quickly, efficient men behind a curtain drawn all around, and the next item came on without delay as if nothing had happened. Four of our best clowns, along with the chimp in tuxedo and wearing spectacles, came on the stage with their special charms and jugglery, and completely diverted the minds of the audience so that no question was asked as to how the preceding item had ended.

Meanwhile I must say I had become unpopular with Captain. He shunned me for a few days and dropped my acts completely from his announcements, explaining to the audience in one of his speeches, "Ladies and gentlemen, I'm sorry to say that Raja's acts have to be suspended for a few days as he has distemper and needs rest and isolation."

"Rest and isolation" meant starving to me. They gave me neither food nor water for three days on end, Captain's usual method of chastening one's temper. I wished I could have explained that what I had done was due to robust health and hunger and in no way to be described as distemper. Distemper indeed! If they had left me alone, I could have helped them forget the existence of the goat completely. At least they should have let me finish off my prize; I had thought I would take it to my cage . . . What right did he have to starve me? I felt enraged at the thought of Captain and his allies and wished the iron bars could yield, and then I could show them another way to celebrate the Jubilee. The isolation hurt me most. I had got used to the company of that wonderful chimp and all the good fellows, gossiping among ourselves from our confinements or tether posts. However, the chimp sneaked in beside my cage unobserved when Captain was away on some business in the town and the keepers were relaxing. He said, "What had come over you?"

"I was hungry, that's all," I said.

"How can you eat a friend with whom you had been on milk-drinking terms, however hungry you might be! Though I am sorry for the poor goat, for he was mild and inoffensive, I'm glad to say that it's done us some good. Captain is talking of closing the Jubilee shows and resting for a few days. I was there when he was talking to his wife at breakfast and she said, 'The first wise act in your life . . . We are all at breaking point, I'm sure.' He didn't dispute her remark as he normally would, but remained moody and gave me a cup of tea to wash down a buttered toast. It was so good. Why can't you also eat these things, so much better than your normal preferences . . . You'll be a good fellow if you learn to eat things that don't move or breathe, and then people will not blame you, but accept you in society and have you around without these iron bars. Then you will be popular, not feared. If you are hungry, I can bring you a banana and some nuts sometimes. Many visitors bring me a lot—I can't eat all of it . . ."

Listening to him made me feel worse. I said, "Don't talk about food, unless you can get me what I can eat. It's no use talking about it. Your talk makes my hunger worse . . ." And the chimp went away with a leer. I was in no mood for jokes.

I suffered hunger another day. When I was lying half-dead Captain came up, peered in through the bars, and said to his companion, "Take a look at him now. Not at his best. He is under treatment for his misconduct. I hope he has learnt a lesson . . ."

"Put up another goat before him and see what he can do. That was a magnificent shot I took in sixteen-millimetre. I was lucky to be there in time to take it. I don't think you could ever repeat it. One-in-a-million situation . . . As I watched, he was so quick no one could have noticed his action. His head shot up like a cobra's and he just pecked at that goat . . . but it was like a—it was snap-action, neat, precise like a surgeon's . . ." That man was so full of enthusiasm and praise for me that he became incoherent and could hardly complete a sentence.

Captain said, "So what?"

"You don't seem to appreciate it . . . It'd be an impossible, unbelievably perfect shot—the kind of thing that a film director would be dreaming about. I shall treasure the shot I've taken and use it somewhere, and if it gets an award in any international film show, don't be surprised . . ."

"Raja is my tiger, and I want a royalty for a show by him . . ."

The other laughed as if he had heard a humorous statement, and then said, "Captain, ever since I saw Raja's surgical performance on the goat, I have been thinking of a story in which I could put him to proper use . . ."

"I have to think it over," said the Captain. "I can't give an instant yes or no. I want two days."

"But I can't force you to give a reply. Think it over, and understand that I can give you a handsome offer . . . but don't starve him further. Feed him. He is magnificent; don't spoil him. You have no idea how he will look in colour." He took another long look at me and said, "Raja the Great. I am sure you will cooperate with us . . ."

Both of them went away. I heard the tinkling of the bucket handle and stood expectantly. My food was come. An attendant placed meat and water in the other half of the cage, locked it, and pulled open the partition. I gave a roar of pleasure, and attained a feeling of well-being very soon. I was able to pace up and down the entire length of the cage in a happy state of mind.

Captain spoke to his wife about the film-maker that night. After the Jubilee he was going through a period of rest for two weeks before starting preparations to move on to Trichy, the next camp. This was just the time when Captain could enjoy a little domestic felicity. Go to bed early and find time to talk to his wife. When he mentioned the film proposal she asked, "What exactly is Raja expected to do?"

"I'll know it soon, but I must know first of all whether we should consider the proposal at all . . ."

"I'll say nothing until I know what you are going to say."

"Why?"

"So that I may save you the trouble of contradicting me."

They were in a pleasant mood of banter without acrimony or any relevance. She asked, "Can they handle Raja?"

"They can't. The idea seems to be that they will tell me what they want, and I get Raja to do it."

She remained in deep thought for a while and said, "I don't know, I've always hated that brute . . . seems undependable . . . I feel uneasy whenever you are out with him."

Captain laughed at her fears. "Let me say he is more docile than a Siamese cat . . . However, I'm not asking for a testimonial, but whether we should consider the film proposal at all."

"Yes, if he will buy this little cat off your hands . . ."

"Nothing of the kind, my dear, I won't part with him as long as I run a circus. I'm looking for another goat to train; until then Raja can be used elsewhere."

"Another poor goat to be made into a ghost?" was all that she could say. "Shocking it was. I realized that if you relax even for a split second he'll, God knows what he will do . . . the way he glares! I feel more easy with your lions . . . they are noble and gentle—I don't know why you should not be satisfied with their work, and want to bother about this tiger or any tiger . . ."

"Given a chance the lion can also bifurcate a goat. Don't take too harsh a view of Raja for it . . . He didn't do it out of malevolence, but a sudden impulse of mischief. That's a way of life in their jungle society."

"What an explanation!" she cried. "I don't know if you will ever listen to me."

"All the time I do nothing but listen. Anyway, the main question is whether Raja should be lent for film work at all. However, there is time to think it over. Instead of idling his time . . ."

The film-maker, whose visiting card, embossed on a thin sandalwood strip that filled Captain's office with fragrance, said,

"Madhusudan, Cine-Director and Producer," came in as promised on the third day.

Captain said, "The scent of your visiting card heralds your arrival even before you appear."

"That's my intention, Captainji. If you keep it in your table drawer, you will not forget me. Call me Madan."

Captain showed him a chair. "I'm a TT, but I can get you a drink, if you would like that sort of thing . . ."

"Never touch a drop when I have to talk business."

"Why?" asked Captain. "I thought for people like you it'd sharpen your negotiations."

"No, sir, I should like to be aware of what I'm saying," said the director.

Captain engaged him in small talk for a while, called for soft drinks, and said, "Now let me hear your proposal."

The director cleared his throat and lit a cigarette. "It's a simple one. Ever since I saw your tiger, I wanted to make a picture with him in the chief role. I have watched his performance for weeks now, while the idea was developing in my mind. But when I saw him the other evening so neatly slicing the goat, I said to myself, 'Ah, here is my material, here is what I have been seeking eternally. I'm at the end of the quest.'"

"The tip of the rainbow where the golden bowl is!" added Captain.

"You are absolutely right, sir," cried the director. "So you understand me! You are a genius, sir."

Captain cried, "You are no less so, now go on. We understand each other."

The director said, "Ever since I saw that act of your tiger in relation to the goat, I felt inspired, particularly after I saw the shot in sixteen-millimetre, which of course is going to be blown up to thirty-five and integrated in the feature, and, oh, boy! it's going to be a sensation."

Captain, being used to the company of monologists, sat patiently without fidgeting or interrupting the other's flow of talk as he went on dilating on his aesthetic and commercial outlook without coming near any actual offer. When he had gone on for

fifteen minutes, Captain felt he should put in a sentence of his
own lest the other take him to be asleep, and said: "You found
the goat scene inspiring, but my wife Rita, although accustomed to circus life, felt sickened by the spectacle and retired;
even now when she recollects the scene, she is in tears . . ."

The other said, "Of course, women are likely to be squeamish, and we have to make allowances for that, but we can't
allow our plans to be guided by them. I always take care to see
that when my picture goes up for the censor's certificate it is
seen only by the male members on the panel . . . After all the
film medium is where Art and Commerce meet—we have to
keep that fact always in mind. All the sentimentalists' outcry
against the so-called sex and violence must be ignored. They
make too much out of it. Life is created and made possible only
through sex and violence, no use fighting against it, shutting
one's eyes to the facts of life . . . Inspired by your circus act I sat
up that night and wrote the outline of the story in which Raja
would be the main feature. The human side in the story will be
a hero called Jaggu. I have already booked him; he was an all-in
wrestler and physical-feats performer and weighs one hundred
kilogrammes, two metres in height. When he is photographed,
his figure will fill a wide screen. I had booked him and was
looking for a story. I was lucky to have got one of your VIP
seats at the show, through a friend in the Collector's office—
that's how I was able to film the goat sequence."

"I didn't notice your camera . . . I'd not have permitted it."

"I know, I know, I wouldn't blame you. But I've a special kind
of camera, which can't be noticed . . . What was I saying?"

"Your last sentence ringing in my ear is 'Goat sequence . . .'"

"Thank you. The goat, brought up as a pet, is constantly being pursued by the tiger, who is accustomed to ripping off goat
heads, but the giant who owns the goat fights it off with his
bare hands. He finally captures the tiger and trains it to live at
peace with the goat . . . Non-violence is India's contribution to
civilization. I got the idea from your own speech before the tiger act; violence can be conquered only by non-violence . . ."

"Then how are you going to fit in the shot you have already
taken?"

The director became thoughtful. "I'll get a story writer to fix all that. After all it should be his business. How can you show non-violence without showing a lot of violence and how bad it is?"

"Sex, how about it?" Captain was enjoying this talk. He found it relaxing after all the strenuous labour of recent days.

"Oh, yes, that part of the story will come through in our story conference and the story writer should be able to work it in properly. Everyone knows how important normal sex is and what an evil sex can turn out to be without a proper philosophy of life."

"With a virile giant running about, it should not be difficult for him to hunt women also . . . Well, that part of it cannot concern me—only the tiger. If we agree on terms and if you would complete Raja's part of the work within the time I specify, it'll suit me."

"I don't know . . . If there should be any retakes?"

"We'll think of it. But let us discuss terms, if we may . . ."

"I hope you will not demand too much. I want your cooperation and encouragement. We are planning on a moderate budget, getting the technicians and crew from Madras, shooting mostly outdoors . . ."

"I can spare Raja for two weeks at the start and for retake extensions, we'll see, we may have to think of special terms . . ."

"What are your terms? You are mentioning only special terms."

"Meet me again three days from now. I'll have to talk to my lawyer."

"There should be no delay . . . We must shoot in the bright season. I am anxious to start the production without delay. I have come to you because you are an animal lover like me; with your cooperation I want to make an international picture. I'm not having a dialogue writer yet, I want to try how far we can go with a minimum of speech, which should make the picture appreciable anywhere in the world . . . I am young—I want your blessing," he appealed.

"I'm not a hermit to give blessings. I'm only a businessman, and expect my terms to be fulfilled if my services are wanted."

At which Madan threw open his briefcase, took out a cheque-book and a pen, poised the point over the cheque, and said, "Mention your figure and I'll put it down and sign. I'm also a businessman."

Captain watched him calmly with a smile. "Put it back. I don't accept a cheque. Anyway, I have said see me again and we can discuss terms. On Friday you will have my terms neatly written down. You will have only to put your signature to it, and then you may schedule your work."

It sounded simple enough, but Madan found it difficult to conclude the transaction. He could not understand what Captain expected him to do to finalize the business. He came almost every morning. He was staying at The Travellers' Bungalow, four miles out, and had to visit the circus camp every day. He had to be satisfied with meeting Anand, who would keep him seated in his office, offer him coffee and soft drinks but no interview with the boss: "He is in the training enclosure," which implied that no one could reach him or watch him at work. Captain knew it was hard on the creature under training, and did not want any sentimental busybody to watch and carry tales to the SPCA. Any visitor who strayed beyond the STRICTLY KEEP OUT board faced the danger of being thrown out.

It made Madan fret while waiting in the front office. "Do you realize that I have to come five miles each day and go back, while all my technical arrangements are ready, but unutilized?" Anand never paid attention to his complaints, but went on with his work at the desk, answering him in monosyllables, and if the visitor seemed too impatient, silencing him with refreshments. Anand just said, "When he is rehearsing, even I cannot approach him, even if the tent should be on fire."

"How long should one wait?"

"That I can't say . . . Sometimes he goes on for eight hours at a stretch. Unless the performer executes what he has in mind, he never lets go. It may take a whole day."

"So how long should I wait?"

"That I can't say . . . In this season of training for the next camp, he is generally not available; even his wife can't disturb him."

"Can I go and watch the tiger in the cage, please?"

"Yes, of course, but we have to have the boss's permission."

"But you can't reach him."

"Yes, that's true," Anand said sadly, which was not helpful in any way.

Madan sat every day at Anand's office for four hours at a stretch, while Anand went about his business at his desk and also outside, leaving Madan alone. Madan soon tired of waiting, bored with the outdated newspapers and illustrated magazines on the table. He felt outraged. He told Anand one day, "I'm a businessman too, sir. I have other things to do than just sit waiting for a *darshan* of the great man."

Anand said with a smile, "You must not get discouraged. Many others have had to wait for weeks to see him. After all, in business matters, one should be calm . . ."

At which Madan lost his temper, stamped his foot, and started shouting. The uproar brought Captain on the scene. He asked, "What is going on?" Madan started a harangue, a long narrative full of indignation. Captain cut it short by saying, as if nothing had happened, neither apologetic nor explaining anything, "Come, come, let us adjourn to my room."

Madan followed him sheepishly, grateful that he could at last have an audience. He opened his briefcase, sending out a whiff of sandalwood perfume from his special visiting cards. He took out a sheet of paper. "Here is my proposal in writing. Please say what you want."

Captain glanced through the proposal and said, "Not suitable. I'm only giving you my tiger for a set purpose, for a limited period, and not surrendering him to you. You will have to re-draft the whole thing."

Madan was aghast. "Nowhere have I said—"

Captain did not allow him to continue. "That's all right. Please listen to my advice, and all will be well . . . It's better we have it out at this stage, rather than later—possibly in a courtroom."

"Oh, I hate to have anything to do with lawyers or courts," Madan said nervously.

But Captain said, "I don't mind such things. In my profession, all the time I have to think of lawyers and courts. Can't help it, if I must survive."

Madan was slightly frightened and completely softened by this time. He took back his document and said, "Captain-*sab*, give me a draft and I'll sign it blindfold . . . Only tell me when to come, so that—"

"So that you don't waste your time? Mr. Madan, my time is not my own. My work lies in getting things done with the co-operation of all sorts of animals . . . and I've to depend upon their time. Anyway, let us say next Friday, at ten o'clock. I'll try to keep myself free, and keep away from the animals." And he laughed as if it were a joke.

Before leaving Madan pleaded, "The technical unit are waiting for a word from us. I can't hold them off indefinitely . . ."

"Next Friday at ten o'clock," said Captain repeatedly, and showed him the door.

Several days had to pass before Madan could finalize the agreement. Captain would not be available, or if available would disagree with some clause and send the document back for re-drafting.

"You see, the artiste [they were referring to Raja] should be present at the location when called."

"No, sir, you have to be specific about time and place. Suppose you have a location in Timbuctoo . . ."

Madan looked desperate. "If it was to be at Timbuctoo, why would I be here, sir?"

"I don't know, I want you to be specific. I don't mean Timbuctoo literally, of course . . ."

"I have not yet fixed the location."

"Why don't you do that first? From what I see you are ready only with the tiger . . . Not adequate for the starting."

"I've Jaggu, the hero of the story; I've booked him and he is staying with me—won't let him out of sight till the picture is completed. I'll keep him for possible retakes too."

"Excellent, your actors are ready, but not your stage."

"Each day's delay is costing—"

"Don't bother to tell me the figures or your calculations. I've enough calculations of my own, God knows . . ." He glanced at his watch. "Now I have to be off, my friend. Come again with practical ideas . . ."

"When? When?" Madan asked anxiously. There could be no specific answer to it; he was not even sure these days about the tiger—a fundamental doubt. Every time he suggested that he should be allowed to watch the tiger, he was put off with some objection or other, until Madan began to wonder if he was to get the real tiger or a stuffed one. In his feverish thinking, anything seemed possible. But it was too late to back out of the project. He had taken custody of the strong man Jaggu, who sat placidly in the front veranda of The Travellers' Bungalow, swatting flies, which somehow were attracted to him in swarms. The technical crew awaiting his orders at Madras kept demanding action. He flourished letters and telegrams from them in the hope of impressing Captain. But Captain viewed them indifferently, only remarking, "After all, technicians are there for our use, not the other way round. Don't let the tail wag the dog. Be firm. They must realize who is the boss; they must not try to rule us. You are a good fellow, full of enterprise—don't be weak in management. You must work on bases which are firm. You know, Dadhaji used to say . . ." He would quote some significant aphorism concerning business management.

Madan felt desperate; when he succeeded in securing an audience with the great man, it was difficult to keep him to the point. He could not make out what Captain was to gain by delaying like this. When he tried to be strict, Captain would just say, "Madan, my friend, know this, I won't be coerced whatever may happen. You bring the answers to my queries, and then you'll have my green signal. It must go on at its own pace. Why should we hurry? I won't be coerced or hustled; and I am quite prepared to drop the whole proposal, if you cannot satisfy my conditions. First fix your location, and then come to me."

"Can't you help me?"

"No," said Captain with an air of finality. "It should be your business and your technicians', not mine."

This placed a big strain on the film producer. The greater the urgency he showed, the more Captain delayed, until he felt challenged and got into a fever of activity which did not cease night or day. When he reappeared before Captain a few days later, he was able to be specific about three locations. The first one was rejected because it was close to the jungle, and Captain explained, "Psychologically unsound, as the tiger may become homesick and behave queerly, if not desert us." He rejected the second location, an open ground across river Sarayu, beyond Nallappa Grove, for the reason that it was too close to the town and might attract crowds. The third location, in the southern direction, a wooded area, where the highway passed within a couple of furlongs, was finally approved, and the contract was signed. Madan felt as triumphant as if he had produced a picture and received the Oscar.

Madan worked night and day to transform the land he had taken on lease—a place which had somehow come to be known as the Ginger Field, possibly because at some remote period someone had cultivated ginger and sent up the crop in wagonloads for extraction to a factory in Madras, and later sold the land to a pawnbroker at the Market Gate. Madan lost no time in preparing the location for shooting. He engaged men and women from a near-by village to remove stones and bumps, and sweep and smooth out the ground. He pressed Jaggu into service, a welcome diversion for him from swatting flies at The Travellers' Bungalow. He uprooted boulders and tossed them off with ease. He lifted heavy articles in the construction of sets (a village street with a row of two-dimensional homes), stockades, and platforms for mounting lights, reflectors, cameras.

When all was ready, Madan could persuade Captain to come up and see it, and felt happy when Captain remarked after his inspection, "You are truly great to be able to transform Ginger Field into a film studio."

"All your blessing and cooperation," Madan replied.

"More than mine, seems to be that giant's cooperation," said Captain. "He is, I suppose, a substitute for power-lifts, steam hammers, cranes, and other stuff of that kind."

"He could carry down that generator as if it were a box of matches. Hauls up stacks of bamboos for the fencing, probably a ton at a time, he just picked them up and set them in place . . . For all his appearance, he is mild and gentle."

Captain cast a special eye on the spot chosen for the tiger, and suggested a few changes: "Get the enclosure close upon this spot, so that the cage is not hit by the evening sun, which is not good for the tiger. Give me twenty-four hours' notice, and I'll have him ready for your call. Your Jaggu is really a find," he said, looking at him while he was unloading a truck-load of property and enjoying the task. "What a mountain of a man! You are lucky. I could have used him in my circus too— for lifting and moving which goes on all the time with twenty hands at the job. After you have done with him, will you please let me try him?"

"Of course, if you like. After all the possible retakes, when the negatives are cut, I'll set him free and you may have him. Perhaps if you include an all-in wrestling show, he'll excel in that . . ."

"Oh, that may not fit into my general programming, but I'll take him on and see what I can do."

Madan explained, "I first saw him at a village market fair. I was travelling from Trichy to Madras, and owing to a tyre-burst and a radiator leak the car stalled at an awkward place, and had to be taken to a wayside mechanic. The nearest village smithy was over a mile away, but everyone was at the weekly market fair when I went along to seek help. At the fair I noticed this fellow standing on a little platform and challenging the people around to come up and wrestle, even four at a time, if they chose. When his challenge was accepted, and a batch of four fell on him, he just brushed them off with the back of his hand. His admirers applauded and cheered, while his challengers picked themselves up from the dust and paid down the wager. That seemed to be his main source of income. The money was collected by a woman; I learned from the crowd that she was his wife. Bouts of wrestling were followed by feats of strength: he snapped chains, bent and twisted iron rods, split a slab of granite with the edge of his palm, and even offered to run a road engine over his chest if someone could arrange it. The puny wife went round collecting money. Now, after his per-

formance, I took him along to the spot where my car had
stopped, and he just pushed it down the road like a perambula-
tor. I paid ten rupees to his wife and they were overwhelmed.
Before he returned to his place at the fair, I noted down his address. He lived in a hut and made money at the market fairs in
the countryside. While I was brooding on a subject for a film,
the sight of this man gave me an idea for a 'strong-man' story
of a giant who could not be contained. When I went back that
way again, I visited his hut and offered him five hundred rupees
a month for one year with food (that was most important) to
join me and do whatever role I gave him. His puny wife was
delighted to let him go, having never seen so much money in
her life. Her condition was that he'd send her money every
month and get back to her at the end of it all. After I saw the tiger act in your circus, I wanted to combine them in my story—
and there we are."

They were seated on folding chairs in the shade of a large
banyan tree. Captain looked happy and relaxed, much to
Madan's relief—very different from what he seemed at the circus ground. Madan asked, "Would you like a cup of coffee,
tea, or fruit juice?"

"You have all that here too?" Captain exclaimed patronizingly.

"First thing I arranged to have was the canteen over there,
where you see the smoke—otherwise no work would go on
here; they'll be going out all the time for a refreshing drink . . .
For stronger refreshments too they have a tavern—fortunately
for us a mile out of here—where I believe they gather at the end
of the day. I don't let them leave this spot during their working
hours . . . though sometimes I notice some transaction going on
across the barrier at the back of the lot . . ."

"Don't notice too much. You must know when not to be too
observant. I have a team of about three hundred at work, I find
all sorts of problems. I can't be too strict or rigid as long as they
do their work, I try not to look too closely . . ."

Captain was relaxed; Madan felt expansive and said, "You
will be welcome to come and spend as much time as you like
here . . . You look more happy here."

The make-up and costume section was in one of the huts, and it could hardly hold the make-up man and his assistants as Jaggu stood in the centre. He was fitted with a leopard-skin covering, which was strapped across his shoulder; his hair was tousled so that it stood like an aura, and they had given him a moustachio, which curved up to his ears. There had been a controversy among the make-up men whether the ends should curve down in pirate fashion or up like a colonel's. They went on arguing about it so hotly that Madan heard their wrangling from under the shade of his banyan tree and came over to ask what the matter was; he stood at the entrance, impressed with the mighty figure, while the make-up men were going round him like pygmies. They went on touching him up here and there as if he were inanimate. Except for a little shifting of his legs, and letting out a deep sigh, he gave no sign of being alive. Madan studied him and cried, "Here, pull off those moustaches. He is all right plain-faced. He is like Tarzan and not like a pirate or Bhima."

"But, sir, there must be some break-up or offset for his face. It's too plain for the large area . . ."

"It's sticky, sir, and scratching, sir," mumbled Jaggu through the gum on his lips.

"Where did you get the idea to give him whiskers? Take them off immediately," Madan ordered while Jaggu looked on gratefully. "Also loosen his robe a bit—it should come down to his knees, even covering his knees. Otherwise, it will look as if he wore a loincloth, and will cut a sorry figure on the screen— enough material in that cloak, loosen all the pleats . . ." It took them over two hours before achieving the results visualized by Madan. Pulling out the moustache was ticklish, literally, and Jaggu moaned and wriggled and was reprimanded by Madan's assistant supervising the operations.

Finally at about nine o'clock the hero was ready: properly painted and costumed, his hair done up in proper style. Madan and his assistant stood around gazing and commenting.

Madan looked satisfied. "An hour or more wasted because of the moustache. I don't know where they got the idea from—

our mythology, I suppose! Jaggu is not a demon . . . We must establish him as a normal human being. Any character with whiskers repels—particularly women and children. Polanski has explained somewhere ["Who is Polanski?" the assistant wanted to ask, but checked himself] the audience's sympathy must be established first—and he has statistics to show that between a character with hair on his lip and one clean-shaven, the latter gains more sympathy . . ." His assistants stood around nodding appreciatively at his knowledge of the *shastras* of cinematography. Madan looked with admiration while Jaggu was brought out. He said, "Go up to that hut. Let us see how you do it. Walk naturally . . . don't swing your arms . . . be natural. Camera rehearsal," he shouted suddenly and a cameraman suddenly sprang into action. "O.K., boss, a little more to the left, please . . . more left . . ."

They made Jaggu return to the starting point, marked it with white paint, and told him to walk up again to the steps of the first cottage. They measured the distance with a tape and marked a circle on the cottage step, and directed him to stand in that circle with his back to the camera. The director ordered, "Don't turn until you hear a cry, 'Tiger, Tiger!' Till that cry is heard don't move even an inch . . ." He was made to walk back and forth repeatedly. He began to perspire and pant, and tried to wipe his forehead, at which a great cry went up, "Oh, no, don't wipe!" and a make-up man dashed up to him and dabbed his face with a towel, and touched it up. Then he was made to stand within the circle with his back to them. "Don't turn. Stare ahead until you hear the shout, 'Tiger! Tiger!' Do you follow me?"

"Yes, sir."

The director allowed a pause and suddenly screamed, "Tiger! Tiger!"

"Where?" Jaggu asked involuntarily in a stentorian voice, looking around in panic: he made a move to spring forward.

The director cried, "Idiot! I told you not to move out of this mark. Get back and stay there . . ." This slight exercise disrupted all the original arrangement. Once again they brought all the measuring tape and stretched it between the starting point and the circle. The cameraman kept saying, "More left, more left, your feet in the circle . . . Now come forward just one foot . . ." Someone came up and held a meter close to his cheek again and went back, and the make-up man was again patting his cheeks with a cotton swab. Jaggu felt tired and confused. Madan said to his assistant, "He must be told the sequence of this scene."

He approached Jaggu as he stood with his back to them, and went round to face him. "Now don't move, only listen. They will now take a shot standing as you are now. Following it, you will hear the cry 'Tiger! Tiger!' When that's heard, you will only say, 'Ah!' as loudly as you can, spin round like this, raise your arm and spring forward with a war-cry and run up to that starting point over there marked white, demolish the tiger and walk back casually . . ." Madan demonstrated every detail of his advice, spinning round with upraised arm and falling forward. He showed the action repeatedly till Jaggu could understand, and then withdrew to his chair marked "Director," called for a glass of water, and sipping it said, "Handling this idiot is proving more difficult than I had expected. However, I'm determined . . . Tell them to be ready to shoot in five minutes. Is the clap ready, 'Shot One Take One?' Check it. Sound and camera . . . ready . . . sequence number . . ."

While this was going on a cry was heard from the other end of the field: "Tiger has come!" On hearing it Jaggu without any warning spun round with a great cry and sprang forward with his arms upraised. A couple of members of the crew who were on duty jumped out of his way to avoid his stormy approach. Madan tore his hair in despair and demanded, "Who cried that?"

"The tiger carriage has come, sir, and they are now bringing the carriage down the field, sir," explained one.

Madan looked at the cameraman and said, "Bloody mess . . . Begin all over again." He said to his assistant, "Take that fool back to his position. Keep him within the circle. Let him not budge even a hair's breadth . . . Otherwise tell him he will be sacked. Touch him up all over again . . ." At this moment, Captain arrived in his small car. Madan rose to receive him.

From my cage I could watch the scene and also hear a great
deal of their conversation after their mutual greetings. I felt
happy to be able to stay in this wood. It reminded me of my
jungle days and revived a craving for freedom. I couldn't complain of anything now; I was protected and fed and looked after by Captain. But that seemed hardly to suffice. I'd enjoy
being able to move about and exercise my limbs as I pleased.
Though well kept, I was still a prisoner. If only they could trust
me and open the door, I'd go out, run, and return to my cage.
But my species has an unfortunate reputation, and one's natural actions are misconstrued. People talk ill of us all the time.
It's our misfortune that neither the denizens of the jungle nor
those of the towns would trust us or behave boldly—the exception being Captain, but he had his own limitations of understanding: he had a wrong philosophy of depending upon the
whip and his terrible voice, not realizing that I could be made
to go through all those meaningless motions even without all
that violence, by just being told what to do. But how to make
him or anyone understand that his style drives one into a panic,
and that left alone a tiger could be as innocent and harmless as
a cow or a chimp?

I heard Madan say to Captain, "This is what I want. It is up
to you to arrange it. Raja must make one spring at Jaggu, who
will ward it off with the back of his hand, and pound his face
with such a cry that Raja will turn back with his tail between
his legs."

"Tucking the tail between legs should be more a dog's
habit . . . I've never seen any *Felis* species doing that."

"But I want it so, it's in the script."

"Change the script," said Captain crisply. "However, what's
so important about the tail business?"

"It enhances the prestige of the hero, if he can make a tiger
lower his tail in deference and crawl . . ."

"Who wrote the script?"

"Well, I did, who else could conceive it? I never allow anyone else to handle the basic script."

"Why don't you talk to the tiger about it? He is over there. Take your script and read it to him and if he agrees I'll have absolutely no objection."

Madan looked desperate and upset. "Captain, you are kidding. This is not how I expect you to cooperate, I didn't grudge the full cash payment in advance you wanted for four weeks of shooting . . ."

"Tut, tut, don't talk like a moneylender. I've brought the tiger as agreed in our contract. I'll open the cage and bring him out to wrestle with your hero . . . I'll release him any moment you say you are ready."

Their talk was interrupted by a plaintive appeal from the giant. "I can't keep standing any longer. I want to rest. At least let me sit down on the floor."

"Hey, stop that. I won't have you moan like this every minute, you are not a baby, not by any means, sir; I'll sack and sue you for damages if you do not cooperate. It's against the contract . . ."

"I'm tired," wailed the giant.

The cameraman came to his rescue. "No harm, sir, if he sits down, we have marked the place; it'll only take a few minutes to adjust again. Anyway we have been behind the camera since the morning, not a single shot. Light is changing—new measurements will be needed."

One from a high platform said, "What are we all supposed to be doing here?"

"Is this a protest meeting? Revolt, Rebellion, Rioting or what?" asked Madan haughtily. "If it is, tell me, and I know how to deal with mutineers. Don't you see we are in a discussion, and I can't proceed without a proper discussion. I won't be coerced under any circumstance; remember that discussion is the most important part of film-making. I don't have to explain to you all that . . ."

"It is not in the contract, and so naturally you don't have to explain to us why our time is being wasted!" remarked the cameraman cynically.

Madan ignored him for a moment, but said as if on an inspiration, "I'm buying your time. If there is talk of waste, it's only my money."

Captain felt that it was time to end this squabble. He appealed to the cameraman. "You are an experienced man and you know how difficult is the film medium; it's where Art and Commerce are combined, as our friend here always says, and it suffers from the disadvantages of both. Once you are caught in it, you are finished. You can go neither back nor forward. That is the situation in which our friend finds himself now. So be patient. We will decide very soon how best to proceed, having come thus far . . ."

"But sir, we like to get on with the work . . ."

"That's of course a good idea. But you know, as an ace cameraman, how difficult it is to get artistes to do right! Here we have no normal actors, but a tiger and one who understands less than a tiger . . . Difficult work, but Madan has invested money and time. You must do your best for him and leave it to him to work it out."

"But, sir, we have positioning and rehearsing again and again. Is there no limit? No wonder the artiste is half-dead. Actually we started at . . ."

A man from the top platform added, "Before seven—and nothing done for four hours, while I'm perched here . . ."

"What can I do? Some fool gave the 'Tiger' cue at a wrong moment."

"You had asked me to keep a look-out for the arrival of the animal, sir, and I did it, that's all. I don't like to be called a fool."

"Silence, no back-talk," ordered Madan. "I don't appreciate it."

Captain continued his good offices, and announced, "Coffee break."

Immediately the atmosphere cleared and relaxed. The crew left their posts happily and swarmed around the canteen, Jaggu foremost among them. Madan watched them all helplessly, and protested, "Too early for a break. They have not done an iota of work . . ."

"Not their fault really, but let us not go into all that now. One has to be flexible when dealing with workers. I know, because I have to contend with three hundred workers and animals of various sorts . . ."

While the crew were away refreshing themselves, Madan and Captain engaged in a discussion. "Madan, I wish to help you, understand that. Stop all that nonsense about Raja's tail. Raja's face should be more important."

"But at some point we must follow the script . . ."

"You mention it as if it were your scripture rather than your script. We will come to that later. Be clear as to what you want Raja to do before he tucks his tail."

"He must stand up on his hind legs and place his forelegs on the giant's shoulder first. Then the giant will knock him off . . ."

"Marvellous conception!" commented Captain. "In all my years of association with wild creatures—" He began his sentence and stopped short. "Does it occur to you at all—that even granting that it's possible, the flesh on that poor fellow's shoulders is likely to be torn out, if nothing worse happens?"

"I depend on you . . . Can't you pull out his nails?"

"Horrible idea! Never."

"But they will grow again . . . that's what they do in Hollywood."

"Why don't you go to Hollywood then?"

"I want to make a hundred-per-cent Indian film. I have taken it as a challenge."

"Who is challenging you?" asked Captain. "Leaving the nail-pulling alone, that's not the worst to happen. Raja may decapitate your giant as he did that goat, an act which you so much admired." Madan was lost in thought. Captain continued, "I'll tell you right now, I won't have his teeth pulled out either. I can't think of it. Let me tell you even if everything is pulled out, Raja could still deliver a concussion with a pat. I want Raja to be restored to me in his original condition after the film shooting. If you look closely, you will find it in our contract. If there is a scar or mutilation on Raja, I'll sue for damages up to ten million dollars in your Hollywood terms."

"Then, in some jungle pictures, what they do is to sew up the lips temporarily—the sutures are easily removed later. That's what they do in Hollywood."

"To hell with Hollywood and stitches and sutures. The tiger must be returned intact."

By this time the sun was going down. And the crew, who had returned to their posts and were watching, asked through their spokesman, "Shall we pack up?"

"Yes, pack up," cried Madan commandingly. He turned to Captain and said, "You must cooperate with me, sir."

"Yes, of course, you have lost a full day, and you will have one day less and I want you to do something worthwhile within the stipulated time."

"Won't you give a little extension?"

"No, our circus is on the move, you know that. I have to send Raja off in advance . . . I'll tell you what we might do. You must utilize the flexibility of the film medium. On my side I'll make Raja stand on his hind legs and place his forepaws on a wrestler who is not there, and you will ask your giant to imagine himself to wrestle with a tiger which is not there. After all he was a wrestler and it must not be difficult for him to imagine an adversary and pound him . . . Shoot them separately and join them through an optical printer. That way it should be easy to show them hugging . . ."

"Marvellous idea," cried Madan. "Next four days, we'll shoot the maximum footage. I'll get a second unit from Madras immediately . . ."

"Better you give your hero a close view of the tiger, so that he may flail and hug and tackle realistically. Has he seen the tiger?"

"Yes, from a distance—always from a distance, that's my problem. I notice that he shuts his eyes and trembles when he has to pass that cage! I was afraid how he would react to the tiger at close quarters . . ."

"How soon will your second unit arrive?"

"Within twenty-four hours."

"No need to hurry," said Captain. "They may take three days. Meanwhile it is important that your giant and the tiger are introduced to each other; your artiste has to know what he is doing. As for Raja, as a general rule, it'll be good to give him a glimpse of his adversary."

Madan was too preoccupied to question the logic of it or the need. It was one of the many routine remarks and suggestions that floated in the air during a film shooting and vanished. Madan summoned his assistant and instructed, "Send a telegram to XL at Madras to dispatch the second unit within two days, one cameraman and a sound unit, and light unit . . ."

"Where is the need, sir," asked the cameraman, overhearing the instruction while packing up, "while you are not utilizing the first unit? What have we achieved the whole day?"

"None of your business to question. Be ready when you are asked," Captain said sternly. Captain felt it was time to support Madan and establish his authority, and said, "Shut your ears to our talk, understand? Open only when you are being addressed. In any event keep your mouth always shut, that'll help us all." The cameraman was cowed by Captain's ringside manner and left, others trooping behind them.

From within his circle, where he had returned after the canteen visit, Jaggu cried, "May I come out too?"

"Oh, poor fellow, they have forgotten you . . . Come."

With a sigh of relief like a released animal Jaggu stepped out of his confinement of the Magic Circle. He was led into the make-up shed, and after a while came out without his costume, clad in a *lungi* and shirt with the paint off his face. There was relief in his face as he sat down on a bench to rest his legs after hours of standing. He lit a *beedi* and smoked it with contentment; he had eaten well at the canteen. One of Captain's circus hands who had escorted the tiger cage came up to him and said, "Chief wants you to come . . ."

"Why?"

"To present you a cat . . ."

"Why a cat?" he asked with extreme innocence. The men who had come to summon him made a few merry jokes about a birthday gift and so forth. They led him through a gate into a stockade built for the cameraman, with platforms for taking top shots and enough gaps between the railings for the camera to follow the action in a larger enclosure. He saw a man with a whip in one hand and a chair in the other standing and commanding, "Raja, come out." The whip cracked and a tiger jumped out of its cage. "Race round," commanded the man. The tiger ran around, while Jaggu stood petrified, unable to believe his eyes.

Madan was watching him with attention and said, "Fellow looks nervous but must get used to the idea even if we are faking the shot . . ." He watched the giant's discomfiture with glee. At one point the tiger lunged forward with a roar in Jaggu's direction and dashed against the stockade. Jaggu let out a howl, "*Amma!* Save me!" calling on his long-dead mother, and blindly smashed his way out.

Madan was saying to the Captain, "This is a thing which you might use in an emergency, but generally to tame any wild thing . . ." He produced a gadget, which when pressed shot out a thin metal rod, and at a touch delivered a shock, working on a battery. Madan explained, "Only fifteen volts, but enough to keep any animal well behaved . . . You can try it if you like."

"On Raja? Never, sir. My whip is enough." He would not touch the gadget. He shook his head. "I'd be ashamed to employ this on any animal. No trainer worth his name can be proud of it if his animal is coerced and beaten down with such a contraption. It's no training. It's stampeding an animal into obedience with electric shock . . ."

"Well, I don't know what you mean: you are doing it all the time."

"If you don't see the difference, it's no use explaining further. I don't want short-cuts and hope that I do not destroy the natural pride an animal possesses . . . I'll take care of it."

Although Madan could not admit that Captain actually practised all this theory, but was only letting his eloquence flow on, he just put away the gadget with, "All I need is your cooperation."

Of that word, he was very fond, as Captain noted with amusement; he repeated, "Cooperation! Cooperation! That you can have in plenty, but not the tiger bullied and stunned with electric shocks . . ."

"Oh, come, come—it's not worse than the whip. In Hollywood they are using it all the time."

"Probably even on the human stars, who may need to be kept awake!"

"I was for a moment lost in the fun of hearing 'Amma' from this mountain of a baby. Where is he gone? Don't let him get away. Stun him if necessary," said Madan, sending his men after Jaggu.

Captain could not help laughing at the huge character running away in panic, shouting for his mother's help. "That fellow didn't even notice that he was in a different enclosure from the tiger—didn't notice the bars intervening. Didn't trust them, I suppose . . ."

Madan began to look concerned when his men did not turn up. "Where could he have gone? Gone only five minutes . . . Where are the fellows who ran after him? They are also gone! Everyone seems to be too ready to desert us today . . ." He was rambling on irrelevantly in his anxiety and trying to put the blame on everyone.

Captain was apparently getting a lot of enjoyment out of it. "If you had kept the camera on and shot this sequence of a giant running away at the sight of the tiger, it'd have been the greatest hit . . ."

"While all the time I want him to be heroic and tackle a tiger in keeping with his size!" Madan said ruefully.

Presently the searching party returned and reported: "Nowhere."

"What do you mean by it?" Madan asked angrily. "He is not a tot to be lost sight of . . . can't be hiding behind a blade of grass."

"We beat about every bush, every ditch and crag. We went up over a mile in three directions."

"He must be found, otherwise I'll be ruined," lamented Madan.

"Just take your car and try," suggested Captain.

Madan started his car and drove down the road recklessly. "If he is not found, I'll be ruined," he kept saying to himself.

Madan was back within an hour with the giant stuffed like a baggage in the narrow back seat of his car, which had only two doors and could release a back-seat passenger only by folding down the front seat. It was like locking up a prisoner. Madan looked happy and relieved. "I found him in old *Mari* shrine. Some instinct told me he must be there; other places could not conceal him." He addressed Jaggu: "The Goddess would not protect you. You know why? Because you tried to cheat me. Goddess doesn't like persons who try to cheat."

"I don't like tigers," Jaggu said.

"We don't care what you like or dislike," Madan said. "You are under contract with me. I told you the story before signing the agreement. If you act like a coward now, I will hand you over to the police."

"But I didn't know it'd be a big tiger, it tried to kill me."

"Didn't you see the bars between you and the tiger? We will see it doesn't touch you. You will be safe."

Jaggu was on the point of tears. "Leave me, sir, I am no good for this. Let me go back to my village. I'll display my strength and make my living."

Madan was unmoved by all this pleading. "They will have you in chains and put you to break stones . . ."

"I won't mind it, sir," he said, habituated to breaking stones and chains for a living at all fairs. As a threat it misfired. While all this talk was going on, Madan hadn't yet released him from the back seat. The giant did not know how to come out of it. He said, "Please, sir, let me out. My knees are paining, I can't sit here . . ." When that had no effect, he said, "I've got to . . ." indicating he had to relieve himself.

Madan opened the door, pushed the seat forward, and hustled him out of the car. The giant got out and raced toward a bush. Madan shouted, "If you try to trick me again, I'll release the tiger out of the cage and set him on you." He directed two men to follow him. When he returned with the two bodyguards, Madan said, "You must cooperate with me and I'll make you rich—a famous man. Your photo will be on all walls and papers . . . They will present their notebooks and beg you to sign . . ."

"No, sir, I was never taught how to read or write . . . If they had only put me to school I would have been different. I don't like tigers. Please save me . . ."

"You have signed or put your left thumb impression to an agreement in which you have agreed to act along with a tiger. But let me tell you, you will not be required to come close to the tiger. I will see that you are not hurt. Also remember the tiger is not all—it's only a part. I have written a story in which you knock down the tiger, kill it, and then marry a beautiful girl . . . I'm sure you will like it."

He was horrified. "Oh, no, I'm married . . . I'll go back to the village to give her money, whatever I earn . . ."

"All right, all right, you can take a lot of money for her."

His bodyguards took him away at a signal from Madan and kept him company, enjoying a lot of jokes at his expense about bigamy. They led him away to a secluded spot on the location and said, "Our boss has a beautiful bride for you . . . and yet you try to run away."

Jaggu was horrified. "Oh! I can't, my wife will—"

"Oh, your wife! Don't mind what she says. She is a country girl, but our boss has reserved for you a princess—oh, you will have to go through with it whether you like it or not. You have signed an agreement . . ."

"Don't you know that a film star should have at least two wives?"

"It is a government order," said another.

"Our hut in the village is small . . ." Jaggu pleaded.

"You are going to be rich and can afford two houses for two wives."

"You can sleep with one half the night, get up and go in a car to the other the other half of the night . . . Lucky fellow!"

"My wife will not like it . . . I don't want two wives."

"Wait till you see the other one . . . You will save her from the tiger, and she'll call you her lord and saviour and darling for your trouble . . ."

Jaggu looked distressed and brooded over the terrible prospects that lay before him. He lit a *beedi* and thought over it. "No, no," he said to himself, "I can't accept a tiger . . ."

"It's all written down like fate, nothing can be changed," they taunted him.

He was rehearsed endlessly and made to go through the motions of wrestling with an unseen tiger. Madan himself was fatigued demonstrating, out of the range of the camera, the gestures, which the giant had to copy while the camera was shooting. Though the hero was the only one in the cast for the present sequence, the film personnel of two units created quite a crowd, and were all over the place.

At the other end of the lot Captain was handling Raja. He had extended the time for shooting by several weeks, since Madan had agreed to pay heavily for the extension, and Captain felt it was a sound way of making money during the interval between two camps. Although he was indifferent generally in money matters, now a certain degree of greed was overcoming him, a gradual corruption through contact with the film world. He began to think, "What a lot of money this film business turns over. Let me collect the loot, while this fool of a Madan is about it." He told his wife, "Possibly after this, Madan may come up with an idea for making a full circus-picture, that'll be a good break for us . . ."

She welcomed the idea. "Don't discourage him. 'Cooperate' with that fellow, as he always says. If he wants more days for shooting, grant it . . . We could always delay the opening of the next camp. Anyway I'm tired and bored with the circus. Let us try something new for a change. We lose nothing. We may be free from all this dust and noise and ticket-selling for some time."

"We have to depend upon Raja now too much, and beg him to 'cooperate,' but his act is rather difficult. He is required to stand on his hind legs and fall forward. Every day I'm trying to make him understand, but it's proving difficult . . ."

"Why don't you try the electrical gadget?"

"I won't hear of it. Impossible."

At this point their pleasantries came to an end and she castigated him for being impractical and sentimental. "After all he'll be limp for a few minutes, when you can manoeuvre him for the camera. I'm prepared to handle your Raja with the electric

staff if you lack the guts. I am confident I can manage. Give
me two men, Sam and the other fellow—what's his name?
Muniswami . . ."

"Very well," Captain said, "I'll keep away tomorrow, you
try . . ."

"I mean it," she said.

"You mind your business," he said. "Tumble on your trapeze and read a novel if you can't spend your time. If you feel
dull without work, why don't you spend a week at Lovedale,
visiting the boys?"

"So that you may breathe freely? You always find my presence irksome!"

"Not always but sometimes. Whatever you want to do, keep
off my animals. They won't obey you because you are my
wife."

"Ah, ah, you are modest, aren't you?"

I did not like it in the least. Day after day I had to do the same
thing over and over again. Captain came up at the same hour.
The whip and the chair were back in use. A motley crowd
around, outside the enclosure, watching me perform acts which
I never understood. In the circus ring also there would be many
men, but they all helped the show, carried out Captain's orders,
brought in whatever was required for the show, and took it
away after the act. They moved slowly and never spoke much.
But here were men who were ordering each other all the time.
A man at the camera was commanding everybody, shouting at
the top of his voice all the time, "More left, no not so much, go
back, light . . ." When he said "light," a blinding radiance would
appear. I missed all the good things I had got used to in the circus. There one performed one's duties and quickly went back
home. The band music, and the men and women seated around
in chairs, and their voices and the lights were very welcome and
became a part of one's life. But here, outside the ring, they behaved as if they were seized with fever . . .

The cameraman ordered even Captain. He was constantly
telling him to shift and move: "Captain, if you want the tiger
alone in the shot, you should step back, and manoeuvre the ti-

ger from out of range." Captain became submissive. It was unbelievable that he should be taking orders from others; I could
not understand what had happened to him. He would crack his
whip and get me out of the cage, and order, "Up, up" every
time and hit my legs till I lifted them; gradually he compelled
me to tilt back and rise—a terrible trial for me and very painful, and I always fell back or forward, and went on bruising
myself. And all the time the cameraman went on bawling out
something or the other and shooting from his protected shelter.
He was never satisfied and wanted me to repeat, improve, further improve and repeat, my Captain blindly carrying out his
orders, whipping, hitting and yelling. This went on day after
day. They neither gave me rest nor showed kindness—Captain
was losing grip over himself and his self-respect. Often Madan
came to watch, gave his own directions along with the cameraman. Between the two they seemed to have enslaved Captain.
All the polished gentleness Madan had displayed till now was
gone. He was gradually gaining the upper hand, often spoke of
the money he had thrown away, and of his enterprise as a blunder. Captain was still calm. He said, "Don't talk nonsense. This
is an extremely intelligent tiger, but you demand impossible actions from him."

"I only expect what you yourself suggested at our discussion.
I never thought a man of your calibre would suggest impossible
things . . ." Thus went on their talks. Soon they devised a method
to stand me on my hind legs. When Captain brought me out of
the cage, I found dangled before me a lamb. As I reached out,
the lamb rose in the air gradually. I was interested now, and
tried to reach it; it went up so slowly that I had to stand up and
try to keep my balance, and then it would go out of my reach
up and up, and no amount of straining on my part would
help—even though I stretched myself fully and stood up like a
human being and fell forward. A creature needs the support of
four legs for stability. Somehow human beings balance on two
legs . . . It's not only difficult but a degradation for a quadruped—
you are too exposed; no wonder humans have to cover their
waists. While they tempted me with a bait to stand up, the camera followed my action, the act repeated till I was sick of it.

Monotonous and tedious it was. Morning till night and some-times with blinding lights at night.

I became desperate. Once at the start of the day, I refused to take note of the lamb dangling before me. I looked at him and looked away indifferently, but Captain would not let me be. If I had had the gift of speech, I'd have said, "Please leave me out of it today, I'm worn out." But I could only growl and roar. Not all his whipping and yelling could move me out of the cage. But now a thing happened which I had never experienced before. He tucked his whip under his arm and brought out a novel object, which shot out a tongue of metal; at its touch I felt blinded with a strange kind of pain and helplessness, and ran out of the cage. Anything to escape the touch of that vi-cious tongue. I just collapsed on the ground outside the cage, my legs aching with all that jumping to catch the dangling lamb of the previous day.

But Captain would not let me lie down. The cameraman and Madan were shouting, "Get him on his legs, the reel is running out. Come on . . ." Captain lashed me in the face, and then quietened down; "Come on, be a good boy. You can rest to-morrow," in the gentlest tone as always between two lashings. When it didn't move me, he assumed a third pitch of voice, which could reach the skies, and hit me on the nose, which would usually drive me to obedience. Today it only stirred my anger. I swished my tail and grunted. He knew what it meant, that I'd not be easy to handle. But he was not the one to care for my inclinations. It was his will that counted, he knew he could finally impose it on me. I shuddered at the idea of going after that elusive lamb again. If I could have spoken, I would have told him, "Go away before any harm befalls you, my good man. After all you have fed me and protected me. I shall hon-our you for it. But please go away and leave me alone. I won't be your slave any more, I'll never go back to my cage; that's all, I won't do any of the meaningless turns these foolish men around want me to do. It was different at the circus, but the present activities appear to me senseless and degrading. I won't go through them. I like this air and freedom. I'm not going to give it up now. Later perhaps, when you have regained your

judgement, I'll return to your circus, but please don't drive me
back to the cage now. Please understand and leave me alone.
Please listen to my advice."

But he was a stubborn fellow with no doubt whatever about
his own notions. He brought his whip down on my nose again,
at a point where it hurt most. I let out a roar, involuntarily,
stung by it. That made him more angry. He took it as a piece of
impudence on my part. He brought his whip again in quick
succession over my eyes indiscriminately. I wanted to scream
loudly, "Oh, Captain, don't be foolhardy, your life is in danger,
go away, leave me before any calamity befalls you." But he was
drunk with authority. I wished he could save himself, but he
was not helping himself at all. He would not rest till he exacted
total submission. I noticed him tucking the whip under his arm
and slipping his free hand in his pocket to bring out the dreadful instrument which would shoot out a metal tongue. He'd only
touch me, as with a feather, to make me dizzy and servile.

I caught myself thinking, "Why should I fear this creature no
bigger than my tail?" First time in my life such an idea was oc-
curring. So far I had never measured him. But today he looked
puny to me in spite of all his yelling and angry gestures. In rec-
ognition of our relationship and as a final warning I growled
and just raised my paw. He cried, "Ah! ah!—you threaten me!"
and forgetting himself enough to approach me beyond the margin of safety which he always maintained for an emergency retreat, he dashed foreward with that vicious metal tongue shooting
out of its sheath. As he stooped down to caress me with its tip, I
just raised a forepaw, taking care to retract my claws, and knocked
the thing out of his hand. The blow caught Captain under his
chin, and tore off his head. It was surprising that such a flimsy
creature, no better than a membrane stretched over some thin
framework, with so little stuff inside, should have held me in
fear so long.

Much confusion and excitement and running. I got up to move
freely for the first time. The crew at first tried to save their
equipment in the pandemonium, but abandoned it and fled. I
heard Madan say, "I'm ruined, mind the cables, don't trip over.

You'll bring down the lights." Lights or something did come crashing; the cameraman disappeared.

When I had moved off some distance from the cage, the giant, who had been in action, suddenly made a dash into the cage I had vacated and pulled down the door. A number of others battered on the door, but filling all the space he would not take anyone in. Madan's voice could be heard over the uproar: "Who has the gun? Where is the fellow in charge of it? Absurd situation . . ." No one had the calmness to answer any question: each was looking to his own safety and escape, while I calmly walked off the lot. The cameraman had abandoned his camera on its stand; while moving away, I brushed against it and sent it toppling down with a bang. Some unseen man was crying, "The zoom is gone. Ruined, ruined . . ."

It was still a busy hour in the city when I entered Market Road. People ran for their lives at the sight of me. As I progressed through, shutters were pulled down, and people hid themselves under culverts, on trees, behind pillars. The population was melting out of sight. At the circus I had had no chance to study human behaviour. Outside the circus ring they sat in their seats placidly while I cowered before Captain's whip. I got a totally wrong notion of human beings at that angle. I had thought that they were sturdy and fearless. But now I found them fleeing before me like a herd of deer, although I had no intention of attacking them. When I paused in front of a tailor's shop, he abandoned his machine and shut himself in a cupboard, wailing, "Alas, I am undone, won't someone shoot that tiger?" A prisoner between two constables, who had been caught for murder and was just emerging from the Court House, got his chance to escape when the constables fled, abandoning him with his handcuffs. I tore a horse from its *jutka* and enjoyed the sight of the passengers spilling out of it and running for their lives. A couple of street dogs invited destruction when they barked madly, instead of minding their business.

Later, I learnt from my Master of the chaos that befell the city when it became known that Captain had been destroyed and that I was somewhere in the city. Sheer hopelessness seems to have seized the townspeople. They withdrew to their homes and even there remained nervous. All doors and windows everywhere were shut, bolted, and sealed. Some even thought that I was some extraordinary creature who might pass through the walls and lie in wait on the roof or in the loft or basement. Poor people living in huts had real cause to worry: I could have taken any of their homes apart. But why should I? One could understand their fears, but why should those living in brick and cement feel nervous? It was due to their general lack of a sense of security and an irrational dread of losing their assets. Why should an ordinary simple tiger have any interest in them either to destroy or to safeguard?

I rested for a moment at the door of Anand Bhavan, on Market Road, where coffee drinkers and tiffin eaters at their tables sat transfixed, uttering low moans on seeing me. I wanted to assure them, "Don't fear, I am not out to trouble you. Eat your tiffin in peace, don't mind me . . . You, nearest to me, hugging the cash box, you are craven with fear, afraid even to breathe. Go on, count the cash, if that's your pleasure. I just want to watch, that's all . . . If my tail trails down to the street, if I am blocking your threshold, it is because, I'm told, I'm eleven feet tip to tail. I can't help it. I'm not out to kill . . . I'm too full—found a green pasture teeming with food on the way. Won't need any for several days to come, won't stir, not until I feel hungry again. Tigers attack only when they feel hungry, unlike human beings who slaughter one another without purpose or hunger . . ."

To the great delight of children, schools were being hurriedly closed. Children of all ages and sizes were running helter-skelter, screaming joyously, "No school, no school. Tiger, tiger!" They were shouting and laughing and even enjoyed being scared. They seemed to welcome me. I felt like joining them, and bounded away from the restaurant door and trotted along with them, at which they gleefully cried, "The tiger is coming to eat us; let us get back to the school!"

I followed them through their school gate while they ran up and shut themselves in the school hall securely. I ascended the steps of the school, saw an open door at the far end of a veranda, and walked in. It happened to be the headmaster's room, I believed, as I noticed a very dignified man jumping on his table and heaving himself up into an attic. I walked in and flung myself on the cool floor, having a partiality for cool stone floor, with my head under the large desk—which gave me the feeling of being back in the Mempi cave . . . As I drowsed, I was aware of cautious steps and hushed voices all around. I was in no mood to bother about anything. All I wanted was a little moment of sleep; the daylight was dazzling. In half sleep I heard the doors of the room being shut and bolted and locked. I didn't care. I slept.

While I slept a great deal of consultation was going on. I learnt about it later through my Master, who was in the crowd—the crowd which had gathered after making sure that I had been properly locked up—and was watching. The headmaster seems to have remarked some days later, "Never dreamt in my wildest mood that I'd have to yield my place to a tiger . . ." A wag had retorted, "Might be one way of maintaining better discipline among the boys."

"Now that this brute is safely locked up, we must decide—" began a teacher.

At this moment my Master pushed his way through the crowds and admonished, "Never use the words *beast* or *brute*. They're ugly words coined by man in his arrogance. The human being thinks all other creatures are 'beasts.' Awful word!"

"Is this the occasion to discuss problems of vocabulary?" asked someone.

"Why not?" retorted my Master. At which they looked outraged.

Someone said, "What a reckless man you are! Who are you?"

"You are asking a profound question. I've no idea who I am! All my life I have been trying to find the answer. Are you sure you know who you are?"

"Crazy beggar—with a tiger in there ready to devour us, but for the strong door . . . There is no time for useless talk. Let us get on with the business . . ."

"What business? What is it going to be?" asked my Master.

Everyone was upset at this question. "We must think of those children shut in the hall," said a teacher.

"Open the door and let them out," said my Master, unasked.

"Not your business to advise us; who are you?"

"Second time you are asking the same question. I say again, I don't know," said my Master.

"Get out of the school premises," said a man who acted for the headmaster in his absence. "You have no business here. We can't have all kinds of intruders . . ."

"Did the tiger come on your invitation?" asked my Master.

"We have to think seriously what to do now. Please leave us alone. Go away, I say," commanded the acting headmaster.

At which my Master said, "A headmaster must be obeyed in his school, even if he is only acting," and slipped back to the farthest end of the veranda.

"Go away," they all shouted.

"I'll stay, but promise not to disturb your consultations . . ." And then my Master withdrew to a far corner to watch them, to observe how they were going to tackle the tiger. They constantly turned their heads and threw furtive looks at him, feeling uneasy to talk in his presence, but at the same time finding it difficult to order him out. They lowered their voices. The acting headmaster said, "Now we have to decide on the next step to take . . ."

"Yes, yes," chorused his assistant masters.

"We must get someone to shoot it. Who has a gun in our town?"

Everyone fell into deep thinking. The mathematics teacher, the most practical-minded in the institution, said, "I'm sure the police will have it. Send someone to fetch the superintendent."

I must have turned in my sleep and knocked over some piece of furniture and that seemed to have scared them further. All of them cried, "Let us go, it is perhaps trying to break open the door!" and started to retreat desperately.

At this point my Master shouted from his corner, "He can't open the door. He has no hands. Only some furniture . . ."

Whereupon they glared at him and said, "If you are going to be here, take care not to interrupt out talks."

My Master, being calm and wise, merely said, "Very well, I won't interrupt."

The mathematics teacher now said, "Shall I call the police to handle the tiger?"

Another teacher had a misgiving at this point: "I doubt if this is a police matter. No law has been broken . . ."

"Is it lawful to let loose a tiger in a public thoroughfare?"

"Who let it loose? No one. It came by itself."

"The circus man is responsible."

"But he is dead . . . They must arrest the film producer for endangering public safety."

"Where are they? They have all vanished—fled before the tiger . . . took their shattered cameras too . . . We can't go after them now. I wouldn't be surprised if the tiger has swallowed them up . . ."

"I wouldn't think so," said my Master again. "He is not a man-eater . . ."

"Isn't he? Have you tested him?" asked the acting headmaster, rather viciously, annoyed at the fact that the man was still there.

My Master said, "I don't notice any progress in your talk. Why don't you let all the children go home without making any noise . . . and all of you may also go home . . ."

"And leave the tiger in charge of the school?" asked the acting headmaster with an untimely irony. And added, "You must go. We don't want you on the premises, whatever we may decide . . ." said the acting headmaster, glaring at my Master.

At which my Master shouted back, "If my presence is the real problem rather than the tiger, I'll go, but you will see me again, I have no doubt," rather mysteriously and went off. All eyes followed him till he disappeared beyond the school gate. My Master was only out of their vision, but was at hand, sitting on a culvert keenly watching the goings-on at the school veranda, not missing a single word of their confused babble. He heard, "Get a gun immediately."

"Does anyone know how to shoot?"

"The Superintendent of Police has a gun . . ."

"But he can't use it unless a magistrate orders . . ."

"Where does he live? He used to be in the New Extension . . . that yellow house in the Third Cross corner."

"Now he has moved to the government quarters . . ."

"Better we get Alphonse. He is a good *shikari*, licensed double-barrelled gun. The walls of his house are covered with bison heads and stuff like that. He's a good shot."

"But he is a declared poacher; they have confiscated his gun."

"Can't be, I saw him yesterday at Market Gate . . ."

"Did you see him with a gun?"

"Why should he take his gun to the market? I spoke to him and he said he was going to camp in the forest the next four days—"

"It is rumoured that they have taken away his hunting licence . . ."

"But he said he was shooting with a camera."

"His camera may shoot bullets, too. Don't you believe such fellows—they are really poachers."

Now I let out a growl, a mild one, and that brought their minds back to the business on hand.

"Better get the D.F.O."

"What is D.F.O.?"

"You mean you don't know D.F.O. means District Forest Officer?" At which the man thus corrected was annoyed, and insults and angry words were exchanged until the acting head-master intervened and reminded them that they were engaging themselves in an untimely wasteful talk. And then he turned to the school servant to ask, "Do you know where the D.F.O. lives?"

"No, sir," he said promptly.

A student came forward—a young fellow who had managed to stay back when all others had rushed into the school hall. "Ravi is my friend, I know where he lives."

"Who is Ravi?" His answer was drowned in a lot of cross-talk.

"Don't forget the H.M. can't come down. How long can he be crouching in that loft?"

"How are you sure that he climbed into the loft?"

"They had a glimpse while shutting the door . . . Don't waste time in this sort of cross-examination."

They seemed to be incapable of reaching any practical solution. My Master, who had been sitting on the culvert, came back to say, "If you keep chatting like this, I'll dash up and let the tiger out . . ."

"Oh, would you? You will be the first fellow to be devoured," said an idiot. And all the members said, "We said you should keep out of here, why have you come back?"

"Just to see if you fellows will do or say anything useful. Pity the children whose education and training are in your hands . . ."

At which the acting headmaster drew himself up to say, "Get out of this place, this is our school. In the absence of the headmaster, I take his place automatically. I have told you that already."

"Yes, yes, I remember; I have also said that when a headmaster, even if he is only acting, gives an order, it must be obeyed instantly," and he went back to his seat on the culvert at the gate, beyond their range of vision but not out of earshot.

Presently he saw a man arrive on a noisy motor cycle, drowning all other sound, carrying a gun. He slowed down near my Master to ask excitedly, "I heard of a tiger being somewhere here—is it true?"

My Master indicated the school, but added, "You can't shoot him, if that's your idea . . ." Ignoring it, the man turned into the gate with a haughty toss of his head.

Now my Master followed a fresh motley crowd drifting in, driven by a mixture of curiosity and fear. Now that they knew the tiger was locked up, throngs of men and women were in the streets purposelessly wandering and vaguely looking for the tiger. All normal activity in the city was suspended. In the crowd one could find lawyers in their black gowns, shopmen who had pulled down the shutters, hawkers with trays on their heads, policemen in uniform, and so forth. The school had never seen such a crowd before in its compound and veranda. An army of anxious parents arrived, desperately searching for their children. They dashed hither and thither and towards the head-

master's room in a body, demanding, "Where are our children?
We want our children safely back. What sort of a school that
they can't protect our children when a tiger is about?"

A teacher was provoked by this remark. "Why do you presume such things? Haven't we a responsibility?"

"Where are our children? My child is only seven years old.
It's a mistake to have sent him to this wretched tiger-infested
school."

"You perhaps are always ready to attack the school . . ."

A burly parent came up shaking his fist. "Don't go on philosophizing. We don't want your philosophy. Where are the
children? You should have closed the school when the tiger was
known to have escaped into the town. If anything happens to
the child, I'll smash you all and set fire to the school."

The teacher looked scared between a bully and the tiger. He
said in a trembling voice, "We let them off early, but they came
back."

Meanwhile a group, having heard the shouts of the children
locked up in the hall, went up and forced open the door, and
the children poured out of the room like flood water released
from a sluice, screaming and roaring with joy. Confusion was
at its maximum.

The man with the gun strode in with the gun in position,
shouting at the top of his voice: "Keep away, everybody. I won't
be responsible if anyone is hurt. I'll count. Before I count ten,
everyone must clear out of the way. Otherwise I shoot and
won't be responsible for any mishap to any individual," and he
held up and flourished his double-barrelled gun, asking, "Is he
in there? I can shoot through the door . . ."

"Oh, no, don't. The headmaster is also in there."

"He went up into the loft and is crouching there . . ."

"I'll aim and hit right on it, only the tiger. You may keep a
flower on its back or even the headmaster himself, but my bullet will leave everything else untouched and bring down the
beast alone."

At this moment my Master came forward to say, "Never use
that word again . . ."

"Which word?" asked Alphonse the gunman.

" 'Beast' is an ugly, uncharitable expression."

"Mind your business."

"This is my business," answered my Master, and people, fearing that he might be shot, pulled him away. The gunman continued his plans.

"But how are you to know where he is in that room?"

"If the door is pushed open slightly, I can immediately—"

"If the tiger dashes out?"

"Oh, a moving target is no problem. I have brought down creatures running at one hundred miles an hour . . ."

"No, no, opening the door is out of the question, impossible."

"Get me a ladder, then. I'll go up and shoot from the roof . . . enough if a couple of tiles are removed . . ." Someone was hustled to fetch a ladder from a neighbouring house. They all waited in silence. Somehow the sight of the gunman seemed to have subdued the crowd. They spoke in hushed voices. "Where is the ladder?" demanded Alphonse. "Who is gone to fetch one?" he asked with an air of command. People looked at each other, and no one came up with an answer. At which Alphonse stamped his foot like a spoilt child, and demanded angrily, "Who is in charge here?" The acting headmaster was unwilling to come forward now, with the tiger on one side and the gun-wielder on the other. He had tried to make himself obscure and slip away unnoticed. But others seized him by his arm and propelled him forward, crying, "Here is the First Assistant, he is in charge when the headmaster is away."

The acting headmaster said, "The H.M. is still there in his room. He is not away actually."

"Oh, oh," someone jeered.

"But is he in a position to issue orders?"

"Perhaps not—may not be audible if he talks from inside the tiger," a wag suggested. And there was giggling all round.

At this my Master came forward to ask, "Is this the time for levity?"

Alphonse turned on him fiercely. "Who are you?"

My Master said, "Oh, once again the same question! I wish I could answer with so many asking the same question."

"I am not prepared to waste time talking to you . . . Now be off. Don't interrupt, I don't care who you are or what you are . . . you loincloth-covered, bearded loon . . ." He then turned his attention to the acting headmaster and asked sternly, "Are you in charge of this school?"

"Yes, only when the headmaster is on leave. Not when he is in there . . ." He pointed at the headmaster's room.

Alphonse glared at him and said, "I know you are trying to be slippery. Heaven help you if you are going to be tricky. I like people to be straightforward and truthful . . . You are the man in charge. If you think you are going to have your chance to take his place by letting him be eaten up, you are mistaken. I am determined to get him out intact—if I have to shoot down everything in my way, I'll do it. Now get me a ladder. It's urgent." The acting headmaster was speechless; the crowed watched in a state of hushed awe. Some persons were trying to leave, unable to judge how the situation might develop and anticipating bloodshed. Alphonse held the acting headmaster with his look and demanded, "Get me a ladder at once."

"We have no ladder in this school," he said timidly.

"Do you mean to say," Alphonse asked contemptuously, "that you run a school like this without a ladder?"

"What is a ladder for in a teaching institution?" questioned the assistant headmaster in a foolhardy manner.

"Don't be impudent," said Alphonse, glaring at him, at which the assistant headmaster took fright and tried to mollify him by saying, "Headmaster requisitioned for one last year, but the D.P.I.'s office are holding up the sanction. Unless they sanction the budget, we can't even buy a pin . . ."

"The procedure is silly," commented Alphonse.

A few others murmured, "True, sir, we all agree with you. We can't buy even a cane except through the D.P.I.'s sanction."

"What do you want a cane for?" demanded Alphonse, going off at a tangent. "Do you mean to say you are using it on the boys? Whenever I find teachers doing that, I give them a taste of it first . . ."

"Oh, no, I just mentioned cane because it came to my mind.

We never do such things . . . We get cattle straying into our garden and we use the stick to drive them away."

"Hmm . . . you had better be careful. If you teachers wish to
save your skins, remember I'll as readily bag wild pedagogues
as I do wild animals of the forest."

"Educational norms are different today."

"What do you mean by it?" Alphonse asked severely, turning
to the speaker.

"We have to handle them psychologically . . ."

"Good for you, keep it in mind."

At this point two boys came through carrying a bamboo ladder
between them and placed it before the crowd. Alphonse was delighted. He patted the boys' heads by turn, one by one, methodically. "Where have you got this from?" he asked, very pleased.

"We ran to a house in Kabir Lane, I had noticed that they
had kept a ladder in their back-yard, to pluck drumsticks from
the tree, and now they had locked themselves in and also shut
all the windows because of the tiger, and so I brought it away
quietly and they did not see us. I was dragging it along, but
Ramu saw me on the way and helped me and both of us carried
it down—because we heard you asking for a ladder, I ran out
at once, remembering the ladder in the next house . . ."

"You are a very intelligent, observant fellow. What is your
name?"

"Shekar," he answered proudly and loudly.

"Shekar," cried Alphonse enthusiastically. "Come and see
me with your friend. I'll have a present for you. I've a wonderful air-gun, with which you can practise. You won't need a licence for it although you can hit and disable a buck at forty
feet . . . Our country needs more boys of your type. You are our
only hope."

"He is the brightest fellow in our school," the assistant headmaster ventured to suggest with some pride, to please the gunman.

"I'm glad you recognize it, if you really mean it. Shekar, you
and your friend take the ladder over there and put it up for me
to go up to the roof . . ."

One couldn't have secured more spirited helpers. Shekar and Ramu felt so flattered that they were prepared to obey any command from Uncle Alphonse. "He has promised me a gun. I'll shoot all the crows and dogs in our street."

"I'll shoot the donkeys," said Ramu.

"How can you?" Shekar asked. "He has only one gun and that is promised to me."

"It's for both of us," Ramu said. "Let us share it."

"How can two shoot with a single gun?" sneered Shekar, but before it could develop into a full-scale argument, Alphonse cried, "Come on, boys, march on with the ladder."

The two boys took the ladder out to the spot indicated, and Alphonse placed it below the eaves of the headmaster's office. He then turned to a small crowd, which followed him. He braced himself for the task, put one foot on the first rung, and turned to face his audience: "You must all be calm and mind your business if you have any. Don't get panicky if you hear gunshots presently. I can shoot straight and finally, of course, but there can be no guarantee how the tiger will behave when he is hit. Before I send the second shot and dispatch him, he may go mad and devilish and storm his way out of the room, he may spring skyward, or dash through the door or break the walls in his fury. One can't foresee what'll happen then, especially when I have not seen the brute—"

"He is no brute," shouted my Master from back of the crowd. "No more than any of us here."

"Ah, ah! You are still here. You were ordered to remain out of range, weren't you? Anyway if you are still here you will see who is a brute when he comes out. However, if you have no business here, get out of this place smartly . . . I want two men up here to come up with me and loosen the tiles. If I see clearly inside, I can finish the job in a moment."

"What about the headmaster, who must be somewhere between your gun and the animal?"

"That's a problem," said Alphonse generously, "but if you have confidence in me, he'll escape the shot."

"But the tiger may spring up, you said, and God knows where he will be caught," said someone.

Alphonse said, "Don't imagine troubles. Have you confidence in me or not?" He paused and waited for an answer. It was Shekar who shouted at the top of his voice, "Don't let them stop you, Uncle, go on and shoot the animal. I'd love to see how you shoot."

"Follow me then and help to remove the tiles. I'll tell you how to do it . . . The grown-ups here are all cowards and ought to wear *saris;* they are afraid to see a tiger even from a rooftop."

"I'm not afraid," said Shekar, and his friend added a confirmation. Alphonse climbed the ladder, followed by the two boys, who were cautioned and admonished by their teachers for their fool-hardiness.

"If I had four arms like some of your gods," said Alphonse from the roof, "I would not have needed the help of these young people. Two of my hands would have pulled the tiles out, while the other two might have been holding the gun and triggering off the shot. Four arms are a most sensible arrangement." And then he proceeded to remove a few tiles and asked the boys to follow his example. They tore up the tiles with zest and threw them down recklessly, enjoying the sight of their elders dodging below.

Soon an opening was made, and a shaft of sunlight entered the room. The headmaster was on the point of collapse, crouching there in the narrow attic, amidst bundles of old papers and files. He looked up and saw the faces of the two boys on the roof and could not make out what they were doing up there. He could not believe his eyes. He tried to stand up, but hit his head on the rafters. Shekar cried, "It's me, sir. My friend is also here, Ramu of Four B. Uncle is here to shoot the tiger . . ." The headmaster had enough wits about him to understand the situation. "Sir, aren't you hungry? If you come out, I'll run up to Pankaja Cafe and bring you tiffin, if someone gives me money . . ." said the boy.

The headmaster took his finger to his lips to warn the boy not to make a noise and wake up the tiger. He spoke in a hoarse whisper. At the mention of the tiger, Shekar was pushed aside and in his place the headmaster found another head. "I'm Alphonse," said the man. "Headmaster, keep cool; we will get you out soon. Ah! I see him there . . . must be eleven-point-five feet . . . a full-grown brute. Wish his head were not under the table. I could dispatch him with one shot then and there. You need have no doubt . . . I could shoot now, but if he is hit in the hind part, he may go mad and spring up. I've seen such beasts go up even fifteen feet in the air under similar circumstances. But first let me get you out of here . . . Keep cool . . . don't fall off the attic." He looked around. "Boy, you must run and get a hacksaw or an ordinary carpenter's saw. Run and get it as smartly as you brought the ladder. If you see a carpenter, snatch it from his bag."

"Yes, you will need more than a carpenter's saw," said a voice, and turning round Alphonse exclaimed, "You, here still!"

"Yes, yes," said my Master. "I could come up a ladder as well as anyone."

"Weren't you told to keep out?" asked Alphonse angrily.

"Yes, yes," agreed my Master amiably, and added, "Who are you to pass such orders?"

"You are a pertinacious pest," remarked Alphonse in disgust. "Now the urgent thing is that you get the saw. You stick like the burr, but at least make yourself useful . . . go and get a saw immediately."

"What for?"

Alphonse suppressed his irritation, and said, "I want to saw off a couple of those crossbars, enough to admit the headmaster's head, and then we could pull him out and tackle the tiger."

"And you expect the tiger to watch the fun while you are at your carpentry?" Master said with a smile.

Alphonse said, "If you do not behave, I'll push you in through this gap. Shekar, get a saw without delay—instead of listening to this mad fellow. He is persistent . . . No way of keeping him off."

"How can you keep me off? Who are you?" asked my Master, and added, "I can ask the same question you asked, who are you? I know enough law to realize that I have as good a right to be on a roof as anyone else!"

"I'm only here to help the headmaster . . ."

"You won't be able to work through the rafters so easily. They are old teak beams. You will have to saw for days before you can make a dent . . ."

"In that case, I'll shoot. I've enough sight now. Let the head-master stay where he is, and take his chance and pray for his life and pray that the tiger does not spring up vertically . . ." He turned to the headmaster, who was peering out like a prisoner behind the bars: "Only be careful that you don't fall off the edge when you hear my gun go off, stick close to the wall so that even if the tiger springs up, you will stay clear of his reach. With the second, I'll get him, even if he is in mid air . . ."

"Oh, here they are," exclaimed my Master, pointing at the school gate. A jeep had arrived at the gate and a number of persons jumped out of it and hurried across the school compound. They pushed their way through the crowd.

"Come down, please, and keep your finger off the trigger. We are Save Tiger Committee. You must hear us first. We are a statutory body with police powers . . ."

Alphonse came down the ladder, saying, "The headmaster is about to be saved. Please give me five minutes, I'll get him out and then we can discuss."

The wild-life committee paused to consider it for a moment, and asked, "Explain how you propose to save the headmaster."

Alphonse explained that he proposed to cut through the rafters and bail out the headmaster.

My Master, who had followed him down, said, "Rafters are of ancient timber, it'll take at least three days to make a notch."

Alphonse glared at him and exclaimed, "You again! Why do you dog my steps like this? I'd knock you down with the butt, but for your age. The animal is there already stirring and growl-ing. How long do you think the headmaster will stand the ten-sion? He may faint and roll off the attic straight into the mouth of the tiger. You won't let me call him a beast. I don't know why I'm being plagued by you . . . you follow me like a shadow . . ."

My Master ignored Alphonse and turned to the visitors: "I'm grateful that you have responded to my call. If you hadn't come, he'd have murdered the tiger. His plan was to make enough noise with a saw or anything to stir up the animal, and shoot, leaving it to chance for the headmaster to survive . . ."

Alphonse ground his teeth and remained silent. Meanwhile Shekar plucked at his sleeve. "Uncle, give me money, I'll buy *idli* and *vadai* at the Pankaja restaurant for the headmaster . . ." Alphonse fished out of his pocket a rupee and gave it to the boy, who at once ran off. Alphonse said, looking after him, "This fellow is the hope of our country. He is fit to ride on the back of a tiger . . ."

The leader of the wild-life group said, "Mr. Alphonse, as you may be aware, I'm the chairman of the local chapter of Tiger Project, affiliated to the Central Committee under the Ministry of Agriculture at Delhi . . ."

"What has agriculture to do with tigers?" asked Alphonse.

"We will go into the question later, but at the moment we wish to emphasize the fact that 'Save Tiger Project,' as its name indicates, is to prevent the decimation of the tiger population which was at one time in the neighbourhood of fifteen thousand; today it's less than fifteen hundred." He went into statistics until Alphonse said, "Is this the time for a lecture, while the headmaster is half dead inside? You think that only tigers are important and not a headmaster . . ."

"And so," continued the chairman, "there is a general ordinance issued by the government which prohibits the shooting of any tiger, in any part of India, and we are given powers to enforce the rules and initiate prosecution if and when necessary; with penalty up to two thousand rupees and one year's rigorous imprisonment and confiscation of the offender's weapon and licence . . ."

"I know all this and more," said Alphonse. "You are opening your eyes on this subject probably only now. But I have been in the tiger business for half a century. There's a provision in the same ordinance, an exemption where a man-eater is concerned . . ."

"Yes, yes, we know all that; where a tiger has been established to be a man-eater, we can permit the shooting, provided you apply for it with proof and evidence . . ."

"What proof? Remains of a poor villager snatched away from the tiger's jaw? I'll also have to file a photograph and write an application in triplicate, I suppose?" he asked, with grim humour. "You and your government regulations. You have no practical sense . . . You'll see half the population destroyed in your zeal to protect the tiger: perhaps that's a ruse to keep down the population of our country! Ha! Ha! Ha! Here's a headmaster struggling to survive and you go on talking rules. You people do not distinguish between what's important and unimportant."

Meanwhile I awoke after a very good stretch of sleep and heard voices outside. I looked up and saw the headmaster cowering in the attic. I stretched myself and roared, for no particular reason except that I felt alive. The poor human being in the loft must have trembled at that moment. I wished to assure him that I was not going to hurt him. If it had been the old jungle days, I'd have gone after him; already a change was coming over me, I think. My Master's presence in the vicinity, though he had not come near me yet, must have begun to affect me. I tried to assure the headmaster by raising myself and putting up my forelegs on the wall and scratching it, and growling softly, which must have shaken the poor man so much that he seemed to lose control of his bowels and bladder. Thereupon I withdrew from the wall and curled myself under the table once again in order to reassure the poor man . . .

Meanwhile, outside, my Master noticed Alphonse taking the chairman aside under a tree, where they spoke in whispers. When they came back, the chairman was a changed man. He took aside, in his turn, his committee members, and spoke to them. Thereupon they took papers out of a briefcase and signed and gave them to Alphonse. All this concerned me. I was declared a man-eater and Alphonse was given written permission to shoot. "In the normal course," explained the chairman, "I should get the sanction from Delhi, but in an emergency, I am empowered to use my discretion." My Master suspected that Alphonse had offered a substantial bribe, as he was known to be engaged in a flourishing business exporting tiger skins.

Shekar was seen coming down the ladder with a packet of
food in hand. He approached Alphonse. "Uncle, I can't see the
headmaster; I held out the *idli*, but he didn't take it. What shall
I do now?"

"You and Ramu shall share the *idli*," said Alphonse.

The boy continued, "I peeped and couldn't see him; I called
and he wouldn't answer. I heard the tiger scratching something
and growling. I came away . . ." He looked sad and anxious,
moved aside and gobbled up the tiffin hurriedly.

The crowd, which watched in silence all along, let out a
moan in chorus: "Aiyo! Never thought our beloved headmaster would come to this end . . ." They all looked bitterly at the
assistant headmaster, who they somehow held responsible for
all the delay. The assistant headmaster probably had confused
feelings, happy at the thought that after all he was getting his
chance to become the headmaster, but also unhappy at the same
time. He wailed the loudest at the thought of the headmaster's
fate.

The commotion was at its height when Alphonse, properly
armed with the permit, gave a final look to his double-barrelled
gun, held it this way and that and looked through the barrel,
and shouted a command; "Your attention, everybody! Everyone must retreat at least a hundred yards before the school gate
which will give you an initial advantage if the tiger should decide to chase. No one can foresee how the situation will develop. The beast when shot may smash the door and rush out,
and God help anyone in its way. I'll count ten and this area
must be cleared; otherwise, I won't be responsible for any calamity. Now all clear out . . . It's an emergency. The headmaster
or whatever is left of him must be saved without delay. Now
clear out, everyone." He jingled the school-key bunch which he
had snatched from the assistant headmaster. "I'm risking my
life . . . I'll push the door open and shoot the same second, normally that should be enough . . ." After this he let out a shout
like a cattle-driver and a stampede started towards the gate, as
he started counting: "One, two, three . . ."

He turned to the chairman and his committee and said, as a
special concession, "You may stay back in that classroom to

your left and watch through the window. I've reconnoitred that area; it'll be safe for you to stay there, and you will get a good view through the window, but make sure to bolt the door." He said to Shekar, "Boy, show them the room and stay there yourself with your friend, until I say 'all clear.' He may need two shots—the interval between the first one and the second will be crucial. Anything may happen. No one can forecast with a hundred per cent certainty."

After all these preliminaries, and before delivering the actual assault, Alphonse sat down on the veranda step and took a flask out of his hip pocket, muttering, "This has been a big strain, must restore my nerves first . . ." He took a long swig out of it, while several pairs of eyes were watching him, smacked his lips, shook his head with satisfaction, picked up his gun and examined it keenly, and conducted a little rehearsal by pressing the butt against his shoulder and aiming at an imaginary tiger. He withdrew the gun and placed it at his side, took out the hip flask again, and took another long swig. He was heard to mutter, "Hands are shaky, need steadying up." And then he stood up with gun in hand, and rehearsed again with the butt against his shoulder. "Still shaky . . . Bloody dilute rum, has no strength in it; I'll deal with that fellow." He sat down again and took another drink, and another drink, till the flask was emptied.

My Master, who had stayed back unobtrusively, came forward to ask him, "Whom were you talking to?"

"You," said Alphonse. "I knew you were here. I knew you'd not go. I saw you—you obstinate devil . . . So, I thought, I thought, what did I 'thought'? I don't know. I have forgotten. No, no, if the beast comes out and swallows you, it'll serve you right . . . that's what I thought. Don't look at me like that . . . I'm not drunk . . . It's only watery rum . . . less than ten per cent proof . . . I'll deal with that cheat yet . . . that bastard . . ."

"Are you relaxing?" my Master asked.

"Yes, sir," he said heartily.

And then my Master asked, "What about the tiger?"

"What about what?"

"The tiger, the tiger in there . . ."

"Oh, yes, the tiger, he is O.K., I hope?"

"Aren't you going to shoot?"

"No," he said emphatically. "My hands must be steadied. I must have another drink. But my flask is empty. The son-of-a-bitch didn't fill it. I'll deal with him, don't worry. This sort of a thing . . ."

"The headmaster, what about him?"

"I don't know. Don't ask me. Am I responsible for every son-of-a-bitch?"

"Where did you learn this rare phrase?"

"In America," he said promptly. "I lived there for many years."

"Would you like to rest?"

"Of course, how did you guess? I got up at four this morning and rode fifty miles. Where is my vehicle?"

My Master gave him a gentle push, and he fell flat on the ground and passed out.

My Master must have turned on him his powers of suggestion. Taking the key-bunch from Alphonse, he went up to the headmaster's room and had just inserted the key into the lock when the chairman, watching through the window, shouted across at the top of his voice, "What are your trying to do? Stop!"

"I'm only trying to get the tiger out, so that the headmaster may come down confidently."

While this was going on Shekar suddenly threw back the bolt of the classroom and rushed out, followed by his friend Ramu. Both of them came and stood over Alphonse, watching him wide-eyed. "He is still breathing," one said to the other.

Both of them asked my Master, "Is Uncle dying?"

My Master said to them, "No, he will wake up—but rather late—don't worry. He will be well again . . ."

"Why is he like this? A nice uncle . . ." the boy asked tearfully.

"Oh, he will be all right," said my Master. "Don't worry about him. He has drunk something that is not good and that has put him to sleep . . ."

"Is it toddy?" asked the boy.

"Maybe," said my Master. "What do you know about it?"

"There is a toddy shop near our house . . ." began the boy, and my Master listened patiently, while the boy described the scenes of drunkenness that he witnessed in the evenings. Finally the boys asked, "How will he shoot the tiger?"

"No one is going to shoot," said my Master. "You will see the tiger come out and walk off with me . . ."

"He won't eat us?"

"No, he will not hurt anyone. I'm going to open the door and bring him out."

"The headmaster?" the boy asked anxiously.

"He must have also fallen asleep. He will also come out . . . don't worry. Would you like to come in with me and see the tiger?"

The boy hesitated and, looking back for a safe spot, said, "No, I'll stand there and watch."

The chairman, who had watched this dialogue, cried from behind the window, "What are you trying to do? You are mad."

"Come out and be with me. You will see for yourself what I plan to do."

"Explain," the other cried. "I do not understand you."

My Master turned round, walked to the window, and asked, "Are you afraid to come out of that room?"

"What a question!" exclaimed the chairman. "Of course, who wouldn't be! We are in a hurry. The headmaster must have help without delay. We must act before the gunman wakes up . . ." He spoke through the window.

"Here, I have the key. I'll unlock the door and bring the tiger out of the room. One of you take a ladder in and help the head-master come down from the attic. That's all . . ."

"Do you mean to say that you are going in as you are, with-out arms or protection?"

"Yes, that's what I'm going to do. We have no time to waste."

The chairman said, "By the powers vested in me in my ca-pacity as the Second Honorary Magistrate in this town, I give you notice that you shall not open or enter that room. My com-mittee members will bear witness to this order. It comes into immediate force, notwithstanding the fact that it's not yet in written form . . ." He looked around at his members, who crowded near the window bars and assented in a chorus.

My Master asked when it subsided, "Why'll you prevent me from going near the tiger?"

They were at a loss to answer: "It's unlawful to commit suicide."

"Maybe," said my Master, "but which law section says that a man should not approach a tiger? Are not circus people doing it all the time?"

"Yes," replied the chairman weakly. "But that's different."

"I can tame a tiger as well as any circus ringmaster. It's after all my life that I'm risking."

"There is no such thing as my life or your life before the eyes of the law: in the eyes of the law all lives are equal. No one can allow you to murder yourself . . ."

"Life or death is in no one's hands: you can't die by willing or escape death by determination. A great power has determined the number of breaths for each individual, who can neither stop them nor prolong . . . That's why God says in the *Gita,* 'I'm life and death, I'm the killer and the killed . . . Those enemies you see before you, O Arjuna, are already dead, whether you aim your arrows at them or not!'"

The chairman was visibly confused and bewildered. "In that case you will have to sign an affidavit absolving us from all responsibilities for your life or death . . ."

"You ignoramus of an honorary magistrate! After all that I have said, in spite of all that urgency . . . All right, give me a paper and tell me what to write."

The magistrate took out a sheet of paper from his briefcase and pushed it through the window bar. My Master sat down and wrote to the chairman's dictation through the window, absolving anyone from any responsibility. He signed the document and returned it with the comment, "Just to respect your magistracy, although I am convinced it's uncalled-for and irrelevant, and you are exercising unnecessary authority. The more important thing for you now would be to take in your custody that gun beside Alphonse. When he wakes up, no one can guess his mood, and it's not safe to leave the gun within his reach."

The chairman looked at the document and said, "Stop, wait.
Tell me what is it that you have written here?"

"Only what you have dictated."

"In a language we don't know, can't accept it . . ."

"It's in Sanskrit, in which our scriptures are written, language of the gods. I write only Sanskrit although I know ten
other languages including Japanese." Without further ado, he
turned round, paused for a second to satisfy himself that Alphonse was asleep, and put the key into the lock on the headmaster's room.

I had felt provoked at the sound of the key turning in the lock.
No one had a right to come in and bother me. I was enjoying
my freedom, and the happy feeling that the whip along with
the hand that held it was banished for ever. No more of it; it
was pleasant to brood over this good fortune. It was foolish of
me to have let the whip go on so long. Next time anyone displayed the whip . . . I would know what to do. Just a pat with
my paw, I realized, was sufficient to ward off any pugnacious
design. What ignorance so far! Now that I knew what men
were made of, I had confidence that I could save myself from
them. The chair, ah, that was different. That was more paralys-
ing than other instruments of torture. But here where I'm lying,
the headmaster's room, there are chairs, much bigger and more
forbidding than what Captain used to wield, but they have
done nothing, they have not moved to menace or hurt me. They
have stayed put. Now I've learnt much about chairs and men
and the world in general. Perhaps these men were planning to
trap me, cage me and force me to continue those jumping turns
with the suspended lamb, shamelessly standing on my hind legs
before the crowd of film-makers. If this was going to be the
case, I must show them that I could be vicious and violent too.
So far I had shown great concern and self-control. Thus far and
no further. The evidence of my intentions should be the headmaster, who I hoped was somewhere above me, unharmed and,
as I hoped, peacefully sleeping. I can't be definite. He makes no
sort of sound or movement, hence I guess he must be sound
asleep. I don't want to be disturbed, nor am I going to let any-

one bother the headmaster. So I have a double responsibility now. Someone at the door. I held myself ready to spring forward.

The door opened quietly and my Master entered, shutting the door behind him. I dashed forward to kill the intruder, but I only hurt myself in hurling against the door. I fell back. He was not there, though a moment ago I saw him enter. I just heard him say, "Understand that you are not a tiger, don't hurt yourself. I am your friend . . ." How I was beginning to understand his speech is a mystery. He was exercising some strange power over me. His presence sapped all my strength. When I made one more attempt to spring up, I could not raise myself. When he touched me, I tried to hit him, but my forepaw had no strength and collapsed like a rag. When I tried to snap my jaws, again I bit only the air. He merely said, "Leave that style out. You won't have use for such violent gestures any more. It all goes into your past." I had to become subdued, having no alternative, while he went on talking. "It's a natural condition of existence. Every creature is born with a potential store of violence. A child, even before learning to walk, with a pat of its chubby hands just crushes the life out of a tiny ant crawling near it. And as he grows all through life he maintains a vast store of aggressiveness, which will be subdued if he is civilized, or expended in some manner that brings retaliation. But violence cannot be everlasting. Sooner or later it has to go, if not through wisdom, definitely through decrepitude, which comes on with years, whether one wants it or not. The demon, the tormentor, or the tyrant in history, if he ever survives to experience senility, becomes helpless and dependent, lacking the strength even to swat a fly. You are now an adult, full-grown tiger, and assuming you are fifteen years old, in human terms you would be over seventy years old, and at seventy and onwards one's temper gets toned down through normal decay, and let us be grateful for it. You cannot continue your ferocity for ever. You have to change . . ."

At this point someone from the other side of the door called, "Sir, *Swamiji*, are you all right?"

"Yes, I am, don't you hear me talking?"

"Whom are you talking to, sir?"

"To a friendly soul," he said.

"Do you mean the headmaster? Is he safe?"

"Yes, he is up there, but I've not begun to talk to him yet . . . he doesn't seem to be awake yet. I'll look to him presently. But at the moment I'm discoursing to the tiger . . ."

"Oh, oh, does it understand?"

"Why not? If you could follow what I've been saying, the tiger should understand me even better since I'm closer to his ear . . ." I let out a roar because I was feeling uncomfortable with some change coming inside me. I was beginning to understand. Don't ask me how. My Master never explained to me the mystery or the process of his influence on me.

"Don't let him out, sir," said the voice. "When you open the door, please warn us first . . ."

"Surely, if you are afraid, but let me tell you, you need not fear; he has only the appearance of a tiger, but he is not one— inside he is no different from you and me." I felt restless and wanted to do something or at least get away from the whole situation, back to my familiar life, back to the jungle, to the bed of long grass—I sighed for the feel of the grass on my belly—to the cool of the stream beside the cave and the shade of the cave with its rugged sandy floor . . . I was sick of human beings; they were everywhere, every inch of the earth seemed to be swarming with humanity; ever since the unfortunate day I stepped into that village in the forest to the present moment I was being hemmed in. How grand it'd be to be back in the world of bamboo shade and monkeys and jackals! Even the supercilious leopard and the owl I would not mind; compared to human company, they were pleasant, minding their own business, in spite of occasional moods to taunt and gossip.

I rose. Master became alert. "What do you want to do now? You want to go away, I suppose! I understand. But there is no going back to your old life, even if I open the door and let you out. You can't go far. You will hurt others or you will surely be hurt. A change is coming, you will have to start a new life, a different one . . . Now lie down in peace, I will take you out. Let us go out together, it'll be safer. But first I must get the headmaster down from his perch. He has been there too long. Now you lie still, move away to the corner over there while I help him."

I understood and slowly moved off to the side he indicated. Whatever its disadvantage, circus life had accustomed me to understand commands. This room was not too spacious to talk of far side and near side, but I obeyed him. I moved to the other wall and crouched there humbly. I wanted to show that I had no aggressive intentions. Now my Master ordered, "Turn your face to the wall and do not stir in the least. If the headmaster thinks you are lifeless, so much the better. The situation is delicate, and you must do nothing to worsen it. God knows how long he has been cooped up there . . ."

He called him loudly but there was no answer. Then he went up to the door, opened it slightly and announced, "I want a ladder and a person to climb to the loft, wake up the headmaster, and help him to come down. Is there anyone among you willing to fetch the ladder and go up?" A subdued discussion arose and a couple of men came forward to ask, "What about the tiger? Where is he?"

"You have all improved to the extent of not referring to him as 'brute' or 'beast,' but I'm sorry to note that you still have no confidence in him or me. Let me assure you that this tiger will harm no one." This had no effect on anyone. There was no response. He said, "All right, I'll manage . . ." He shut the door again, pulled the table into position, and put up a chair on it, then another chair and a stool, and went up step by step and reached the loft, saying to himself, "How the headmaster reached here will remain a mystery . . ." He grasped the edge of the loft and heaved himself up.

Presently I heard him waking the headmaster and coaxing him to climb down. I could not see his actual coming down as I had to lie facing the wall; I could only hear movements and words. My Master exerted all his power to persuade him to step down. I sensed what was happening and though curious to watch, did not turn round, as I did not want to disobey my Master. The first thing the headmaster did on coming down was to cry, "Oh, it's still here!" and I heard some scurrying of feet, and my Master saying, "Don't look at him, but step down; he will not attack." The headmaster groaned and whimpered and was possibly trying to go back to the loft, at which my Master must have toppled the pile of chairs and pulled him down. I heard a thud and guessed that the poor man had landed on firm ground. I could hear him moaning, "It is still there, how can I?" My Master kept advising, "What if it is still there? Don't look in its direction, turn away your head, come with me . . ." He led the headmaster as he kept protesting, a sorry spectacle, in disarray, still in the coat and turban which he had worn in the morning. My Master propelled him to the door and pushed him out saying to those outside, "Here he is, take care of him. Not a scratch, only shock . . ." and shut the door again as a medley of comments, questions, and exclamations poured into the room.

Now he addressed me. "Now turn round, get up, and do whatever you like." I stretched myself, yawned, and rose to my feet. That was all I could do. I felt grateful, but I could not make out his form clearly. There was a haze in which he seemed to exist, a haze that persisted all through our association. At no time could I be certain of his outline or features—except what I could gather from his talk. He said, "Let us go out now. You must realize that human beings for all their bluster are timid creatures, and are likely to get into a panic when they see you. But don't look at them. This is one of the rules of yoga to steady one's mind, to look down one's nose and at nothing beyond. That's one way not to be distracted and to maintain one's peace of mind. I would ask you to keep your head bowed and cast your eyes down and make no sort of sound, whatever may be the reaction of the people we pass. We are bound to meet crowds during our passage through the town. People are likely to get excited at the sight of us, but you must notice nothing."

This was a necessary instruction since our emergence from the room created a sensation and a stampede, in spite of the warning cry my Master had given: "Now I am coming out with the tiger. Those who are afraid, keep away, but I assure you again that Raja will not attack anyone. He will walk past you, and you will be quite safe as if a cat passed by. Believe me.

Otherwise keep out of the way. I'll give you a little time to decide." When he opened the door, he said, "Keep close to me."
As he stepped out of the room, I was at his heels, saw no one,
but only heard suppressed, excited comments and whispers from
different corners. The veranda was empty, not a soul in sight,
with the exception of Alphonse lying on the top step. Without
a word my Master walked on briskly. We had to brush past Alphonse. The breeze of our movement seemed to have blown on
his face, and he immediately sat up, rubbed his eyes to see
clearly, blinked, shook his head and muttered, "Crazy dream!"
and laid himself down and apparently went back to sleep. But
he sat up again to watch us go. We had gone past him a little
way when he cried, "Hey, you bearded one, you again! Won't
leave me alone even in a dream! Ah! What is this?"

"Tiger," answered my Master.

"Is it the same or another one?" asked Alphonse.

"Same and another," answered my Master cryptically.

"How? Oh, yes, of course," he muttered, puzzled.

"You may touch the tiger if you like."

"No, no! Go away." He waved us off angrily and resumed
his sleep.

At first, when the Master emerged from the school gate with
the tiger, the crowds in the street stood petrified. Cycles, automo-
biles, lorries and bullock-carts hurriedly withdrew to the side;
even street dogs slunk away under culverts after whining feebly.
As advised by the Master, the tiger never lifted its eyes but followed his steps. The Master passed down quickly, reached the
Market Gate, turned to his right, proceeded northward on the
highway, and vanished at dusk towards the mountains.

Gradually lorries and bullock-carts began to move, cyclists
resumed their wobbly courses, and crowds reappeared on Market Road; at street corners people stood about in clusters regal-
ing each other with sensational accounts of the day's events,
while mischievous urchins continued to run up and down Market Road screaming, "Tiger! Tiger! It's here again!"

At Anand Bhavan, which had already had a visitation, the

main door was closed, but guests were admitted through a back door, the proprietor whispering as they entered, "Finish your business soon and be off . . . remember, no talk of tiger any more . . . have had enough . . ."

At the Boardless, however, it was different. The din in the hall was deafening, but Mr. Varma, the proprietor, who, from the eminence of his cash desk, always enjoyed listening to his clients' voices, felt especially gratified today with the medley of comments, questions, and arguments falling on his ears while his fingers ceaselessly counted cash.

"That hermit must have come from the Himalayas. I have heard that there are many extraordinary souls residing in the ice caves, capable of travelling any distance at will, and able to control anything by their yogic powers."

"How could the yogi have known that there was a tiger in the headmaster's room, and why should he have wanted to protect it?"

"Probably they were family friends!" They laughed at the joke.

"It may be no laughing matter. I was at the school and could overhear his conversation with the tiger as if it were his younger brother."

"Don't be too sure. Suppose that tiger makes a meal of his brother and turns round for more. We must be watchful—where are the police? Why can't they come out of their hiding and patrol the streets?"

"I tried to see the headmaster in Vinayak Street; after all he had kept longer company with the tiger than anyone else. But he was incoherent and still nervous lest the tiger should spring out of the next room. He had to be carried home in Gaffur's taxi, you know."

"The question remains, who is this tiger-tamer—the terrible animal trots behind him, while the circus-wallah for all his expert control could not save himself in the end."

"Whenever we questioned 'Who are you?' he quipped and dodged, you know," said a pedagogue.

Jayaraj, who framed pictures sitting in a cubicle at the Mar-

ket Arch, observed the goings-on in the town from his position
of vantage, and had spent a lifetime commenting and gossiping
while his hands were busy nailing picture frames. He was now
explaining to a company at the centre table, "At first I didn't
close my shop. I was not going to be frightened into thinking
that the tiger would come to eat me or the glass sheets in my
shop. But when I saw the crowd flooding past, I too caught the
frenzy, and went there rather late but just in time to see that
man come out of the school with his pet. The crowd pressed me
against the gate post, I could not back away farther when the
tiger almost brushed past my legs and I shivered, wedged as I
was between the animal and the wall. When he noticed my
fright that man just said, 'Don't fear,' and passed on, but in that
instant I recognized him—the shape of those eyes, the voice,
and those features were familiar, and through all that shrunken
frame and sunburnt, hairy face, I could see who he was. After
all I had started life as a photographer, and when one has
looked at faces through a lens, one can never forget a face.

"At one time I used to see him cycling up the Market Road
every morning to his college. He lived in Ellamman Street in
one of those solid houses built by an earlier generation. I can't
remember that man's name now, Govind, Gopal, or Gund? I
don't know. He was arrested during the Independence Movement for climbing the Collector's office roof and tearing down
the Union Jack, and then again for inscribing on the walls, with
brush and tar, 'Quit India,' aimed at the British. I was told that
he drove his mother mad by his ways. She would cry her heart
out every time he was sent to prison. He didn't pass his B.A.—
too busy, mixed up as he was in every kind of demonstration in
those days. When things quietened down after Independence,
he came to me one day to have his passport photo taken, but
never collected it, though he had paid for it in advance. His
photo must still be there somewhere in those piles of stuff un-
claimed by my customers for reasons best known to them. I
must put them all to the fire some day before all that junk
drives me out of my own shop . . .

"Later on, I used to see him occasionally coming to the market with his family, driving a motor car. At this stage, he was completely changed, looked like a fop with his tie and suit and polished shoes. One day I had the hardihood to hail him and to say that he should take away his passport photograph, since he had paid for it. I'm not the sort to keep other people's property. He halted his steps but before I could pick up his stuff and pack it, he muttered 'I will come again' and hurried out. He was perhaps a busy man, as he was said to be holding a big job in a foreign insurance firm which had its office in New Extension.

"I never thought of him again until I heard one day that he had vanished, abandoning his wife and children. The police came seeking his photograph but I didn't give it. If that man chose to disappear, that was his business, why should I be involved?"

"Any reason why he went away?"

"I know as much as you do. Why ask me? Enough . . . talk of something else . . . Let us forget him and his tiger. Something uncanny about him . . . unsafe to talk about such men, who may be saints or sorcerers. Who knows what will happen? Remember the ancient saying, 'Don't probe too far into the origin of a river or a saint! You will never reach the end.'" With that Jayaraj abruptly got up, paid for his coffee, and went away.

"Extraordinary how that animal could not be shot at all," mused someone after Jayaraj left. "Alphonse, who had hunted tigers all his life, fell into a stupor when he lifted his gun today."

"Oh! Oh! Stupor indeed," someone said, laughing.

Late in the evening Alphonse woke up on the school steps, looked around, and muttered, "Not a soul in sight. Where is everybody gone? They have bluffed me." He got up, went over to his motor cycle, and kicked the starter viciously. Entering the Market Junction, he noticed people standing in knots and slowed down to shout, "Why don't you keep out of the way?"

"The tiger is gone," someone ventured to inform him over the roar of his motor cycle. He replied, "Oh, shut up, all that nonsense about the tiger! It is over a year since I saw one. Those bastards have April-Fooled us. They would not even let me peep through the keyhole to see for myself. I will deal with them yet."

"But it seems you did see the tiger from the rooftop?" ventured his listener.

"You don't have to tell me what I see or don't see, understand? None of your business. If ever you see a real tiger with a tail at the right end, call me; otherwise it is a waste of time." With that Alphonse was off.

We passed through many villages, big and small, towards I don't know where, as I followed my Master; everywhere people made way for us, retreated hurriedly, staring in wonder and disbelief, afraid even to breathe. Crowds which would normally be noisy and jostle looked intimidated by the spectacle, which made my Master remark, "What our country needs most is a tiger for every village and town to keep people disciplined . . ." In some places someone would call out from afar, "Tiger-man, put a collar and chain around your pet—we are terrified . . ."

"Come and do it yourself," my Master said. "I will have no objection and I can tell this tiger to remain still while you collar it . . ."

We passed on while I stuck close to his heels and moved along without lifting my head or looking at anyone too long. My Master told me, "The eye is the starting point of all evil and mischief. The eye can travel far and pick out objects indiscriminately, mind follows the eye, and rest of the body is conditioned by the mind. Thus starts a chain of activity which may lead to trouble and complication, or waste of time, if nothing else; and so don't look at anything except the path." Sometimes I could not resist looking at cattle or other creatures, which I would normally view as my rightful prize. But I'd immediately avert my eyes when I realized what I was doing.

We were about to descend the slope of a hillock when we noticed in the valley below a procession passing. People were dragging a flower-decorated chariot with pipes and drums. The chariot carried the image of God, and there was much rejoicing and dancing and singing, and scattering of flowers. Vendors of fruits or sweets were doing a brisk business with the children swarming around. But the moment we were seen, everyone ran for safety. God's chariot was abandoned in the middle of the road; the drummers and pipers abruptly stopped their music and, clutching their instruments, ran madly. My Master said to me, "Stay here, and don't move even if people come near or touch you." He left me there and ran forward and said to those on the run, "Come, come back, don't abandon your God. Draw the chariot along. Come on, come on. My tiger is godly, and loves a procession." He went after the piper and the drummer, and brought them back forcibly, saying, "That tiger of ours is musically inclined, and won't like to be cheated out of it. Go on, play your pipes. This tiger is no real tiger at all. He just looks like one, that's all. He loves you all. Go on . . ." With their gaze fixed in my direction they played nervously. The chariot wheels moved again and the crowd followed, although in a subdued spirit. The children did not laugh or dance; the sweet-sellers did not cry their wares. "This pains me very much, how can I prove you are a friend?" said my Master, falling back. We took a detour and went forward.

At another place we went into a rioting mob—groups of people were engaged in a bloody strife, attacking each other with stone, knife, and iron rod, and screaming murderous challenges. In their frenzy they had not noticed us, but when they did, they dispersed swiftly. My Master cried to them, "If I find you fighting again, I'll be back to stop it. Take care. You should not need a tiger to keep the peace."

When we reached the foot of Mempi range, he looked up with joy at a towering peak in front of us and said, "That ought to be our home, but it is inaccessible, so we will stop here . . . I was here before, and once saw a flash of light on the very tip of that peak and felt overwhelmed by its mystery since no human being has ever set foot there. Although I realize now that it might be no more than a touch of the moon rising behind it, I will still watch for it: I have a great desire to see that flash again . . ."

He searched and found his spot. A rock jutting over a ledge seemed to him adequate shelter. He said, "Here we will stay." He broke some twigs and swept the floor. Farther off there was a spring bubbling up from a cavity in the rock. "You can have a drink of water here, but I cannot tell you where you should seek your food. I don't know and I do not wish to think of it, as I cannot give you any help. I know I cannot persuade you to eat grass or live on roots and greens. God has decided for you a difficult diet. I can help your mind and soul, but I cannot affect your body or its functions. Now I should leave you free to go where you like, but don't go too far away from here or too long . . ."

I accepted his advice. All day long I lay across the entrance of his shelter. It was enough for me that I was near him, while he sat with his eyes shut in prayer. I cannot say how long he would sit thus. In the evenings he would open his eyes, and then talk to me on life and existence and death, and help my understanding. More than once he mentioned God. The word "God" had been unheard of by me. We who live in the jungle have never known the word. He explained God; most of it was beyond my understanding, but he said, "You may not understand the word. But let it sink in your mind and ring on your ears, and then tell me later how you feel." He described God in his own terms as the Creator, the Great Spirit pervading every creature, every rock and tree and the sky and the stars; a source of power and strength. Later when my Master questioned me about it, I said that God must be an enormous tiger, spanning the earth and the sky, with a tail capable of encircling the globe, claws that could hook on the clouds, and teeth that could grind the mountain, and possessing, of course, immeasurable strength to match. On hearing my notion of God, my Master burst into a laugh and said, "It's often said that God made man in His own image, it's also true that man makes God in his own image. Both may be right; and you are perfectly right in thinking of your God as a super tiger. Also it may be true. What we must not forget is that He may be everything we imagine and more. In *Bhagavad Gita* He reveals Himself in a mighty terrifying form which pervades the whole universe in every form of life and action. Remember also He is within every one of us and we derive our strength from Him . . ." He did not treat me as an animal which sat before him in respectful silence trying to understand his words; I only felt grateful that he was trying to transform me in so many ways. How he could do it was his own secret.

At dawn, it was his habit to go to the spring and bathe, wash his single piece of cloth, and wear it, allowing it to dry on his body. He would then pray and meditate, and break off to go into the forest and return with an armful of roots, herbs, and leaves which provided him nourishment. Except those moments when he discoursed to me, he remained silent and often went into deep meditation. Nowadays the keenness of my hunger was also gone, and I slipped away into the jungle, not too often, only when I felt I could not stand hunger any more. When I returned from my hunt, I kept myself away until he summoned me. I would be oppressed with a sense of guilt in spite of the fact that when I hunted and killed, I was lost in the thrill of the moment and relished the taste of warm flesh and blood, a luxury I had missed at the circus, where stale meat was thrown out of buckets at feeding time, by butchers on contract. It might be any meat, no way of knowing, might be a dog's or a donkey's, dull-tasting since the contractor soaked the meat in water to give it weight. So all along I could not help craving for fresh kill. But nowadays, the moment I had eaten my fill I'd be seized with remorse. And so, when I returned from the jungle I'd lie low, out of sight of my Master.

Even for drinking water, I chose another stream within the forest, since I did not want to sully the spring in which my Master performed his morning ablutions. Nor would my Master shame me by referring to my night expeditions. I tried to attain some kind of purification by reducing the frequency of seeking food. Nor did I kill recklessly as I used to in my jungle days—any game of any size or bulk, I used to slaughter, consume it partly, and return to the fly-covered remnant again the next day. I could not bear to recollect this habit: it nauseated. Nowadays, I went into the jungle and stalked the littlest game, just sufficient enough to satisfy my hunger of the moment and not my gluttony. And then I didn't go into the forest again for several days, prolonging the intervals as much as possible. I suffered hunger for consecutive days before seeking food again, but felt nobler for it. I felt I had attained merit through penance, making myself worthy of my Master's grace. How I wished I had learnt the art of living on sugar cane and rice, like the elephant and the hippo of the circus; the chimp would explain how they ate nothing else, which lesson I should have taken from them. How mighty the hippo and the elephant looked, although they ate no meat.

At night I quietly returned to a spot beyond a screen of vegetation not far from my Master, ready to reach his side in a few bounds if summoned. This phase of life I found elevating: the change churning internally was still felt by me, but did not bother me now as it did at the beginning. I was getting accustomed to many changes. If I could have shed the frightening physical encasement God has chosen for me, I could have lived on air, or dry leaves, and I'd have felt more blessed. Understanding the turmoil in me, my Master said, "Do not crave for the unattainable. It's enough you have realization. All in good time. We cannot understand God's intentions. All growth takes place in its own time. If you brood on your improvements rather than your shortcomings, you will be happier."

While I learnt a great deal from my Master, enough to know myself, understand the world in which I lived, feel and express my thoughts (although understood only by my Master), one thing he would not teach me was the art of reckoning. Numbers and figures were still beyond my grasp. To my questioning, he said, "Why do you want to know how long ago or before or how much later or earlier? Not necessary for you. A sense of time may be required for human beings engaged in worldly activities. But why for you and me? I shun all activities and you have none. You have freed yourself from all duties which had been forced on you. And so you need not know what time of the day or what time of the week, or numbers, reckoning of before and after, when and how far; in short you don't have to know the business of counting, which habit has made us human beings miserable in many ways. We have lost the faculty of appreciating the present living moment. We are always looking forward or backward and waiting for one or sighing for the other, and lose the pleasure of awareness of the moment in which we actually exist. Time is not for you or for that matter

me, although at some stage of my life . . ." Here was some hint
of his past life and I pricked up my ears. He understood that I
wished to know more about him. "Why do you want to know
what I was or how or where? It'd be unnecessary knowledge.
Knowledge, like food, must be taken within limits. You must
know only as much as you need, and not more. All the thousands of human beings you have encountered since leaving the
shelter of your forest life suffer from minds overburdened with
knowledge, facts, and information—fetters and shackles for the
rising soul.

"I was a man of the world, busy and active and living by the
clock, scrutinizing my bank book, greeting and smiling at all
and sundry because I was anxious to be treated as a respectable
man in society. One day it seemed all wrong, a senseless repeti-
tion of activities, where one's head always throbbed with the
next plan, counting time or money or prospects—and I abruptly
shed everything including (but for a bare minimum) clothes,
and fled away from wife, children, home, possessions, all of
which seemed intolerable. At midnight, I softly drew the bolt of
our back door, opening on the sands of Sarayu behind our
house at Ellamman Street, while others slept and left very much
in the manner of Siddhartha . . . They searched but gave up
eventually, concluding that I was washed off in the Sarayu,
which was in flood at that time . . . I trudged and tramped and
wandered through jungles and mountains and valleys not caring where I went. I achieved complete anonymity, and shed
purpose of every kind, never having to ask what next. And so
here I am, that's all you need to know."

Although my Master had taken the trouble to choose a remote
part of the jungle to live in, people seemed to have got scent of
us, of the novelty of our life—a man living in the company of a
tiger—and began to visit us. The news must have spread from
village to village. One morning, watching from his ashram, a
sort of table at an elevation, which could give one a view of the
surrounding country, we saw a file of peasants approaching at
a distance. My Master remarked, "No escape from humanity!
They'll pursue you even if you hide yourself in the bowels of

the earth. Anyway, you keep yourself out of view so that they may approach without fear." I had been lying on the ground while he sat on the slab of stone. I got up in obedience to his command and moved off to my cave behind the screen of creepers and *lantana* shrubs. Presently I noticed from my spot some men arrive, carrying baskets of flowers and fruits. They stood away at a distance and hallooed: "*Swamiji,* are you there?"

"Yes, I'm here, but I am no *Swamiji.*"

"May we approach you?"

"Why not? Anyone is welcome."

"But you have the tiger with you still?"

"Yes, naturally, but he is not a tiger."

"He looks like one, we are afraid."

"Then why do you want to come?"

"For your *darshan,* sir." This kind of talk went on for a while.

"Don't use the word *darshan,*" he shouted back.

"Why not, master?"

"Because the word is not appropriate . . ."

"What does *darshan* actually mean, sir? We do not wish to offend you."

"Why don't you come up and ask, so that I may not have to shout through my answer."

"Of course, sir, we are naturally here to sit at your feet . . ."

Master uttered an exclamation of impatience. "Oh, at my feet! Where have you picked up these phrases of mental slavery? Come up if you are not afraid. What makes you think you are safe there if it's the tiger that frightens you? He can easily come there too—nothing to hold him back."

"Have you not tied him up, sir?"

"Certainly not, I live freely too . . . so there is no place in my system for any rope or chain or bond of any kind. If you don't muster enough courage and confidence, turn back and go."

"We have come a long way, sir, for your *dar*—" They were about to say "*darshan*" again but restrained themselves.

"I leave you to your discretion. Go back if you like . . ."

But they hesitated uncertainly, and consulted among themselves. Having taken the trouble to come so far, they didn't

want to waste the visit, and perhaps feeling that they might encounter the tiger in any case even while retreating, in a short
while they came up and placed their offerings before my Master. When he noticed their preparations to prostrate before him,
he said emphatically, "I won't allow you to prostrate." They
would not listen to his objection. In spite of it, they threw
themselves full-length on the ground and tried to touch his feet.
He shrank back from them and threw himself on the ground as
a counter-measure and tried to take the dust off their feet. They
scrambled up in great confusion. "Oh, *Swamiji*, you could not
do it. We are small men, but you are great."

"How? Because I'm unshaven and shirtless? I don't shave because I find it easier not to. I don't wear a shirt because I don't
have one. But for these, I go about with the tiger because it's
God's will. I am not different from you, we are equals and no
need to pay homage to me. It has no meaning. You must prostrate only before God. You should seek only God's *darshan*, we
must not misappropriate the word that belongs to him, in a
temple. Even that I doubt, since the same God resides within all
of us. When you address a prayer to God, you are only praying
to yourself . . . or at least you are entitled to half that prayer;
and if you are offering a flower, again half is yours, as a famous
mystic poet sung . . ." At this point he suddenly lifted his head
and delivered a full-throated song, his voice rebounding from the
rocks. "When I bring my palms together and raise my arm in
prayer, I'm only half-praying to you. Is it right to pray thus?"

His visitors were overwhelmed, but suddenly remembered
the tiger and asked timidly, "Where is the tiger?"

"Don't think of him. Sit down with an easy mind and tell me
your purpose. Why do you spoil your mind with thoughts of
the tiger? Having come all this distance . . ."

They placed the basket of flowers and fruits before him and
appealed, "Please accept these."

He took just a single flower and a small banana. "Yes, these
will do. Take them back to the children in your village, and the
flowers to the womenfolk."

They sat down again on the ground in front of my Master
and began to explain. "We are from both the sides you found

fighting the other day. We have come to assure you that we will
not fight again. When your honour passed through our village
that day, you saw us in a shameful state . . . We are here to beg
your forgiveness."

"Ask God's forgiveness rather than mine."

"The cause of our fight that day—"

"Don't tell me what—all causes of rivalry and clash are
senseless and so need no defining or explanation . . . Don't ever
fight. No cause is worth a clash."

"We pledge never to fight again. Your gracious presence
helped us the other day . . ."

"That's good. You should not depend upon a tiger or a bearded
man again to help you settle your differences. If you are ready
to hate and want to destroy each other, you may find a hundred
reasons—a diversion of canal water in your field, two urchins of
opposite camps slapping each other, rumours of molestation of
some woman, even the right to worship in a temple, anything
may spark off a fight if you are inclined to nurture hatred—only
the foolish waste their lives in fighting . . ."

One morning I was lying at the feet of my Master; he was sitting in meditation. Nowadays he encouraged me to remain
close by when he meditated as it might help me too. At such
moments a profound silence prevailed, and the sublime state to
which he had raised his mind carried mine also along. At such
moments I felt lighter at heart and my physical self also became
secondary. My sight became clearer; if I lifted my gaze to the
horizon, the sun shining on the land filled me with joy: the
leaves of the mighty banyan trees sparkling like gems, the bamboos swaying their golden stems with their filigreed leaves—I
felt I could ask for nothing more in life. When he read the state
of my mind, my Master explained. "No one would credit a tiger with so much poetic joy, it is inconceivable. Looking back,
I would say that in one of your previous births you might have
been a poet, and your deeper personality retains that *vasana*
still. Whatever one had thought or felt is never lost, but is buried in one's personality and carried from birth to birth. You

must have been a poet, perhaps many centuries ago in the court
of a king, your shoulder wrapped in a resplendent shawl, a diamond bracelet on your arm, seated beside the throne stirring
royal hearts with songs of nightingale, moon, roses or of an
aching heart pining away for the lost love . . . Oh, Raja, I see a
visitor coming up, of all things a woman, go, hide yourself before she sees you, she may faint in my arms . . ." I rose and
went behind the screen of *lantana* bush and the rock.

Presently the visitor arrived, panting. I could see her through
the foliage. I couldn't describe a human being. My Master never
taught me how to distinguish one from another. All humans look
alike in my eyes, and my Master has confirmed that it is the right
view. I could, in a rough manner, identify some special person-
alities like Captain or the clowns or Rita by prolonged association, and especially by their functions. If I needed to know the
looks of any person, I would know it only through my Master's
description. When he understood my curiosity about this woman,
he explained that she was over fifty years old, medium height,
dark, round cheeks, with grey hair tied up at the back.

The lady advanced towards my Master, seated on his slab of
stone, and prostrated.

"Madam, you should not prostrate before me, please get up.
I never like anyone to touch my feet."

She got up, saying, "One has the right to show one's venera-
tion for a sublime soul, a saint perhaps."

"Please sit down, madam. I am unhappy that I can offer you
only the bare ground to sit on, no carpet or mat."

"They're immaterial, the great thing is to be blessed with
your *darshan*."

"Calm yourself, rest for a while, you don't have to say anything. Feel completely free to remain silent. You don't have to
utter a single word."

The lady smiled. "I've not come all the way to observe a vow
of silence."

"Perhaps I may be under a vow not to hear a word . . ."

"Quite likely . . . even then I will speak since I have come all
the way."

"By all means. Go ahead. I have not shut off my ears yet. First let me ask what brought you here?"

"I heard of a remarkable person who went out with a tiger, as if he had taken a dog out, and I told myself I must see this *Swamiji*, it's only this remarkable man who can help me in my search . . ."

"Don't you see what risk you face by going after a *sadhu* you have only heard about? He might be a fake."

"Yes, I fear that too," she said.

"You might be endangering your virtue, too . . ."

"At my age and condition, my virtue is quite safe. No one will be tempted to molest a grey-haired fat hag. Only they robbed me of the money I had, and also a chain and bangles; while crossing a lonely forest path, three men accosted me, and relieved me of my jewellery and a bundle of clothes, too, and went their way quietly. Good men, they only robbed, which seems to me less heinous than deserting one's family and home for no reason."

"How can you say 'no reason'? An inner compulsion is enough to make one take fateful decisions."

How I wished I could join their conversation. Not only could I not speak, but I had to keep my cursed form concealed behind the *lantana* bush in order not to scare the visitor. If permitted, I would have asked, "How did you come to know about my Master?"

As if in answer to my question, she was saying, "On that day when a tiger was at school, I went there with a neighbour who was searching for her son. The crowd was pressing and suffocating, pushing us about. Everybody was terrified, and yet wanted to get a glimpse of the tiger, with the result no one could ever go in. My companion broke down and wept helplessly. Some mischievous persons were enjoying the situation by suddenly crying out, 'Run, run, the tiger has come, the tiger is coming,' and kept the crowd running back and forth. I and my friend got separated in the mêlée. Later when we met, she told me how she was comforted and helped by a bare-bodied *sadhu* who was calmly sitting on a culvert outside the school gate."

"In what manner did the *sadhu* help her?"

"He told her that the tiger was locked in and would not harm anyone, and also that her son must be with the other children safely sheltered in the school hall. Was that *sadhu* you?"

"Could be, or might be any other bare-bodied, bearded person. There must be hundreds of them everywhere."

"But there was only one in that place and he was offering to lead away the tiger."

"Oh, did he?"

"And something that she had noticed about him which she mentioned made me think."

"What could it be?"

"He was in the habit of rubbing his finger across his brow while thinking, as you are doing now . . ."

It was true, when my Master was listening or thinking he always drew his finger across his brow as if writing something there. The mention of this mannerism seemed to disturb my Master's equanimity, but only for a moment; he laughed and said, "This is my habit, surely I know it. I do it and a hundred others may also be doing it, just to probe what's written there by fate, like a blind man's running his finger over an etching, and are we not all blind where our fates are concerned?"

"By the time I learnt about the *sadhu*, he was gone with his tiger. I went back home and kept thinking. The picture came up before me as to how I had not seen anyone else do it. How when he sat in the veranda, reclining in his easy chair, reading a newspaper, he'd hold it in one hand so as to leave the other free to trace his forehead; or before going out to his office, if I asked for cash for some domestic shopping, he would always say, 'If I could conjure up the money,' and while uttering the word 'conjure,' he'd send his fingers dancing across his forehead—whether joking or serious, he always took his fingers to his forehead. I have also felt sometimes irritated by it and told him, 'Oh, keep off your fingers from your head, it's very distracting!' When our son had a problem in his college, you could not listen to him without these fingers almost skinning your forehead."

"Did he help his son at all?"

"The boy was in constant trouble with a particular master who was rather vindictive, but you went up to their principal and spoke to him and from that day—"

"You are beginning, I now notice, to use the word 'you,' which is not proper; keep to 'he.'"

"Even now I notice your fingers going to your brow . . ."

"Many people have that habit, you see of all organs, it is the hand that's most active and independent. The hand acts by itself when you are not watchful—it can tease you by hiding the keys . . . It's the hand that goes forward first to strangle a throat, fondle a lover, or bless or thieve . . . If God had devised the hand differently, the world and human actions and attitudes would have been different."

She was listening with adoration. At this moment I sneezed, some insect having settled on my nostril. She asked in alarm, "What is that?"

"Oh, some jungle noise, don't worry about it."

"Oh, husband, how can you forget the years we have spent together, twenty years, twenty-five, thirty—I have lost count . . ."

"Don't say 'husband,' it is a wrong word . . ."

"Husband, husband, husband, I'll repeat it a thousand times and won't be stopped. I know to whom I'm talking. Don't deceive me or cheat me. Others may take you for a hermit, but I know you intimately. I have borne your vagaries patiently for a lifetime: your inordinate demands of food and my perpetual anxiety to see you satisfied, and my total surrender night or day when passion seized you and you displayed the indifference of a savage, never caring for my health or inclination, and with your crude jocularities even before the children, I shudder!"

"You should have felt happy to lose such a husband. Why have you gone after him? No reason, especially when he has left for you and your children a comfortable home, all the money he had, and every kind of security in life. If you think over it, you will realize that the surrender has been rather on his part: it was total, he took nothing for himself except a piece of loincloth for all the wealth he had accumulated! However, please know that he left home not out of wrath, there was no cause for it, but out of an inner transformation."

"You have a strange way of talking now."

He said with a touch of firmness, "Time for you to start back if you must reach the nearest village before nightfall. I'll take you down and from the village you can go on."

"I can't go without you—or let me stay with you . . ."

"Impossible. What you see is my old shell; inside it's all changed. You can't share my life."

"Come home with me, I'll accept you as you are, keep your beard and loin-cloth, only let me have my husband at home . . ."

"Listen attentively: my past does not exist for me, nor a future. I live for the moment, and that awareness is enough for me. To attain this state, I have gone through much hardship. I don't have to explain all that now. I have erased from my mind my name and identity and all that it implies. It would be unthinkable to slide back. You must live your own life and leave me to live mine and end it my own way."

She broke down and wailed aloud. He calmly watched her. "I wish I could help you, as I managed to help Raja and calm his turbulent soul. I can only pray for your well-being."

"Let me stay in that village, so that I'll at least be near you."

"Why should you? You can't. You have your own home and family."

"Have you no feeling or even an ordinary sense of duty?"

"I do not understand these phrases. I have forgotten the meaning of many words. Please do not force me to talk so much about myself. Because of my sympathies and a real desire to help you, I have spoken. Otherwise I never revive the identity of the past in thought or word; it's dead and buried."

"You are callous; you talk of sympathy just with the tip of your tongue. You have no real feeling, you are selfish, you are . . ." She went on until sheer exhaustion overcame her.

He listened to her in stony silence. At some point he even failed to look at her; closed his eyes and went into meditation. He just said, "I'll take you down to the village. Let's get there before sunset."

"Why should you take the trouble?"

"You will have to pass through the jungle all alone."

"I can go alone, as I came . . ."

"Yes, we come into the world alone, and are alone while leaving. Your understanding is becoming deeper."

She repeated, "I didn't need your help while coming. Why should you bother about a stranger? You and your tiger—if he is there in the jungle and meets me, I shall be grateful if he ends my misery then and there, or couldn't you tell him?"

"You will reach home safely."

She sprang to her feet. "Finally, is there no way I can persuade you?"

"I need no persuasion . . . God be with you."

She wiped her eyes with the end of her sari, turned round, hurried down the hill, and disappeared into the jungle. He sat motionless in his seat and closed his eyes in meditation.

I did not wish to disturb him; I kept away until he should call me. I didn't go out to hunt that night, preferring to go without food. I didn't want to go prowling in the forest for fear that if that lady happened to be there and saw me, she might die of shock.

My Master never mentioned her visit again. He sat continuously in meditation for a few days, and then our normal life was resumed. He bathed in the pool, went into the forest to gather roots and leaves for his nourishment, meditated and discoursed to me in the evenings seated on his slab of stone.

Thus life went on. As I have said I have no reckoning of time. I could only measure it by my own condition. Gradually I realized that I was becoming less inclined to get up and move, preferring to spend long hours in my own corner hidden behind the shrub. I preferred to go without food rather than undergo the strain of chasing game. I could not run fast enough to catch anything. Many creatures eluded me with ease. Most of my old associates, the langur, the jackal, and others who used to watch me and annoy, were missing, perhaps dead or not frequenting this particular part of the forest. My claws sometimes stuck and most of my teeth had fallen. It was difficult for me to tear or chew. My movements were becoming so slow and clumsy that I was often outwitted; and when I succeeded in cornering some animal, I could not kill it successfully. I took a long time to consume it. The result was that in due course, I was under-feeding myself and my skin fell in folds.

My hearing was also impaired. Nowadays I could not hear when my Master summoned me. And his discourses were much reduced as he understood that I could not hear him properly. He told me, "Raja, old age has come on you. Beautiful old age, when faculties are dimmed one by one, so that we may be rest-ful, very much like extinguishing lights in a home, one by one, before one goes to sleep. Listen attentively. You may live a maximum of five years; I don't think we should risk your suf-fering starvation or attack from other creatures or hunters. Once they know you are old and weak, they will come for you and you are going to be alone because we are about to part. Last night I realized that the time for my attaining *samadhi* is near at hand. I must prepare for it by releasing myself from all bondage . . . As a first step, I'm releasing you. Tomorrow a man will come to take charge of you. He is the head of a zoo in the town. You will spend the rest of your years in the company of animals. You will be safe in a cage, food will be brought to you, and they will open the door and let you out to move freely in an open-air enclosure, and look after you." Never having been in the habit of questioning my Master, I accepted his plans, though with a heavy heart. He explained his philosophy: "No relationship, human or other, or association of any kind could last for ever. Separation is the law of life right from the moth-er's womb. One has to accept it if one has to live in God's plans."

Very soon we had a visitor from the town. It was noon. The visitor looked to me a kindly person; he held no whip in hand. He had a companion and down below on the forest track there was a cage on wheels. My Master and the visitor were engaged in a long talk. My Master was saying, "Keep him well. Remem-ber he is only a tiger in appearance . . . He is a sensitive soul who understands life and its problems exactly as we do. Take him as a gift from God; only please don't put him in rough company. He is magnificent though he is not at his best now.

After a few days of regular feeding at the zoo, he will get back the shine on his coat."

"We'll take care of that," the other said.

"Raja, come," commanded my Master for the last time.

I came out of the shrubberies and covering. The visitor was rather startled at first and remarked, "Oh, truly the most magnificent of his kind, regal, of grand stature, although you think he is faded. We have our own system of feeding and improving with tonic and he'll be record-breaking. Our zoo can then claim to have the largest tiger for the whole country."

My master assured him, "He is quite safe."

At first sight, I could understand that this man was fearless and used to the company of animals, and had sympathy, and was not another Captain. He asked my Master, "May I touch him?"

"Yes, certainly," said my Master, and patted my back. The man came near and stroked my back, and by his touch I could see that I had a friend.

"May we go?" he asked.

My Master said to me, "Raja, will you come with me?" and I followed him. He opened the cage and said, "You may get in now, Raja, a new life opens for you. Men, women, and children, particularly children, hundreds of them will come to see you. You will make them happy." The others got into the jeep to which the cage was yoked. Before we drove off my Master thrust his hand through the bars and whispered to me, "Both of us will shed our forms soon and perhaps we could meet again, who knows? So goodbye for the present."

THE MAN-EATER
OF MALGUDI

CHAPTER ONE

I could have profitably rented out the little room in front of my press on Market Road, with a view of the fountain; it was coveted by every would-be shopkeeper in our town. I was considered a fool for not getting my money's worth out of it, since all the space I need for my press and its personnel was at the back, beyond the blue curtain. But I could not explain myself to sordid and calculating people. I hung up a framed picture of Goddess Laxmi poised on her lotus, holding aloft the bounties of earth in her four hands, and through her grace I did not do too badly. My son, little Babu, went to Albert Mission School, and he felt quite adequately supplied with toys, books, sweets, and any other odds and ends he fancied. My wife, every Deepavali, gave herself a new silk sari, glittering with lace, not to mention the ones she bought for no particular reason at other times. She kept the pantry well-stocked and our kitchen fire aglow, continuing the traditions of our ancient home in Kabir Street.

I had furnished my parlour with a high-backed chair made of teak-wood in the style of Queen Anne, or so the auctioneer claimed who had sold it to my grandfather, a roll-top desk supported on bow-legs with ivy-vines carved on them, and four other seats of varying heights and shapes, resurrected from our family lumber-room.

Anyone who found his feet aching as he passed down Market Road was welcome to rest in my parlour on any seat that happened to be vacant. While they rested there, people got ideas for bill forms, visiting cards, or wedding invitations which they asked me to print, but many others came whose visits did not mean a paisa to me. Among my constant companions was

a poet who was writing the life of God Krishna in monosyllabic
verse. His ambition was to compose a grand epic, and he came
almost every day to recite to me his latest lines. My admiration
for him was unbounded. I was thrilled to hear such clear lines
as "Girls with girls did dance in trance," and I felt equally excited when I had to infer the meaning of certain lines; that happened when he totally failed to find a monosyllable and achieved
his end by ruthlessly carving up a polysyllable. On such occasions even the most familiar term took on the mysterious quality of a private code. Invariably, in deference to his literary
attainments, I let him occupy the Queen Anne chair, while I sat
perched on the edge of my roll-top desk. In the next best seat,
a deep basket-chair in cane, you would find Sen, the journalist,
who came to read the newspapers on my table, and who held
forth on the mistakes Nehru was making. These two men and
a few others remained sitting there till six in the evening when
the press was silenced. I had no need to be present or attend to
them in any way. They were also good enough to vacate their
chairs without being told and to disappear when anyone came
to discuss business with me.

Between my parlour and the press hung a blue curtain. No
one tried to peer through it. When I shouted for the foreman,
compositor, office-boy, binder or accountant, people imagined
a lot of men working on the other side; if I had been challenged
I should have gone in and played the ventriloquist. But my
neighbour, the Star Press, had all the staff one could dream of,
and if any customer of mine insisted on seeing machinery, I led
him not through my curtain, but next door to the Star, where I
displayed its original Heidelberg with pride as my own acquisi-
tion (although in my view the owner had made a mistake in
buying it, as the groans of its double cylinder could be heard
beyond the railway yard when forms were being printed). The
owner of the Star was a nice man and a good friend, but he
hardly got any customers. How could he when all the time they
were crowding my parlour, although all I could offer them was
an assortment of chairs and a word of welcome? But as few
had ever stepped beyond the blue curtain, everyone imagined
me equipped for big tasks, which I certainly attempted with the

help of my well-wisher (I dare not call him staff) Sastri, the old man who set up type, printed the forms four pages at a time on the treadle, sewed the sheets, and carried them for ruling or binding to Kandan four streets off. I lent him a hand in all departments whenever he demanded my help and my visitors left me alone. On the whole I was a busy man, and such business as I could not take up I passed on next door to be done on the original Heidelberg. I was so free with the next-door establishment that no one knew whether I owned it or whether the Star owned me.

I lived in Kabir Street, which ran behind Market Road. My day started before four in the morning. The streets would be quite dark when I set out to the river for my ablutions, except for the municipal lamps which flickered (if they had not run out of oil) here and there in our street. I went down Kabir Street, cut through a flagged alley at the end of it, trespassed into the compound of the Taluk office through a gap in its bramble fencing, and there I was on the edge of the river. All along the way I had my well-defined encounters. The milkman, starting on his rounds, driving ahead of him a puny white cow, greeted me respectfully and asked, "What is the time, master?"—a question I allowed to die without a reply as I carried no watch. I simpered and let him pass suppressing the question, "Tell me the secret of your magic: how you manage to extract a milk-like product out of that miserable cow-like creature to supply thirty families as you do every morning. What exactly are you, conjuror or milk-vendor?" The old asthmatic at the end of our street sat up on the *pyol* of his house and gurgled through his choking throat, "Didn't get a wink of sleep all night, and already it's morning and you are out! That's life, I suppose!" The watchman at the Taluk office called from beneath his rug, "Is that you?"—the only question which deserved a reply. "Yes, it's me," I always said and passed on.

I had my own spot at the riverside, immediately behind the Taluk office. I shunned the long flight of steps farther down; they were always crowded, and if I went there I was racked with the feeling that I was dipping into other people's baths, but this point upstream seemed to me exclusive. A palmyra-tree loomed over the bank of the river, festooned with mud pots into which toddy dripped through a gash in the bark of the tree. When it fermented, it stank to the skies, and was gathered in barrels and sold to the patrons who congregated at the eighteen taverns scattered in the four corners of the city, where any evening one could see revellers fighting or rolling in the gutters. So much for the potency of the fluid dripping into the pot. I never looked up at the palmyra without a shudder. "With his monopoly of taverns," I thought, "Sankunni builds his mansions in the New Extension and rides about in his four American cars driven by uniformed chauffeurs."

All the same I was unable to get away from the palmyra. At the foot of the tree was a slab of stone on which I washed my dhoti and towel, and the dark hour resounded with the tremendous beating of wet cloth on granite. I stood waist-deep in water, and at the touch of cold water around my body I felt elated. The trees on the bank stood like shadows in the dusk. When the east glowed I sat for a moment on the sand reciting a prayer to the Sun to illumine my mind. The signal for me to break off from contemplation was the jingle of ox-bells as country carts forded Nallappa's grove, bringing loads of vegetables, corn and fuel from the near-by villages to the market. I rose and retraced my steps, rolling up my washing into a tight pack.

I had more encounters on my way back. My cousin from the fourth street gave me a cold look and passed. She hated me for staying in our ancestral home, my father having received it as his share after the division of property among his brothers. She never forgave us, although it had all happened in my father's time. Most of the citizens of this area were now moving sleepily towards the river, and everyone had a word for me. The lawyer, known as the adjournment lawyer for his ability to prolong a case beyond the wildest dream of a litigant, came by, a sparse hungry-looking man who shaved his chin once a fortnight. When I saw him in the distance I cried to myself, "I am undone. Mr. Adjournment will get me now." The moment he saw me he cried, "Where is your bed? Unless you have slept by the river how can you be *returning* from the river at this unearthly hour?"

There was one whom I did not really mind meeting, the septuagenarian living in a dilapidated outhouse in Adam's Lane, who owned a dozen houses in our locality, lived on rent, and sent off money-orders to distant corners of the Indian sub-continent, where his progeny was spread out. He always stopped to give me news of his relations. He looked like a new-born infant when he bared his gums in a smile. "You are late today," I always said, and waited for his explanation, "I sat up late writing letters. You know how it is with one's children scattered far and wide." I did not mind tarrying to listen to the old man, although my fingers felt cramped with encircling the wad of wet clothes I was carrying home to dry. The old man referred to four sons and their doings and five daughters, and countless grandchildren. He was always busy, on one side attending to the repairs of his dozen houses, about which one or the other of his tenants was always pursuing him; on the other, writing innumerable letters on postcards, guiding, blessing, admonishing, or spoiling with a remittance of cash one or the other of his wards.

I was content to live in our house as it had been left by my father. I was a youth, studying in Albert Mission, when the legal division of ancestral property occurred between my father and his brothers. I well remember the day when his four brothers marched out with their wives and children, trundling away their share of heirlooms, knick-knacks and household articles. Everything that could be divided into five was cut up into equal parts and given one to each. Such things as could not be split up were given to those who clamoured the loudest. A rattan easy chair on which my grandfather used to lie in the court-yard, watching the sky, was claimed by my second uncle whose wife had started all the furore over the property. She also claimed a pair of rosewood benches which shone with a natural polish, and a timber wooden chair that used to be known as the bug-proof chair. My father's third brother, as compensation for letting these items go, claimed a wooden almirah as his own and a "leg" harmonium operated by a pedal. The harmonium was also claimed by another uncle whose daughter was sup-

posed to possess musical talent. It had gathered dust in a corner
for decades without anyone's noticing it. No one had even asked
how it had come to find a place in our home, although a little
family research would have yielded the information. Our grandfather had lent a hundred rupees to a local dramatic troupe and
attached their harmonium as their only movable property after a
court decree, lugged it home, and kept it in a corner of our hall.
He died before he could sell and realize its value, and his suc-
cessors took the presence of the harmonium in the corner of the
hall for granted until this moment of partition.

All the four brothers of my father with their wives and children, numbering fifteen, had lived under the same roof for
many years. It was my father's old mother who had kept them
together, acting as a cohesive element among members of the
family. Between my grandmother, who laid down the policy,
and a person called Grand-Auntie, who actually executed it,
the family administration ran smoothly. When my grandmother
died the unity of the family was also gone. The trouble started
with my father's second brother's wife, who complained loudly
one day, standing in the passage of the house, that her children
had been ill-treated and that she was hated by everyone; her
cause was upheld by her husband. Soon various other differences appeared among the brothers and their wives, although
all the children continued to play in the open courtyard, un-
mindful of the attitude of the elders to each other.

Before the year was out, on a festival day, they had their biggest
open quarrel, provoked by a minor incident in which an eight-
year-old boy knocked down another and snatched a biscuit
from his mouth. A severe family crisis developed, as the mother
of the injured child slapped the offender on his bare seat. My
father and his brothers were sitting around, eating their mid-
day meal. My father muttered mildly. "If Mother were alive she
would have handled everyone and prevented such scenes."

Two of his brothers, incensed at the incident, got up without
touching their food. My father commented, without looking at
anyone in particular, "You need not abandon your food. This
is a sacred day. Such things should not be allowed to happen."
My mother, who was bending over him, serving ghee, whis-

pered, "Why don't you mind your business? They are not ba-
bies to be taught how to conduct themselves on a festive day."

My father accepted her advice without a word and resolved
at that moment to break up the joint family in the interests of
peace. The next few days saw our family lawyers, assisted by
the adjournment expert, walking in and out with papers to be
signed, and within a few weeks the house had become empty. It
had been a crowded house since the day it was built by my father's grandfather, numerous children, womenfolk, cousins, relations and guests milling in and out all the year round, and
now it became suddenly bare and empty. The household now
consisted of my parents, Grand-Auntie, me and my two sisters.
My brother was away in Madras in a college hostel. As he grew
older my father began to spend all his time sitting on the *pyol*,
on a mat, reading *Ramayana* or just watching the street. Even
at night he never went beyond the *pyol*. He placed a small pillow under his head and stretched himself there. He hardly ever
visited the other parts of this immense house. Occasionally he
wandered off to the back yard to pluck the withered leaves off
a citrus tree, which had been his favourite plant. It had been
growing there for years, and no one knew whether it was an
orange- or lime-tree; it kept people guessing, never displaying
on its branches anything more than a few white flowers now
and then. This plant was my father's only concern. He hardly
ever looked up at the six tall coconut-trees that waved in the
sky. They were my mother's responsibility and Grand-Auntie's,
who regularly had their tops cleared of beetles and withered
shoots, sent up a climber once a month, and filled the granary
with large, ripe coconuts. There were also pumpkins growing
in the back yard, and large creepers covered the entire thatched
roof of a cow-shed, which used to house four of Malgudi's
best-bred cows, years before.

After my father's death my mother lived with me until Babu
was a year old, and then she decided to go and live with my
brother at Madras, taking away with her her life-companion
Grand-Auntie. Thus I, with my wife and little Babu, became
the sole occupant of the house in Kabir Street.

CHAPTER TWO

Sastri had to go a little earlier than usual since he had to perform a *puja* at home. I hesitated to let him go. The three colour labels (I prided myself on the excellence of my colour-printing) for K.J.'s aerated drinks had to be got ready. It was a very serious piece of work for me. My personal view was that the coloured ink I used on the label was far safer to drink than the dye that K.J. put into his water-filled bottles. We had already printed the basic colour on the labels and the second was to be imposed today. This was a crucial stage of the work and I wanted Sastri to stay and finish the job.

He said, "Perhaps I can stay up late tonight and finish it. Not now. Meanwhile will you . . ." He allotted me work until he should be back at two o'clock.

I had been engrossed in a talk with the usual company. On the agenda today was Nehru's third Five-Year Plan; my friend Sen saw nothing but ruin in it for the country. "Three hundred crores—are we counting heads or money?" His audience consisted of myself and the poet, and a client who had come to ask for quotations for a business card. The discussion was warming up, as the client was a Congressman who had gone to prison fourteen times since the day Mahatma Gandhi arrived in India from South Africa. He ignored for the time being the business that had brought him and plunged into the debate, settling himself inexorably in a corner. "What's wrong with people is they have got into the habit of blaming everything on the Government. You think democracy means that if there is no sugar in the shops, Government is responsible. What if there is no sugar? You won't die if you do not have sugar for your morning coffee some days." Sen disputed every word of the patriot's speech.

I listened to the debate until I noticed Sastri's silhouette beyond the curtain. Sastri, when there was any emergency, treated me as a handy-boy, and I had no alternative but to accept the role. Now my duty would be to fix the block on the machine and put the second impression on all the labels and spread them out to dry, then he would come and give the third impression and put the labels out to dry again.

He explained some of the finer points to me, "The blocks are rather worn. You'll have to let in more ink."

"Yes, Mr. Sastri."

He looked at me through his small silver-rimmed glasses and said firmly, "Unless the labels are second-printed and dry by three o'clock today, it's going to be impossible to deliver them tomorrow. You know what kind of a man K.J. is . . ."

What about my lunch? Sastri did not care whether I had time for food or not—he was a tyrant when it came to printing labels, but there was no way of protesting. He would brush everything aside. As if reading my mind he explained, "I'd not trouble you but for the fact that this *satyanarayana puja* must be performed today in my house; my children and wife will be waiting for me at the door . . ." As it was he would have to trot all the way to Vinayak Street if his family were not to starve too long.

Wife, children. Absurd. Such encumbrances were not necessary for Sastri, I felt. They were for lesser men like me. His place was at the type-board and the treadle. He produced an incongruous, unconvincing picture as a family man. But I dared not express myself aloud. The relation of employer and employee was reversed at my press whenever there was an emergency.

I accepted the situation without any fuss. According to custom my friends would not step beyond the curtain, so I was safe to go ahead with the second impression. Sastri had fixed everything. I had only to press the pedal and push the paper on to the pad. On a pale orange ground I had now to impose a sort of violet. I grew hypnotized by the sound of the wheel and the dozen kinks that were set in motion by the pressure I put on the pedals. Whenever I paused I could hear Sen's voice, "If Nehru is practical, let him disown the Congress . . . Why should you undertake projects which you can't afford? Anyway, in ten years what are we going to do with all the steel?" There was a sudden lull. I wondered if they had been suddenly struck dumb. I heard the shuffling of feet. I felt suddenly relieved that the third Five-Year Plan was done with.

Now an unusual thing happened. The curtain stirred, an edge of it lifted, and the monosyllabic poet's head peeped through. An extraordinary situation must have arisen to make him do that. His eyes bulged. "Someone to see you," he whispered.

"Who? What does he want?"

"I don't know."

The whispered conversation was becoming a strain. I shook my head, winked and grimaced to indicate to the poet that I was not available. The poet, ever a dense fellow, did not understand but blinked on unintelligently. His head suddenly vanished, and a moment later a new head appeared in its place—a tanned face, large powerful eyes under thick eyebrows, a large forehead and a shock of unkempt hair, like a black halo.

My first impulse was to cry out, "Whoever you may be, why don't you brush your hair?" The new visitor had evidently pulled aside the poet before showing himself to me. Before I could open my mouth, he asked, "You Nataraj?" I nodded. He came forward, practically tearing aside the curtain, an act which violated the sacred traditions of my press. I said, "Why don't you kindly take a seat in the next room? I'll be with you in a moment." He paid no attention, but stepped forward, extending his hand. I hastily wiped my fingers on a rag, muttering, "Sorry, discoloured, been working . . ." He gave me a hard grip. My entire hand disappeared into his fist—he was a huge man, about six feet tall. He looked quite slim, but his bull-neck and hammer-fist revealed his true stature. "Shan't we move to the other room?" I asked again.

"Not necessary. It's all the same to me," he said. "You are doing something? Why don't you go on? It won't bother me." He eyed my coloured labels. "What are they?"

I didn't want any eyes to watch my special colour effects, and

see how I achieved them. I moved to the curtain and parted it
courteously for him. He followed me. I showed him to the Queen
Anne chair, and sat down at my usual place, on the edge of my
desk. I had now regained the feeling of being master of the situation. I adopted my best smile and asked, "Well, what can I do
for you, Mr. . . . ?"

"Vasu," he said, and added, "I knew you didn't catch my
name. You were saying something at the same time as I mentioned my name."

I felt abashed, and covered it, I suppose, with another of those
silly smiles. Then I checked myself, suddenly feeling angry with
him for making me so uneasy. I asked myself, "Nataraj, are you
afraid of this muscular fellow?" and said authoritatively, "Yes?"
as much as to indicate, "You have wasted my time sufficiently;
now say quickly whatever you may want to say."

He took from his inner pocket a wad of paper, searched for a
hand-written sheet and held it out to me. "Five hundred sheets of
note-paper, the finest quality, and five hundred visiting cards."

I spread out the sheet without a word and read, "H. Vasu,
M.A., Taxidermist." I grew interested. My irritation left me.
This was the first time I had set eyes on a taxidermist. I said,
assuming a friendly tone, "Five hundred! Are you sure you
need five hundred visiting cards? Could you not print them one
hundred at a time? They'd be fresh then."

"Why do you try to advise me?" he asked pugnaciously. "I
know how many I need. I'm not printing my visiting cards in
order to preserve them in a glass case."

"All right. I can print ten thousand if you want."

He softened at my show of aggressiveness. "Fine, fine, that's
the right spirit."

"If you'd like to have it done on the original Heidelberg . . ."
I began.

"I don't care what you do it on. I don't even know what you
are talking about."

I understood the situation now; every other sentence was
likely to prove provocative. I began to feel intrigued by the
man. I didn't want to lose him. Even if I wanted to, I had no
means of getting rid of him. He had sought me out and I'd have

to have him until he decided to leave. I might just as well be friendly. "Surely, whatever you like. It's my duty to ask, that's all. Some people prefer it."

"What is it anyway?" he asked.

I explained the greatness of Heidelberg and where it was. He thought it over, and suddenly said, "Nataraj, I trust you to do your best for me. I have come to you as a friend." I was surprised and flattered. He explained, "I'm new to this place, but I heard about you within an hour of coming." He mentioned an obscure source of information. "Well, I never give a second thought to these things," he said. "When I like a man, I like him, that's all."

I wanted to ask about taxidermy, so I asked, looking at his card, "Taxidermist? Must be an interesting job. Where is your er . . . office or . . ."

"I hope to make a start right here. I was in Junagadh—you know the place—and there I grew interested in the art. I came across a master there, one Suleiman. When he stuffed a lion (you know, Junagadh is a place where we have lions) he could make it look more terrifying than it would be in the jungle. His stuffings go all over the world. He was a master, and he taught me the art. After all we are civilized human beings, educated and cultured, and it is up to us to prove our superiority to nature. Science conquers nature in a new way each day; why not in creation also? That's my philosophy, sir. I challenge any man to contradict me." He sighed at the thought of Suleiman, his master. "He was a saint. He taught me his art sincerely."

"Where did you get your M.A.?"

"At Madras, of course. You want to know about me?" he asked.

I wonder what he would have done if I had said, "No, I prefer to go home and eat my food." He would probably have held me down.

He said, "I was educated in the Presidency College. I took my Master's degree in History, Economics and Literature." That was in the year 1931. Then he had joined the civil disobedience movement against British rule, broken the laws, marched, demonstrated and ended up in jail. He went repeatedly to prison and once when he was released found himself in the streets of Nagpur. There he met a *phaelwan* at a show. "That man could bear a half-ton stone slab on his cheek and have it split by hammer strokes; he could snap steel chains and he could hit a block of hard granite with his fist and pulverize it. I was young then, his strength appealed to me. I was prepared to become his disciple at any cost. I introduced myself to the *phaelwan*." He remained thoughtful for a while and continued, "I learnt everything from this master. The training was unsparing. He woke me up at three o'clock every morning and put me through exercises. And he provided me with the right diet. I had to eat a hundred almonds every morning and wash them down with half a *seer* of milk; two hours later six eggs with honey; at lunch chicken and rice; at night vegetables and fruit. Not everyone can hope to have this diet, but I was lucky in finding a man who enjoyed stuffing me like that. In six months I could understudy for him. On my first day, when I banged my fist on a century-old door of a house in Lucknow, the three-inch panel of seasoned teak splintered. My master patted me on the back with tears of joy in his eyes, 'You are growing on the right lines, my boy.' In a few months I could also snap chains, twist iron bars, and pulverize granite. We travelled all over the country, and gave our shows at every market fair in the villages and in the town halls in the cities, and he made a lot of money. Gradually he grew flabby and lazy, and let me do everything. They announced his name on the notices, but actually I did all the twisting and smashing of stone, iron, and what not. When I spoke to him about it he called me an ungrateful dog and other names, and tried to push me out. I resisted . . . and . . ." Vasu laughed at the recollection of this incident. "I knew his weak spot. I hit him there with the edge of my palm with a chopping movement . . . and he fell down and squirmed on the floor. I knew he could perform no more. I left him there and walked out, and gave up the strong man's life once and for all."

"You didn't stop to help him?" I asked.

"I helped him by leaving him there, instead of holding him upside down and rattling the teeth out of his head."

"Oh, no," I cried, horrified.

THE MAN-EATER OF MALGUDI

"Why not? I was a different man now, not the boy who went to him for charity. I was stronger than he."

"After all he taught you to be strong—he was your guru," I said, enjoying the thrill of provoking him.

"Damn it all!" he cried. "He made money out of me, don't you see?"

"But he also gave you six eggs a day and—how much milk and almonds was it?"

He threw up his arms in vexation. "Oh, you will never understand these things, Nataraj. You know nothing, you have not seen the world. You know only what happens in this miserable little place."

"If you think this place miserable, why do you choose to come here?" I was nearest the inner door. I could dash away if he attempted to grab me. Familiarity was making me rash and headstrong. I enjoyed taunting him.

"You think I have come here out of admiration for this miserable city? Know this, I'm here because of Mempi Forest and the jungles in those hills. I'm a taxidermist. I have to be where wild animals live."

"And die," I added.

He appreciated my joke and laughed. "You are a wise guy," he said admiringly.

"You haven't told me yet why or how you became a taxidermist," I reminded him.

"H'm!" he said. "Don't get too curious. Let us do business first. When are you giving me the visiting cards? Tomorrow?" He might pulverize granite, smash his guru with a slicing stroke, but where printing work was concerned I was not going to be pushed. I got up and turned the sheets of a tear-off calendar on the wall. "You can come tomorrow and ask me. I can discuss this matter only tomorrow. My staff are out today."

At this moment my little son Babu came running in crying "Appa!" and halted his steps abruptly on seeing a stranger. He bit his nails, grinned, and tried to turn and run. I shot out my hand and held him. "What is it?" I asked. He was friendly with the usual crowd at my press, but the stranger's presence somehow embarrassed him. I could guess why he had come; it was either to ask for a favour—permission to go out with his friends, or cash for peppermints—or to bring a message from his mother.

"Mother says, aren't you coming home for food? She is hungry."

"So am I," I said, "and if I were Mother I wouldn't wait for Father. Understand me? Here is a gentleman with whom I am engaged on some important business. Do you know what he can do?" My tone interested Babu and he looked up expectantly.

Vasu made a weary gesture, frowned and said, "Oh, stop that, Mr. Nataraj. Don't start it all again. I don't want to be introduced to anyone. Now, go away, boy," he said authoritatively.

"He is my son . . ." I began.

"I see that," Vasu said indifferently, and Babu wriggled himself free and ran off.

Vasu did not come next day, but appeared again fifteen days later. He arrived in a jeep. "You have been away a long time," I said.

"You thought you were rid of me?" he asked, and, thumping his chest, "I never forget."

"And I never remember," I said. Somehow this man's presence roused in me a sort of pugnacity.

He stepped in, saw the Queen Anne chair occupied by the poet, and remarked, half-jokingly, "That's my chair, I suppose." The poet scrambled to his feet and moved to another seat. "H'm, that's better," Vasu said, sitting down. He smiled patronizingly at the poet and said, "I haven't been told who you are."

"I'm I'm . . . a teacher in the school."

"What do you teach?" he asked relentlessly.

"Well, history, geography, science, English—anything the boys must know."

"H'm, an all-rounder," Vasu said. I could see the poet squirming. He was a mild, inoffensive man who was unused to such rough contacts. But Vasu seemed to enjoy bothering him. I rushed in to his rescue. I wanted to add to his stature by saying, "He is a poet. He is nominally a teacher, but actually . . ."

"I never read poetry; no time," said Vasu promptly, and dismissed the man from his thoughts. He turned to me and asked, "Where are my cards?"

I had a seasoned answer for such a question. "Where have you been this whole fortnight?"

"Away, busy."

"So was I," I said.

"You promised to give me the cards . . ."

"When?" I asked.

"Next day," he said. I told him that there had been no such promise. He raised his voice, and I raised mine. He asked finally, "Are we here on business or to fight? If it's a fight, tell me. I like a fight. Can't you see, man, why I am asking for my cards?"

"Don't *you* see that we have our own business practice?" I always adopted "we" whenever I had to speak for the press.

"What do you mean?" he asked aggressively.

"We never choose the type and stationery for a customer. It must always be the customer's responsibility."

"You never told me that," he cried.

"You remember I asked you to come next day. That was my purpose. I never say anything without a purpose."

"Why couldn't you have mentioned it the same day?"

"You have a right to ask," I said, feeling it was time to concede him something. The poet looked scared by these exchanges. He was trying to get out, but I motioned him to stay. Why should the poor man be frightened away?

"You have not answered my question," said Vasu. "Why couldn't you have shown me samples of type on the first day?"

I said curtly, "Because my staff were out."

"Oh!" he said, opening his eyes, wide. "I didn't know you had a staff."

I ignored his remark and shouted, "Sastri! Please bring those ivory card samples and also the ten-point copper-plate." I told Vasu grandly, "Now you can indicate your preferences, and we shall try to give you the utmost satisfaction."

Sastri, with his silver-rimmed glasses on his nose, entered, bearing a couple of blank cards and a specimen type-book. He paused for a second, studying the visitor, placed them on the table, turned and disappeared through the curtain.

"How many are employed in your press?" Vasu asked.

The man's curiosity was limitless and recognized no proprieties. I felt enraged. Was he a labour commissioner or something of the kind? I replied, "As many as I need. But, as you know, present-day labour conditions are not encouraging. However, Mr. Sastri is very dependable; he has been with me for years . . ." I handed him the cards and said, "You will have to choose. These are the best cards available." I handed him the type-book. "Tell me what type you like."

That paralysed him. He turned the cards between his fingers, he turned the leaves of the type-book, and cried, "I'm damned if I know what I want. They all look alike to me. What is the difference anyway?"

This was a triumph for me. "Vasu, printing is an intricate business. That's why we won't take responsibility in these matters."

"Oh, please do something and print me my cards," he cried, exasperated.

"All right," I said, "I'll do it for you, if you trust me."

"I trust you as a friend, otherwise I would not have come to you."

"Actually," I said, "I welcome friends rather than customers. I'm not a fellow who cares for money. If anyone comes to me for pure business, I send them over to my neighbour and they are welcome to get their work done cheaper and on a better machine—original Heidelberg."

"Oh, stop that original Heidel," he cried impatiently. "I want to hear no more of it. Give me my cards. My business arrangements are waiting on that, and remember also five hundred letter-heads."

CHAPTER THREE

An attic above my press was full of discarded papers, stacks of old newspapers, files of dead correspondence and accounts, and, bulkiest of all, a thousand copies of a school magazine which I used to print and display as my masterpiece and which I froze in the attic when the school could not pay the printing charges.

I called up a waste-paper buyer, who was crying for custom in the streets, and sent him up the rickety staircase to make a survey and tell me his offer. He was an old Moslem who carried a sack on his back and cried, "Old paper, empty bottles," tramping the streets all afternoon. "Be careful," I told him as I sent him up the stairs to estimate. "There may be snakes and scorpions up there. No human being has set foot in the attic for years." Later, when I heard his steps come down, I prepared myself for the haggling to follow by stiffening my countenance and assuming a grave voice. He parted the curtain, entered my parlour and stood respectfully pressing his back close to the wall and awaiting my question.

"Well, have you examined the lot?"

"Yes, sir. Most of the paper is too old and is completely brown."

"Surely you didn't expect me to buy the latest editions for your benefit, or did you think I would buy white paper by the ream and sell it to you by weight?" I spoke with heavy cynicism, and he was softened enough to say, "I didn't say so . . ." Then he made his offer. I ignored it completely as not being worth a man's notice.

At this point, if he had really found my attitude unacceptable, he should have gone away, but he stayed, and that was a good sign. I was looking through the proofs of a cinema programme and I suddenly left him in order to attend to some item of work inside the press. I came out nearly an hour later, and he was still there. He had set his gunny sack down and was sitting on the door-step. "Still here!" I cried, feigning astonishment. "By all means rest here if you like, but don't expect me to waste any more time talking to you. I don't have to sell that paper at all. I can keep it as I have kept it for years."

He fidgeted uneasily and said, "The paper is brown and cracks. Please have consideration for me, sir. I have to make one or two rupees every day in order to bring up my family of . . ." He went into the details of his domestic budget: how he had to find the money for his children's school-books, food, and medicine, by collecting junk from every house and selling it to the dealers for a small margin of profit, often borrowing a loan at the start of a day. After hearing him out, I relented enough to mention a figure, at which he picked up his sack and pretended to go. Then I mitigated my demand, he raised his offer, and this market fluctuation went on till three o'clock. Sastri came at three with a frown on his face, understood in a moment what was going on and muttered, "Sometimes it's better to throw old paper into a boiler to save firewood than sell it to these fellows. They always try to cheat," thus lending support to my own view.

Presently Vasu arrived in his jeep, and unpacked his valise, mumbling, "Let me note something before I forget it." He sat in the Queen Anne chair, took out a sheet of paper and wrote. Both of us, the parties to the waste-paper transaction, watched him silently. A lorry was passing down the road, raising a blanket of cloud; a couple of *jutkas* were rattling along on their wooden wheels; two vagrants had stretched themselves on the parapet of the fountain, enjoying a siesta; a little boy was watching his lamb graze on the lawn which the municipality was struggling to cultivate by the margin of the fountain; a crow sat on top of the fountain, hopefully looking for a drop of water. It was an ideal hour for a transaction in junk.

Vasu stopped writing and asked, "What's going on?"

I turned to the waste-paper man and said, "You know who he is? I'll have him to explain to if I give the paper away too cheap."

Vasu raised his eyes from the paper, glared at the Moslem and asked, "What are you supposed to be doing? Have a care!" The trader grew nervous and said, "My final offer, sir. It's getting late; if I get nothing here I must at least find another place for my business today."

"All right, go," I said. "I'm not stopping you."

"Twenty-five rupees, sir."

"If this gentleman approves," I said. Vasu seemed pleased at being involved. He tapped the table and hummed and hawed. The ragman appealed to him, "I'm a poor man. Don't squeeze me. If I invest it . . ."

Vasu suddenly got up, saying, "Let's have a look at your loot anyway," and, led by the Moslem, passed beyond the curtain and clambered upstairs. I was surprised to see Vasu enter the spirit of the game so completely.

Presently the Moslem came down with a pile of paper and took it to the front step. He came up to me, holding twenty-five rupees in currency, his face beaming, "The master has agreed." He made three more trips upstairs and barricaded my entrance with waste paper. He beckoned to a *jutka* passing down the street and loaded all the bundles into it. I asked, "Where is that man?"

"He is up there."

"What's he doing there?"

"I don't know," said the old man. "He was trying to open the windows."

Presently Vasu called me from the attic, "Nataraj, come up."

"Why?" I cried. I was busy with the cinema programme. He repeated his command, and I went up. I had not gone upstairs for years. The wooden stairs creaked and groaned, unused to the passage of feet. There was a small landing and a green door, and you stepped in. Vasu was standing in the middle of the room like a giant. He had opened a little wooden window with a view of the fountain, over the market road; beyond it was a small door which led to a very narrow terrace that looked southwards on to the neighbouring roof-tiles. The floor was littered with pieces of waste paper; age-old dust covered everything.

Vasu was fanning around his ears with a cover of the school magazine. "That fellow has done you a service in carrying away all that waste paper, but he has dehoused a thousand mosquitoes—one thing I can't stand." He vigorously fanned them off as they tried to buzz about his ears. "Night or day, I run when a mosquito is mentioned."

"Let us go down," I said, flourishing my arms to keep them away from my head.

"Wait a minute," he said. "What do you propose to do with this place?"

I ruminated for a moment; I had no plans for it, but before I could say so he said, "I'll clean it up and stay here for a while. I want some place where I can throw my things and stay. The important thing will be to get a mosquito-net for sleeping in, a bed and one or two chairs. The roof comes down too low," he added. He swung his arms up and down and said, "Still a couple of feet above my arms, not too bad."

I gave him no reply. I had never thought of the attic as habitable.

He asked, "Why are you silent?"

"Nothing, nothing," I said. "I shall have to . . ."

"What?" he asked mercilessly. "Don't tell me you want to consult your seniors or partners, the usual dodge. I will stay here till a bungalow is vacated for me in the New Extension. I wouldn't dream of settling here. So don't be afraid. After all you would only put junk into it again."

I said nothing and went down to my office. He followed me, drove away in his jeep and returned an hour later with four workmen carrying brooms and buckets. He led them past the curtain, up the stairs. I heard him shouting and bullying them and the mops and brooms at work. He discovered the water-closet below the staircase and made them carry up buckets of water and scrub the floor. Next day he brought in a builder's man and spent the whole day washing the walls of the attic with lime. He passed in and out, and hardly found time for a word with me. I watched him come and go. Two days later he brought a bedstead and a few pieces of furniture. Since I found it a nuisance to have Vasu and his minions pass up and down by the press I opened a side gate in the compound, which admitted his jeep into a little yard from Kabir Lane and gave him direct access to the wooden stairs. It took me another week to realize that without a word from me Vasu had established himself in the attic. "After all," I thought to myself, "it's a junk-room, likely to get filled again with rubbish. Why not let him stay there until he finds a house?"

He disappeared for long periods and would then suddenly drop in. I had no idea where he went. Sometimes he just came and lounged in my parlour. My other visitors always tried to run away at the sight of him, for they found it difficult to cope with his bullying talk. The poet left if he saw him coming. Sen, the journalist, who was always loudly analysing Nehru's policies, could not stand him even for a minute. He had been unwittingly caught the very first day, while he was expatiating on the Five-Year Plan. Vasu, who had come in to collect some stationery, listened for a moment to the journalist's talk and, turning to me, asked, "Who's he? You have not told me his name."

"A good friend," I said.

Vasu shook his head patronizingly and said, "If he is so much wiser than Nehru, why doesn't he try to become the Prime Minister of India?"

The journalist drew himself up haughtily and cried, "Who is this man? Why does he interfere with me when I am talking to someone? Is there no freedom of speech?"

Vasu said, "If you feel superior to Nehru, why don't you go to Delhi and take charge of the cabinet?" and laughed contemptuously. Words followed, Sen got up in anger, Vasu advanced threateningly. I came between them with a show of courage, dreading lest one of them should hit me. I cried, "All are friends here. I won't allow a fight. Not here, not here."

"Then where?" asked Vasu.

"Nowhere," I replied.

"I don't want to be insulted, that's all," the bully said.

"I am not going to be frightened by anyone's muscle or size. Do you threaten to hit me?" Sen cried. He pushed me out of the way and stepped up to Vasu. I was in a panic.

"No, sir," said Vasu, recoiling. "Not unless I'm hit first." He raised his fist and flourished it. "I could settle many problems with this, but I don't. If I hit you with it, it will be the end of you. But that doesn't mean I may not kick."

Vasu sat in my parlour and expounded his philosophy of human conduct. "Nataraj!" he would say. "Life is too short to have a word with everyone in this land of three hundred odd millions. One has to ignore most people." I knew it was just a fancy speech, because his nature would not let him leave anyone in peace. He'd wilt if he could not find some poor man to bully. If he found someone known to him, he taunted him. If he met a stranger or a new face, he bluntly demanded, "Who is he? You have not told me his name!" No maharaja finding a ragged commoner wandering in the halls of his durbar would have adopted a more authoritative tone in asking, "Who is this?"

Vasu's habit of using my front room as an extension of his attic was proving irksome, as I had my own visitors, not to speak of the permanent pair—the poet and the journalist. For a few days Sen and the poet left the moment they heard the jeep arrive, but gradually their views underwent a change. When Vasu came in, Sen would stick to his seat with an air of defiance as if saying, "I'm not going to let that beefy fellow . . ." The poet would transfer himself without fuss from the high-backed Queen Anne chair to a poorer seat. He had developed the art of surviving Vasu's presence; he maintained a profound silence, but if he were forced to speak he would confine himself to monosyllables (at which in any case he was an adept), and I was glad to note that Vasu had too much on his mind to have the time for more than a couple of nasty, personal remarks, which the poet pretended not to hear. Sen suppressed the expression of his political opinions in Vasu's presence (which was a good thing again), but it did not save him, as Vasu, the moment he remembered his presence, said, "What are the views of our wise friend on this?" To which Sen gave a fitting reply, such as "If people are dense enough not to know what is happening, I'm not prepared to . . . ," which would act as a starting point for a battle of words. But the battle never came, as on the first day, to near-blows—it always fizzled out.

I left everyone alone. If they wrangled and lost their heads and voices, it was their business and not mine. Even if heads had been broken, I don't think I'd have interfered. I had resigned myself to anything. If I had cared for a peaceful existence, I should have rejected Vasu on the first day. Now it was like having a middle-aged man-eater in your office and home, with the same uncertainties, possibilities, and potentialities.

This man-eater softened, snivelled and purred, and tried to be agreeable only in the presence of an official. He brought in a khaki-clad, cadaverous man one day, a forestry officer, seated him and introduced me, "This is my best friend on earth, Mr. Nataraj; he and I are more like brothers than printer and customer or landlord and tenant."

"Actually, I am not a landlord and don't want to be one," I said, remembering how much more at peace I used to be when my attic was tenanted by junk. Woe to the day I had conceived the idea of cleaning it up.

Vasu said, "Even among brothers, business should be business."

"True, true," said the forester.

Now Vasu turned to the art of flattery. I would never have guessed his potentialities in this direction. He said, "I have brought Mr. . . . because I want you to know him. He is a very busy man, but came with me today."

"Do you live in the forest?"

Before the forester could speak, Vasu answered, "He *is* Mempi Forest. He is everything there. He knows and has numbered every beast, and he has no fear. If he were a coward he would never have joined this department."

The forester felt it was time for him to put in a word about himself, "I have put in thirty years in the department. They gave me a third extension of my service only two weeks ago."

"See how he looks? Can you guess his age?" (I wanted to say that I could do so unerringly.) "He is like a teak-tree—thousands of those trees in Mempi Range are in his charge, isn't it so, sir?"

"Yes, yes, that's a big responsibility," he said.

"And you know, he looks wiry, but he must be like a teak log in strength. I am a strong man, as you know, but I'd hesitate to challenge him. Ha! Ha! Ha!" Vasu stopped laughing and said, "Seriously, he is one of the best forestry officers in India. How many times has he been attacked by a rogue elephant?"

"Eighteen times," said the man statistically.

"And you just gave it a four-nought-five charge at point-blank range?"

"Yes, what else could one do?" asked the hero.

"How many tigers has he tracked on foot?"

"An average of at least one every half-year," he said.

"And in thirty years you may guess how much he must have done and seen," Vasu said. He asked the hero, "What did you do with all those skins?"

"Oh, presented them here and there," said the man. "I don't fancy keeping trophies."

"Ah, you shouldn't say that. You must let me stuff at least one animal for you, and you will know the difference," said Vasu. "Nataraj," he added suddenly, "the main reason why I have brought him to you is he wants a small book printed." My heart sank. It was terrible enough to have Vasu for a customer, and now to have to work for someone he was championing! The three-colour labels were still undelivered. "Nataraj, you will have to clear your desk and do this."

I held out my hand mechanically. The forester took out of his bag a roll of manuscript, saying, "I have made a habit of collecting Golden Thoughts, and I have arranged them alphabetically. I wish to bring them out in book form and distribute them to schoolchildren, free of cost. That is how I want to serve our country."

I turned over the manuscript. Virtues were listed alphabetically. "My Tamil types are not good," I said. "My neighbour has the best Tamil types available and his original Heidelberg . . ."

"Oh," Vasu groaned, "that original again!"

I looked at him compassionately. "As a man of education, Vasu," I began, "you should not shut your mind to new ideas."

"But why on earth should I know anything about the original what's-its-name?" he cried with mild irritation; it was evident that he was struggling to be on his best behaviour before the man in khaki.

"It's because," I replied with the patience of a saint explaining moral duty to an erring soul, "it's the machine on which fast printing has to be done. For instance work like our friend's here—Golden Thoughts—the right place for it would be the original Heidelberg—a lovely machine. What do you say, sir?" I said, turning to the man. I had spent a lifetime with would-be authors and knew their vanities from A to Z.

The forester said, "Yes, I want the best service possible—the book must look nice. I want to send a specially bound copy to our Chief Conservator at Delhi through our chief at Madras."

"So you want two special copies?" I asked.

"Yes, yes," he agreed readily.

I looked through the pages of the manuscript. He had culled epigrammatic sentiments and moralizings from every source—*Bhagavad-Gita, Upanishads,* Shakespeare, Mahatma Gandhi, the Bible, Emerson, Lord Avebury and Confucius—and had translated them into Tamil. It was meant to elevate young minds no doubt, but I'd have resented being told every hour of the day what I should do, say, or think. It would be boring to be steadfastly good night and day. All the same the book contained most of the sentiments Vasu had missed in life and it would do him no harm to pick up a few for his own use. I told him, "I'm sure you will enjoy going over the manuscript, in case our friend does not find the time to give it a final look-over."

"Oh, yes, yes, of course," Vasu said faintly.

I was confident now that I could dodge, at least for the time being, the responsibility of printing the golden book, but I couldn't judge for how long. If I took it on, with Vasu living overhead, he would storm the press night and day when the man in khaki was out of sight. There was going to be no money in it; I was positive about that. The whole transaction, it was patent, was going to be a sort of exchange between the two:

Vasu wanted to win the other's favour through my help. I had already printed stationery for Vasu, and he had shown no signs of paying for the work.

I told the man, handing back the manuscript, "Please go through it again and make all the final revisions and additions. Then if you are satisfied with the final form, we'll do something with it. I do not want you to incur any unnecessary expense later—corrections are rather expensive, you know. All the time you can give for revision in manuscript will be worthwhile." Once again my experience of would-be authors saved me: authors liked to think that they took infinite pains to attain infinite perfection.

I could see Vasu's bewilderment: he could not make out whether it was a good thing or a bad thing that had happened: the manuscript had changed hands too swiftly. He looked at my face and then at the other's. I was a seasoned printer. I knew the importance of shuffling off a manuscript without loss of time. Once the manuscript got lodged with you, you lost your freedom, and authority passed to the writer. Vasu began to argue, "How can you get him to come again? Do you know the distance he has to come—from Peak House, where he is camping." Very encouraging! Sixty miles away. It would not be often that he would find the time, or the conveyance, to come downhill.

"He won't have to come here! You can fetch the manuscript," I said, and Vasu agreed with alacrity. "Yes, yes, that's a good idea. I'll always be round you, you know," he said with servility.

A week later, a brown envelope from the Forest Department arrived for Vasu. His face lit up at the sight of it. "Must be my game licence. It was embarrassing to go into the jungle without it. Now you will see what I shall do . . . The swine!" he cried when he had read the contents. "They think I want to go sightseeing in the forests and permit me to shoot duck and deer—as if I cared!" He remained in thought for a while. "Now they shall know what I can do." He carelessly thrust the paper into his pocket.

CHAPTER FOUR

A month later Vasu stopped his jeep in front of my office and sounded the horn; he sat at the wheel, with the engine running. I looked up from a proof of a wedding invitation I was correcting. The adjournment lawyer was sitting in front of me—his daughter was to be married in two weeks and he was printing a thousand invitation cards. This was one piece of work I was obliged to deliver in time, and I didn't want to be interrupted. I shouted back to Vasu, "Anything urgent?"

"Yeah," he said. He seemed to have picked up his American style from crime books and films.

"I am busy," I said.

"Come on," he said aggressively. I placed a weight on the proof and went out. "Jump in," he said when I approached him.

"I really can't," I said. "That man is waiting for me."

"Him! Don't be silly. Jump in."

"Where are you going?"

"I'll bring you back in ten minutes," he said. "Can't you spare ten minutes for my sake?"

I said, "No, I can't spare ten minutes."

"All right, five minutes then." I climbed into the jeep and he drove off. We crossed Nallappa's Grove and drove for ten miles on the trunk road; he drove recklessly. I asked him where he was going.

"I thought you might enjoy a visit to Mempi."

"What . . . what's the meaning of this?" I asked angrily.

"So you don't like being with me! All right. Shall I stop? You may get down and go back."

I knew it would be futile to exhibit temper. It'd only amuse him. I concealed my chagrin and said, "I certainly should enjoy walking back ten miles, but I wish I had had the time to pick up my shirt buttons before leaving." I had mislaid my buttons at home. My shirt was open at the chest.

He cast a look at me. "No one will mind in the jungle," he said and rocked with laughter. Now that I was at his mercy, I thought I might as well abandon myself to the situation. I only wished I had not left the adjournment lawyer sitting in my chair. How long was he going to be there and what was to happen to the marriage of his daughter without invitation cards? I said, assuming the most casual tone possible, "It was a matter of an urgent marriage invitation."

"How urgent is the marriage?" he asked.

"It's coming off in fifteen days, and they must have time to post the invitation cards. A printer has his responsibilities."

"If the man is willing and the woman is willing—there is a marriage. What has a printer to do with it? It's none of a printer's business. Why should you worry?"

I gave up all attempts to explain; he was not prepared to pay any attention to my words. He was the lord of the universe, he had no use for other people's words. "Why should you worry?" he asked again and again. It was so unreasonable and unseasonable that I didn't think fit to find an answer. I noticed that the speedometer needle was showing a steady sixty. "Mind the road," I said, as I saw villagers walking in a file, stepping aside as the jeep grazed them. Lorries and buses swerved away, the drivers muttering imprecations. Vasu enjoyed their discomfiture and laughed uproariously. Then he became suddenly serious and said, "More people will have to die on the roads, if our nation is to develop any road sense at all!" A peasant woman was sitting on the roadside with a girl whose hair she was searching for lice. He saw them and set his course to run into them, swerving away at the last moment after seeing them tumble over each other in fright.

"Oh, poor creatures," I said. "I hope they aren't hurt."

"Oh, no, they won't be hurt. These women are hardy and enjoy a bit of fun. Didn't you see how they were laughing?"

I felt it best to leave his words without comment. Even that seemed to annoy him. After we had gone a couple of miles, he said, "Why are you silent? What are you thinking about? Still worrying about that invitation?"

"Yes," I said to be on the safe side.

"Only fools marry, and they deserve all the trouble they get. I really do not know why people marry at all. If you like a woman, have her by all means. You don't have to own a coffee estate because you like a cup of coffee now and then," and he smiled, more and more pleased with his own wit.

I had never known him so wild. He had seemed to practise few restraints when he visited me at my press, but now, in his jeep on the highway, his behaviour was breath-taking. I wondered for a moment whether he might be drunk. I asked testily, "What do you think of prohibition, which they are talking about nowadays?"

"Why?" he asked. As I was wondering what to say, he said, "Drink is like marriage. If people like it, it's their business and nobody else's. I tried to drink whisky once, but gave it up. It tastes bad." He sat brooding at the wheel for a moment and said, "I wonder why anyone should want to drink."

My last hope that the man might be drunk was gone. A man who could conduct himself in this way dead sober! I shuddered at the thought. When we arrived at Mempi village I was glad to jump out. Riding in the jeep with one leg dangling out had made me sore in all my joints and my head reeled slightly with the speed of his driving.

Mempi village, at the foot of the hills, consisted of a single winding street, which half a mile away disappeared into the ranges of Mempi. A few cottages built of bamboo and coconut thatch lined the wayside; a tea-shop with bananas dangling in bunches from the ceiling was a rallying point for all buses and lorries plying on this road; a touring cinema stood in the open ground flanking the road, plastered over with the picture of a wide-eyed heroine watching the landscape. The jungle studded the sides of the hill. A small shrine stood at the confluence of the mountain road with the highway, and the goddess presiding was offered coconut and camphor flames by every driver on the mountain road.

Vasu pulled up his jeep and asked the man at the tea-shop, "What's the news?"

The man said, "Good news. There was a prowler last night, so they say. We saw pug-marks on the sand and sheep were bleating as if they had gone mad. Not where I live, but I heard Ranga talk of it today."

"Did he see anything?" asked Vasu; and added eagerly, "What did he see?"

The tea-shop had a customer waiting, and the owner mechanically handed him a bun and drew strong, red tea from a sizzling urn and poured it into a glass tumbler. I had been starving. I cast longing looks at the brown buns arranged on a shelf, although normally I would not have dared to eat anything out of a shop like this, where flies swarmed over the sugar and nothing was ever washed or covered; road dust flew up whenever a car passed and settled down on the bread, the buns, the fruit, sugar, and milk. The shop had a constant crowd of visitors. Buses and lorries halting on their way up to the coffee estates, bullock carts in caravans, pedestrians—everyone stopped here for refreshment.

When I put my fingers in my pocket, I did not find a single coin, but only the stub of a pencil with which I'd been correcting the proof of the wedding invitation. I called pathetically like a child at a fair tugging at the sleeve of his elder, "Vasu!" He was busy discussing the pug-marks and the circle round him was growing: a coconut-seller, the village idiot, the village wag, a tailor, and a man carrying a bundle of tobacco on his head. Each was adding his own to the symposium on the tiger's visit.

Vasu did not hear me call him. I had to cry out, "Vasu, lend me some cash; I want to try the tea here."

He paused. "Tea! Why?"

I felt silly with my shirt open at the chest and the dhoti around my waist. "I'm hungry. I had no time for breakfast this morning."

He looked at me for a minute and resumed his discussion about the pug-marks. I felt slighted. Hunger had given an edge to my temper. I felt indignant that I should have been dragged out so unceremoniously and treated in this way. I called out, "Have you or have you not any loose coin on you? I'll return it to you as soon as I am back home."

"So you think we are going back home, eh?" he said irresponsibly. I was struck with a sudden fear that this man was perhaps abducting me and was going to demand a ransom for releasing me from some tiger cave. What would my wife and little son do if they were suddenly asked to produce fifty thousand rupees for my release? She might have to sell the house and all her jewellery. I had not yet paid the final instalment on that gold necklace of hers that she fancied only because someone she knew had a similar one. Good girl, this had been her most stubborn demand in all the years of our wedded life and how could I deny her? Luckily I had printed the Cooperative Bank Annual Report and with those earnings paid off half the price of the necklace. But, but, that necklace cost in all only seven hundred rupees—how would she make up fifty thousand? We might have to sell off the treadle; it was rickety and might fetch just thirteen thousand, and then what should I do after my release, without my printing machinery? What was to happen to Sastri? He'd be unemployed, or would he go over to operate the Heidelberg? If my wife appealed to him would he have the sense to go to the police and lead them to the tiger cave guarded by this frightful man with the dark halo over his head? Suppose he mounted guard over me and the tiger returned to the cave and found him, would the beast have the guts to devour him first and leave me alone, retching at the sight of any further food?

All this flashed through my mind. It made me swallow my temper and smile ingratiatingly at Vasu, which had a better effect than any challenge. He relented enough to say, "You see, when I'm out on business I rarely think of food." ("Because you'll not hesitate to make a meal of any fool who has the ill-luck to go with you," I remarked mentally.) Suddenly he left me, got into his jeep and said, "Come on," to someone in the group, and was off. I felt relieved at his exit, but cried like a lost child, "When . . . ? When . . . ?" He waved to me saying, "Stay here, I'll be back," and his jeep raced up the mountain road and disappeared round a bend. I could hear the whining of its gears for a while.

I looked down at my chest, still unbuttoned. I felt ridiculous, standing there. This was no doubt a very beautiful place—the hills and the curving village road, and the highway vanishing into the hills. The hills looked blue, no doubt, and the ranges beyond were shimmering, but that could hardly serve as an excuse for the liberties Vasu had taken with me. I sat down on a wooden plank stretched over two empty tins, which served for a bench, and addressed myself to the tea-shop man, "Is there a bus for Malgudi from here?"

"Yes, at two o'clock coming from Top Slip."

It would be a good idea to catch it and get back to town, but how was I to pay for the ticket? I didn't have even a button to my shirt. I cursed myself for entertaining and encouraging Vasu, but I also felt relief that he had gone away without a word about the ransom. I explained my situation to the tea-shop man. He was very happy when he heard that I was a printer. "Ah, I'm so happy, sir, to know you. Can you print some notices for me, sir?"

"With pleasure," I said, and added, "I'm here to serve the public. I can print anything you want. If you prefer to have your work done on a German machine, I can arrange that too. My neighbour has an original Heidelberg, and we are like brothers." I became loquacious at the unexpected opening offered for a friendly approach.

The man explained, "I have no time to leave this place and attend to any other business in the town, and so I have long been worrying how to get some printing work done."

"Oh, you don't have to worry as long as I'm here. Your printing will be delivered to you at your door, that's how I serve my customers. I print for a wide clientele and deliver the goods by bus or train, whichever goes earlier."

"Ah, that's precisely how I would like to be served," he said. Then he launched on his autobiography. He was a self-made man. Leaving his home in Tirunelveli when he was twelve years of age, he had come to Mempi in search of work. He knew no one, and he drifted on to the tea plantations in the hills and worked as an estate-labourer, picking tea-leaves, loading trucks, and in general acting as a handy-man. In the August of 1947, when India became independent, the estate, which had been owned by an English company, changed hands, and he came downhill to look for a new job. He established a small shop, selling betel nuts, peppermints and tobacco, and expanded it into a tea-shop. Business prospered when a new dam construction was started somewhere in a valley ten miles out; engineers, ministers, journalists, builders, and labourers moved up and down in jeeps, lorries and station-wagons, and the place buzzed with activity night and day. His tea-shop grew to its present stature. He built a house, and then another house, very near the shop in a back street. ("I can go home in five minutes for a nap or a snatch of food," he boasted.) He began to take an interest in the shrine at the confluence of the mountain and the plains. "Hundreds of vehicles go up to those summits and to this day we have never heard of an accident—although some of those roads are narrow and twisting, and if you are careless you'll dive over the ridge. But there has not been a single accident. You know why?" He pointed at the little turret of the shrine showing above the roadside trees. "Because the Goddess protects us. I rebuilt the temple with my own funds. I have regular *pujas* performed there. You know we also have a temple elephant; it came years ago of its own accord from the hills, straying along with a herd of cattle returned from the hills after grazing. It was then about six months old, and was no bigger than a young buffalo. We adopted it for the temple. His name is Kumar and children and elders alike adore him and feed him with coconut and sugar cane and rice all day."

After all this rambling talk he came to the point. He was about to celebrate the consecration of the temple on a grand scale, carrying the Goddess in a procession with pipes and music, led by the elephant. He wanted me to print a thousand notices so that a big crowd might turn up on the day.

I readily agreed to do it for him, and asked, "When do you want it?"

He was flabbergasted. "I don't know. We shall have to discuss it at a meeting of the temple committee."

I was relieved to note that it was only a vague proposal so far and said, "Write to me as soon as your plans are ready, and I will do my best for you. I will print anything you want. By the way, why don't you let me taste your tea and a couple of those buns? Who is your baker in the town? He has given them a wonderful tint!" He concocted a special brew of tea for me and handed me a couple of brown buns on a piece of old newspaper. I felt refreshed and could view my circumstances with less despair now. At the back of my mind was a worry as to whether the adjournment lawyer might still be sitting waiting for my return. Return home? Ah, there was no such prospect. I would have been wiser if I had written my will before venturing out with Vasu. "I'll pay your bill next time I visit you," I said, "maybe with the printed notices. You see, I had to come away suddenly and didn't know I'd come so far." And then I made another request, "Do you know these bus people? What sort are they?"

"Every bus must stop here for tea," he said boastfully.

"I knew it'd be so. Can you do me a favour? Could you ask one of the conductors to take me back to town and collect the fare at the other end? The bus has to pass in front of my press, and I could just dash in . . ."

"Why do you want to go away? Aren't you going to wait for Vasu?"

I felt desperate. Was this man in league with Vasu? Probably they had plans to carry me to the cave at night—all kidnappers operated at night. They were saving me up for their nocturnal activities. I said desperately, "I must get back to the press today; the lawyer will be waiting for me. A wedding invitation. You know how important it is."

"But Vasu may ask why I didn't keep you here. I know him, and he is sometimes strict, as you may know."

"Oh," I said casually, "he is a good fellow, though his speech is blunt sometimes. We are very close, and he knows all about this marriage invitation. He'll understand and . . . he is a good friend of mine. The trouble is I came away without picking up my buttons or cash." I laughed, trying to import into the whole situation a touch of humour. "I wonder when Vasu will be back!"

"Oh, that nobody can say. When he hears about a tiger, he forgets everything else. Now he'll be right in the jungle following the pug-marks, and . . ."

"A fearless man," I cried in order to please the tea-seller. "What is your name?" I asked.

"Muthu," he said. "I have four children, and a daughter to marry . . ."

"Then you will understand better than anyone else how anxious that lawyer will be."

"Which lawyer?" he asked.

"Our adjournment lawyer, whom I left sitting in my office."

"I'm sure you will help me to find a good bridegroom for my daughter." He lowered his voice to say, "My wife is scheming to marry her off to her own brother's son, but I have other ideas. I want the girl to marry a boy who is educated."

"She must marry someone who is at least a B.A.," I said.

He was so pleased with this that he gave me a third bun and another glass of tea. "This is my treat. You don't have to pay for this cup," he said.

Presently his customers began to arrive—mostly coolies carrying pick-axes, crow-bars and spades on their way to that mysterious project beyond the hills. Caravans of bullock carts carrying firewood and timber stopped by. Loudspeaker music blared forth from the tent-cinema, where they were testing their sound again and again—part of some horribly mutilated Elvis Presley tune, Indianized by the film producer. I sat there and no one noticed me: arms stretched right over my head for glasses of tea; sometimes brown tea trickled over the side of the glass tumbler and fell on my clothes. I did not mind, though at other times I'd have gone into a rage at any man who dared to spill tea over my clothes. Today I had resigned myself to anything—as long as I could hope for a bus-ride back to town on credit and good will. I glanced at the brown face of a very old timepiece kept on a wooden shelf inside the tea-shop. It was so brown that I could hardly make out the numerals on it.

Still an hour before the bus arrived and two hours since Vasu had gone. I only hoped that he would not return before the bus arrived. I prayed he would not: I reassured myself again by asking, over the babble of the tea-shop, if Muthu could tell when Vasu would be back, and he gave me the same reply as before. This was the only silver lining in the cloud that shrouded my horizon that day. Even so my heart palpitated with apprehension lest he should suddenly appear at the tea-shop and carry out his nefarious programme for the evening. He could pick me up between his thumb and first finger and put me down where he pleased. Considering his enormous strength, it was surprising that he did not do more damage to his surroundings. I sat in a trembling suspense as men came and went, buying tobacco, betel leaves, and cigarettes and tea and buns. I could hardly get a word with Muthu. I sat brooding over what I'd have to face from Sastri or my wife when I got back . . . Get back! They very phrase sounded remote and improbable! The town, the fountain, and my home in Kabir Street seemed a faraway dream, which I had deserted years ago . . .

The crowd at the tea-shop was gone. I sat on the bench and fell into a drowse. The hills and fields and the blindingly blue sky were lovely to watch, but I could not go on watching their beauty for ever. I was not a poet. If my monosyllabic friend had been here, perhaps he would have enjoyed sitting and staring; but I was a business man, a busy printer. I bowed my head and shut my eyes. I felt weak: I might eat all the buns in the world, but without a handful of rice and the sauce my wife made I could never feel convinced that I had taken any nourishment. The air far off trembled with the vibration of an engine. Muthu declared, "The bus should be here in ten minutes." Amazing man with ears so well attuned; I said so. I wanted to do and say anything I could to please this man, whom at normal times I'd have passed as just another man selling tea in unwashed tumblers.

The bus arrived, on its face a large imposing signboard announcing "Mempi Bus Transport Corporation," although the bus itself was an old one picked off a war surplus dump, rigged up with canvas and painted yellow and red. It was impossible

to guess how many were seated in the bus until it stopped at the
tea-shop and the passengers wriggled and jumped out as if for
an invasion. They swarmed around the tea-shop, outnumber-
ing the flies. The conductor, a very thin man, in a peaked cap
and khaki shirt over half-shorts, emerged with a cash-bag
across his shoulder, and the driver jumped out of his seat. Men,
women, and children clamoured for attention at the tea-shop.
The driver and the conductor exchanged a few words, looked
at the cash-bag, took out some coins for themselves. The conductor then addressed the gathering in a general manner, "I am
not stopping for more than five minutes; if anyone is left behind he will be left behind, that's all. I warn you all, don't blame
me later," and he looked around like a schoolmaster watching
his erring pupils and passed into the tea-shop. He was given a
seat of honour beside the owner. He called for a glass of tea and
buns. He lit a cigarette. After he was well settled, I went to
show myself to Muthu, who, I feared, might forget me in the
midst of his booming business—a fear which was well-founded,
for as soon as he saw me he said, "Ah, I'd forgotten about our
printing master." Then he told the conductor, "Brother, give him
a seat to the town; he will pay at the other end." The brother
took time to grasp the meaning of the proposition. He looked
at me with sour suspicion. "Why should he not pay now?"

"Because he has left all his cash in town."

"Then why did he come here? You know how many tell me
that each day?" He moistened his upper lip with his tongue as
smoke emerged from his nostrils. "Another monster in league
with Vasu," I thought, and felt desperate. He demonstrated
with his hands the act of wringing a neck. "I'd like to do this to
anyone who comes up with such a proposal. If our inspector
checks mid-way, it'll end my career, and then I and my family
will have to take a begging bowl and go from door to door."

The man had a far-fetched imagination. Having always lived
within the shelter of my press, I had probably grown up in
complete ignorance of human nature, which seemed to be vicious, vile, vindictive and needlessly unfriendly everywhere. I
went up to him with chest thrown out and said haughtily, "I'll
guarantee that you will not have to carry a begging bowl. To-

day I am stuck here, but generally I'm not a passenger in any bus, having a car—if not mine, my friend's which is as good as mine."

"What car do you use?"

"Well . . . ," I said, reflecting, "a Morris, of course," mentioning the first make that came into my head.

"Model?" he asked, pursuing the subject.

"Fifty one, I think . . ."

"Four-door?"

"Yes."

"Oh, you are lucky; it's worth its weight in gold, that particular model. I know several people who are searching for one desperately. Do you think you would care to quote a price for it?"

I shook my head. "Oh, dozens of persons ask me that every day, but I want to keep it till it falls to bits, you know. I don't want to sell."

He had now developed a wholesome respect for me as a member of the automobile fraternity. He was prepared to overlook my unbuttoned shirt and dishevelled appearance and ticketless condition; I wished I had some more jargon to impress him further, but I had to manage as best I could with whatever rang in my memory as a result of the printing I had done for Ramu of Ramu's Service Station, who sometimes dropped in to talk of the state of the nation in the motoring world.

The bus-conductor said, "Any time you want to dispose of your Morris, you must tell me." He turned to Muthu and confided, "Sooner or later I want to give up this endless ticket-punching and drive a baby taxi—I know a man who earns a net income of fifty rupees a day with just one baby vehicle. I have saved enough to buy a car now."

Muthu nudged him in the midriff and muttered, "Don't I know!" darkly, at which both of them simpered. I knew at once they meant that the conductor made money by pocketing a lot of the cash collected from passengers. I said, to add to the mood of the hour, "One has to make money while one can. Otherwise, when one is old or down and out, who would give a paisa?"

When the conductor started nearly half an hour later, I

walked along royally beside him and took my seat in the bus. I had taken leave of Muthu briefly but in touching terms; he assured me that he would write to me for any help he might need. I sat in the royal seat, that is, beside the driver. The conductor leaned over my shoulder from behind, to say, "You will have to move and make space at the next stop. The Circle is expected." The word "Circle" in these circumstances indicated the inspector of police for this circle, whose seat at the front was always reserved. If another passenger occupied it, it was a matter of social courtesy to vacate it or at least move up closer to the driver and leave enough space at the end of the seat for the Circle. Once, long, long ago, a planter returning to his estate created a lot of unpleasantness by refusing to make way for the Circle, with the result that the Circle was obliged to travel in one of the ordinary seats inside the bus, with the rabble, and at the next stop he impounded the whole bus with the passengers for overcrowding.

The bus travelled for an hour. I felt happy that after all I'd slipped away from Vasu. I cast a look behind once or twice to see if his jeep was following us. Coming back from tracking the tiger, he might want to embark on the bigger expedition of tracking a printer who had escaped from a tea-shop.

The bus stopped under a tree on the road and the conductor issued a warning, "We are not stopping for more than a minute. If anyone is impatient to get out, let him get out for ever. Don't blame me afterwards." In spite of this threat a few of the passengers wriggled out and disappeared behind the bushes by the roadside. A constable in uniform was seen coming across a maize field, sweating in the sun and bearing under his arm a vast load of papers and files. He gesticulated from a distance to catch the eye of the driver. He arrived and placed the files on the seat next to me. I moved up to the inferior side of the seat close to the driver and cleared a space for the Circle. I couldn't, after all, be choosy as I was there on sufferance.

The constable said to the driver, "The Circle is coming; you'll have to wait."

"How long?" asked the conductor. The constable clung to the rail, rested his feet on the step, pushed his turban back on

his head, and spurned answering. Instead he said, "Give me a
beedi," and held out his hand. The driver produced from his
pocket matches and a *beedi*. The constable smoked: the acrid
smell of *beedi* leaf and tobacco overpowered the smell of petrol. The constable's face shone with perspiration. He said, "I
feared I might lose the bus; the Circle would have chopped off
my head." A couple of children started crying, a woman sang a
soft but tuneless lullaby, someone was yawning noisily, someone else was swearing, a couple of peasants were discussing a
litigation, someone asked wearily, "Are we going to go on at all?"
and someone else made a joke about it. I looked back furtively for
Vasu's jeep coming in pursuit. I grew tired of the policeman's face,
and the road ahead, and everything. I was beginning to feel hungry, the buns having been assimilated into my system long ago.
All the passengers subsided into apathetic, dull waiting.

Finally the Circle turned up, a swarthy man in a khaki uniform, appearing suddenly beside the bus on a bicycle. As soon
as he jumped off, work started: the constable held the handlebars; the conductor heaved the bicycle up to the roof; the Circle
climbed into his seat and said, "Start." The driver squeezed the
bulb of the rubber horn, and its short raucous bark resounded
along the highway, past the hill, and brought a dozen passengers at the run who had strayed away from the suffocating bus
into the surrounding country. For a brief while there was the
disorder of people trying to clamber back to their original seats.
One heard grumblings and counter-grumblings—"I was sitting
here," "No, this was my place," until the conductor said, "Keep
quiet, everyone," in deference to the presence of the Circle. The
Circle, however, sat stiffly looking ahead; it was evident he did
not want to embarrass the conductor by noticing the overcrowding.

I was overwhelmed by the proximity of this eminent person,
who smelt of the sun, sweat and leather. I hoped he'd not take
me for an ex-convict and order me out. He had a nice downward-
directed short moustache. He wore dark glasses and his nose
was hooked and sharp; his Adam's apple also jutted out. The
driver drove with great caution; he who had been swerving
away from collisions for over an hour (a pattern of driving

which Vasu had already accustomed me to), now never exceeded twenty miles an hour, applied the brake when a piece of paper drifted across, and gently chided any villager who walked in the middle of the road. At this rate, he would not reach the town before midnight. His speed depended on where the Circle was getting out. I felt it imperative to know at once his destination. "You are going to town, I suppose?" I said to him. Where was the harm in asking him that? There was no law against it.

He turned his sun-glasses on me and said, "I'll be getting off at Talapur."

"Is that where you stay?" I asked.

"No. I'm going there for an investigation," he said, and I shuddered at the thought of the poor man who was going to be investigated. He talked to me about crime in his area. "We've a lot of cattle-lifting cases in these parts, but the trouble is identification when the property is traced; they mutilate the animals, and then what happens is the case is dismissed and all the trouble one takes to frame a charge-sheet is simply wasted. We have a few murders too, and a certain amount of prohibition offences around the dry-belt areas." I found that he was a friendly sort of man, in spite of all his grim looks. "This is a difficult circle," he said finally. "Offenders often disappear into the jungles on Mempi, and sometimes one has to camp for days on end in the forests."

At the Talapur bus-stand, which was under a tree, with a replica of Muthu's tea-stall, a constable was there to receive the Circle and haul down his bicycle from the roof. The Circle got on his cycle and pedalled away. Talapur was a slightly larger town than Mempi and was regarded as an important junction. It had more shops lining the street. The conductor uttered the usual warning to the passengers and vanished into the tea-shop. Most of the passengers followed suit and some dispersed to various corners of the city. I sat in the bus, nursing my hunger in silence, having no credit here.

When the bus started again, it was obvious that the Circle was no longer there to impede its freedom. It was driven recklessly and brought to a dead stop every ten minutes, to pick up a wayside passenger. The conductor never said "no" to anyone.

As he explained to me, "These poor fellows will get stranded on the highway if we are not considerate. After all they are also human creatures." He was a compassionate conductor, who filled his pockets with the wayside fare, never issuing a ticket. "At this rate he could buy a Rolls-Royce rather than a Morris Minor," I thought. The bus left the highway and darted across devious side-tracks through corn-fields in search of passengers. It would draw up at a most unexpected spot, and, sounding the horn, the driver would cry, "Come on, come on, Malgudi, last bus for the town." The bus penetrated into the remotest hamlet to ferret out a possible visitor to the town, and all the passengers had to go where the bus went and sit there patiently watching the antics of the driver and conductor, who seemed to have a fixed target of income for the day and to be determined to reach it. That was how a three-hour jeep ride in the morning was stretched out to eight on the return journey and it was eleven at night when the bus came to a halt in the public square beyond the market in Malgudi.

At eight o'clock next morning I sat correcting the proof of the adjournment lawyer's invitation. Sastri came in half an hour after I had opened the door of the press. He stood transfixed at the sight of me and said, "We all waited till nine last night."

"I've always told you that you should lock up the door at your usual time whether I am in or out," I said grandly, and added, "Sometimes I get so much else to do."

"But that lawyer would not move. He kept saying you promised to be back in five minutes, in five minutes, and then there were the fruit-juice labels. He was very bitter and said . . ."

"Oh, stop that, Sastri," I said impatiently. I did not like the aggrieved tone he was adopting. I'd had enough of nagging from my wife all night, after she had been forced to get up from sleep and feed me at midnight. "If I disappeared abruptly it was my own business. Why should I be expected to give an explanation to everyone? If the fruit-juice man wants to print his labels elsewhere, let him clear out, that's all. I can't be dancing attendance on all and sundry. If he can find any other printer to bring out his magenta shade in the whole of South India . . ."

Sastri did not wait for me to finish my sentence but passed into the press, as it seemed to me, haughtily. I sat correcting the proof: the corrections were in the state I had left them on the previous day. "Mr. . . . requests the pleasure of your company . . ." Wrong fonts, and the bridegroom's name was misspelt. "Company" came out as "cumbahy." I never cease to marvel at the extraordinary devils that dance their way into a first proof. The sight of "cumbahy" provoked me to hysterical laughter. I was light-headed. I would not have to beg at a tea-shop and starve or go about without a button to my shirt. I had a feeling that I was in an extraordinarily fortunate and secure position, enough to be able to say "fie" to Sastri or anyone. Life in Market Road went on normally. It was good to watch again the *jutkas* and cycles going round the fountain and the idlers of our town sitting on its parapet and spitting into it. It produced in me a great feeling of security and stability. But that lasted only for a few minutes. The adjournment lawyer, looking unshaven as ever, his shoulders draped in a spotted *khadi* shawl, a dhoti above his knee, and an umbrella dangling from his arm, stepped in, his face set in a frown.

"Do you think . . . ," he began.

One look at him and I knew what he was going to say, "Won't you come in and take a seat, first?"

"Why should I?" he asked. "I'm not here to waste my time."

I was still motioning him to a chair, but he seemed afraid that once he sat there I'd abandon him and disappear again for the day.

He said, "I'm printing my invitation elsewhere, so don't trouble yourself."

"Oh, no trouble whatever. This is a free country, you are a free man. Our constitution gives us fundamental rights. How can I compel you or anyone to do what you may not want to do?" I knew he was lying; if he had wasted his time till nine last evening and was back so soon, when had he found the time to seek a printer? Anyway it was not my business; this was a free country, fundamental rights, every citizen was free to print his daughter's marriage card where he pleased, but if he had his wits about him he'd watch out where he got the best results.

"Sastri!" I called aggressively. "Bring this gentleman's original draft—Lawyer so-and-so's daughter's wedding." Sastri from his invisible world responded with his voice, but made no effort to bring the original. This gave everyone time to cool. The lawyer edged a step nearer the chair.

"Won't you take a seat, please? Mr. Sastri should be with us in a minute." He sat down, but remained in a state of hostile silence. I said, "I suppose all your other arrangements are ready?"

He shook his head. "How truly have our elders said . . ." He quoted a proverb to the effect that building a house and conducting a marriage were the two Herculean tasks that faced a man. I added a further sentiment that a man who marries off his daughter need perform no other meritorious acts in life as he is giving away his most precious treasure—which moved the lawyer so deeply that the tears came to his eyes. He said, blowing his nose, "Susila is the gentlest of my children. I hope she will have no trouble from her mother-in-law!" He sighed deeply at the thought and I said consolingly, "Mother-in-law! 'Down with them,' says the modern girl, college-educated and modern-minded."

"I've given her the best possible education," he said morosely. "What more could I do? I pay her music master fifteen rupees a month, her school fees amount to fifteen rupees, and I pay ten rupees for her school bus . . ."

"And you have to manage all this," I thought, "by securing endless adjournments." But I said aloud, "Yes, life today is most expensive."

After this agreeable *tête-à-tête*, I cried suddenly, "Sastri, this gentleman is waiting to take away his invitation copy. After all we must give him time to print elsewhere."

The lawyer behaved like one who has been stung. "Oh no. Oh no," he cried. "Even if it means stopping the marriage, I will not go anywhere else for my printing."

I said, "I'm here to help humanity in my own humble way. I will never say no to anyone. Don't hesitate to command me for anything you may want me to do." He took my offer promptly, and said, "A thousand cards—or do you think we could do with less?"

Late that evening Vasu's jeep drew up before my press. It was past eight and the traffic in the street was thin. Vasu looked at me from his driving seat. His hair was covered with dust and stood up more like a halo than ever. He beckoned to me from his seat. I was overworking in order to finish the lawyer's invitations, and I had even undertaken to address and distribute them if he so ordered. He had acquired so much confidence in me that he did not feel the need to sit up with me, and had gone home. I shouted back to Vasu, "Why don't you come in?" I was now on my own ground, and had no fear of anyone. He said, "Hey, come on! I want you to see what I have here." I went out, making up my mind not to step into the jeep, whatever might happen. I'd stand at a distance to see whatever it was that he was going to show me. There was dust and grime on his face, but also a triumphant smile exposing his teeth; his eyes had widened, showing the whites. I edged cautiously to the jeep. I only hoped that he would not thrust out his arm, grab me and drive off. He took a flashlight and threw the beam on to the back seat, where lay the enormous head of a tiger. "How did you manage that?" I asked, there being no other way of talking to a man who had brought in the head of a tiger. A couple of curious passers-by slowed their pace. Vasu shouted to them, "Get away and mind your own business." He started his car to take it through the side gate and park it in the yard. I went back to my seat and continued my work. I could hear his steps go up the wooden stairs. When the breeze blew in from his direction, there was already a stench of flesh—it might have been my imagination.

The curtain parted; he came in and took a seat. He lit a cigarette and asked, "Do you know what he measures? Ten and a half tip to tip; the head is almost eighteen inches wide! I got him finally in the block, you see; they will have a surprise when they next check the tiger population in their block." He then described how he got information from various people, and had followed the foot-marks of the tiger from place to place. He had to wander nearly six miles within the jungle, and finally got it at a water-hole, at about two in the morning. He showed me the bleeding scratches on his feet from having to push his way through thickets; at any moment it might have sprung on him from some unsuspected quarter. "I was prepared to knock him down with my hands and ram the butt of my rifle between his jaws if it came to that," he said. It was evident that he was not going to wait for others to pay him compliments. He showered handfuls of them on himself.

"What about the permit? You didn't have one?"

"The tiger didn't mind the informality." He laughed aloud at his own humour. "That swine double-crossed me! Probably because you didn't print Golden Thoughts for him." He never let slip an occasion to blame me or accuse me. I gave no reply, but I became curious to see his animal.

He took me to his room. This was my first visit there since he had occupied it. He had his bed draped over with a mosquito-net, a table in a corner, heaped with clothes and letters, and a trunk with its lid open with all his clothes thrown about. He had tied a string across the room and had more clothes hanging on it. On the little terrace he had put out some skins to dry; there was a tub in a corner in which the skin of the tiger was soaking. Skins of smaller animals lay scattered here and there, and jungle squirrels and feathered birds were heaped in corners. A lot of wooden planks and moulds and all kinds of oddments lay about. Ever since I had given him the attic, I had left him fairly alone, not wanting to seem an intrusive host, and all the while he had been surrounding himself with carcasses. The room smelt of decaying flesh and raw hide; he had evidently been very active with his gun, which now rested on his bed. ("I'm a man of business, and I cannot afford to waste my time. Each day that I spend without doing my work is a day completely wasted.") There was a resinous odour in the air which made me retch. I couldn't imagine any human being living in this atmosphere. Sastri now and then in the past weeks had complained of a rotting smell somewhere. We had searched our garbage cans and odd corners of the press to see if the paste we were using had gone bad. Once I had to speak severely to our binder; I called him names for possibly using some nasty slaughterhouse material in binding. He was apologetic, although he had used no such material. Even after his promise to improve his material, the smell persisted. It was pervasive and insistent and Sastri found it impossible to stand at the type-board and compose. Then we thought a rat might be dead somewhere and turned up every nook and corner of the press, and finally we blamed the health department. "Next time that fellow comes around for votes, I'll make him stand at the type-board and perform inhaling exercises," I said bitterly. Sometimes my neighbour of the original Heidelberg came to ask if I noticed any smell around. I said emphatically that I did and asked his views on the municipal administration, little thinking that the fountainhead of all the stink was the attic over my own machine.

I sat down on an iron chair because the whole problem loomed enormously before me. If this man continued to stay here (I had really no idea how long he proposed to honour me with his presence), what was to happen to me and to my neighbourhood?

Vasu was stirring the broth in the tub with a long pole, at which the stench increased. I held my nostrils with my fingers and he ordered, "Take your fingers away. Be a man." When I hesitated, he came and wrenched my fingers apart. "You are imagining things," he said. "What do you think that tub contains? Tiger blood? Ha! Ha! Pure alum solution." He began to instruct me in the higher realms of carcass treatment. "Actually the whole process of our work is much more hygienic and clean than paring the skin of vegetables in your kitchen." I shuddered at the comparison. "After all one takes a lot of care to bleed the animal, and only the skin is brought in. In order to make sure that there is no defect, I attend to everything myself. The paws and the head are particularly important." He lifted the paw of the dead tiger and held it up. "If there is the slightest flaw in the incision you will never be able to bring the ends together. That is what Suleiman taught me; he was an artist, as good as a sculptor or a surgeon, so delicate and precise! I killed the tiger last night. What do you think I was doing till tonight?"

"Hiding yourself and the carcass from the eyes of forest guards," I thought.

"Bleeding, skinning, and cleaning it so that sentimentalists may not complain. To make still surer, we pack, or rather pickle, the skin in tins of salt immediately after flaying. So you will understand it is all done under the most hygienic conditions." He swept his hand around, "I do everything myself, not because I care for anyone's comments, but . . ."

"There are bits of flesh still there," I said, pointing at the new tiger-skin.

"What if there are! Don't you have flesh under your own skin? Do you think you have velvet under yours? This was his idea of humour and I had no way of matching it. I looked around. On his work bench in a corner stood a stuffed crow, a golden eagle, and a cat. I could recognize the cat as the one that used to prowl in my press hunting for mice. "Why did you shoot that cat? That was mine!" I cried shuddering. I fancied I could still hear its soft "mew" as it brushed its back against my legs at the treadle.

"I didn't know," he said, "I only wanted it for study; after all, it's the same family as the tiger. I am trying to make a full mould of the tiger. There are some problems of anatomy peculiar to the *Felis* family in this area and I needed a miniature for study and research. Without continuous application one cannot prosper in my line."

"What did that crow do to you?" I asked.

"It's to serve as a warning to other crows to let Vasu's skins alone and not to peck at them when they are put out to dry."

"And that golden eagle?"

"It was wheeling right over this roof four days ago; it's only five days old and do you notice any smell?" he asked victoriously. He had such a look of satisfaction and victory that I felt like pricking it a little.

"Yes, of course, there is a smell."

"Oh, come on, don't be a fussy prude, don't imagine that you are endowed with more sensitive nostrils than others. Don't make yourself so superior to the rest of us. These are days of democracy, remember." I was appalled at his notion of democracy as being a common acceptance of bad odours.

"What did that poor eagle do to you?" I asked. I could not bear to see the still, glazed look of the bird. "See its stare!" I cried.

"Aha!" he said. He picked it up and brought it closer to me. "So you think it's looking at you with its eyes!" Its dilated black pupils, set in a white circle, seemed to accuse us. He was convulsed with laughter and his voice split with mirth. "So you are taken in! You poor fool! Those eyes were given it by me, not by God. That's why I call my work an art." He opened a wooden chest and brought out a cardboard carton. "See these." He scooped out a handful of eyes—big round ones, small ones, red ones in black circles. The ferocious, striking, killing glare of a tiger, the surprise and superciliousness of an owl, the large, black-filled softness of a deer—every category of gaze was there. He said, "All these are from Germany. We used to get them before the war. Now you cannot get them for love or money. Just lenses! Sometimes I paint an extra shade at the back for effect. The first thing one does after killing an animal is to take out its eyes, for that's the first part to rot, and then one gives it new eyes like an optician. I hope you appreciate now what an amount of labour goes into the making of these things. We have constantly to be rivalling Nature at her own game. Posture, look, the total personality, everything has to be created." This man had set himself as a rival to Nature and was carrying on a relentless fight.

"You have no doubt excelled in giving it the right look, but, poor thing, it's dead. Don't you see that it is a *garuda*?"

"What if it is?"

"Don't you realize that it's sacred? That it's the messenger of God Vishnu?"

"I want to try and make Vishnu use his feet now and then."

"You may be indifferent, but haven't you seen men stopping in the road to look up and salute this bird when it circles in the sky?" I wanted to sound deliberately archaic and poetic.

He ruminated for a second and added, "I think there is a good business proposition here. I can supply them stuffed eagles at about fifty rupees each. Everyone can keep a sacred *ga-*

ruda in the *puja* and I'll guarantee that it won't fly off. Thus they can save their eyes from glare. I want to be of service to our religious folk in my own way."

I shivered slightly at the thought and the way his mind worked. Nothing seemed to touch him. No creature was safe, if it had the misfortune to catch his eye. I had made a mistake in entertaining him. I ought to send him away at the earliest possible moment. His presence defiled my precincts. My mind seethed with ideas as to how to throw him out, but he noticed nothing. He settled himself down on the easy chair, stretched his legs, and was preparing for a nice long chat. "This is a minor job. I really don't care for it. My real work you will see only when the tiger is made up. You see it now only as a beast with a head and a lot of loose skin soaking in alum, but I'll show you what I can do with it."

CHAPTER FIVE

He was a man of his word. He had said that he never wasted his time. I could see that he never wasted either his time or his bullets. Whenever I heard his jeep arrive, I would see some bloody object, small or big, brought in, if I cared to peep out. But nowadays, as far as possible, I tried to shut my eyes. I was having a surfeit. Not in my wildest dream had I ever thought that my press would one day be converted into a charnel house, but here it was happening, and I was watching helplessly. Sometimes it made me very angry. Why couldn't I ask him to get out? This was my own building, laboriously acquired through years of saving and scraping, and the place would not have come to me but for a good Moslem friend who migrated to Pakistan and gave me the first offer. If I opened the back door, I stepped into Kabir Street, and right across it to my own home. But all this had come about only to harbour the murderer of innocent creatures.

I had been brought up in a house where we were taught never to kill. When we swatted flies, we had to do it without the knowledge of our elders. I remember particularly one of my grand-uncles, who used the little room on the *pyol* and who gave me a coin every morning to buy sugar for the ants, and kept an eye on me to see that I delivered the sugar to the ants in various corners of our house. He used to declare, with approval from all the others, "You must never scare away the crows and sparrows that come to share our food; they have as much right as we to the corn that grows in the fields." And he watched with rapture squirrels, mice, and birds busily depleting the granary in our house. Our domestic granary was not built in the style of these days with cement, but with a bamboo matting stiffened with mud and rolled into cylinders, into whose wide mouth they poured in the harvest, which arrived loaded in bullock carts. That was in the days before my uncles quarrelled and decided to separate.

I was appalled at the thought that I was harbouring this destroyer, but I hadn't the courage to go up to him and say, "Take yourself and your museum out of here!" He might do anything—bellow at me, or laugh scornfully, or rattle my bones. I felt dwarfed and tongue-tied before him. Moreover it was difficult now to meet him; he was always going out and returning late at night; sometimes he was away for three days at a stretch. He returned home late because he did not want his booty to be observed. When he was at home he worked upstairs with the broth and moulds; one heard the hammering, sawing, and all the other sounds belonging to his business, and sometimes during the day he hauled down packing cases and drove off to the railway station. I noted it all from my seat in the press and said to myself, "From this humble town of Malgudi stuffed carcasses radiate to the four corners of the earth."

He worked single-handed on all branches of his work. I admired him for it, until I suddenly realized that I too laboured single-handed at my job, with the slight difference that Sastri was with me; but Vasu had, I suppose, all those ruffians of Mempi lending him a hand in his nefarious trade. I do not know why I should ever have compared myself with him, but there it was. I was getting into an abnormal frame of mind. There was no person in whom I could confide, for I had always played that role myself. My visitors were, as usual, the journalist and the poet, both of them worthless as consultants. All the same I made an attempt to ascertain their views.

The journalist was frankly dumbfounded when he realized that there was no aspect of this particular problem which he could blame directly on the Government. He merely snapped, "Why do you tolerate such things? As a nation, we are what we are today because of our lack of positive grip over our affairs. We don't know where we are going or why. It is part of the policy of drift, which is our curse." I paid no attention to what he was saying; it was all too vague and round-about and irrelevant to the present case; the idea of Vasu provoked Sen into incoherent unpredictable statements. I left him alone. After all one should learn to bear one's burdens.

Still, two days later, the oppression on my mind was so great that I buttonholed the poet when he was struggling to start on the seventh canto of his opus and asked what he would do in my place. I feared that he might suggest reading poetry aloud as a possible step towards driving out the killer. He took time to comprehend my problem; even to myself, the more I attempted to speak of my problem, the more incomprehensible it seemed. I was left wondering if I were making too much of a very simple matter.

When he did understand, the poet asked, "Why don't you try to raise the rent?"

I beat my brow, "Oh, Kavi! Do I have to tell you that I am not a *rentier*? I let him in as a friend and not as a tenant. Do you want to heap on my head the reputation of being a man who takes rent for his attic space?"

The poet looked bewildered and said, "Then you could surely tell him to go. Why not?"

It was impossible to explain. My wife also said the same thing. In my desperation I had turned to her, though I rarely discussed my problems with her. I had become abnormal. I was brooding too much on Vasu. His footsteps on the wooden stairs set my heart racing. I knew that it was involuntary anger which stirred my heart; the trouble was that it was both involuntary and suppressed! My wife said simply, sweetly, as she served my supper, "Ask him to go, that's all. Babu is frightened of him, and refuses to go when I send him to you."

All this worked on my mind. I waited for a chance to have a word with the man. It was like waiting for my father, in my childhood. I often had to spend days and days hoping to catch my father in a happy mood to ask him for a favour, such as cash for purchasing a bat or ball or permission to go out scouting. Most times he was preoccupied and busy, and I lost the taste for food until I was able to have a word with him. I would confide in my grand-uncle and he would help me by introduc-

ing the subject to my father at the appropriate moment, when
he was chewing betel-leaves after a contented dinner. When my
father turned to question me, I would squirm and find myself
tongue-tied, unable to go on with my proposition. I was in a
similar predicament now, with the added handicap of not having my grand-uncle around. I recollected that on the day I saw
his dead body stretched out on the bier my first thought was,
"Oh Lord, who is going to speak for me hereafter?"

At last I stuck a note on Vasu's attic door when he was away,
"May I have a word with you when you have the time?" and
waited for results. One morning, three days later, he parted the
curtain and peeped in while I was at the treadle, printing the
monosyllable forms. I had now barricaded the passage beyond,
from the attic stairs to my treadle, with steel mesh, so that Vasu
always had to come by the front door whenever he wanted to
see me. The first thing he said was, "You take a pleasure in
making me go round, is that it?" My heart sank at the sight of
him. There was a frown on his terrible brow. "Perhaps he
missed a target or his gun backfired!" I thought to myself. It
was more dangerous than asking for a concession from my father. He flourished the note and asked, "Is this for me?" He
seemed to possess a sixth sense. He looked grim and unfriendly.
I wondered if someone had been talking to him. I looked up
from my proof and just said, "Nothing urgent. Perhaps we could
meet later, if you are busy."

"If *you* are busy it is a different matter, but don't concern
yourself with my busyness. I am always busy."

"Yes," I added mentally, "as long as the forests are full."

He added, "I cannot afford to lounge about, if you know
what I mean. If I had the same luck as your other friends who
congregate in your press, reading verse or criticizing the Government, I might . . ."

That settled it. He was in a challenging mood. I suppressed
the qualms I had all along and said, "Will you kindly take a
seat? I will join you in a moment." He was sitting in his chair
when I came to him two minutes later, after taking enough time
to put away the paper in hand. He said, "You have made a fe-

tish of asking people to sit in this room." This was a surprise attack.

"I like to observe the ordinary courtesies," I said.

"Do you mean to say that others don't?" he asked with his face puckering into the usual lines, and I knew he was getting back into his old mood of devilish banter. I felt relieved. I might have even gone to the length of inquiring about his dead or dying animals, but I checked myself, feeling an aversion to the subject. I said, "Vasu, I don't want you to mistake me. Have you been able to secure a house?"

"Why?" he asked, suddenly freezing.

"I just thought I might ask you, that's all."

"Not the sort of question a supposedly hospitable person should ask of his guest. It is an insult."

I fought down my racing heart and my tongue which was ready to dart out like a snake's. I said very casually, "I asked because I require the place for . . ."

"For?" he asked aggressively, cocking his ear, and waited for my answer.

"Someone is coming to stay with us, and he wants . . ."

"How many rooms in your own house are occupied?"

"Should one go into all that now?"

"Yes, the question is of interest to me," he said, and added, "Otherwise I would not mind if you had all your relatives in the world come and live with you."

I suppressed the obvious repartees. Aggressive words only generate more aggressive words. Mahatma Gandhi had enjoined on us absolute non-violence in thought and speech, if for no better reason than to short-circuit violent speech and prevent it from propagating itself. I toned my repartee down to a cold business-like statement, "My guest is a man who likes to stay by himself."

"Then why should he seek solitude in this noisy press?"

I had no answer, and he said after some reflection, "For years you did nothing more than house old decaying paper there; now I have made it slightly habitable you are getting ideas. Do you know how much it has cost me to make it livable in? The mosquitoes and other vermin would eat you up if you were slightly careless, the roof-tiles hit your head, there are cobwebs, smoke, and in summer it is a baking oven. No one but a fool like me would have agreed to live there!"

I remained silent. All I could say was obvious, such as, "Is this the return I get for giving you shelter?" "If you remember, you volunteered to stay," and the most obvious one, "After all you are living on my hospitality; get out if you do not like it." "You are not obliged to be here, you know," etc. etc. I swallowed all such remarks. Instead I said sentimentally, "I never expected you would be so upset."

"Who says I am upset? You are fancying things. It takes a lot more to upset me. Well, anything else?" he asked, rising.

Not until his jeep moved did I realize that he had given me no answer to my question. He had treated it lightly, viciously, indifferently, but all to no purpose. He was gone; my problem remained unsolved, if anything made worse by my having irritated the man. Stag-heads, tiger-skins and petrified feathers were going to surround me for ever and ever. My house was becoming a Noah's Ark, about which I had read in our scripture classes at Albert Mission. There was going to be no help from anywhere. Nobody seemed to understand my predicament. Everyone ended up with the monotonous conclusion, "After all, you invited him to stay with you!" I felt completely helpless. Sastri alone grasped the situation and now and then threw in a word of cheer such as "These things cannot go on for ever like this, can they?" Or sometimes he was brazen enough to say, "What can he do after all, if you really want him to clear out?" as he stuck alphabet to alphabet on his composing stick. He felt it necessary to cheer me up as nowadays I was involving him in a lot of worrying transactions with our customers. The co-operative society report and ledgers were overdue because I could not muster enough sharpness of mind to check the figures. The cash bill of Anand Bhavan Hotel remained half done for the same reason, and it was he who had to battle with the customers and send them back with a convincing reply. Anyway it was a slight comfort in a world where there seemed to be no comfort whatever. I was lulled into a state of resignation. Vasu saw me less and less. I could hear his steps treading the staircase more emphatically than ever. I detected in that stamping of feet a challenge and a sense of ownership. I raged within myself every time I heard those footsteps and I knew I had lost him as a friend. From now on our relationship was going to be of the coldest. I would be grateful if he left me alone and did not think of bringing that terrific fist of his against my chin.

That he had not been idle came to light very soon. Five days passed uneventfully, and then came a brown envelope brought by a court process-server. I received it mechanically, signing the delivery note. Opening it, I read, "You are hereby asked to show cause why proceedings should not be instituted against you . . ." etc. It was from the House Rent Controller, the most dreaded personality in the town. The charges against me were: one, that I had given part of my press for rent without sanction to one Mr. Vasu; and two, that I was trying to evict a tenant by unlawful means. It took me time to understand what it meant. Vasu had filed a complaint against me as a landlord. There were also other minor complaints, such as that I was not maintaining the house in a habitable condition, and was involving the said tenant in great loss, damage, and expense.

This involved me in a set of new activities. Up till now I had not known what it was to receive a court summons. I really did not know where to start and what to do next. Litigation was not in my nature. It was a thing I avoided. I had a shuddering fear of courts and lawyers, perhaps from the days when my uncles let them loose on my father and there was no other topic of discussion at home for months on end. I hid the summons away: they had given me three days' time to attend to it—a sort of reprieve. It gave me a feeling of being on parole. I did not confide even in Sastri. I realized that it would be futile to speak about it to anyone: no one was going to understand. Everyone would treat me as if I had done some unlawful act on the sly and was now caught, or trot out the old advice, "After all it was *you* who agreed to take the man in. You have only yourself to blame."

The situation seemed so dark that I surrendered myself to a

mood of complete resignation. I even began to look relaxed. I attended to my work, listened to jokes and responded to them normally at my press. I counted the days—seventy-two hours more, sixty, twenty-four ... "Tomorrow, I shall probably be led off straight from the court to the jail." Everyone was going to have a surprise. Vasu would chase out Sastri and my customers and utilize my front room and all the rest of the space for arranging his "art" pieces. People would get used to it in due course, cease to refer to the place as a press, and rather call it a museum. My wife and child would fend for themselves and visit me in prison on permissible days. A strange sense of relief came over me when my mind had been made up on all these issues and I knew where I was going to end. People would no doubt sympathize with me, but always conclude with, "Who asked him to encourage the man anyway? He brought it all on his own head. Let him not blame others."

On the last day of my freedom, at dawn, I had gone as usual to the river for a bath and was returning to my house at five-thirty. As usual the adjournment lawyer was on his way to the river. An idea came to me: it had never occurred to me until now that he could be of use. I had only viewed him as a printing customer. Since I had printed his thousand cards, he had been avoiding me—because of the unpaid bill. The marriage was over, and the bill and become stale: after all I didn't charge him more than ninety rupees for the entire lot. These days I never saw him even on my morning walk back from the river. Perhaps he detoured and took a parallel road. But today, as my luck would have it, I came face to face with him.

A great feeling of relief came over me at the sight. "Ah, my friend," I cried. "Just the person I was hoping to meet."

He looked panic-stricken. Luckily I cornered him at the bend of Kabir Street where the house of the barber abuts the street, and with the storm drain on the other side a man cannot easily slip out if his path is blocked. He said awkwardly, "Just today I was planning to see you at the press. You know, with one thing and another, after my daughter's marriage ..."

I felt overjoyed at meeting him, and asked him, "How is

your daughter? Has she joined her husband? How is your son-in-law? How do you fare in the role of a father-in-law?"

He said, "Most people think that with the wedding all one's troubles are over. It's only half the battle! Ha! Ha!" I laughed in order to please him. I didn't want him to think that I had accosted him so early in the day for my unpaid bill. He said, "It's only after a marriage that one discovers how vicious one's new relatives can be. How many things they demand and keep demanding! Oh, God."

"That's true," I said. "Taking your daughter up and down to visit her mother-in-law."

"That I wouldn't mind," he said. "After all she is our child; it's my duty to help her travel in comfort."

"Yes, yes," I said, wondering what it was that he really minded.

His answer was not long in coming. "All sorts of things, all sorts of things." The first rays of the sun touched up the walls of the barber's house with the morning glory. Sparrows and crows were flying already in search of grain and worms. As I watched them a part of my mind reflected how lucky they were to be away from Vasu's attic windows. The lawyer was talking, habituated to rambling on until the court rose for lunch. "The presents demanded are enough to sink one," he was saying. "The new son-in-law must be propitiated all the year round, I suppose," he went on with grim humour. "He must be given a present because it's the sixth month after the wedding, because it's the month of Adi, because it is Deepavali, because it is this and that; every time you think of the great man, you must part with a hundred rupees in cash or clothes! It's all an old, silly custom; our women are responsible. I would not blame the young man; what can he do? It's his mother who demands these things and the bride's mother at once responds by nagging her husband. These women know that if a man is sufficiently nagged, he will somehow find the cash."

"So," I thought, "can the good lady be made to take an interest in the payment of my bill?"

The lawyer, as if reading my thought, said, "Now you know

why I could not really come over to see you. In spite of one's best efforts, small payments get left out. In all I had to find about ten thousand rupees for the marriage—savings, borrowings, loans, all kinds of things. Anyway it is all over. I will not have to face a similar bother for at least a decade more. My second daughter is just six years old."

"That gives you a lot of time," I said, and I hoped he would now let me say a word about my own problem. But he added, "I am sorry I kept your bill so long; it escaped my notice."

"Oh, that's all right," I said reassuringly. "I knew you must have been busy. Some of my customers are like a safe-desposit for me; I can ask for my money whenever I want. Don't worry, sir, I would not mistake you. Don't trouble to come to my press. I can send Sastri to collect the amount from you." This I added out of a sudden apprehension that he might think I was writing off the account. The sun had grown brighter now, and still I had not told him of my problem. I did not know how to make a beginning. He was on the point of moving off, having had his say, when I said quickly, "I want to see you on a legal matter."

He drew himself up proudly now. He was on his own ground. He asked brusquely, "Any more problems coming out of your property matters? I thought they had all been settled once and for all."

"No, no, it's not that," I began.

"Or are you thinking of a partnership deed? A lot of business men are having them now, you know."

"Oh, no, I am not such a big business man."

"Or estate duty; have you any trouble on that account?"

I laughed. "Fortunately I own nothing to bring the estate duty on my head."

"Or Shop Assistants' Act or Sales Tax? You know, half the trouble with Sales Tax problems is due to a lack of definition in the phrasing of the Act. Today I could tweak the nose of any Sales Tax Official who dared to tamper with my client, with all their half-digested manuals!"

"I have a summons from the Rent Controller."

"What for?" he asked. "Do you know how many people . . ."

he began, but I wrested the initiative from him and cut in. "It is some fancy summons as you'll see. Can I meet you at home?"

"No," he said. "Come to my office." His office was above a cotton warehouse, or rather a bed-maker's shop, and cotton fluff was always flying about. Clients who went to him once never went there again, as they sneezed interminably and caught their death of cold; asthmatics went down for weeks after a legal consultation. His clients preferred to see him as he lounged about the premises of the district court in search of business, and he tackled their problems standing in the veranda of the court or under the shade of a tamarind tree in the compound. But he liked his inexperienced clients first to meet him at his office and catch a cold. I tried to dodge his proposal, but he was adamant that I should meet him in the narrow room above the cotton shop.

I went sneezing up the wooden stairs. The staircase was narrower than the one leading to my attic devoted to dead wild life, and creaked in a way which dimmed the sneezings of a visitor. Although I was born and bred in the district, this was the first time I had trod Abu Lane, which was only four blocks away from my press, conveniently tucked away from the views and turmoil of Market Road. There you saw his signboard, bleached by time and weather—Mr. . . . , Pleader—nailed to a pillar on which a more aggressive board announced Nandi Cotton Corporation. Inside you saw nothing at first except bales and bales of cotton, and then a heap in a corner with some women beating them into fluff for bed-making. It was this process which spread tuberculosis and asthma among would-be litigants. Our lawyer's chamber was right on the landing, which had been converted into a room, with one table, one chair, and one bureau full of law-books. His clients had to stand before him and talk. The table was covered with dusty paper bundles, old copies of law reports, a dry ink-well, an abandoned pen, and his black alpaca coat, going moss-green with age, hung by a nail on the wall. Down below, the cotton-fluffers kept up a rhythmic beating. He had a very tiny window with wooden bars behind him, and through it one saw the coconut tree by a neighbouring house, a kitchen chimney smoking, and a number of sloping roof-tiles, smoky and dusty, with pieces of tinsel thrown away by someone gleaming in the bright sun.

"Allergy?" he cried on seeing me. My sneezings had announced my arrival. I stepped in, blowing my nose and rubbing my eyes. There was a beatific smile on his face, and his single tooth was exposed. He sat at the table and commented, "Some people suffer from allergy to dust and cotton. But I never notice such things." He seemed to feel that his superior physique had come about through a special arrangement between himself and God, and he enjoyed the sight of allergy in others as if it gave him an assurance that God was especially good to him. "Allergy, they say, is just mental, that's all," he said. "It is something you should overcome by your own resolution," he added grandly. I stood in front of his table like a supplicant, and placed before him the brown document. He put on his spectacles, opened the paper, spread it out with the palm of his hand, put a weight on it (the inkless bottle), reared back his head in order to adjust his vision, and read. His unshaven jowl and chin sparkled as if dusted over with silver powder.

He sighed deeply. "Of course, you have given him no sort of receipt?"

"Receipt? What for?" I asked.

"For the rent, I mean. I suppose you have been sensible enough not to take a cheque from him?"

I was appalled. He was falling into the same pattern of thought as a dozen others, including my wife. I declared, "I have not rented him the house."

"Have you taken a lump sum?" he asked.

"Look here, he is not my tenant."

"Whose tenant is he then?" he asked, cross-examining me.

"I don't know. I can't say." I was losing my equanimity. Why were people so pig-headed as not to know or want to understand my position? My legs felt heavy with climbing the ladder, and he would not give me a seat. He seemed to delight in punishing people who came to see him. I could hardly recognize my own voice, it sounded so thick with cotton dust.

The man was pursuing his inquiry. "If he is not your tenant, what is he?"

"He is not a tenant, but a . . . friend," I said, almost unable to substitute any other word.

He was quick to catch it. "Friend! Oh! Oh! What sort of friend is he to file a complaint against you! This is a fairly serious offence according to the present Housing Act. Why could you not have straightaway gone through the usual formalities, that is . . ."

"Stop! Stop!" I cried. "I swear that I gave him the attic free, absolutely free, because he asked for it."

"If I were a judge, I would not believe you. Why should you let him live with you? Is he a relative?"

"No, thank God; it's the only thing that is good about the present situation."

"Are you indebted to him in any way?"

"No. On the contrary, he should feel himself in debt to me, and yet he doesn't hesitate to have me hanged!" I cried. I explained to him at length how Vasu had come in search of me and how it had all come about. Feeling that perhaps the lawyer was too sympathetic to my enemy, I tried to win him over by saying, "You remember that day when you came to have the wedding invitations printed, and how he pulled me out and left you—that's how he does everything. Now you understand what he is capable of."

That prejudiced him. He reflected with bitterness. "And I had to sit there and waste a whole day to no purpose." He spoke to me on many legal technicalities, and took charge of my summons. He pulled out of a drawer a sheet of paper and took my signature. Then he put everything away with relief, "I'll deal with it; don't worry yourself any more about it. How much money have you now?"

"Not an anna," I said, and emptied my pockets to prove it. He looked gloomy at this bankruptcy.

"I would not charge more than a minimum, you know. Some routine charges have to be paid—stamp charges, affidavit charges, and coffee charges for the bench clerk. He is the man to help us, you know."

"Oh, how?"

"Don't ask questions. Now I'm wondering how to pay these

charges, absolutely nominal, you know. Even if you can spare about five rupees . . ."

"I thought since . . . since you have . . . you might adjust your accounts."

He threw up his arms in horror, "Oh, no, absolutely different situations. Don't mix up accounts, whatever else you may do. It always leads to trouble. Can't you send someone to your press to fetch your purse, if you have left it there?"

I felt like banging my fist on his table and demanding immediate settlement of my account, but I felt humbled by circumstances; the lawyer must save me from prison. So I said, "If you will manage it somehow, I will send the amount to your house as soon as I'm back at the press."

"I am not going home. There is no time today for me to go to court if I go home, and so, I don't want to seem to trouble you too much, but one oughtn't to start out on a business like this without cash of any kind."

"I came only to consult you," I said.

"I hope you have found it satisfactory," he replied ceremoniously.

"Yes, of course," I said. I felt like a pauper petitioning for help. How long would he keep me standing like this? I could not afford to be critical. So I asked breezily, "Now what is to be done?"

"First things first." He studied the sheet of paper intently. "The summons is for 11 a.m. Tuesday the 24th; today is Monday the 23rd. It is 10.30 now. I must file your application for non-appearance almost at once. The ruling gives twenty-four hours if a summons is to be non-responded. It would have been a different matter if you had dodged the summons. Did you sign that little paper the fellow had?"

"Yes, of course."

"Ah, inexperience, inexperience," he cried. "You should have consulted me before touching it or looking at it."

"I had no idea it was coming," I said, putting into my voice all the shock I had felt at Vasu's treachery.

"That's true, that's true," he said. "You must have thought it was some printing business from the district court, ha?"

"Now, is that all?" I asked.

"H'm, yes," he said. "I can always depend upon the bench clerk to help me. I'll do what I can. You must feel happy if you are not on the list tomorrow. I'll have to plead that you are away and need more time or notice."

"But everybody can see me at my press," I pleaded.

"Oh, yes, that's a point. But how can the court take cognizance if you are there? In any event, it'll be better if you don't make yourself too conspicuous during the hours of the court sitting."

"Except when I am called out, I'm usually behind the blue curtain," I said.

"That's good, it is always helpful," he said.

"And what's the next step?"

"You will be free for at least four weeks. Rent court is rather overworked nowadays. They won't be able to re-issue the summons for at least four weeks." I felt grateful to the man for saving my neck for four weeks; but now he added a doubt. "Perhaps the complainant will file an objection."

"He may also say that I've not gone anywhere, as he lives right over my head."

"But the court is not bound to take cognizance of what he says. It's not that way that your *mala fides* can be established."

I didn't understand what he meant.

"I have some work now," I said apologetically. I did not want to hurt his feelings with the least hint that I didn't like to be kept standing there while he talked; as a matter of fact my legs were paining me.

"You may go," he said grandly. "I'll be back home at three o'clock. I will manage it all somehow. If you are sending anyone at all to my house, send an envelope with ten rupees in it. Anyway I'll give you a complete accounting when it is all over."

The proof of the lawyer's handiwork: I was sitting unscathed at my press, printing three-colour labels, on the day following my D-day. I gladly sent him ten rupees through Sastri. He would account for it all at the end. I was not to mix up accounts. Great words of wisdom they seemed to me in my fevered state.

CHAPTER SIX

Fifteen days passed uneventfully. We left each other alone. I heard Vasu come and go. His jeep would arrive at the yard, I could hear that mighty fist pulling at the brake, and feet stumping upstairs. Amidst all his impossible qualities, he had just one virtue: he never tried to come to my part of the house; he arrived and departed as he liked. Only the stench of drying leather was on the increase. It disturbed the neighbourhood. I had a visitor from the health department, one fine day—a man in khaki uniform. He was a sanitary inspector whose main business was to keep the city clean, a hard job for a man in a place like Malgudi, where the individual jealously guarded his right to independent action.

The sanitary inspector had the habit of occasionally dropping in at my press and sitting in a chair quietly when his limbs ached from too much supervision of the Market Road. He would take off his pith helmet (I think he was the only one in the whole town who had such headgear, having picked it up at an army disposal store), place it on the chair next to him, wipe his brow with a check-coloured handkerchief, sigh and pant and call for a glass of water. I could not say he was a friend, but a friendly man. Today, he leaned his bicycle on the front step of my press, and came in saying, "There is a complaint against you." He produced an envelope from his pocket and took out a sheet of paper, and held it to me.

I was beginning to dread the sight of brown envelopes nowadays. A joint petition from my neighbours, signed by half a dozen names, had been presented to the municipal authority. They complained that on my terrace they noticed strange activities—

animal hides being tanned; the petitioners pointed out that the tanning and curing of skins should be prohibited in a residential area as it gave rise to bad odour and insanitary surroundings. They also complained of carrion birds hovering around my terrace. One part of my mind admired my neighbours for caring so much for sanitation; the rest of it was seized with cold despair.

I requested the inspector to take a seat and asked what he expected me to do. He said, "Can I have a glass of water?" I called Sastri to fetch water. The sanitary inspector said, after gulping it down in one mouthful (he was the most parched and dehydrated man I had ever seen in my life), "By-law X definitely prohibits the tanning of leather indiscriminately in dwelling areas; By-law Y specifies exactly where you can conduct such a business. I did not know you were engaged in this activity. Why? Is your press not paying enough?"

I slapped my brow with my palm in sheer despair. "I have not turned tanner!" I cried. "I am still a printer. What makes you think I'm not?"

"Where is the harm?" asked the inspector. "There is dignity in every profession. You don't have to be ashamed of it, only you must carry it on at the proper spot without violating the by-laws."

"All right, I'll do so," I said meekly.

"Oh, good, you will co-operate with us! That is the difference between educated people and uneducated ones. You can grasp our problems immediately. Of course people will do wrong things out of ignorance. How can we expect everyone to be versed in municipal by-laws? I never blame a man for not knowing the regulations, but I'm really upset if people don't mend their ways even after a notice has been issued. May I have another glass of water, please?"

"Oh, surely, as many as you want. Mr. Sastri, another glass of water." I could hear Sastri put away the urgent job he was doing and prepare to fetch the glass.

The inspector emptied the second supply at one gulp and rose to go. He said in parting, "I'll send off an endorsement to the parties, something to silence them."

"What will you say?" I asked, a sudden curiosity getting the upper hand.

"We have a printed form, which will go to them to say that the matter is receiving attention. That is enough to satisfy most parties. Otherwise they'll bombard us with reminders."

I saw him off on the last step of my press. He clutched the handlebars of his bicycle, stood for a moment thinking and said, "Take your time to shift, but don't be too long. If you get a notice, please send a reply to say that you are shifting your tanning business elsewhere and pray for time."

"Yes, sir," I said, "I'll certainly do all that you say." I was beginning to realize that it was futile to speak about any matter to anyone. People went about with fixed notions and seldom listened to anything I said. It was less strenuous to let them cherish their own silly ideas.

The septuagenarian came along, tapping his stick; he stood in the road, looked up through his glasses, shading his eyes with one hand, and asked in a querulous voice, "Is Nataraj in?" The usual crowd was there. "Now is the testing time for Nehru," the journalist was saying. "If the Chinese on our border are not rolled back—" The poet had brought the next canto of his poem and was waiting to give me a summary of it. The septuagenarian asked again, "Is Nataraj here?" unable to see inside owing to the glare.

"Yes, yes, I'm here," I cried, and went down to help him up the steps.

He seated himself and looked at the other two. "Your friends? I may speak freely, I suppose?" I introduced them to him, whereupon he expatiated on the qualities of a poet, and his duties and social relationships, and then turned to me with the business on hand. "Nataraj, you know my grandson had a pet—a dog that he had kept for two years. He was very much devoted to it, and used to play with it the moment he came back from school." I almost foresaw what was coming. "Someone killed it last night. It lay under the street-lamp shot through the heart; someone seems to have shot it with a gun. Who has a gun here in these parts? I thought no one but the police had guns."

"Why did you let it out?"

"Why? I don't know. It generally jumps over the wall and goes around the neighbourhood. It was a harmless dog, only barking all night, sitting under that street-lamp. I don't know what makes these dogs bark all night. They say that ghosts are visible to the eyes of a dog. Is it true? Do you believe in ghosts?"

"I haven't been able to see any," I began.

"Oh, that's all right. Most people don't see them. Why should they? What was I saying?" he asked pathetically, having lost track of his own sentence. I was loath to remind him. I hesitated and wavered, hoping that he'd forget the theme of the dead dog and concentrate on the ghosts. But the journalist said, "You were speaking about the dog, sir."

"Ah, yes, yes. I could not bear to see its corpse, and so I asked the scavenger to take it away. I don't know what you call that breed. We called it Tom and it was black and hairy, very handsome; someone brought it from Bombay and gave it to my son, who gave it to this little fellow—quite a smart dog, very watchful, would make such a row if anyone tried to enter our gate, would wait for me to get up from my morning prayer, because he knew he would get a piece of the bread I eat in the morning. For the last three years doctors have ordered me to eat only bread, one slice of it. Before that I used to take *idli* every day, but they think it's not good for me. My father lived to be a hundred and never missed *idli* even for a single day." He remained silently thinking of those days.

I was glad he was not asking to be reminded of his main theme. I hoped he would get up and go away. Everyone maintained a respectful, gloomy silence. If it had continued another minute, he would have risen and I'd have helped him down the steps. But just at the crucial moment Sastri came in with a proof for my approval. As soon as he entered by the curtain, instead of handing me the proof and disappearing he stood arrested for a minute, staring at the old man. "What was all that commotion at your gate this morning? I was coming to the press and had no time to stop and ask. But I saw your grandchild crying."

"Oh, is that you, Sastri?" asked the old man, shrinking his

eyes to slits in order to catch his features. "How are you, Sastri? It's many months since I saw you. What are you doing? Yes, of course I know you are working with Nataraj. How do you find his work, Nataraj? Good? Must be good. His uncle was my class-mate, and he had married the third daughter of . . . He used to come and play with my nephew. Where do you live, Sastri? Not near us?" Sastri mentioned his present address. "Oh, that is far off Vinayak Street; ah, how many centuries it seems to me since I went that way. Come and see me some time, I'll be pleased."

Sastri seemed pleased to be thus invited. He said, "I must, I must come some time."

"How many children have you?" Sastri mentioned the number, at which the old man looked gratified and said, "Bring them also along when you come. I'd like to see them."

Instead of saying "Yes" and shutting up, Sastri said, "Even this morning I could have come for a moment, but there was too much of a crowd at your gate."

"Oh, idiot Sastri! What on earth are you becoming so loquacious for?" I muttered to myself. "Leave him alone to forget this morning's crowd."

But he had stirred up mischief. "Didn't you know why there was a crowd?"

"No, I only saw your grandchild crying. I was in a hurry."

The reminder of his grandchild nearly brought the septuagenarian to the verge of a breakdown. The old man almost sobbed, "That boy is refusing to cheer up. I can't bear to see the youngster in such misery."

"Why? Why? What happened?" asked Sastri.

"Someone had shot his pet dog," said the journalist.

"Shot! Shot!" cried Sastri as if he had been poked with the butt of a rifle. "When? Was it shot dead? Oh, poor dog! I have often seen it at your gate, the black one!" Why was he bent upon adding fuel to the fire? "Do you know who could have shot it?" he asked menacingly.

"For what purpose?" said the old man. "It's not going to help us. Will it bring Tom back to life?"

But Sastri insisted on enlightening him. He gave the old man the killer's name, whereabouts, and situation, and added, "He is just the man who could have done it."

The old man tapped his staff on the floor and shouted at me, "And yet you said nothing? Why? Why?"

"It didn't occur to me, that is all," I said hollowly. The old man tapped the floor with his staff and cried, "Show me where he is, I'll deal with him. I'll hand him over to the police for shooting at things. What's your connection with him? Is he related to you? Is he your friend?" I tried to pacify the old man, but he ignored my words. "In all my eighty years, this is the first time I have heard of a shooting in our street. Who is this man? Why should you harbour him? Tomorrow he'll aim his gun at the children playing in the street!"

Knowing Vasu's style of speech with children, I could agree with the old man's views. The old man's hands and legs trembled, his face was flushed. I feared he might have a stroke and collapse in my press—anything seemed possible in my press these days. I said, "Be calm, sir, it will not do to get excited. It's not good for you."

"If it's not good for me, let me die. Why should anything be good for me? Death will be more welcome to me than the sight of my unhappy grandson."

"I'll get him another dog, sir, please tell him that, a beautiful black one. I promise."

"Can you?" asked the old man, suddenly calming down. "Are you sure? You know where one is to be found?"

"Oh, yes," I said, "the easiest thing. I know many planters who have dogs, and I can always get a puppy for our little friend."

"Will you accompany me now and say that to him?"

"Oh, surely," I said, rising.

Sastri chose just this moment to thrust the proof before me and ask, "Shall I put it on the machine?"

I didn't want anything to stop the old man from getting up and going, so I said, "Wait a moment, I'll be back." But Sastri would not allow me to go. "If you pass this proof, we can print it off, everything is ready. They are shutting off power at eleven o'clock today. If we don't deliver . . ."

"Oh, Sastri, leave everything alone. I don't care what happens. I must see the child first and comfort him." I was desperately anxious that the old man should be bundled off before someone or other should offer to point Vasu out to him.

As Vasu became more aloof, he became more indifferent, and everything that he did looked like a challenge to me. I was, I suppose, getting into a state of abnormal watchfulness myself; even the sound of his footstep seemed to me aggressively tenant-like, strengthened by the laws of the rent-control court. He pretended that I did not exist. He seemed to arrive and depart with a swagger as if to say, "You may have got an adjournment now, but the noose is being made ready for you."

He brought in more and more dead creatures; there was no space for him in his room or on the terrace. Every inch of space must have been cluttered with packing-boards and nails and skins and moulds. The narrow staircase, at which I could peep from my machine, was getting filled up with his merchandise, which had now reached the last step—he had left just enough margin for himself to move up and down. He had become very busy these days, arriving, departing, hauling up or hauling down packing-cases, doing everything single-handed. I had no idea where his market was. In other days I could have asked him, but now we were bitter enemies. I admired him for his capacity for work, for all the dreadful things he was able to accomplish single-handed. If I had been on speaking terms, I'd have congratulated him unreservedly on his success as a taxidermist—his master Suleiman must really have been as great as he described him. He had given his star pupil expert training in all branches of his work. Short of creating the animals, he did everything.

Vasu was a perfect enemy. When I caught a glimpse of him sometimes when I stood at the treadle, he averted his head and passed, perhaps stamping his feet and muttering a curse. He seemed to be flourishing. I wondered why he should not pay me the charges for printing his forms and letterheads. How to ask him? I did not want to do anything that might madden him further and worsen our relationship.

I was beginning to miss his rough company. I often specu-

lated if there could be some way of telling him that all was well,
that he should not give another thought to what had happened
between us, that he could stay in my house as long as he pleased
("only don't bring too many carcasses or keep them too long,
this is a fussy neighbourhood, you know"). I could never be a
successful enemy to anyone. Any enmity worried me night and
day. As a schoolboy I persistently shadowed around the one
person with whom I was supposed to be on terms of hate and
hostility. I felt acutely uneasy as long as our enmity lasted. I
was never more than a few paces away from him as we started
home from school. I sat on a bench immediately behind him
and tried to attract his attention by coughing and clearing my
throat or by brushing against his back while picking up a pencil
deliberately dropped on the floor. I made myself abject in order
to win a favourable look or word from my enemy and waited
for a chance to tell him that I wanted to be friends with him. It
bothered me like a toothache. I was becoming aware of the
same mood developing in me now. I was longing for a word
with Vasu. I stood like a child at the treadle, hoping he would
look at me and nod and that all would be well again. He was a
terrible specimen of human being no doubt, but I wanted to be
on talking terms with him. This was a complex mood. I couldn't
say that I liked him or approved of anything he said or did, but
I didn't want to be repulsed by him. My mind seethed with
plans as to how to re-establish cordiality. I was torn between
my desire to make a grand gesture, such as writing off his print
bill, and my inability to adopt it—as I didn't like the idea of
writing off anything. I liked to delude myself that I collected
my moneys strictly and never let anyone get away with it. So I
decided not to rake up the question of the bill with Vasu until
a smiling relationship could once again be established between
us and I could refer to the question in a humorous way.

While I was in this state of mental confusion, Sastri came up
with a new problem. There was a hyena at the foot of the stairs,
the sight of which upset him while he was composing the admission cards of Albert Mission High School. I was sitting at
my usual place when he parted the curtain and cried, "How can

I do any work with a wolf and a whatnot staring at me? And there's a python hanging down the handrail of the stairs."

"Sastri, I saw it; it is not a wolf but a hyena. Don't you think it surprising and interesting that we should have all this life around us in Malgudi? They are all from Mempi hills!"

The educational value of it was lost on Sastri. He simply said, "Maybe, but why should they be here? Can't you do something about it? It's repulsive and there is always a bad smell around—all my life I have tried to keep this press so clean!"

I could see that Sastri was greatly exercised. It was no use joking with him or trying to make him take a lighter view. I feared that he might take steps himself, if I showed indifference. He might call to Vasu through the grille that separated us and order him to be gone with the wolf. I didn't want Sastri to risk his life, so I said placatingly, "Sastri, you know the old proverb, that when your cloth is caught in the thorns of a bush, you have to extricate yourself gently and little by little, otherwise you will never take the cloth whole?"

Sastri, being an orthodox-minded Sanskrit semi-scholar, appreciated this sentiment and the phrases in which it was couched; he set it off with another profounder one in Sanskrit which said that to deal with a *rakshasa* one must possess the marksmanship of a hunter, the wit of a pundit, and the guile of a harlot. He quoted a verse to prove it.

"But the trouble is that the marksmanship is with him, not with us. Anyway, he'll soon deplete the forest of all its creatures, and then he will have to turn to a tame life, and our staircase will be clear again."

"He shows all the definitions of a *rakshasa*," persisted Sastri, and went on to define the make-up of a *rakshasa*, or a demoniac creature who possessed enormous strength, strange powers, and genius, but recognized no sort of restraints of man or God. He said, "Every *rakshasa* gets swollen with his ego. He thinks he is invincible, beyond every law. But sooner or later something or other will destroy him." He stood expatiating on the lives of various demons in *puranas* to prove his point. He displayed great versatility and knowledge. I found his talk enlightening, but still felt he might continue with the printing of the school admission cards, which were due to be delivered seventy-two hours hence; however, I had not the heart to remind him of sordid things.

He went on; his information was encyclopaedic. He removed his silver-rimmed spectacles and put them away in his shirt pocket as being an impediment to his discourse. "There was Ravana, the protagonist in *Ramayana,* who had ten heads and twenty arms, and enormous yogic and physical powers, and a boon from the gods that he could never be vanquished. The earth shook under his tyranny. Still he came to sad end. Or take Mahisha, the *asura* who meditated and acquired a boon of immortality and invincibility, and who had secured an especial favour that every drop of blood shed from his body should give rise to another demon in his own image and strength, and who nevertheless was destroyed. The Goddess with six arms, each bearing a different weapon, came riding for the fight on a lion which sucked every drop of blood drawn from the demon. Then there was Bhasmasura, who acquired a special boon that everything he touched should be scorched, while nothing could ever destroy him. He made humanity suffer. God Vishnu was incarnated as a dancer of great beauty, named Mohini, with whom the *asura* became infatuated. She promised to yield to him only if he imitated all the gestures and movements of her own dancing. At one point in the dance Mohini placed her palms on her head, and the demon followed this gesture in complete forgetfulness and was reduced to ashes that very second, the blighting touch becoming active on his own head. Every man can think that he is great and will live for ever, but no one can guess from which quarter his doom will come."

Vasu seemed to have induced in Sastri much philosophical thought. Before leaving, his parting anecdote was, "Or think of Daksha, for whom an end was prophesied through the bite of a snake, and he had built himself an island fortress to evade this fate, and yet in the end . . ." and so on and so forth, which was very encouraging for me too, as I felt that everything would pass and that my attic would be free. I hoped we would part on speaking terms, but Sastri did not think it necessary. I was glad he left me suddenly without asking me to throw out the hyena, having found a solution to his problem through his own research and talk. He vanished behind the curtain as he suddenly remembered that he had left the machine idle and that the ink on the plate was drying.

My aim now was to save the situation from becoming worse and gradually to come back to a hallo-saying stage with Vasu. I was glad I had warded off the danger emanating from Sastri, but this gratification was short-lived. Sastri himself seemed to take a detached, synoptic view of the hyena and other creatures on the other side of the grille. He got quite busy with the admission cards and left me alone, and I thought I had given a rest to the problem of Vasu and might some time be able to greet him. But it was not destined to be. One fine morning, the forester came to my press to ask if Vasu was still with me. I thought he had come to get his book of morals printed, and said, "I have not forgotten my promise, but just as soon as I am able to complete all the work . . ."

He didn't seem interested, but said, "All right, I am in no hurry about anything, but I am here on official work. Is Vasu still here? If he is I'd like to speak to him." A sudden doubt assailed me whether it would be safe to be involved in this. The forester might have come as a friend, or he might not. So I said dodgingly, "I'm not seeing much of Vasu nowadays, although he lives upstairs. He seems to be very busy nowadays . . ."

"With what?"

I became cautious. "I don't know, I see him coming and going. He has his own business."

"Has he? That's what I want to find out. Would you answer some questions?"

"No," I said point-blank. "I wish to have nothing to do with anything that concerns him."

"Rather strange!" he said. He had seemed such a timid moralistic man some months ago when he visited me. It was a surprise for me to find him adopting a tough tone. He continued,

"He is your tenant, as everybody knows, and he claims your friendship, and yet you disclaim all knowledge of him? Is it believable?"

"Yes. You should believe what I say. Won't you sit down and talk?"

"No, I'm spending Government hours now. I'm here on official duty, and they are certainly not paying me to lounge in your chair. I must get busy with what I came for." This thin cadaverous man, whose neck shot straight out of his khaki like a thin cylindrical water-pipe, was tough. He said, "Any man who violates the game laws is my enemy. I wouldn't hesitate to shoot him if I had a chance. A lot of game has been vanishing from our reserves and even tigers disappear from the blocks. Where do they go?"

"Perhaps to other forests for a change," I said.

He laughed. It was a good joke in his view. I hoped that humour would establish a bond between us.

"That shows your ignorance of wild life."

I felt relieved that he recognized my ignorance. That would certainly induce him to view me with greater toleration and absolve me from all responsibility for what Vasu was doing. He recovered his composure, as if he realized that he ought not to spoil me by smiling too much, and suddenly compressed his lips into a tight narrow line and became grim. He said, "Joking apart, I shall lose my job if I don't track down this mischief going on in the forests of Mempi. Somebody is busy with his gun."

"Can't you keep a watch?" I asked.

"Yes, but in a forest of hundreds of miles you can't watch every inch of ground, especially if the thief operates at night. Some of our guards are none too honest. We rely in some places on the jungle dwellers, and they are not wholly dependable. I must first have a talk with your tenant."

"He is not my tenant. I take no rent from him."

"Then he must be your friend." I recognized the pincer-movement in which this man was trying to trap me as all the others had done.

I said, "He is not even my friend. I never knew him before he came here." This sounded even worse—much better remain his friend or landlord than his business associate. I could see the cadaverous face hardening with suspicion.

He thought over the situation for a moment, and asked, "Why don't you help me?"

"In what way?"

"I want to get at this man who is destroying game. Can't you give me some clues?"

We had come around to the same starting point, and I said, "I wish to have nothing whatever to do with this business of yours. Leave me out of it. What makes you think I should have anything to do with it?"

"Since you are not his friend, why don't you help me?"

"I am not your friend either," I said.

It seemed silly to carry on a vague talk on friendship like this early in the day, while the Market Road traffic was flowing by and the treadle was rolling nicely on the admission cards. I said with an air of finality, "If you like to rest, come in and take a chair."

"Do I go through here to reach his room?"

"No, it's blocked this way. He has his own door . . ."

He stepped down without a word and went away. I could read his mind. He was now convinced that I was a joint owner of the poaching and stuffing factory. He went out with an expression that said when the time came he'd round up the gang.

I heard him go up the staircase and knock on the door. Vasu was unused to having visitors. He shouted from inside, "Who is it?"

I heard the other reply, "I wish to see you for a minute. Open the door, please."

"I asked who you are; what is your name?"

"I am Ramaswami. I want to see you."

"Ramaswami, whoever you may be, go down and wait near my jeep. I will be coming down in a short time."

"Why don't you let me in now?"

Vasu shouted from inside, "Don't stand there and argue. Get out and wait."

I heard the forester go down the stairs, pausing for a moment to study the hyena. Half an hour later, steps once again came tumbling down the stairs, and voices sounded from the yard where the jeep was parked. "So you are Ramaswami, are you? To what do I owe the honour of this visit?"

I had to follow all the conversation through the wall at my back and it filtered their exchanges into the lower octaves. I stood on a chair and opened a ventilator high up on the back wall in order to follow their conversation better. The cadaver was repeating his statement about the disappearance of game from Mempi Forest. All that Vasu said was, "Why not?" The other merely remarked, "Game in the sanctuaries is expected to be preserved."

"Of course it will be preserved if you get help from a taxidermist who knows his job," said Vasu jocularly.

The cadaver seemed a match for Vasu. "Well, we may not get the taxidermist's services, but the taxidermist himself."

By this time Vasu had climbed into his seat in the jeep, the forester standing beside it. What a contrast to the first day when he brought the forest official into my office and sat him down and flattered him as a noble writer!

"We will watch, and when we get at the man who is depleting the reserve, well, the law is pretty clear on that—"

"If your department needs my co-operation in any matter, don't hesitate to tell me," said Vasu with that crude cynicism he was capable of. The forester ignored it, but said, "How do you account for the hyena you have on the staircase?"

"The hyena came in search of me. I shot it right where you are standing now," he said.

"What about . . . ?"

"What about what? Nothing that's all. I am not bound to say anything."

"From which forest did you get them?"

"Not from your jungle. Go and look again and see if there is any trade-mark on them proving that they are from Mempi. India is a big country with many jungles, and you can get everything everywhere. For your information, I've also some tiger-skins. Are they yours? Claim them if you can. I am hungry, and am going out for breakfast. No time to waste. Don't bother me unless you come with some more practical proposition." He drove off unceremoniously. The forester stood where he was for a second and moved away.

Nothing happened for two days. I was in my usual chair one afternoon when Vasu's jeep pulled up at my door. My heart gave a thump. He sat in his jeep and said, "Nataraj, come here." I had an impulse to drop whatever I was doing, rush up to him and seize the chance to make friends with the monster again. But my pride was stronger. I suddenly resented all the trouble he had caused me. "Come and speak if you have anything to say." I was amazed at my own temerity.

He grinned, "Ah, you are showing some spirit after all, that's good."

I didn't like the paternal tone he adopted. I asked again, "What is your business with me? I'm rather busy."

"Yes, yes," he said mockingly. "I see it, and it's good to see a man do an honest job at his office instead of chatting away the time with friends who treat the place as a club lounge." This was a reference to my two friends who had come to see me after a long time. He went on shouting from his jeep, "I appreciate your guts, Nataraj. I had thought that you were rather spineless. I now know that you have a spine. I'd never have dreamt that you would set that ghost in khaki on me! You were smart to think it up. So that's your move; you want to know what I'll do next?"

"No, I'm not interested. I'm busy."

"You showed him the way to my room. He sees all the things there. What of it? Ask your friends to put a rubber-stamp on the backs of all the beasts in Mempi, so that he may identify them later and not make a fool of himself, and not make a fool of you either." He drove off.

Sen said, "I don't envy your luck in getting a man like that to live with."

I wondered what Vasu's menacing words might mean. Legally he had trapped me at the Rent Controller's court, and the adjournment lawyer was handling the case, every now and then tapping me for a five or ten, but I found that he was satisfied even if I gave him just a couple of rupees, and made no mention of the money he owed me for printing his daughter's wedding card. I thought Vasu had done his worst, but now what did he mean? I hoped he was not planning to abduct my son and hold him to ransom. He might be up to anything. That evening I told my wife, "If you have any urgent business to call me, wait till I come home. Don't send the little fellow across."

She grew nervous and asked, "Why?"

I just said, "I don't want him to come there and make a fuss, that's all."

"You see so little of him," she complained, and added, "You leave before he wakes, and come home after he is asleep, and if he wants to see his father he mustn't even come to the press, I suppose?" Then I had to explain and she grew really frightened.

She was in a panic. She kept the front door shut. She was completely demoralized if the boy did not come home at six. She behaved as if the monster would be unleashed and come rushing in to swallow up the family if the back door of my press was opened. My son seemed to enjoy the thrill of the situation as long as there was daylight. He spoke to his friends about the dangers that surrounded his life, and I saw batches of schoolboys standing around in knots in front of my press, looking up at the attic window during the afternoon recess at school. I became curious and beckoned to a couple of children to come in. "What are you all doing here?"

"Nothing," said one of them. "We are going home from school."

"What are you looking for?" I asked.

"Babu said there was, was . . . some giant here . . ."

"You want to look at him?" They nodded. "Better not. Go home, boys. There is no such creature here." I was anxious they should not see Vasu, as they might shout and circle round him and infuriate him. Knowing his attitude to children, I did not want to risk a meeting between them. One of them asked, slyly, "Is it true that he eats dogs?"

"Oh, no," I said immediately. "He eats rice and other stuff just as we do. That's all false."

"Then why did he shoot Ramu's dog?"

"Oh, that! It was shot by mistake. He was expecting a black

bear and had his gun ready, but at the same time this dog
came . . ."

"It was called Lily," said one boy. The other contradicted,
"No, it was Tom."

"No, it's Lily," persisted the first. "Yes, what'll you give me
if it is Lily? Shall we go and ask Ramu?"

"Yes, come on," and both ran off as if they were a couple of
birds that had alighted at the window and were flying off. Two
other children who were watching the scene also ran off happily shouting, "Let us ask Ramu."

My son came up with Ramu one afternoon two days later.
Ramu said, "My grandfather asked me to see you." My son
added, "He has come to ask for his dog." Several weeks had
gone by since I had promised the septuagenarian that I'd re-
place his grandson's dog. Although at that time it had seemed
a perfectly feasible thing to find another dog, as days passed it
began to look more and more difficult. I had promised in a moment of emotional stress, and now in the cold light of day it
appeared to me an unreal, impossible task. I did not know how
to acquire a puppy or where one was to be had. I had no doubt
mentioned some planter with a dog. I had had in mind Achappa,
a coffee planter on Mempi, for whose estates I used to do printing work at one time. I remembered his saying that he had a
Great Dane pair with nine puppies. Did I need one? That was
years ago. Achappa was not to be seen nowadays; occasionally
his manager was observed at my neighbour's press.

I walked across to the Star and said, "If you see anyone from
Consolidated Estates, please call me." He replied that it was
months since he had seen anyone from Consolidated Estates
and suspected that Achappa was getting his printing done at
Madras. So there it was. The dog-sources were drying up. I
needed some expert help in the matter. My sincerity was un-
questionable, but my resources were poor. I had no time either.
Every day the boy came to my press and said, "My grandfather
asked me to see you." And every day I gave him some reply and
sent him off. It was becoming a mechanical action. And the boy
went away satisfied with any answer I gave. My intentions
were absolutely honest, but the press work was heavy nowa-

days and I did not have a moment to spare. In addition to other
work Sen was giving me manifestoes to print and the poet was
fetching his cantos with greater speed. With one thing and another my time flew swiftly each day. I had to work hard and
make enough money at least to pay the lawyer whenever he
held his hand out for cash! I had not given up hopes of recover-
ing my dues from him, but I obeyed his advice not to mix up
accounts.

I had no time actually to go out and seek a dog for the boy,
but I had several plans in my head. I'd make a list of all my
friends with dogs, tabulate each breed, note down their breed-
ing time, make one of them promise to give one of the litter to
me, make a round of visits every Sunday afternoon, and finally
pick up a dog for the young fellow. My son asked me at nights
while he nestled close to me (when night advanced the fear of
the monster grew in him and he refused to sleep in a separate
bed), as if he were a sharer of my dream, "Get me a puppy too,
Father, when you get one for Ramu."

"Yes, yes," I said. "Why not?"

At the hyena's corner one day Sastri heard the jingling of bangles and turned to see a woman go down the steps and out of
the building. He had been at the machine. I was in the front office, and presently the curtain parted and he peeped in. A look
at his face and I knew something was wrong—some matter referring to Vasu. His face was slightly flushed and his spectacles
wobbled as he raised and lowered his brow. There was no need
for preambles and so I asked straightaway, "What is the latest?"

He swallowed once or twice before saying, "All sorts of low-
class women are wandering around this press nowadays . . ."

"Where? Who are they?"

He flourished his arms upward, and I knew he was indicating not the heavens, but Vasu. I did not like to pursue the subject because I had a couple of visitors waiting to discuss a
printing job. "Sastri, I will be with you in a moment . . ."

He took my hint and vanished into the wings. After persuad-
ing my would-be customers to patronize the original Heidelberg, I went in to conduct the research with Sastri. He was

printing the leaves of a bank ledger with a sullen face. I had never seen him so worried before. Even the first shock of finding a hyena beyond the grille had been nothing to what he seemed to face now. I stood beside him without a word except to sound bossy, "There is too much ink. Watch the inking."

He ignored my fussy advice and said, "If this sort of thing goes on, our reputation in the town will be ruined. I saw Rangi going downstairs. Is she the sort of person we should encourage here? Is this a printing press or what?"

"Who is Rangi?"

He looked desperate, shy, and angry. I was enjoying his discomfiture immensely.

"Oh, you are asking as if you didn't know!"

"How should you expect me to know anything of Rangi, Sastri? I have so much to do!"

"As if I had nothing else to do."

"I don't know anything about these people."

"Best thing under the circumstances . . . We should not have this kind of person seen in a place like this, that's all."

"I don't know what you are saying, Sastri. What is it all about?"

"That man has started bringing disreputable people here; where shall we be?"

I had no answer. Little by little I got it out of him. Rangi was a notorious character of the town. She lived in the shadows of Abu Lane. She was the daughter of Padma, an old dancer attached to the temple of God Krishna four streets off, our ancient temple. Padma herself had been an exemplary, traditional dedicated woman of the temple, who could sing and dance, and who also took one or two wealthy lovers; she was now old and retired. Her daughter was Rangi. Sastri darkly hinted that he knew who fathered her into this world, and I hoped it was not himself. His deep and comprehensive knowledge of the dancer's family was disconcerting. I had to ask him to explain how he managed to acquire so much information. He felt a little shy at first and then explained, "You see my house is in Abu Lane, and so we know what goes on. To be frank, I live in a portion of the house, the other half is occupied by Damodar, who has a wholesale grain shop in the market. For many years he was keeping Padma, and after this daughter was born he suspected Padma's fidelity and gave her up, but she threatened to go to court to prove that he was the father, and finally he had to accept the situation and pay her a lot of money to get out of her clutches. He used to be a chum in our schooldays and he would never conceal his exploits from me." Padma was now retired, being old, fat, and frightening like the harem guards of Ravana, and her daughter Rangi had succeeded her at the temple. Before that she had studied in a school for a while, joined a drama troupe which toured the villages, and come back to the town after seducing all the menfolk she had set eyes on. According to Sastri, she was the worst woman who had ever come back to Malgudi. She was a subject of constant reference in Abu Lane, and was responsible for a great deal of the politics there.

Next morning I was at the machine, after sending away Sastri to the binders to look to something. I heard the sound of bangles and there she was—Rangi, stepping between the hyena and the mongoose and making for the door. She was dark, squat, seductive, overloaded with jewellery; the flowers in her hair were crushed, and her clothes rumpled; she had big round arms and fat legs and wore a pink sari. She evidently didn't care how she looked now, this was her off-hour, and I could imagine no other woman who would be prepared to walk along the streets in this *déshabillé*. I felt curious to know what she would look like in the evenings—perhaps she would powder her face, the talcum floating uneasily over her ebonite skin. Anyway whatever might be the hour, every inch of her proclaimed her what she was—a perfect female animal. How did she get home? When did she come in? When did she go out? She went about her business with such assurance, walking in and out of a place like a postman. My mind seethed with speculations. Did Vasu bring her in his jeep at the darkest hour? Not likely. What a man he must be who could turn his mistress out in cold blood when morning came!

My further speculations on the theme of lust were cut short by the arrival of Sastri, who said, "The binder says that one of his office boys is down with mumps, and that he cannot do the ruling until Friday." He said this in a tone of utter fatalism.

"The sky is not going to fall because he holds it off till Friday," I said.

"Unless the ruling is done, the bank ledger won't be ready and they'll come down on us."

Why was Sastri always in a state of panic lest we should fail one or the other of our customers? He had no trust in my ability to manage things and no sort of confidence in me. I felt indignant. "No need for panic! I have run this press for how many years? I've managed to survive and flourish, and so far not made a fool of myself. So why do you worry?" I could not conclude my sentence. There was no conclusion to it as there was no basis at all for beginning it. My mind was busy following the fleshy image of Rangi and perhaps I resented the intrusion.

I was mistaken in thinking that Rangi was the only woman. I had only to stand there between seven and eight in the morning, and it became a sort of game to speculate who would be descending the stairs next. Sometimes a slim girl went by, sometimes a fair one, sometimes an in-between type, sometimes a fuzzy-haired woman, some morning a fashionable one who had taken the trouble to tidy herself up before coming out. Most times Rangi came along also with one or the other of them, or by herself. Brisk traffic passed on the staircase. I guessed that after the challenge from the cadaver, Mempi Forest was being watched more carefully, and, his activities there neutralized, Vasu had turned his tracking instinct in another direction. I had had no notion that our town possessed such a varied supply of women.

CHAPTER SEVEN

It took me time to make him out. His face was familiar. I had seen those slightly fin-like ears and round eyes somewhere. He stood on my threshold and brought his palms together and cried, *"Namaskaram."* On that voice, with its ring—I knew it. It was the afternoon hour. The Market Road was sleepy, a donkey was desultorily chewing an old newspaper at the fountain parapet, the black cow and its friend the free bull had curled up for a siesta right in the middle of the road, obstructing the traffic as was their wont. A couple of late schoolchildren were dawdling along the edge of the road, gazing with fascination into the gutter; a bright scalding sun was beating down; the woman sitting under the acacia selling a ripped-up jack fruit was waving a stick over its golden entrails, trying to keep off a swarm of flies; a *jutka* was rattling along on the granite metalled road; a sultry, sleepy hour. I had returned to my seat after lunch; Sastri had not yet arrived. My brain was at its lowest efficiency as I had to battle within myself to wrench myself away from a siesta. I had arrears of work to clear. I sat on the Queen Anne chair and stretched my legs on the ancient table as a compensation for forgoing my siesta.

"Come in, come in," I said as a general courtesy to whoever it might be that said *"Namaskaram."* He came in hesitantly, with an umbrella tucked under his arm, and lowered himself gingerly into the first chair.

"I came by the morning bus, not the one that brought you but the earlier one."

Oh, yes, now it came like a flash. "Oh, Muthu!" I cried, almost jumping up and hugging him. "Whom have you left to mind the tea-shop?"

"Oh, the boys are there, they can manage it. I am returning by tonight's bus."

"How is your business?"

"Doing very well, sir."

"How are your children? Have you found a bridegroom for your daughter?" His face fell at the mention of it. I would normally not really have troubled him with any reminder of his daughter's marriage, but in order to cover my initial lapse I now tried to show off my knowledge of his problems. I could not be blamed for my lapse. At his tea-shop he had been bareheaded; now he had donned a white khaddar cap, a long mull jibba and a dhoti, and had a lace upper cloth over his shoulder—he had dressed himself to come to town, I suppose. I was very happy to see him. He had rescued me from Vasu that day. I had always anticipated another meeting with him at least in order to pay off the tea bill. I opened the drawer of my table and took out a rupee and held it to him. I was suddenly inspired by the lesson taught by my adjournment lawyer not to mix accounts.

He looked at the rupee with some surprise and asked, "What is this for?"

"I have long wanted to pay you that bill for the tea and buns . . ." Even as I was speaking, I realized how silly it sounded. The lawyer had taught me a rather coarse lesson. Muthu looked rather hurt as he said, "I have paid a bus fare of fourteen annas for coming and will pay fourteen annas for going back; do you think I am spending all that in order to collect—how much was it?"

I was abashed, but said, "My duty, you know. Can I get you coffee or tiffin or anything?"

He shook his head. "I never eat anywhere outside, when I travel, and it keeps me fit. I like and enjoy a good meal when I go home."

Now that all the awkwardness was gone, I asked, "What's your command? Tell me what I can do for you." A sudden fear assailed me lest he should ask me to go up to tell Vasu that his old friend was come. I said to test him, "I saw Vasu go out in his jeep."

"We see him at Mempi going up the hill now and then, but he doesn't stop to speak to us nowadays."

I was pleased and relieved. "What is the reason?" I asked.

"Why go into all that?" he said gently, tapping his umbrella on the floor. "He is a man with a gun," he said. "Why speak of him? He doesn't care for us now."

"He may have no more use for you," I said, adding fuel to the fire.

"He has other people, who are more suitable to his temperament," he said, hinting at a vast army of undesirable men, trailing behind Vasu, looking for mischief.

I didn't want to pursue the subject further. I merely said, "He may drop them off when he finds someone more useful," a sentiment on which we both immediately concurred. "After all it may be for the best; it would be best to be forgotten by him and have nothing whatever to do with him," I said, and then I tried to elaborate the statement with an account of all the happenings ever since he stepped over my threshold. I said in conclusion, "He stood just where you stood; I welcomed him, he sat where you are sitting now. I make no distinction between men . . ."

Muthu sprang up as if he had occupied a wrong place, and said, "I am not that kind."

"I know, I know," I said. "Don't I know? You are a helpful man. You cannot see a man stranded. I know you."

He was pleased and said, "We helped that man so much. Now he thinks we have informed against him, and he came and created a scene at my shop and threatened us with his gun." He laughed at the memory of it. "As if we wouldn't know what to do, as if we would sit back and let him shoot us! We don't want to bother about him and so we leave him alone. He still passes up and down, but never stops for tea and doesn't seem to carry home much from the forests either—and he thinks we are responsible for it! Why, there are hundreds of people going up and down to the project on that road and anyone was bound to notice his activities."

"It's all for the best if a *rakshasa* ceases to notice you," I said and that put an end to our discussion of Vasu. I was very happy that he was no longer liked by Muthu. My enemy should be the enemy of other people too, according to age-old practice.

After all this preamble, he mentioned his business. "You remember our temple elephant I spoke to you about, though you couldn't see him that day? He had gone into the jungle for grazing? He's sick; and we want your help to see a doctor!"

Our doctor, Dr. Rao of Town Medical Stores, how would he react to the presence of an elephant in his clinic? I said doubtfully, "I don't know if our doctor knows enough about elephant-sickness."

"Oh, no," he said. "We have heard of a Government hospital for animals recently opened. We want your help to get our Kumar treated there."

I remained speechless—a new set of circumstances seemed to be approaching me in an enveloping movement. This was the first time I had heard of an animal hospital. I could have just said, "I don't know anything about it," and ended the matter there, but my nature would not permit it. I always had to get into complications. So I said, "All right, let us see what we can do for poor Kumar. What is the matter with him?"

"He is not taking his food at all, nowadays. He shuns it."

The enormity of the problem oppressed me. This was not something I could evade by suggesting that they looked over the Heidelberg. At the same time I felt flattered. That someone should think of me to tackle such a problem was itself an honour. I felt too proud to say that I knew nothing about elephant doctors; after all the man who had come all this way expected me to do something about it. Suppressing my astonishment at being involved, I asked, "Is there any hurry? I mean, can't the elephant wait?"

He looked doubtful. "I came to you because, more than others, I knew you would be able to do something for me. You were kind enough to say I could ask you for any help. Poor Kumar, he used to be so lively, playing with all the children and now, for the last ten days, he is suffering, he accepts no food; I don't know, something is wrong with him. There is a fellow there in Top Slip, an elephant trainer, who looks after some of the elephants working in the timber yards, but he says that he cannot really judge what is the matter."

"All right. I'll do my best. Now what are his symptoms? At least tell me that."

"Oh." He thought it over for a moment and said, "He seems to get cramps—he lies down on his belly and howls. Have you ever seen an elephant lie down? I have never seen it; he has to be coaxed and cajoled to accept a ball of cooked rice."

I felt genuinely concerned about poor Kumar now. I said, "I'll go and meet this doctor you mentioned, and we will see what we can do. How shall I communicate with you?"

"Please drop a card, or send a note with any of the Mempi bus drivers, and I'll be here immediately."

I noted down various details officiously. Before leaving he said, "Nothing is more important to me than this, sir."

I had to overlook the responsibilities on hand. Kumar's welfare became an all-important issue. The visiting cards that I was printing could wait, but not Kumar.

Later in the day I asked Sastri, "Where is the animal hospital that was recently opened?"

"No idea," he said. "Lost interest in animals five years ago; after the death of my cow I vowed never to have another. I'm the first person in our whole family to buy milk from street vendors! My relations laugh at me for it."

I inquired here and there. Two days were gone. I had the feeling of being a defaulter. As each hour and day passed I grew nervous and finally on the flash of an idea sought my friend Sen, who lived all alone in a converted garage in the compound of a house in Lawley Extension. I had to hire a cycle for this expedition. Sen was pleased to see me in his shed. He had surrounded himself with books and stacks of newspapers, which were all over the floor. He sat on a rush mat and worked by a small kerosene light.

I burst in on him at about seven in the evening. He had a sloping board on which was fixed a sheet of paper for writing. It had been a warm day, and he sat bare-bodied. He was delighted to see me. I sat on his mat.

"I can't give you coffee or anything, but, if you like, let us go to a restaurant. There is one not too far off." He was visibly overwhelmed by my visit. He was used to visiting, but this was one of the rare occasions when he was receiving.

I said, "I don't need coffee, thank you. I have come for some information; as a newspaper man, you'll be able to help me." He liked to be called a newspaper man, and I hoped sincerely that some day he would see his views in print. He was always saying that he was about to secure the finances for a paper, he was on the verge of it, but something always happened, and he sat back, wrote his editorials and waited for the next financier. He was equipping himself for the task all the time. Part of his equipment was knowing what was going on in the town. I asked him about the animal hospital.

"Oh, yes, I remember something about it . . ." He frowned for a moment at all the accumulation of the past, got up, pulled down some stacks of old papers, turned them over, blowing the dust in my face. He thrust an old newspaper under my nose and tapped his finger on a news item. It gave a description of how a Deputy Minister had laid the foundation for a veterinary college and animal welfare hospital on the other bank of the Sarayu, for which ten acres of land had been gifted by the municipality; some foundation had given dollars and equipment for a start, and the Government had promised to take the hospital under its wing during the third Five-Year Plan and so on and so forth. A lengthy speech was reported in which the Deputy Minister dwelt on the importance of *ahimsa* and of animals in human economy, after which he was garlanded and made to tread the red carpet. I wondered how I had missed it.

"Do you know how you missed it?" Sen said. "They mismanaged the whole thing. The printed invitations went out late and reached most people a day too late."

"I wonder where they got them printed," I said to ward off any suspicion that I might be responsible for the mess.

"The result was that no one turned up at the function except the organizers and the Deputy Minister—and he was furious. They had a platform, decorations, and an elaborate tea, but only a handful of audience; the Deputy Minister made his speech all the same. It looks dignified and impressive in print anyway," he said fondly, looking at the printed column. "However, the doctor is already on the scene, although little else is ready."

Next afternoon I went in search of the animal doctor, crossing Nallappa's Grove on my cycle. It was about one o'clock and the sands were hot. A few bullock carts were crunching their wheels along the sand. The mango-trees cast a soft shade and the air was thick with the scent of mango blooms. The river flowed on with a soft swish. It was so restful that I could have set my bicycle against the trunk of a tree and gone to sleep on the mud under the shade of a tree. But duty impelled me on. I cycled up the other bank across a foot-track, and suddenly came upon a bare field enclosed within barbed wire. The gate was barricaded with a couple of bamboo poles. A tablet on a bit of masonry commemorated the laying of the foundation. The south side of the barbed wire enclosure was bounded by one wall of the cremation ground, where a couple of funeral parties were busy around smoky pyres. A howling wind blew across the fields. There was a single palmyra-tree standing up in the middle of this desert, although across the road, tops of green corn rippled in the air.

A signboard stood over the entrance. I left my bicycle at the gate and walked around to read, "Department of Animal Welfare, World Q.R.L. (World Quadruped Relief League, Calif.)." I saw the roof of a hut shining in the sky and sent a shout in that direction, "Hi! Who is there?" I was enjoying the hunt. I shouted without any hope, expecting the Mempi hills shimmering on the horizon to echo back my call without an interruption. But "Who is there?" a voice called back from the hut.

"I have come for the doctor," I said.

It seemed absurd to be calling for a doctor out of empty space, but it worked. A man appeared at the door of the hut and gesticulated. He cried, "Come along!"

"The gate is barred," I cried.

"Come through the fence," he called. I slipped through the fence, the barbed wire slightly gashing my forearm and tearing my dhoti. I swore at it, but it gave me a feeling of shedding my blood for a worthy cause.

The man stretched his hand. "I'm Dr. Joshi."

"My name is Nataraj," I said, as the wind howled about my ears.

Dr. Joshi wore a shirt over white pants; he was a short man, with a small face and a brow knit in thought. "Come in," he said, and took me into the hut. A tin roof arched overhead; he had a bamboo table and a couple of folding chairs, a charpoy with a pillow, a few books in a small wooden rack, a kerosene lamp and a stove and pots and pans in a corner. Here definitely was a man with a mission. He seated me in a chair and drew the other close to me and said, "Yes, Mr. Nataraj? What can I do for you, Mr. Nataraj?"

I looked around; there was very little of the hospital or dispensary or college about it. I told him about the elephant. He listened to me with the characteristic patience of a doctor and said, "H'm, I would like to have it under observation and then I'll see what we can do."

I had not visualized this prospect. I had thought that he would come over and examine the elephant. I suggested it. He said, "It's impossible. The equipment for tests is here."

"He is sick and keeps throwing himself down. How can we bring him so far?"

The problem looked frightening, but he had an absolutely simplified view. He brushed aside all my doubts and said, "He has his mahout, hasn't he? Tell him that he must come here and prod him and prick him and make him walk. Animals, once they realize the pleasure of sitting, will always sit down," he added. "It doesn't mean anything. It'll be our business to prod him and keep him on his feet. Unless I have him here, I shall have no means of handling him or testing him. You see there . . ." He walked over to a chest and threw it open—it was crammed with all kinds of shining instruments, tubes, bottles, and a microscope. "This is the standard equipment that our League ships to every centre; it contains everything that a veterinarian can need, but you see, we are doing very little with it now."

"Why so?" I asked.

"Our League provides equipment and a basic grant for a

doctor like me, but the local organizations also have to do their bit. For instance the college and the hospital must be built before we can do anything."

"When do you expect it all to be ready?"

"How can we say? The question is full of politics. People do not want it here, but somewhere else. Our Deputy Minister has no interest in the project and so it goes on at its own pace. The Public Works should give us the building and the sheds for the animals, but they are still in the stage of estimates and sanctions. I really cannot imagine when we shall start or what we can do. I alone am ready, because I'm being maintained by the League and there's a lot of equipment to guard. As matters stand, I'm just a watchman. I'm sticking on because I feel that if I leave even this will be gone. I have a hope that things will be O.K. some time. I'm not allowing things to rust, you know. All the time I'm bombarding the headquarters with letters and so forth . . . I'm happy that you have heard about us and want our service."

"It was in the papers," I said knowledgeably.

"Bring your elephant over. I'll do what I can for the poor creature. I have always wanted to try my hand at an elephant."

"What could be wrong with him?"

"Well, anything. Colic, or an intestinal twist, or he might have swallowed a sugar cane without chewing it and that sometimes causes trouble."

"Do you know all about all animals?"

"Oh, yes, about most of them. Our League headquarters in California has one of the biggest collections of animals in the world and I went through a four-year course. Although our main job will be to treat the cattle of our country, we like to do our best for any creature. Most animals and men are alike, only the dosage of a medicine differs," he said. He was a man completely serious, living in a world of animals and their ailments and diseases.

At Mempi the affair caused a sensation. The village elders gathered together in front of the tea-shop and a great debate started over the question of the elephant. Muthu was all for bringing the elephant over. After carrying on their discussion in front of the tea-shop, everybody trooped to the little temple. Lorries and cars passed by. I marched with them to the little shrine at the cross-roads; the four-armed Goddess watched our proceedings serenely from her inner sanctum. Within the yard of the temple the elephant was tied by his hind leg to a peg under a very large tree. He had flopped himself down like a dog, with his legs stretched out. His trunk lay limp on the ground; his small eyes looked at us without interest; his tail lay in the dust; his tusks seemed without lustre. Muthu patted his head and said, "He has been like this for three days now." He looked unhappy. A few boys stood outside the ring of elders and watched the elephant, and commented among themselves in whispers.

Everyone looked at me sourly as a man who had come to abduct their elephant and make things worse for them. I said, "If you do not send the elephant along, what is the alternative?"

"Bring the doctor here," said the tailor, who kept his machine next to the tea-shop and who was one of the trustees of the temple. There was a schoolmaster in their gathering who was not sure what he wanted to say but kept interrupting everyone with his reminiscences. "There was once," he began, "an elephant," and he narrated a story which was considered rather inauspicious as by the end of it the elephant had become incurably ill. "Oh, master!" appealed Muthu. "Should I teach a wise one like you what to speak and when, and what not to speak?" He looked sadly at the teacher.

I began afresh to outline the whole proposition by stages. "Our main business will now be to see that the elephant Kumar gets well." This was the only part of my statement which received universal and immediate accord. "And so," I began, "what is most important is that we should see that he gets on to his feet and moves freely." It was the same sentiment in another form; they hesitated for a moment, examined it critically, and accepted it also as one without a trap. Now I mentioned something really dangerous. "And so he should be made to get up and move in the direction of the doctor."

"No," said the obstinate tailor. "The doctor must come here.

Have you no pity? How can a sick animal tramp fifty miles? It'd be cruel." For a moment, everyone made noises of sympathy for the tailor. This brought the question back to its starting point. The tailor had won his point; he looked triumphantly obstinate, and moved away.

I felt desperate among an immobile elephant, an equally immobile doctor and a mentally immobile committee; there seemed little to do except pray for the elephant. I realized that in a committee there was likely to be no progress, and so I didn't press the point. I knew that the tailor would not go on standing there for ever; sooner or later someone would come to his shop and demand his clothes back. So Muthu and I spent the time morosely watching the recumbent elephant, suppressing the suggestions which occurred to our minds, but which we knew would be thrown out in no time. The ring of children grew smaller as they had grown bored with watching the gloomy elders and had exhausted themselves in suppressed giggles (for fear of the elders who were constantly turning to them and ordering them to shut up). There were really five on the committee of the temple, but except Muthu and the tailor the rest were men of no consequence. All they did was to simper and evade any commitment.

I had not too much time to waste today; I had come by the first bus in the morning and the last bus was leaving at six. At four o'clock there was still no sign of an agreement. I was still hoping that the tailor would be called off; and as if some customer of his had been hit by a thought-wave from me, an errand boy from the shop came up panting with the statement, "The trouble-maker is back, and won't go until he can talk to you."

The tailor lost his head at the mention of the trouble-maker, whoever that beneficent soul may have been. "Has he no other business than bothering me for those miserable jackets of his wife's? This is the fifth time he has visited me!"

"Perhaps his wife has barred the house to him until he brings home the jacket," I commented under my breath.

"Throw his pieces out. Fling his pieces in his face," cried the irate tailor.

"But you have locked them up," said his errand boy seriously.

"That settles it. I'll be back soon," the tailor said and rushed out in a rage. I felt relieved, lighter in my chest. This was my chance. Now I had the committee in my pocket. I told Muthu hurriedly, "Before my bus leaves, I must see this elephant on his feet. We will discuss the other things later."

"But how to get him up? Kumar," he appealed, "please, please stand up!"

One of the stragglers, a young urchin who had been watching us with a thumb in his mouth, took out his thumb and said suddenly, "I know how to make an elephant get up."

"How? How? Come on, do it!" I said eagerly, pulling his hand from his mouth and propelling him forward.

He grinned, showing a toothless gum, and said: "If you get me a frog, I can make him get up."

"What! How will you do it?"

"When a frog is put under an elephant, it'll jump, and the elephant will jump with it," he said.

I was even prepared to dig a crowbar under Kumar and lever him up if necessary, but a mahout arrived at the crucial moment. He was attached to the timber yard five miles up in a mountain jungle. They had sent a desperate summons to him four days ago by a lorry-driver who passed that way, and only today had the man found time to turn up. He arrived just when we were hesitating between applying a jumping frog or a crowbar, wanting to do something before the tailor should return. The mahout wore a knitted vest and over it a red sweater and a white dhoti coming down to his knees, a combination calculated to strike terror into the heart of any recalcitrant elephant. He pushed his way through the ring of watching loungers, and looked us all up and down questioningly. "Why is he lying down?" he asked.

"That is what we would like to know," said Muthu. "He has been like this for four days." The mahout looked at Kumar questioningly, put his face close to the elephant's and asked, "What is your secret?" in a soft murmur. He told us, "Keep away. He doesn't like a big audience for his speech, you understand? Move off, and he will tell me." We moved away. He put his face close to the large trunk of the elephant, murmuring something, and after a while we turned to look as we heard a swish proceeding from a very thin green switch in his hand, which lashed the underside of the elephant within his reach. He repeated it at intervals of a second and the elephant was on his feet. He flourished the green switch (it looked no different from any trailer of a plant), and said, "This is . . . ," he gave us the name of some obscure plant grown in mountain thickets. "This is more serviceable than one's own brothers emanating from the same womb," he explained. "I have still to see an animal that does not respect this stick." As he flourished it the elephant blinked and gave a loud trumpet. I only hoped that it would not bring the tailor scrambling in. The trumpeting was loud and prolonged.

The mahout leaned on the side of the elephant as if posing for a photograph and smiled at the gathering. He seemed to fall into a mystic trance as he drew the switch across his nose. "Now get me a broken coconut and a little jaggery and a piece of sugar cane."

We sent a youngster running to fetch these. While waiting for his return, the mahout leaned on the elephant and regaled us with his memoirs; he recounted the tales of all the elephants that he had coaxed and taken to the various zoos in the country and he spoke of a chance that he once had of taking an elephant to Tokyo or New York, which was frustrated by his brothers who did not like the girl he had married and wanted to punish him for not marrying according to their own arrangements. From Kerala, far-off Kerala, this mahout had brought a girl to marry, but his brothers advised him to pay off the woman and raised among themselves two hundred rupees. The mahout went up to her with the money and asked her to go back to Kerala. She quietly said, "Keep your money, only tell me if there is any deep well or tank near by where I can drown myself. I want you to know that I have come to you not for your money. If I can't be worthy of being your wife, I shall be quite happy to be dead at your feet, rather than go back to my village with two hundred rupees." He explained, "Two hundred rupees, not just two rupees, and she did not want it. I immediately told my brothers that I did not care for them, told them to do their worst and married the girl. You think that I married her on the money from them? Not me. I returned it to them. I actually threw it out of the door and told them to pick it up, and borrowed a hundred rupees on which I am still paying interest of five rupees a month, and married her. Such a wonderful woman. She won't eat her food unless I am back home, even if it is midnight. What can I do? Sometimes I have to be out for days and days, and what does she do? She starves, that is all," he said, and added, "A dutiful wife."

He never finished his narrative to tell us how it prevented his going to Tokyo or New York, for at this moment the elephant coiled his trunk around his back, and he patted it and said, "Now we are friends, he wants me to sit on his back." He tapped the elephant's knee, and took hold of its ear, and pulled himself up even as he was talking. By this time the youngster had brought the coconut and jaggery. The mahout stooped down to take them, and held them out to the elephant, saying something. The elephant just picked up the bamboo tray, raised it and sent it flying across the field. Muthu was crestfallen, "See, that's what he does to food!"

"Never mind," said the mahout. "He is not hungry, that is all. I would myself fling the dinner plate at my wife's face if I did not feel hungry and she persisted. Now I am ready, where is he to go?"

"Ride him to the town," I said promptly. "I will meet you at the toll-gate outside the city." And before we knew what was happening, he had flourished his green switch and was off, all of us trooping along behind. All the children let out a shout of joy and ran behind the elephant. I was not very happy about the amount of public notice the whole business was receiving. It might stir the tailor up once again. Muthu walked with a look of triumph beside the elephant. I felt triumphant too in a measure.

To put our ideas in proper perspective the mahout leaned down to say, "Because he is trotting don't imagine he is not ill. He is very sick. I have my own medicine for his sickness, but you want to see an English doctor; try him and come back to me. I never stand in anybody's way of doing something, although I know what English doctors can do. They will sooner or later call me . . ."

This made Muthu once again thoughtful. He suddenly remembered that he had come out without thanking the goddess. He ran back to the temple, lit a piece of camphor before the Goddess and rejoined the procession. At the Market Road, when the procession passed in front of the tea-shop, he invited the mahout to stop for a moment, and ran into his shop.

The mahout said, "If you can, reach me a glass of tea here, otherwise I can't get down. If I get down, Kumar will also sit down immediately, that is his nature." Kumar seemed to understand this, I could detect a twinkle in his small red eyes, and he swayed his head in appreciation. Muthu brought out a tray covered with buns and a tumbler of tea, and held it to the mahout. The flies that swarmed in his shop sought a diversion by settling in a mass on the back of the elephant for a ride. The mahout sat comfortably in his seat, set the tray before him and started to drink his tea. And now the tailor came flouncing out of his shop, demanding, "Everyone get out of the way and tell me what is happening."

The mahout thought the remark beneath his notice and looked down from his eminence with indifference. This irritated the tailor. He repeated, "This is our elephant. Where are you taking him?" The tailor's sense of ownership was comical, and everyone laughed. Muthu, who had gone back to his seat at the counter, now said, "He knows how to handle the elephant, don't worry. He is taking it out for its own good."

"What? To the city? I will never have it, never, never . . ." He stamped his feet like a petulant child.

The mahout was confused. He looked puzzled and asked, tying a towel around his head as a turban, "What does it mean? Am I stealing an elephant?"

Muthu came out of his shop, put his arm around the tailor, and said, "Come and have tea," and managed to say at the same time to the mahout, "Yes, yes, you go, it is getting late, remember where you will be met . . . We will look to other things."

The mahout flourished his green switch ever so gently and the elephant was on the move again, with the trail of children behind it. Soon his green turban vanished from the landscape around a bend.

The tailor was disconsolate until Muthu poured oblatory tea into him, unwashed glass after unwashed glass. "At this rate," I said to myself, "Muthu will be a bankrupt, if he has to treat all his elephant associates to tea. He will close down his business, and then who will pay for the elephant doctor at the other end?"

I sat on the plank bridging two empty kerosene tins in front of Muthu's shop, watching the scene with detachment. Now that the elephant was gone, a big worry was off my mind. I didn't care what the tailor thought or said. Refreshed by tea and buns, he came out of the shop, wiping his mouth with the sleeve of his shirt, and passed me without a word. But his look, the brief one that he cast in my direction, was enough to indicate what he thought of me—an abductor of elephants. He was soon out of view in his own shop four doors off. I could hear him say to someone, "Take away those pieces if you cannot wait. I promised you the jackets only at the end of this week."

I could not hear the rest of his sentence as the dreaded jeep drew up in front of me on the road. Vasu had come down the hill. He looked at me from his seat and said, "Coming along? I am going back to the town."

I hesitated for a moment. The bus had been due any time the last ninety minutes. Still there was no sign of it. But how could I go with this man? We were facing each other for the first time after months. I didn't like to tell him about myself or my mission here. I would be at his mercy if I climbed into his jeep. I said, "I am not coming back yet."

"Why not?" he asked persistently. "What do you want here? You want to spend the night here?"

He was blocking the road; a lorry was trying to pass, the driver sounding his horn impatiently. Vasu merely waved his arm, "You have enough clearance, get along."

"There is a ditch."

"All right, get into the ditch. Don't disturb me now. Don't you see that I am talking to a gentleman?"

The lorry-driver edged close to the drain and passed. Vasu said to me, "I will take you back home."

"You may go," I said.

He indicated the back seat. "I have nothing there today. I knew that you would swoon at the sight of a dead creature. That is why I came without any today."

How did he know my movements? Perhaps he had been watching me all the time. In any case I did not like to talk to him about it. I merely said, "I have another conveyance. You may go, thank you."

"What other conveyance?" he persisted. "Your bus has broken down at the tenth mile up, axle gone. Men, women and children are sitting by the roadside. They will have to be there until . . . I don't know. If anyone has a gun there he may shoot a tiger or a rogue elephant that may prowl around tonight. If you are keen on catching the bus, I will take you there and leave you with that crowd."

I wondered for a moment if there might be truth in his report. As I hesitated he commanded, "What are you waiting for? If you want to spend the night with that tea-shop crowd, go ahead, please yourself. I have things to do, if you don't mind," he said cynically.

He had irritated me at first, but I suddenly realized that this was a good chance to establish contact with him again. He spurned me and picked me up again as it suited his fancy: this was a galling thought no doubt, but it was better than being continuously ignored. So I climbed into the jeep without a word. He drove off. We remained without speaking for some time; he drove at his usual reckless speed, swearing at bullock carts, threatening to smash them up and calling insults at passers-by. He was disappointed when they accepted his bullying unprotestingly, but when one or other of the cartmen turned round with a frown or a swear-word, he was delighted, and he nudged me and confided, "That is how I like to see my countrymen. They must show better spirit; they are spineless; no wonder our country has been a prey to every invader who passed this way."

I could not accept his view, and so I asked, "Do you want everyone to be a blustering bully in this country?"

"Yes," he said simply. He was in an extraordinarily good humour. I wished he would continue thus. It was becoming dark and the lights were on in the homesteads on the way. He said, "How busy are you nowadays?"

"Well, the usual quantity of work."

"And the usual quantity of gossip-mongering?"

"What do you mean?" I asked rather sharply.

"No offence, no offence," he said with mock humility. "Just my fun, that is all. I meant those chair fixtures in your press."

"Why can't you leave them alone?" I asked. "They hardly ever think of you; why should you bother about them?"

"No offence meant, no offence meant," he said with a great display of humility. "I just wanted to know. I am their well-wisher, and I just wanted to know how they are faring, that is all."

"Look here, Vasu," I said, with a sudden access of foolhardiness, "you should leave others alone; it will make for happiness all round."

"I can't agree with you," he said. "We are not lone dwellers in the Sahara to live self-centred lives. We are members of a society, and there is no point in living like a recluse, shutting oneself away from all the people around."

There was no use arguing with him. I once again became aware of my mounting irritation and wanted to guard against it. I said, moderating my tone, "After all the poet has done a remarkable performance with his life of Krishna. He is completing *Radha Kalyan,* that is the marriage of Krishna with Radha, and his book will be out soon."

"H'm," Vasu said with a half-interest, "and what about the other?" He was referring to his favourite target, the journalist.

"Well," I said, with considerable pride, "his plans are almost ready for starting a small news-sheet in this town; he is already issuing printed manifestoes."

He remained thoughtful for a moment and said, "I like people to do something, whatever it may be."

So the journalist and poet had secured this man's approval, I reflected. I wanted to tell him, but could not, that it was impertinence on his part to think that the world waited for his approval. He was pleased to think that humanity could move only after securing a clearance certificate from him. There was no use arguing with him as he was one of those strong men who had no doubt at all about their own conclusions. He asked suddenly, "I want to know if you are willing to print a book I am writing. I have been busy with it for some weeks now."

"Aha!" I cried unable to restrain myself. It was unthinkable that he could be busy with a literary composition. He brightened up on hearing my interest and said, "It is a monograph on wild life. Every day our papers are full of speeches and meetings on the problem of preserving wild life, and most people don't know what they are talking about. I have some very important points to make on the subject. What has happened in this country is that amateurs have invaded every field. People just talk their heads off. I have made many important points in my book, and I want it to be ready for the conference on wild life at the end of this year."

"But that conference will be for the preservation of wild life?" I asked.

"What if it is? My book is also about better methods of preserving wild life. This cannot be achieved by refusing game licences to honest folk, or by running behind animals with cries of sympathy."

I restrained my interest. I did not want to get involved in his affairs again. I dreaded the prospect of having him again in my parlour, sharpening his wits against the poet and my other visitors. I maintained my reserve and silence for the rest of the journey as the jeep sped along the dark highway.

CHAPTER EIGHT

The poet was in a grand exalted mood. He had completed the portion of his poem where Krishna meets his future wife Radha, and their marriage is to be celebrated. He had written several hundred lines of crystal-clear monosyllables; he had evolved his own prosody and had succeeded. His manuscript was ready, several little exercise books stitched by himself and wrapped in brown paper, closely filled with writing in green ink. He had written till late on the previous night. His eyes were red with sleeplessness, but his face glowed with triumph. With the marriage, the book would make about ninety-six pages. Sastri had printed the book at the rate of four pages a month over a space of countless months and it had now assumed the shape of a volume. Sastri himself was excited at the completion of the volume with the marriage episode. He brought in the proofs of some pages, and hesitated for a moment. When Sastri stood thus I always knew he had something to say, and I hoped that if I did not turn round and meet his eyes he would be gone. As I bent over my paper, I was aware of his shadow behind me. "What is it, Sastri?" I asked sharply. He looked at the poet and both of them smiled. So I knew it was a good piece of news, and felt relieved. "When a poet has arrived at the stage of the marriage of a god, it would be auspicious to celebrate the occasion." He went on to explain how the celebration was to be conducted. I was fond of the poet and anything that was going to give him a place in our society was welcome to me.

Enormous preparations began. Once again, my normal work of composing and printing was pushed to the background. The fruit-juice man had prospered more than ever and wanted four

thousand more of the three-colour labels, but I was not prepared to give him his labels yet. I had only time to print the first
basic grey. I put it away to dry and said so every time the messenger came from Fruit Juice. Let him try and print it elsewhere
and I should not object. But where would he get the magenta,
that thirst-creating shade which drew people in a rush to wherever his bottles were displayed? The sixth time when I turned
back the boy, K.J. himself came thundering in, and shouted at
Sastri beyond the curtain. He did not know I was also there,
helping Sastri to compose an appeal for our celebrations, for
which we needed funds. We were also in conference with an astrologer in the composing room. We did not want to be disturbed. There now hung a thickly-woven bamboo mat which
screened us off from whatever might be on the other side of the
grille. Vasu might have all the dead animals in creation on the
other side, but it was not going to affect us. All the prostitutes
in the town might be marching up and down the steps, but that
was not going to distract either me or Sastri. We could hear
footsteps moving, but that didn't distract our attention. We
went on with our jobs, although if I felt too curious I could always peer through a pin-hole in the bamboo curtain and get a
lovely circular vision of a hyena's snout or the legs of some
woman or the hefty feet of Vasu himself stumping upstairs. But
it was a luxury I permitted myself only under very special or
extraordinary conditions, never when Sastri was around, as I
did not want him to get into the habit. I don't think he even
knew of the existence of the peep-hole.

The astrologer was sitting on the floor beside the treadle. He
had a page of an almanac open before him, held far away at
arm's length for better focus, and was explaining, "On the full
moon, the moon is in the sixth house, which is the best place
we can have for the moon, and the presiding star that day is . . . ,
which means—," he shrunk his eyes to catch the figure in the
column and muttered, "I've left my glasses at home," whereupon Sastri took his own glasses off his nose and handed them
to him. He put them on and said, "You see this here . . . What's
the number?" It was now Sastri's turn to snatch the almanac
from the other man's hand and hold it at arm's length. Still not

being able to see, he held his hand out for the glasses, which the other removed from his nose and handed back. Now Sastri saw the number and said something, and the other, wanting to verify it, held his hand out and thus they bandied Sastri's silver-rimmed glasses back and forth. The conference proceeded on these lines—I'd not much to do, a veritable ignoramus among the stars. The idea was to fix a day suitable to the poet, also coinciding with the spring festival at the Krishna temple.

A loud voice called through the curtain, "Sastri!" I was offended by the commanding tone. I signalled to Sastri to find out who it was, but before Sastri could take a step forward the voice continued, "Are you delivering the labels or not? If you can't, say so, instead of making our boy run to you a dozen times." Now I knew who it was. He went on in a big way cataloguing his grievances, our lapses, and threatening us with dire consequences. Sastri and the astrologer looked intimidated. I could notice on Sastri's face a slight satisfaction too at the realization that I had not heeded his warning.

It was time for me to show myself. I said, "Who is it? Is it K.J.?"

There was a pause and the man said from the other side of the curtain, "Mr. Nataraj, you are letting me down. How can you expect us to deliver our bottles when . . ."

I could have spoken for him. I knew all his points. So I cut him short with, "Why don't you take a seat, my friend? I'll be with you in a minute." I had hesitated for a moment whether I should tell him to come through the curtain as a special gesture, but abandoned the idea for fear it might create a bad precedent. People respected the curtain, and it was better so. Vasu alone had pierced its privacy and this had turned out to be a nuisance in every way. I did not want it to happen again, and so I said to the angry fruit-juice seller, "Sit down comfortably in that big chair, and I'll join you in a moment."

He made no reply. A silence ensued and I heard the movement of a chair and guessed he must have acted on my advice in a mood of sullen compliance. I allowed him to wait, giving him time to cool off. We resumed our conference with the astrologer, who sat carrying on his investigation among the planets, unruffled by the happenings round him. After half an hour's silent calculations, with Sastri's spectacles perched over his nose, the man lifted his head slightly but would not yet speak. He behaved like one still in a trance. I knew that the man in the other room was impatient. He was kicking the floor and clearing his throat in order to attract my attention. I felt satisfied that I had cowed him. The astrologer sat beside the treadle and still said nothing. Sastri stood respectfully looking down at him. I asked, "What are we waiting for?" The astrologer merely looked up. The visitor in the other room again cleared his throat. Sastri said, "He may take another fifteen minutes." I thought it would be best to dispose of the visitor. I passed through the curtain.

The drink-seller sat cross-legged in the Queen Anne chair, his sandals abandoned on the floor under the chair. He was an old-type orthodox, who wore a red caste-mark on his forehead. It was clear that he was there to see this thing through and to have it out with me. Initiative was half the victory in a battle, and so before he could open his mouth I remarked, wearing a look of grievance, "What's the use of my friends losing their temper here? I never delay anyone's business without a reason."

"What's it this time?" K.J. asked cynically, and added, "Blocks not ready? Ink not available? That's why I made sure of sending with my order that can of ink which I got from Madras."

"And your can of ink is perfectly safe here," I said, producing it out of my drawer. I turned the can in my hand, scrutinized the label and gave it to him. "This is unsuitable. If I had used it, people would have run away from your bottles. Do you know what it looks like when it dries? It assumes the pink of an old paper kite picked out of a gutter."

"I got it from Madras, the same brand as you suggested."

"But I use only the imported variety. This is canned in Delhi, did you know that?"

This was good, as it made K.J. look so ignorant, wrong, and presumptuous that he remained dumb. I said, "I wouldn't use stuff like this on your work even if you forced me at the point of a gun. I have my responsibility."

He asked like a child, "So what shall we do about it now?"

"Well, I won't let you down, an old valued customer. If you have trust in me, I'll never let you down," I said as if I were a god speaking to a sinner. "Sastri!" I shouted. "Please bring that magenta ink." Turning to K.J. I said, "You can see the difference for yourself . . ."

There was some vague movement of response inside the curtain. I knew Sastri would not pay any attention to my call unless I called him again. K.J. grew interested and asked, "Is Sastri in?"

"Why?" I asked.

"He never answered, although I called him."

"He is a very busy man," I said. "He carries a hundred things in his head."

"Except my work, I suppose," K.J. said with a sort of grim humour.

"Don't blame him. He has a hundred different things to do."

"May I know the nature of his hundred activities?"

I could easily have snubbed him, but I said quietly, "A poet is going to be launched on the world soon, and he is busy with the arrangements connected with it." I realized that in the last resort truth was more convincing and effective than any fabricated excuse.

K.J. looked stunned on hearing it, and asked, "Does it mean that nothing has been done about our labels?"

"Yes," I said, "the main reason being that we could not use your ink and had to wait for our usual brand. The other reason was that this poet's business came up suddenly. We are in search of a good day for the function; as soon as the date is settled, we'll approach you. It's a good cause for which everyone should do his best."

"How? How? What do you expect me to do? Give money?"

"Yes, that'd be best, but we leave it to you. The only thing is that a good man like you must share the honour with us in doing this noble task; in what way, we leave it to you."

He was afraid to ask further questions for fear of involvement, but still he was curious to know. "How am I concerned? What do you want me to do?" he asked.

I could see that he was scared. He was not one who gave a

donation cheerfully, or mustered the courage to say no straightaway. He was an in-between type. So I said, "Some people give
a hundred rupees, some have promised to give more. How can
anyone set a limit on these things?"

He mumbled faintly, "A hundred rupees! I'm not so big,
sir . . ."

"What is a hundred rupees to you?" I asked. "You make it
every hour. Don't I know how you sell?"

He looked forlorn. He felt sorry that he had walked into this
trap, and wished that he hadn't ventured out of his orbit. He
looked as if he were facing the Income Tax Commissioner.

"No compulsion, no compulsion," I said. "Whatever is given
must be given out of free will, otherwise the money will be
worth nothing. Another thing, even in accepting donations we
are selective. We don't care to take money from all and sundry.
Money is not our main consideration. I mentioned the matter
to you because your name is first in our list, and you came just
when we were discussing you."

He began to fidget in his seat: he was eager to get up and get
out of sight. I was unwilling to let him go. I practically held him
down and enjoyed it immensely. I said, "What do you propose
to do for us? It's always easy to adjust these things, and I'd hate
to trouble you unnecessarily. What exactly would you like to
do for us?"

"I'm very busy just now. I am going round organizing our
sales in the surrounding country, where we are facing a certain
amount of competition. A host of imitators have come into the
field . . ."

"It's perfectly all right. We are not suggesting that you should
disturb yourself. All we want is encouragement from people
like you. After all you are an important citizen of this town,
and we feel honoured when people like you are associated with
us." I laid it on thicker and thicker till he became panic-stricken.
He got up suddenly and dashed out, muttering that he would
see me again.

After he was gone the astrologer and Sastri emerged from
their seclusion. The astrologer clutched a sheet of paper and
the open page of his almanac in his right hand, and in his left

dangled Sastri's silver spectacles. "I have a date for you . . . No, actually I have three dates: good, not so good, and half-good," he said. "You may make your choice according to your convenience. Each man should choose what is convenient."

The good date was five months hence; the poet would never survive such a delay. I knew him. He was impatient to launch his work within the next twenty-four hours. We rejected the half-good date, so there remained only the not so good day, which was four weeks hence, when the full moon came up a second time over the municipal tower and, more important, coincided with the festival at the temple. The astrologer said, "This is as good a date as the best one, but do you know why it's classed not so good? You see, there is a slight aspecting of Jupiter, and the poet's ruling star is——, and it might not prove so beneficial after all. Jupiter's aspects remain for four and a half hours; that will be until 5.25, and it may mean a slight setback in one's efforts, that's all."

"What sort of a setback?" I asked, rather worried.

"Well, it's hard to describe. It may be nothing more serious than a stubbed toe. Or the milk kept for coffee may turn sour. Are you going to give coffee for all the guests that day?"

"Certainly not," I said.

He was wondering how he should describe the impending setback. "Or the water in the tap might suddenly stop flowing."

"Or flow into K.J.'s bottles a little too much," I said. "K.J. was here and he may probably offer to serve drinks to all the visitors and fill up his bottles with just water and nothing more."

"Oh, that's possible," the astrologer echoed. "Or anything else in a general way."

Sastri now interpreted, "You see in astrology anything is a setback. If a fly settles on your nose at a crucial moment and annoys you, you may treat it as one astrological setback worked off." He laughed, and the astrologer laughed, and both of them said more or less simultaneously, "When it comes, it comes; when it goes, it goes; but it is useful to know ahead approximately." "Or the ink in the pen may not flow," added the astrologer. "Or it may be . . ." They were now at the game of drawing up a list of minor annoyances. The list grew. Jupiter's aspecting seemed to bring about a set of minor worries. The astrologer probably felt that he was belittling the planet too much, and suddenly drew himself up to explain, "He could be very vicious, left to himself—bring enough harm to a man's life itself or to his limbs; but when the presiding planet is Saturn, he yields place to him. You understand me? Saturn has more powers, although Saturn will not actually interfere with Jupiter's activities."

I had to send people to be served by Heidelberg, as neither myself nor Sastri had any leisure to attend to our profession. I sent my printing customers in a steady stream next door. Sastri and I had a hundred things to do, morning till night. I kept walking in and out of my office. I saw very little of my wife and child. I went home for dinner late every night. We printed appeals for donations in the form of a letter, setting forth our cultural heritage and so forth. We had to gear up our press to compose the final forms in readiness for the great day. I went out to meet the townfolk and get their subscriptions for our function, by no means an easy job as everyone of our citizens had the same temperament as K.J.—affluent, afraid to reject an appeal, but unwilling to open the purse. We needed a lot of money. We were planning an elaborate ritual, a procession, and a feast for a thousand. A few of the people we approached asked pointblank why we wanted to do anything at all if we had no money in hand—a reasonable question, but we did not contemplate a retreat. We had to keep going on, and the city was flooded with my notice. Sen was good enough to compose it for me. He wrote a few hundred words, beginning with the origin of the world; then he went on to the writer's duty to society, the greatness of the tale of Krishna and our cultural traditions, the merits of monosyllabic verse, concluding with some spicy remarks on the Nehru government's attitude to creative writing. These were totally erased by Sastri himself before he set up type. "Let Sen write a separate book on Nehru, if he chooses. Why should he try to display his wisdom at our cost?"

Our appeals were scattered far and wide and its effect was to draw Vasu into our fold again. He caught me late one evening as I was opening the door of my press in order to pass through to the back door. His jeep stopped at my door and he followed me in. I hadn't even switched on the lights. I was for passing straight in. He followed, asking, "Are you in a hurry?"

"Yes . . . I'm . . ."

"Then slow up. Such frenzy will do your heart no good. Slow down, or slow up. Why stand in the dark and talk? Switch on the light. Where is the switch?" He fumbled along the wall and found the switch. He sat in his usual chair and ordered me to be seated too.

I said, "I'm hungry, I've to go in and have my dinner."

"I too am hungry," he said. "You are not the only man who eats, are you?"

I sat down reluctantly on the edge of my table. "Well, what is it?" I asked.

"Look, Nataraj, I'm trying to be good to you. Don't be naughty. I don't like anyone to talk to me in that tone."

"Can't we meet some time tomorrow? I am very tired, that's all," I said.

"What has tired you? Being a busybody? Do you think I don't know what's going on?"

"What do you know?"

He produced one of our notices from his pocket and flourished it. "I'm as good a citizen as any, and even if you don't send me one I can always get one. You print it right under my floor" (I winced at his expression "my floor") "and yet no one has the courtesy to send me a copy! Strange world!"

I had no answer. While we had posted several hundred envelopes, I had deliberately avoided sending him one. Though our cold relationship was slightly improved, I could not bring myself to send him an invitation. There was an uneasy thought at the back of my mind that something might go wrong if this gunman was called in. But he was not the kind who would wait to be called. I merely said, "I knew you would get it, and so I did not think it was particularly . . ."

"Important?" he said while I was fumbling for an expression. "Why? Did you think I'd not be good enough to give you money, that I have no money?" This was really crushing. Why was he trying to have a fight with me?

"Do you want to find a reason for a fight with me?" I asked.

He said, "I'm not going to fight with anyone. If I had to fight, there'd be no half measures and it would not be at all good for the man who asked for it. You want to fight?" he asked solicitously as if he were asking "Would you like to wash or take a cup of coffee?"

I adopted diplomacy and said, "I thought of coming to you late, because I knew you would be here."

"That's better," he said. "Now you sound better. H'm. I had no notion that the poet had gone so far. A hard-working fellow!" he added with a sort of appreciation. He took out his purse and held out to me a ten-rupee note, holding it carelessly at the tips of his fingers. "Well, this is my contribution, although you wouldn't ask for it."

I stared at the note uncomprehendingly for a while and then said, "Is this all? I was going to ask you for a hundred."

"A hundred! H'm, that's interesting. If my business were as good as it used to be . . . Those bastards are trying to lock away the animals, very unhelpful," he said, thinking of the big army of forest guards. "Still, they can't put me down, you know. It only makes my business a little complicated, that is all. Who are they to tell me how to shoot or when!"

"You are right in a way," I said in order to sound agreeable, without bothering to think what I meant—without thinking of the river of animal blood which would have flowed if he had had his way.

He looked at me for a moment. "Nataraj! You really think so? I don't really need anybody's support or encouragement. I can get on very well by myself." The ten-rupee note still fluttered at his fingers' ends. "Well, do you want this or not?" he asked with sudden aggressiveness.

My mood began to match his. "I said I want a hundred from you, not less."

"Okay," he said and put the money back into his pocket.

"Now you can tell me how much you have collected in one hundred rupees."

It was a challenge and I said, "So far I have got fifty donors of the hundred-rupee class." That made him thoughtful.

"So! Five thousand rupees! How much of it is in your hands?"

That was a point. I said, "I don't want to take it yet. Nearer the time of the function. Why should we burden ourselves with the custody of so much cash?"

He made a sound of deprecation with his tongue and said, "Such a lot of cash! After all it's five thousand rupees, not five lakhs!"

"It is big enough from our point of view," I said, "Someone else's money is always a burden to carry."

"That's an unphilosophical way of looking at things. Money is only a medium of exchange and has no value by itself, and there can be no such thing as your money and my money. It's like the air, common to mankind."

"Then why not let me take your purse?"

"Why not indeed!" He took it out of his pocket and dropped it on my lap, rose, strode away to his jeep, and drove off. I sat transfixed. It was a large, well-stuffed purse, the size of a lady's handbag. I sat for a while wondering what to do with it. I couldn't guess where he was gone. I had never expected that I would be charged with the custody of the man's purse. Its flap was buttoned with an old-type metal head which could be pressed in. If you applied your thumb in the gap under the flap and lifted your finger, the flap snapped open. It had several compartments. It was stuffed with letters and currency. There was a photograph, plastic-covered, of a brawny young man with wavy hair standing up like a halo ear to ear, and bushy eyebrows. If you scrutinized it for a few minutes, you could easily recognize the face—Vasu at eighteen or twenty; you could recognize him by his bull-neck. There was a larger side-flap into which were stuffed currency, some letters, bills to be paid, and one letter in a blue envelope. The colour blue always arouses my curiosity. I pulled it out, toyed with the idea of go-

ing through it, but put it back. I lacked the courage to read it.
If he came back suddenly and caught me reading, he might perhaps break my spine or hold me upside down and rattle my
teeth out of my skull. I also wanted to know urgently how
much money he had in his purse and what were the unpaid bills
standing in his name, but I lacked the courage to undertake the
research now. I folded back the purse, pressed down the metal
buttons, and put it carefully in my drawer and locked it. I shut
the front door and went in for the night.

Three days later Vasu came to claim his purse. He peeped
into my roll-top desk when I was looking through a list of persons who had promised us funds, snatched the list from my
hand, glanced through it, and asked, "How much money do
you expect to collect?" I opened a green folder in which all the
papers relating to accounts, receipts and cash already collected
were kept. I examined the account and mentioned a figure.
"Give it here," he said, snatching away the green folder too. "I
will double it for you. You mind the other things."

I stammered, "But . . . but . . . ," and stretched my hand for
the folder. He pushed away my hand. "Leave this to me, and attend to other matters." I tried to argue with him, but he didn't
stop to hear me. He walked briskly to his jeep and drove away.

A week later he came into my office with a triumphant look.
He flourished the green folder and asked, "Can you guess how
much I have managed to get out of all the tight-fists in your
town?" I mentioned a figure. He said, "You are wrong. Try
again," and went away.

After that, during my round of visits I met people who remarked, "What a money-gatherer you have engaged! One will
have to sell the vessels in the kitchen and find the money, only
to be rid of him! What a specimen!" There could be no doubt
that he was extremely active.

I had to know exactly what he was up to. I waited patiently.
When he came in one afternoon I asked him straightaway,
"Where is the green folder?"

"It is locked up in an iron safe," he replied.

I ceremoniously showed him the Queen Anne seat, and

began, "We are all grateful to you for your help. You know a poet is . . ."

"Oh, no!" he cried. "I can't stand all this thanksgiving rigmarole."

"You are doing so much," I said ignoring the insult. "Part of the collections will be utilized for expenses connected with the festival, and then whatever is left over . . ."

"Why do you tell me all this?" he snapped.

I said, "We need funds now for making a few advance payments."

He thundered, "So what?" He cooled suddenly and asked, "How much do you want anyway?"

"At least five hundred rupees," I said.

"All right, you shall have it." He made no movement to fulfil his promise.

I asked, "When? When shall we . . . ?" He was trying to swat flies with a piece of cardboard.

He said, "Why do you let these flies swarm here? Have you stored sweets in your desk for your favourite poet?"

"It is important we should know how much you have been able to collect and from whom," I said firmly.

"All in proper time," he said. "Meanwhile, observe proper manners, keep your expenses down. Don't imagine you are millionaires!" He rose abruptly, glared at me for a moment, and was off.

CHAPTER NINE

We were a grim and silent trio that night. I had never worked harder as a printer. Details connected with the celebration had kept us so busy that I had had to neglect the most important item—the book to be dedicated on the day of the spring festival at the temple. I had to have at least one copy of the first volume ready in a special binding of hand-woven cloth. We still had a thousand lines of verse to be printed to bring it up to the end of the marriage of God Krishna with Radha. The poet had given us the last instalment of the manuscript weeks before, but it had lain in storage. I found no time even to open the cover. The poet was patient. He could not hustle me as this was practically a free service I was doing. He had always said that if the whole of it could not be got ready, they could always make use of the manuscript for the ceremony. But it was a matter of prestige for me as a printer to get through it and have at least one bound copy ready.

So we were working on this desperately tonight—myself, Sastri, and the poet: Sastri to compose each page, the poet to pass the proof, and I to print off the page as it came through. We had between us a large flask of coffee. We were weary and tired. All speech between us had ceased. During the earlier part of the night we had discussed the various aspects of the function and cracked a few jokes, but an hour before midnight we were irritated by each other's presence. My legs ached, my eyes smarted and I longed for bed. There were moments when I wondered why I had involved myself in all this, when I could have spent the time profitably printing K.J.'s fruit-juice labels. The poet sat in the Queen Anne chair and nodded; the sight of him provoked wild thoughts; I felt like flinging a tumbler of cold water over his head; I felt furious at seeing him nod, as I sat in the chair opposite him. "We are doing all this for your sake. How dare you sleep?" was my thought. And I took a pleasure in shouting in his ear, "Here, should it be—or—?" a doubt, a query, any excuse to pull him out of sleep. Looking at his mild face one would never imagine that he was a fanatic, but he was an implacable foe of all disyllables, and this drove him to attack and pulverize polysyllables so that they might fit into his scheme. A new syntax had grown from this, which caused Sastri endless headaches. Every few minutes Sastri called out to me from the composing room to clear his doubts and I in my turn prodded the poet to give me an answer. Strange problems faced us. The poet had used too many K's and R's in his composition, and the available poundage of K and R in our type-board was consumed within the first twenty lines; I had to ask him whether he could not use some other letters in order to facilitate our work. Sometimes he was obliging and sometimes he refused point-blank. At these moments we managed to put in a star in place of K or R and continue. Whenever he saw a star, the poet went mad and asked, "What does it mean?" I answered pugnaciously, "Don't worry, we will take care of it while printing. Otherwise we may add a footnote to readers to say that whenever they see a star . . ." All this upset the poet very much, and kept him awake.

When I threw on the poet's lap a particular complicated, star-filled galley, I watched him from my chair with calm satisfaction for a while. I always told him, every time, monotonously repeating myself, "Proof-correcting is like child-bearing. It is to be performed by you and you alone; no one else can step in and help you," and I sat down and rested my neck on the high back of the Queen Anne chair and watched him. He was a man of few words, probably because most expressions are polysyllabic, and he just glanced at me and got absorbed in proof-correcting. He held between his fingers a very small, white-handled pencil, and often nibbled its tip and brushed it against his cheek. The sight somehow annoyed me and made me say, "Is your cheek a pencil-sharpener?"

"I do that whenever I think."

"Stop thinking when you correct a proof. Let only your eye watch the word, letter, punctuation. If you start thinking, we shall have to go on with corrections and proofs till eternity." I suddenly felt that I sounded like Vasu, and added softly, "If we had had more time I would not have minded anything, you know."

"That's why I said . . . ," he began and I cut him short with, "Let's not waste the midnight hour. Go on, go on with the proof. Only when you have passed it, can I print it." Watching him working under the twenty-five-watt bulb, my eyes swam. I ceased to notice anything. A radiant light gathered around him and isolated him as if he were within an illuminated capsule or cocoon. His frayed jibba and dhoti, and the silly jute bag on his lap in which he carried his papers, were no longer there; they became smudgy and vague. I could see only his face—unshaven (he was saving up a blade for the great day); the light fell on his nose-tip and the rest receded in shadow.

The policeman's whistle sounded far off somewhere, and everything conduced to a dopy state of mind. I felt light and floated and sank into sleep, forgetting everything for the moment—Sastri, the temple, the poet, the celebrations, and the funds locked up with Vasu, the pipe and drum, the feeding arrangements and garlands. Like a dagger-jab, I heard the words "Shall I stop with this line on this page?" Sastri stood over me and bellowed his question, and all the fine fabric of my oblivion was completely torn and messed up. Evidently Sastri got jealous when he saw me asleep and invented a doubt in order to pull me out of it.

Then it was Sastri's turn to seek a corner chair. He arranged it perfectly; after turning a chair to face the wall, he curled up in it. His deliberate preparations to sleep upset me, but I could do nothing about it, as he had an unchallenged right to doze. It was my turn to work, for until I printed off the forms he had no types left to compose; for the poet's work had swallowed up all the contents of the type-case and left them blank. Until I released the types there was nothing for Sastri to do but sleep, and of course the poet was entitled to sleep because until Sastri gave him a galley . . . I wished I could make them do something instead of letting them sleep, but my devilish brain was too dead at this hour to devise anything, and so I stuck the types on the treadle, adjusted, and operated the pedal. I could hear them snore in the other room beyond the curtain, but there was nothing I could do about it. Perhaps I might have splashed a bucket of water over them, had I felt able even to contemplate the lifting of a loaded bucket. The sound of the treadle parts came in a series, *chug, gluck, pat* and *tap.* I was trying to classify their sounds. I poured out a little coffee in the thermos lid, and paused ever so slightly to sip it.

Now over the *chug, gluck, pat* and *tap* I heard a new sound: a repeated tap on the grille that separated me from Vasu's staircase. I hoped that the stuffed hyena had not come to life. I tried to ignore it and go on with my printing. *Tap, tap,* on the steel mesh. I applied my eye to the private pin-hole and saw a vague outline stirring. "Oh, the ghost of the hyena has come back!" I cried. A thrill of fear lifted the hair on my scalp and forearm. I wondered if I should wake up the other two—it was a perfect excuse—and make them share my fright.

"Sir, sir," whispered the animated hyena, "this is urgent—listen."

I lifted the edge of the bamboo curtain. The light from the treadle fell on the other side and illuminated the face of Rangi. My hair stood on end. Rangi! The woman to avoid.

My first reaction was one of thankfulness that Sastri was on the other side of the curtain, facing the wall. It was impossible—that woman whom I saw going down the steps every morning with the flowers crushed in her hair, the awful fleshy creature whom Sastri considered it a sin to look at! Was it possible that I was a prey to hallucinations? Perhaps overwork and the strain of the last few weeks had done their trick. I turned away to my treadle, smiling indulgently at the pranks my mind was playing. But the phantom sounded husky as it called again, "Listen to me." Was the woman trying to seduce me at this hour? I looked around. If my wife happened to come in, it would be the end of my domestic career. Although Rangi was black as cinders and looked rugged, there was an irresistible physical attraction about her, and I was afraid that I might succumb to her charms. But there was the safety of the grille between us. I asked, with needless sternness in my voice, "Why do you disturb me at this hour of the night? Have you no . . . ?"

"Sh! Sh!" she said, gesturing with her fingers to cover her mouth. "You will wake him up if you talk so loudly. Listen to me, sir," she said. "I have very urgent news for you."

"What is it? Couldn't you have spoken to me earlier in the day?"

When I saw her nearer, she wasn't so rugged. The light touched her high cheek-bones, and I found myself saying to myself, "Not bad, not bad. Her breasts are billowy, like those one sees in temple sculptures. Her hips are also classical." I resented the attraction she exuded from a personality so rough. She wore a thin reddish sari. She interrupted my midnight dreaming with, "I must get back before he awakes. Listen: he is talking of shooting your Kumar tomorrow. Be careful."

I took a little time to grasp the sense of her information. The name Kumar stirred up in me all the necessary memories, from the first day when we had made him get up on his legs, through all our effort to restore him to health, to this day, when he was peacefully swaying and crunching all the sugar cane that the children of the neighbourhood brought him.

During his convalescence Kumar had become our own temple elephant and was living in the compound. He was to be a main feature of our festival, and afterwards he would be returned to Muthu.

"I am also a woman of the temple and I love that elephant. It must not be shot. Sir, you must somehow see that he doesn't do it. Please save the elephant."

"How? How can I shield the elephant? What sort of an armour can we provide for him?" I asked. And then on a sudden doubt I whispered, "Are you in your senses? Or have you been taking opium or something of that kind?"

She glared at me angrily, "Sir, I am only a public woman, following what is my *dharma*. I may be a sinner to you, but I do nothing worse than what some of the so-called family women are doing. I observe our rules. Whatever I may do, I don't take opium."

I felt apologetic for uttering so outrageous a remark and said, "What you say is so unbelievable."

She looked nervously up the stairs, as there was a slight stirring noticeable above. "If he wakes up...," she whispered. "Wait here, don't go away," and she ran up the steps. My blood tingled with an unholy thrill. I let my mind slide into a wild fantasy of seduction and passion. I was no longer a married man with a child and home, I was an adolescent lost in dreams over a nude photograph. I knew that I was completely sealed against any seductive invitation she might hold out for me, but, but, I hoped I would not weaken ... My mind speculated on how I was to neutralize the grille between us if it came to that; the grille had a lock, and the key was in the drawer of my table in the other room. I stepped up to the curtain, parted the edge of it, and was relieved to see Sastri continuing his sleep, his position unchanged. The poet slept equally soundly, but he had drawn up his legs and curled himself in the Queen Anne. If I approached the desk for the key, it was bound to disturb the sleepers. Anyway, I left the problem alone, resolved to tackle it somehow at the right moment.

When I tiptoed back to my place beside the grille, there she was, ready as it seemed to swallow me up wholesale, to dissolve within the embrace of her mighty arms all the monogamous chastity I had practised a whole lifetime.

I found her irresistible. She stood on the last step, a goddess carved out of cinder. The shadows cast by the low-powered lamp were tricky and created a halo around her. I pressed my hands on the grille and put my face close, and, adopting the appropriate tone of a man about to succumb to seduction, I said, "Oh, you are back!" I tried to put into the sentence all the pleasure I was anticipating.

She looked at me indifferently and said, "I only went up to see if he was sleeping; he was just rolling over, he won't get up till five, I know him." She sat down on the last step, took out of the folds at her waist a pouch and from it a betel-nut and leaf and two inches of tobacco, put them into her mouth and started chewing. She looked completely relaxed. In my fevered state I wanted to ask her if she was aware that the grille was locked and the key was where Sastri was sleeping.

She asked, "Are you going to save that elephant or not?"

"Why do you ask? Tell me all about it."

"He will kill me if he knows I have been talking. But I don't care. He has been telling me his plans. Tomorrow night, what time does your procession pass this way?"

"You should know, you are in it."

She was to perform her original function of a dedicated woman, and dance in front of the God during the procession, although her dance would consist only of a few formal flourishes of her arms. She was perhaps the most indifferent dancer in India, but no one expected anything else of her. People were used to seeing her before the God and no one cared how she performed. Her place would be right between the decorated chariot and the group of pipers and drummers.

"He doesn't want me to go in the procession tomorrow," she said, "because he says it'll not be safe for me." She giggled slightly, and threw the end of her sari over her face, feeling shy at the thought of Vasu's considerateness.

I asked in a panic, "Aren't you joining the procession?"

"Yes, I'll be there. It will be my duty."

"But, but, what about Vasu?"

"Oh, let him say what he pleases; no man so far has stopped my doing what I like," she said proudly.

"Why doesn't he want you there?"

"He doesn't want me there when it happens."

"What happens?"

"When he shoots the elephant from his window."

"I never thought Vasu cared for anyone so much."

"He cares for me very much, although sometimes he is completely mad and picks up all kinds of women and expects me to quarrel with them—but not me. Let any man do what he fancies. I don't care what anyone does, so long as he doesn't dictate to me what I should do." She chewed her tobacco contentedly.

"He wants to take me with him to Bombay—that's why he doesn't want me to get lost in the crowd."

"What will you do in Bombay?" I asked, my curiosity roused.

"Cook for him. He likes the *pulav* I make, so he wants to take me along with him. I want to see new places too when the time comes. In a year or two who will care to have me?"

"Oh, you will have your charms," I wanted to say in my impassioned state, but I restrained myself. She treated me with much respect, always addressing me as "sir," and she would have been shocked if I had spoken to her like a lover. Even at that mad hour, I am glad to think, I kept my head and tongue. "Good man," I said, "he cares for you so much!"

"He is tired of his restaurant food, he says, and he doesn't want me to risk my life in the crowd when he shoots the elephant from his window."

"Why shoot the poor thing?" I persisted. "Does he think I will let him do it?" I asked heroically. "I will tell the police."

"Oh, sir," she begged, "don't do that. How will it help? The police themselves may ask him to shoot it. They may want someone able to shoot." And then she explained, "When the elephant is passing here, it may go mad and charge into the crowd."

"Oh, God. Why?"

"Well, elephants are easily excited; and then he will take aim from his window and shoot it. He is certain that he can finish it. His aim is always accurate, you know," she said.

I said, angrily, "If he is such a good shot, the place for him to demonstrate it is elsewhere, not here."

"Master," she implored, "don't be angry. Think calmly what you should do, and act before it's too late."

"Anyway, why does he want to shoot the elephant?" I asked.

"He says it's more useful dead. He may kill me for speaking, but I don't care. I want to save poor Kumar."

"Neither you nor Kumar need have any fear. The time has come for me to hand him over to the police, the devil!" I said with a lot of passion but little idea of what I could do about it.

———

I finished printing the forms, woke up Sastri to do more, woke up the poet to proof-read, printed four more pages, and it was nine o'clock in the morning when I saw the last page off the machine and one set of forms was assembled ready for the binder. The sacred copy was to be bound in Benares silk and kept in the temple. I said to the poet, "It's all right, go home and wash and be here in time. We have to be at the temple before three."

He yawned, scratched the back of his head and went down the road muttering, "I'll be back soon. Tell me if there is anything more I can do."

I sent Sastri with two copies to the binder. Sastri hesitated for a second. "Can't I go home for half an hour—for a wash?"

I was irritated. "Why not me? I also would like to go home and sleep and wash and relax." As I was talking my little son came running down the road. "Father, Mother says . . ." Even before he finished his sentence, I said, "Tell your mother not to call me for the rest of the day. Tell your mother that even Sastri is not going home today. We are all very busy." I handed him a bunch of coloured notices. "Give one of them to your mother and the rest to your friends or anyone you like—let them all turn up at Krishna's temple. We'll all meet there. Tell Mother I'll come home, but I don't know when." Even as I spoke I remembered Rangi, and for a moment I wondered whether to ask my son and wife to keep out of the crowd. "Damn it!" I said to myself. "Nothing shall happen. I shall have Rangi and that paramour of hers in the police lock-up." This thought gave me strength although I had no notion how I was going to achieve it practically. The police would not listen to my orders if I said, "Lock up that man." Why should they?

Every hour of that day was like a tenth of a second to me, it was so compressed and so fleeting. After sending everyone away I sat down to take stock of all I had to do between now and the grand function. I found my head in a whirl. I didn't know where to make a start in drawing a schedule. Every item appeared to be important and clamoured for immediate attention. I could now understand why Government officials liked to stack up on their desks trays marked Immediate, Urgent, and Top Priority. Everything today was on the top-priority level.

Although we had been working madly for weeks, everything seemed to be crowded into the last minute. First I must remind the flower-dealer to get us the first supplies for decorating the chariot by eleven. We had engaged two specialists, brothers from Talapur, who were in demand all over South India. Given the foliage and the quantity of chrysanthemums they demanded, their decoration of a chariot was a masterpiece, but they needed a clear eight hours to arrange the flowers. The chariot must be ready for the procession at eight in the evening, and they would have to begin their work at eleven in the morning. I had paid a visit to them at Talapur ten days before. They accepted the engagement only because the police inspector with whom I had influence interceded; otherwise they had a much bigger job to do at Madras. I gave them an advance of fifty rupees and noted down their indent: seven thousand yellow chrysanthemums, four thousand of a certain green plant, two thousand red oleanders, two hundred thin bamboos splintered according to their specification, which they'd loop around the pedestal of the God, working the flowers into them, and seventeen bundles of banana fibres thinly torn off for binding the flowers. In addition to these basic requirements they had asked for a thousand roses, twenty measures of jasmine buds, and bouquets and garlands ready-made to be strung according to their specifications. These latter items could arrive after six, but the first supply of chrysanthemums must be there before eleven. The brothers were arriving by the bus at ten o'clock behind the market depot, and they were stars who expected to be received on arrival. I was the only one who had seen them, and it meant that I would have to wait for them at the market stand. Also I had to visit the florist who had his shop at the farthest corner of Market Road, a man amenable only to my influence. He waited in his turn on the suppliers from the surrounding gardens. We were taking all the flower supplies coming into town that day, and the price of flowers for common folk shot up.

I had also to make sure that our piper and the drummer, who lived not too far away, would arrive in time. Our chief piper blew through a silver-covered pipe, and the drummer had gold beads around his neck and beat his drum with ivory-tipped fingers; they were stars in their own line, and so expected personal attention from the organizers as represented by me. They were in demand all over South India for marriage and temple festivals, but they had condescended to accept a local engagement because it was the first of its kind in our town. They lived right on the edge of the town, the last house in Ellaman's Street, but, since they were cousins of our barber whose house abutted Kabir Street, we were able to exert pressure on them through him and set him to bring them to the temple at three in the afternoon.

We had an enormous programme of feeding the public too. We had planned to offer the God rice cooked with jaggery and spiced with cardamom and coconut and distribute it to the crowd following the procession. One of the rice merchants had donated us all the rice that would be needed together with the coconut and jaggery. All that he wanted in return was that, in any public speech, his shop should be mentioned. We had a kitchen in the temple, and an enormous cauldron was fetched and mounted over a fireplace with half a ton of chopped wood burning under it. Four professional cooks were engaged, and several thousand little receptacles made of banana bark would be filled with sweetened rice and distributed. And then there were the Kitson lights and petrol lamps for the illumination of the temple and the procession, in addition to torches soaked in oil. And above all fireworks.

The whole town was at it. The Chairman of our Municipal Council had agreed to preside over the function, the advantage in that being that the municipal services were easily secured for us! When it was known that the Municipal Chairman would be there, the roads were swept and watered, and the licence for a procession was immediately given. Along the corridor of our Krishna temple we had erected a *pandal* and a dais, on which the Mayor (he liked to be called Mayor) would stand and harangue the gathering before the dedication.

All the public relations and the general arrangements at the temple were undertaken by Sen, who never left the temple precincts for seven days, working at it night and day. He had man-

aged to get a band of young volunteers from Albert Mission
College and High School to assist him and run small errands;
he had managed to erect a *pandal* with coconut thatch and
bamboo; he saw to the decorations, and kept a hold on the
Municipal Chairman by writing his speech for him. He had
also arranged to keep in readiness hand-outs and photographs
for newspapers. K.J., our aerated-water specialist, had set up a
booth at the temple gate and had offered to open a thousand
bottles free of cost and thereafter charge only half-rate to the
public gathered at the temple. There were three donors who
had offered five hundred rupees each, and they expected me to
fetch them by car, although one had to be brought from New
Extension, the other from Gandhi Park and a third from Lawley Road. I had fortunately the assistance of Gaffur, who ran
his 1927 Chevrolet as a taxi. It was always available around
the fountain. "Any time, anywhere, this car is yours," he had
declared. I had only to fill the petrol tank, ask him to drive and
give him ten rupees at the end of the day.

"First things first, and I have to be at the temple at three," I
told myself. There was Dr. Joshi, the elephant doctor beyond
Nallappa's Grove, who wanted a car to be sent for him. "I
must remember to take with me six bottles of rose water and
the sandalwood paste, and then . . ." Items kept coming to
mind, like the waves beating on a shore. "Oh, when Muthu
and his party arrive, I must leave a guide at the bus-stand to
take them to the temple." Everything was important and clamoured for first attention.

I dropped what I was doing, dashed through the press,
opened the back door and stepped across to my house. I'd have
no time to visit the river today. I went straight into the bathing-
room, saw that there was cold water ready in a brass cauldron,
undressed and poured the cold water over my head, shouting
through the door to my wife, "Bring me my towel and a change
of clothes." She thrust the towel through the half-open door,
and I cried, "I forgot to shave; bring me my safety razor and
mirror. I'll shave here." She ran back to fetch these, and presently my son entered, bearing them in his hand. I shouted, "You
should not handle razor blades."

"Mother asked me to carry them."

I called his mother urgently and told her, "After this never let the young fellow handle razor blades."

"He insisted upon fetching them himself."

"That's no excuse," I said, "You must watch him."

"What else do you think I am doing?" she asked. "But now I have your breakfast on the fire, and I know how you will dance for it and make us dance who serve you, the moment you come out of the bathroom."

"No time for arguments today."

Within fifteen minutes I was leaving home again, completely refreshed by my bath and food. I took leave of my wife. "Try and manage to come to the temple at five with Babu. I'll give you a good place for watching the show, then you can go back home and come again before the procession. The decoration will be the finest. Come with some of our neighbours." I was off.

Across the street, back at my press, I was troubled with a secret uneasiness that perhaps I should have asked her to stay at home in view of Rangi's warnings. "First things first . . ." If I devoted four minutes to each task, I could get through everything and reach the temple in time before the Chairman arrived. But, but, I had to get this affair of Vasu straightened out; I braced myself to face him. I did not want to give myself any time. If I began to think it over, I'd find an excuse to go ahead with all the other tasks, while the lives of thousands of men and women might hang by a thread depending on my interview with Vasu, not to speak of the survival of poor Kumar who had proved such a delight to our neighbourhood!

I dashed home for a minute to ask my wife to pack up and give me some eatables that she had prepared, and then turned to go to Vasu. I went around to the yard. Until I turned the corner I had a hope that the jeep might not be there. But there it was. My steps halted for a second at the bottom of Vasu's staircase, where I noticed the plaster on the walls peeling off. "I must attend to this," I said to myself, and immediately felt a pang at the thought of how little I had to do with this part of my property. At the foot of the stairs the hyena was still there. "There seems to be no demand for stuffed hyena nowadays," I said to myself. The python was gone, but a monitor lizard, a crocodile, and a number of other creatures, looking all alike in death, cluttered the staircase. I went up to the landing, making as much sound as I could. It was about eleven and I knew Rangi would not be there. I stood on the landing and called, "Vasu, may I come in?" I didn't knock on the door as I felt it might upset him. "How can I find time today for this?" I thought. "I hope they'll remember the rose-water bottles." I stood brooding, waiting for Vasu. The door opened.

"What an honour!" he cried ironically. I passed in, took my seat on his iron chair, and settled myself for a talk with him, although one part of my mind went on repeating, "Where is the time? Rose-water, sandal-paste, New Extension, Gandhi Park . . ." We had avoided each other since the day I asked for my accounts and thus entered a second phase of our quarrel. Last time it was he who had come with peace overtures; this time I was initiating them. My heart swelled with pride; I was performing a mighty sacrifice on behalf of God and country. By approaching him and humbling myself I would be saving humanity from destruction . . .

I said, "Vasu, I have no time today for anything, as you know, but I've come to invite you personally to our function this evening." He received my words coldly, without even thanks, and made no reply. I looked around; the room was once again cluttered with hides and stuffed creatures and packing-sheets and materials. I noticed a small tiger cub in a corner. I tried to win him by saying, "A pretty cub that!"

He picked it up and brought it closer, "Someone picked it up right in the centre of a road while coming from . . ."

"Its mother?"

"Will miss her, of course. I was busy with other things, and could start on it only last week."

"You could have kept it alive and brought it up," I said, trying to discover ways of pleasing him.

"Me? No. I've spent a lifetime trying to make you see the difference between a zoo-keeper and a taxidermist," he said with weariness as if I'd been trying to place him among an inferior caste of men. "Anyway it's easier to rear a dead animal. For one thing it saves complications with a landlord."

I felt proud that he still recognized me as the lord of this attic. Vasu without a live tiger was quite problem enough, and I had made the suggestion only to please him. In the hope of pleasing him further I added, "Of course, a baby anything is a beauty. I'd have loved to have him around."

"It was a she," he corrected.

"What is the safe age?"

"What do you mean?"

"Up to what age can a tiger be kept as a pet?"

"Until it starts licking the skin off the back of your hand," he said, "Anyway, how should I know? I am not a zoo-keeper."

I tried to find something nasty to say about zoo-keepers, that odious tribe of men whom he loathed, but failed. I merely said, "Most peculiar profession. I would not be a zoo-keeper for all the wealth in the world."

He set the tiger cub before me on a stool. I shivered slightly at the thought of anyone taking so young a life. "Doesn't she look cute? I have had more trouble shaping this than a full-grown one. Guess what I am charging for it?"

This was really a problem for me. If I undervalued it, I might antagonize him. If I mentioned a fantastic figure, he might despise me, seeing through the trick. While my mind was working fast, I stole a glance through the little window over the street. Yes, the fountain would be within his range. From the fountain, down the road, branching off to Lawley Road—he could aim anywhere within the perimeter.

"What are you watching?" he asked suddenly.

"Nothing. I always look at far-off things when I have to do a calculation. I've been thinking over your question. If you charge five thousand rupees, as you told me once . . ."

"Oh, the question is unimportant, leave it alone," he said. He carried the cub off and put it back, covering it over with a piece of cloth.

I was not to be quenched so easily. I said, "About two thousand? The labour of shaping it must have been equally great."

"You are right. It's slightly less. I never charge a round sum. My bill for it would be eighteen hundred and twenty-five, packing extra."

I gave appropriate cries of admiration for his cleverness, and after talking a little more on the same line we came to business. "Why don't you come along with me at three o'clock?"

"To your wonderful function? I have had enough of this tomfoolery."

"Well, you were enthusiastic about it once!"

"That's why I want to keep away. Let me alone, enjoy it yourself."

He had still to render us an account, but this was not the time to tackle him about it. There was enough time ahead— after tonight, after the elephant was safely returned to Muthu. I wanted to assure him now that I had not come about the accounts. I said, "Everyone is bound to ask why you are not there. You have done so much for us already."

"I have had to spend over two thousand rupees out of my pocket. You have no idea how much of my business I have had to set aside. Time is money. I can't be like some of your friends."

"Let us not talk of all that," I said.

"Who are you to ask me to shut up!" he cried.

We were coming dangerously near another clash. I did not want to lose my head and lose the chance of keeping him with us and saving the elephant. This was the only tactic I could think of. He spurned me again and again as I repeated my invitation, and finally said, "Your whole crowd sickens me! You are a fellow without any sense. Why you are so enthusiastic about a poetaster obsessed with monosyllables I don't know. And then that local Nehru. Who does he think he is? All of you joining to waste everyone's time and money! If I had any authority I'd prohibit celebrations of this kind as a waste of national energy."

I did not want to say that he could keep out if it didn't suit him. I wanted to stretch my capacity for patience to the utmost in the cause of God and country. He was abusive and angry. I wanted to assure him that I was not going to mention accounts for a considerable time to come. So I said, "Vasu, I have come to you as a friend. I thought it would be fun to have you around. We could see things together and laugh at things together. Perhaps you are worried we might ask about those collections . . ."

"Who? Me, worried!" He laughed devilishly. "A hundred of you will have to worry before you can catch me worried."

I laughed pretending that he was joking. I looked at the time. I had wasted nearly three-quarters of an hour in the *tête-à-tête*, and still I had not come to the point. How was I to ask him for an assurance that he would not shoot the elephant?

I now took the rice cake and sweets out of my bag, and placed the packet before him. "Ah, I forgot about this," I said. "I have brought you something to eat. I found it at home and I thought you might like it."

"What is it?" he asked. He opened the packet and raised his brow. "You want to practise kindness on me! All right. This is my first experience of it from you. All right, all right, while it lasts." He put a piece in his mouth, chewed it with critical seriousness and said, "Not bad, but tell the person who made it to fry the pepper a little more before putting it in. Anyway better than nothing." He transferred the whole of it, and swallowed it at one gulp, accepting it as something rightfully due to him. I was a little upset to see him take it so casually and critically, and was especially hurt to think that he couldn't pay a compliment to my wife even for courtesy's sake. He merely said, "If you want to find this stuff at its best, you must taste it at . . . ," and he mentioned some exclusive place of his own.

"This was prepared by my wife," I said, trying to forestall any nasty statement he might make. But he merely said, "Modern women are no good at this. Modern women are no good at anything when you come to think of it." I did not want him to elaborate the subject as I feared he might say something nasty about my wife, so I desperately changed the subject to the real issue. I said, "Vasu, I have come to appeal to you not to harm our elephant tonight."

"How can anyone harm an elephant, of all things? Don't you know that even if you drive a bodkin into its skin, it will only break the point? Anyway, what are you trying to tell me?"

This was challenging. He had risen from the cot, which

showed that he was agitated by my question. He tried to look calm, but I found that he was roused. "Who has been gossiping, I wonder." He paced up and down, then stood for a moment looking out of the window—as I guessed, at the market fountain. "Has that bitch been talking to you?"

"Which bitch?" I asked.

"That woman Rangi," he said with heat.

"Who is Rangi?" I asked.

"You pretend you don't know her!" he cried. "Why all this show? I'll wring her neck if I find . . ." He didn't finish the sentence. He asked suddenly, "Well, suppose I decide to shoot that elephant, what can you do about it?"

I had no answer. I only asked, "What has the poor elephant done to you?"

"Has it occurred to you how much more an elephant is worth dead? You don't have to feed it in the first place. I can make ten thousand out of the parts of this elephant—the tusks, if my calculation is right, must weigh forty pounds, that's eight hundred rupees. I have already an order for the legs, mounted as umbrella stands, and each hair on its tail can be sold for twelve annas for rings and bangles; most women fancy them and it's not for us to question their taste. My first business will be to take out the hairs and keep them apart, while the blood is still hot; trunk, legs, even the nails—it's a perfect animal in that way. Every bit of it is valuable. I've already several inquiries from France and Germany and from Hong Kong. What more can a man want? I could retire for a year on the proceeds of one elephant."

"Why don't you go and shoot one in the forest?"

"Forest! I want to show them that I can shoot anywhere. I want to teach those forest men a lesson."

A strange way of teaching a lesson to foresters. I said weakly, "Shoot a wild one, and no one will blame you."

"This will be wild enough, don't worry."

"What do you mean?"

"You watch out," he said. "You will thank me for my services. That Kumar is mad already; none of you have noticed it. Have you ever observed his eyes? See the red streak in his little eyes; that means at the slightest provocation he will fly off. . . ."

"What sort of provocation?" I asked.

"How can I say? Elephants are really crazy animals. Anything, any slight . . ." He did not explain.

I felt worried. What was he planning? How was he going to excite it? "Have you plans to excite it?" I asked point-blank.

He laughed diabolically. "You want to know everything, my boy. Wait, and you will know. Whatever you have to know will be known one day," he said in a biblical manner.

I said, "Whatever horrible plans you may have, remember there will be thousands of people around—men, women, and children dragging the chariot."

"Let them go home like good citizens before midnight. They can have all the fun they want until midnight."

"Who are you to say when they should go or come?"

"Now, now, don't try to be nasty. Let them stay or go, that's their business. If the elephant runs wild . . ." He ruminated.

"A few will be trampled and choked in a stampede," I said.

"You are saying things I don't say. You have a morbid mind." He said a moment later, "The elephant has been promised me when it's dead. I have it in writing here."

"Who has promised?"

"Why should I tell you everything? As far as I'm concerned, you have no business with me at all. How are you concerned with the elephant? It's not yours. I'm not bound to tell you anything. I'm an independent man. You keep it locked away, if you like; that's not going to bother me. Why come and talk to me? Get out of here and mind your morning's work."

I trembled with excitement and helplessness. I dared not say anything more, lest he should hit me. I pleaded, "Vasu, you are a human being with feelings like any of us. I am sure you are only pretending to be so wild." He laughed. He seemed delighted at the way he had brought me down.

"All right, keep your own view of me. I don't mind. You are . . . Shall I tell you what's the matter with you? You are sentimental. I feel sickened when I see a man talking sentimentally like an old widow. I admire people with a scientific outlook."

"What's scientific about the terrible plans you have?"

"Ah, you see! You use the word 'terrible' and are carried

away by it. You allow your mind to be carried away by your own phrases. There's nothing terrible in shooting. You pull your trigger and out goes the bullet, and at the other end there is an object waiting to receive it. It is just give and take. At one time I was squeamish like you. It was Hussein who broadened my outlook. He used to tell me the way to be broad-minded is to begin to like a thing you don't like. It makes for a very scientific outlook."

"It may be science, but the object at the other end does not deserve to be brought down. Has that occurred to you?"

"How can you say? What do you do with an animal which goes on a rampage? Should the public not be protected?"

"This is not that kind of animal," I said weakly. It was idiotic to try to change his mind, but I wanted to try to the last.

"Unscientific! Unscientific!" he cried. "What's the premise for your conclusion? Normal behaviour is one thing and the abnormal behaviour of a beast is another. Exactly when a beast will cross the frontier is a matter that's known only to those who have studied the subject. If you had printed my book on wild life, you'd have found it profitable. I've devoted two chapters to animal behaviour. But you chose to busy yourself with monosyllables."

I said placatingly, "I'll take it tomorrow and finish it," carefully avoiding a mention of the original Heidelberg which was rising to my lips.

"I don't believe your promise," he said. "Did you think I'd wait on your pleasure indefinitely? It's already being printed."

I felt jealous. "Here, in this town? Who could do it?"

He laughed at my question and said, "Now I've given you all the time I can. You'll have to leave me. This is my busy day."

I shuddered at the implication.

The interview knocked out all the joy I had felt in the festival. I had looked forward to it for weeks, and now I felt like a man working towards a disastrous end and carrying a vast crowd with him. I'd have willingly stopped the entire celebration if it had been practicable. But we had started rolling downhill and there was no way of checking our momentum.

———

It was four o'clock when I managed to reach the temple at Vinayak Street. Men, women, and children thronged the street and the courtyard of the temple. Sen had put up a few bamboo barriers here and there to allow some space for the Mayor and his entourage. He had dressed himself in a dhoti at his waist and had wrapped a red silk upper cloth around his shoulder and his forehead was blazoned with sacred ash, sandal-paste, and vermilion. He was nearly unrecognizable in his holy make-up. The poet had donned a pink bush-coat for the ceremony, and it hurt my eyes. It reminded me of the labels for K.J.'s drinks. K.J. had spread out his coloured water on a wooden platform, and was doing brisk business. Since he had not specified when the free drinks would be supplied, he was freely plying his trade. The babble of voices was deafening. A few shops had sprung up—paper toys, fried nuts, and figurines in red and green sugar, on little trays at the temple gate. The back of the temple was filled with smoke rising from the enormous cooking. Some of the temple priests were busy in the inner sanctum, decorating the God and lighting oil lamps.

Kumar was chained to a peg at the end of the temple corridor, under a tree. A crowd of children watched him; and he was briskly reducing to fibre lengths of sugar cane held out to him by the children. The mahout from Top Slip was perched on his back, painting his forehead in white, red and green floral patterns, to the huge delight of the children, to whom he was appealing, "Don't make so much noise, give us a chance, give us a chance. Kumar can't hear me if you keep making so much noise." He had scrubbed and cleaned Kumar's tusks so that the ivory gleamed in the sun. He had decorated the tusks with bronze bands and rings; he was very happy because someone had promised him the loan of gold head-ornaments and brocades. The elephant seemed to enjoy it all immensely and was in a fine mood. My heart sank at the sight of the happy animal.

I found Dr. Joshi standing near him, stroking his trunk. In all the rush of work, my promise to fetch him had gone out of my head, but he had somehow arrived. I approached him, pushing my way through the crowd of sightseers. I wanted to apologize for my lapse. But the moment he saw me, he said, "Sorry I couldn't wait for you. I had to come to the town on business and have stayed on."

"Oh, that's all right, Doctor, I'm happy to see you. How do you find Kumar?"

He said, "He is in good shape, I think."

"Will he stand all the crowd and excitement?"

"Surely. What else do you think he is good for? You will find him at his best in such surroundings."

"I was wondering whether he would tolerate the fireworks and the band?"

"Why not? But don't let sparks fall on him from the torches or the fireworks. Some elephants get a fright when a flare is held too close. Keep an eye on the torch-bearers, and that should be enough."

"Do you think he'll go wild if something happens?"

"Why do you ask?" asked the doctor.

"I've heard some people say that an animal can suddenly charge into a crowd."

He laughed at my fear. "Don't talk about such ideas. People might get into a panic and that would be really bad in a crowd like this." We surveyed the jam of humanity. Any rumour might ruin the occasion, and create a stampede. The distribution of the offerings was planned for the end of the procession, when we returned to the temple. That meant that most of the crowd would wait for it. One way of reducing the crowd would be to distribute the sweet rice as soon as possible. I sought out the chief priest of the temple to ask if it could be managed. He said immediately, "No. The offering is for the eleven o'clock service. How could we distribute anything before that?"

I was obsessed with plans to save the lives of the people who had come out for enjoyment: little girls had dressed themselves in bright skirts, women wore their jewellery and flowers in their hair, and men had donned their best shirts and bush-coats and dhotis and silks. My wife and son were somewhere in that crowd. I had no way of reaching them either. The air was charged with the scent of the jasmine and roses which decorated the chariot.

———

The Mayor's speech was drowned in the babble in spite of a microphone and loud-speaker. This was the journalist's domain, and I kept away from the dais. I saw from far off the pink bush-coat of the poet rising. He was respectfully presenting the silk-bound copy of the book to the priest. The crowd demonstrated unmistakably that they hadn't assembled there to listen to a speech. The piper and the drummer were providing a thunderous performance. The priest was busy placing offerings at the feet of Krishna and Radha, and Rangi was dancing and gesticulating before the golden images. She had draped herself in a faded brocade and wore a lot of tinsel ornaments on her head and around her neck. I wanted to speak to her—it was urgent—but it would be improper to be seen engaged in a talk with the woman, and the enormous crowd might boo me. I toyed with the idea of sending an emissary to her, any young urchin, but if the fellow was bent on mischief he could expose me and make me the laughing-stock of the crowd. The crowd was in a mood to enjoy anything at anybody's expense.

What did I want to see her for? I wasn't very clear. It seemed vulgar to share a secret with her. If Sastri came to know of it, he would denounce me and leave my service. All the same I wanted to attract her attention, why I couldn't say. I could glimpse her only over several heads and through gaps between shoulders. She was agitating herself in such a way as to make it impossible for anyone to catch her eye. All the same I edged closer, pushing my way through the crowd. The incense smoke and camphor, the babble of the priest's recitations over, the babble of the crowd suddenly proved too oppressive. All night I had sat up working on the forms, and after all this trouble the whole business seemed to be unimportant. I found it strangely irritating to think of the pink-coated poet and all the trouble he had caused me.

The God was beautifully decorated. He wore a rose garland, and a diamond pendant sparkled on his chest. He had been draped in silk and gold lace, and he held a flute in his hand; and his little bride, a golden image draped in blue silk and sparkling with diamonds, was at his side, the shy bride. The piper was blowing his cheeks out, filling the air with "Kalyani Raga," a lovely melody at this hour. The temple was nearly a century old, built by public subscription in the days when my grandfather and a few others had come here as pioneers. Beyond the temple had been a forest extending to the river; today all the forest was gone; in its place were only a number of ill-built houses, with tiles disarranged by time and wind, straggling houses, mainly occupied by weavers who spread out their weaving frames all along the street. But the temple, with its tower and golden crest and carved pillars, continued to receive support.

The story of Krishna and Radha was now being recited in song-form by a group of men, incoherently and cacophonously, while they acted as vocal accompanists for Rangi's dance, as she swayed and gesticulated. With all the imperfections, the effect of the incense and the chants made me drowsy and elated, and I forgot for a moment all my problems. Vasu was like an irrelevant thought. He should have no place in my scheme of things. People I had never seen in my life acted as a padding to my right and left and fore and aft. I had lived a circumscribed life and had never thought that our town contained such a variety of humanity—bearded, clean-shaven, untidy, tidy; women elegant, ravishing, tub-shaped and coarse; and the children, thousands of them, dressed, undressed, matted-haired, chasing each other between the legs of adults, screaming with joy and trying to press forward and grab the fruit offerings kept for the Gods. Half a dozen adults had set themselves the task of chasing the children away and compelling them to keep out of the main hall of the temple, but when they overflowed into the corridor and the veranda, half a dozen other people set themselves a similar task of keeping them out of the assembly listening to the Chairman's perorations. They chased them back into the hall with equal vigour, and the gang of children came screaming in, enjoying immensely the pendulum swing back and forth.

Through all this babble, the music went on. But I had withdrawn from everything and found a temporary peace of mind. The sight of the God, the sound of music, the rhythm of cymbals and the scent of jasmine and incense induced in me a temporary indifference to everything. Elephant? Who could kill an elephant? There came to my mind the tale of the elephant

Gajendra, the elephant of mythology who stepped into a lake and had his leg caught in the jaws of a mighty crocodile; and the elephant trumpeted helplessly, struggled, and in the end desperately called on Vishnu, who immediately appeared and gave him the strength to come ashore out of the jaws of the crocodile. "In this story," I told myself, "our ancestors have shown us that an elephant has a protected life and no one can harm it." I felt lighter at heart. When the time came the elephant would find the needed strength. The priest was circling the camphor light before the golden images, and the reflections on the faces made them vibrate with a living quality. God Krishna was really an incarnation of Vishnu, who had saved Gajendra; he would again come to the rescue of the same animal on whose behalf I was . . .

Unknowingly I let out a terrific cry which drowned the noise of children, music, everything. "Oh, Vishnu!" I howled. "Save our elephant, and save all the innocent men and women who are going to pull the chariot. You must come to our rescue now." Unknown to myself, I had let out such a shout that the entire crowd inside and outside the hall stood stunned, and all activity stopped. The Chairman's speech was interrupted as my voice overwhelmed the loud-speaker. Rangi stopped dead in her dance. I was soon surrounded by a vast crowd of sympathizers. I felt faint and choked by the congestion.

"Did you shout like that? The Chairman's speech . . ." It was Sen speaking, to whom the only thing that mattered was the Chairman's speech. He was angry and agitated. I heard someone remark, "This man is possessed, listen to him." My shout had brought round me all the friends I had been looking for in the crowd. Muthu, the tea-stall keeper, was very tender. He said, "Are you feeling well?" I felt not unwell but foolish to have brought on myself so much attention. "Where have you been all along? I've been looking for you." I had now lost the initiative in my affairs. A number of busybodies carried me out to the veranda under the sky and fanned my face. The veterinary doctor felt my pulse and injected a drug into the veins of my arm. The poet had my head on his lap. "Doctor, don't give me an elephant dose of anything. I have never seen you curing human ills." The crowd that stood over me was enormous. Faces everywhere, to my right, left, above and aside. A glut of breathing, sighing, noisy humanity, packing every inch of space. The journalist suddenly lost his head and charged madly into the crowd crying, "If you don't leave him alone, he'll die of lack of air," and people made way. The incomplete speech of the Chairman seemed to have given an edge to his temper.

The Chairman sailed in with a lot of dignity. He stooped over to ask, "Are you feeling better?"

"I'm absolutely well, nothing is the matter with me. Please go and continue your speech. Don't stop it on any account."

The Chairman looked pleased at the importance given to his speech. He cackled like a shy adolescent. The Chairman of the Municipal Council was actually a man who owned a sweet-meat shop and had risen to his present position through sheer hard work. He was supposed to have started life as a servant and ultimately became the owner of the sweetmeat shop. He always wore (even in his sleep, so people said) a white Gandhi cap as an unwavering member of the Congress Party; a chubby, rosy-cheeked man, who evidently consumed a great deal of his own sweets. Seeing his face so close to mine, I felt reassured. Here was a man who could save the elephant. I said, "You must protect the elephant."

"Which elephant?" he asked, rather startled.

I explained. I took my head off the lap of the pink coat and said to the poet, "Take him to where the elephant is kept." The poet demurred, the Mayor dodged the suggestion, but I was adamant. The Mayor was being watched by a big circle of the crowd; he did not want to be embroiled in a scene with me and so left. The poet was glad to be out of the spotlight too. I could now sit up. I realized that I had an odd commanding position. People were prepared to do anything I suggested. I felt better. At this moment my wife entered the scene, accompanied by my little son. Both of them rushed to me with agonized cries. I didn't like such a dramatic show, so I told my wife, "Why are you behaving like this? I only felt a little choked in there and so came out to sit here."

"You were lying flat on Uncle's lap," said my boy.

"Only because they would not let me rise to my feet." My wife burst into tears and remained sobbing. "Now, now, don't be ridiculous; people will laugh at us for creating a scene and spoiling their day for them. Now, now, go and enjoy yourselves."

I was on my feet again, and went out of view of the crowd, so that they might carry on normally. I felt rather foolish to have drawn so much attention to myself. I left the temple swiftly by a back door and went home through the lanes. My wife and son accompanied me. I felt bad about depriving them of the pleasure they had come to enjoy at the temple. My son was openly critical. "Why should we go home so soon? I want to stay and watch the fun." On our way we saw the schoolmaster going towards the temple, and I handed over the boy to him with "Please don't let him join the procession, he must come home for supper."

"I'll bring him back," said the teacher.

We were not gone long before we heard the piper resume his music, and the loud-speaker's mumbo-jumbo over the babble of the crowd, and that made me happy. Life had become normal again at the temple.

CHAPTER TEN

At home my wife unrolled a mat, spread a soft pillow and insisted upon my lying down to rest, turning a deaf ear to all my pleading that I was in a perfectly normal condition. She went in to make coffee and nourishment for me. She grumbled, "Not eating properly, not sleeping, not resting. God knows why you wear yourself out in this way?" How could I tell her about Rangi? It would be awkward and impossible. But if I tried to explain it would be impossible to talk of the matter, leaving out Rangi. And if my wife should ask, "When and where did Rangi meet you?" I would be unable to reply. I thought it best to accept the situation and rest my weary body on the mat and consume whatever was placed before me. Anyway no one was going to miss me, and nothing in the programme was going to be altered because I wasn't there. The whole programme was so well organized that nothing could be halted. That was the chief trouble now; neither Vasu nor the temple authorities seemed prepared to relax their plans ever so slightly. Each was moving in a fixed orbit as if nothing else mattered or existed.

After the refreshment she had provided me, I fell into a drowse. What had really been the matter with me was lack of food and sleep; now I was having both and benefiting by them. I enjoyed the luxury of floating off through the air on drifting cotton-wool immediately I shut my eyelids. My wife sat at my side, fanning me. She was very anxious about me. I don't know what she had heard. I myself had no notion what my state had been before I let out the shout about the elephant. My wife had dressed herself in her heliotrope silk sari, which she reserved for special occasions; it showed that she considered the temple function a most important one, and it depressed me to see her forgo it. I had implored her, "Please go and enjoy yourself at the temple. I can look after myself quite well. Don't worry about me."

She ignored my advice and replied light-heartedly, "I went there only because you were there," which pleased me. She added, "Not that I care for these crowds. Babu was crazy about it, and has taken out all the savings in his money box for sweets and toys."

"Oh, I should be with him. I could give him such a nice time," I said remorsefully.

"You will do us all a favour if you keep away from the crowd," she said, and added, "Now sleep a little."

"Why am I being treated like a baby?" I protested. She did not answer and I fell asleep, until I heard soft hammer-strokes on the walls of cotton-wool which had encased me. When the hammer-strokes ceased, I heard voices, and then my wife stood over me. A ray of evening sun thickened with iridescent specks of dust came in through the ventilator of our dining-hall. It used to have a red glass pane when we were young, and made me sick when the evening sun threw a blood-red patch on the wall. Luckily the red pane had been smashed by a stone thrown by a street urchin one mango season, who had actually aimed at the fruits ripening on the trees in our garden, and the pane was never replaced.

My wife said, "Someone to see you." She did not like any visitor to disturb me. Her tone was hostile. She added, "His name is Muthu. Seems to be from a village."

Immediately I was on my feet. "Ah, Muthu! Muthu! Come in, please."

He had his umbrella hooked as usual to his forearm. "I wanted to see you and so came. I told the mistress of the house that I would wait until you were awake. Why did you disturb yourself? Go back and rest. I will wait."

I resisted his suggestion, but he was so firm and insistent that I had no alternative but to go back to my mat. He followed me and sat down on the edge of the mat, carefully laying his umbrella on the floor beside his feet. He looked round appreciatively and cried, "What a big house you have! Do you live in the whole of it or have you rented out a portion?"

I lay back on my pillow, and hotly repudiated the idea. "I never want to be or ever wanted to be a rent-collector. We have always entertained guests rather than tenants." I put into my sentence all the venom I wanted to inject into the memory of Vasu.

"It all depends," Muthu said. "There is no harm in making a little money out of the space you really do not need."

"It depends," I echoed. "My wife would never permit me, even if I wanted to."

"Then you can do nothing about it," he said. "It's best to listen to the advice of one's wife—because sooner or later that's what everyone does, even the worst bully. Take my own uncle, such a bully for forty years, but at sixty he became a complete slave to his wife. If people are not slaves before sixty, they become slaves after sixty," he said. He was trying to amuse me—a sick man. It was obvious that he was trying to steer away from the topic of the procession and the temple ceremony. "He waits for her command every moment, and even stands and sits according to her direction," he said and laughed. It really amused me, this picture of the bully fawning on his wife at sixty, and I cried to my wife, "Coffee for my friend!" at which he shouted, "Good lady, no, don't trouble yourself, no coffee for me."

"Don't listen to him, but bring the coffee or make it if you haven't got it ready," I cried. He called in turn, "Good lady, if you must be troubled, let it be just cold water, a glass of water."

"Is it impossible for me to offer you anything?" I cried.

"Yes, yes, I never need anything. I have told you I never take anything outside my home."

"And yet you want everyone to come and ask for tea in the village!" I said complainingly.

"I never force it on anyone," he said.

There was another knock on the door, and presently my wife ran across to open it and came back, followed by Sen. "Another cup of coffee," I cried as she went back to the kitchen. Sen cried, "So good to see you again in this state; the speech went off very well in spite of the interruption. You really gave a shout which could have gone to heaven, you know."

"Why talk of all that now?" said Muthu.

"Why not?" cried the journalist aggressively. "He is all right. And he was all right. Why shouldn't a man let out a shout if it pleases him? This is a free country in spite of all the silly rules and regulations that our Government is weaving around us."

By the time my wife was ready with two cups of coffee, there was a third knock on the door, followed by another one a moment after: the pink-coated poet, followed by the veterinary doctor. So there was a full assembly on the mat at my house. My wife had to prepare coffee again and again. She accepted the situation cheerfully; the important thing was to keep me in good humour at home. The veterinary doctor felt my pulse and cried, "You are in perfect gear, you must have had some temporary fatigue or something of the kind, a sudden attack of nerves."

"I have never felt better," I said, although the thought kept troubling me that the veterinarian was trespassing unwarrantedly into human fields.

"Haven't you noticed a dog let out a sudden howl, or an elephant trumpet out for no known cause? It's the same mechanism in all creatures. In our institute we spend a course of six months on comparative anatomy and psychology. Only the stimuli and medicinal doses differ between human beings and animals."

As we were talking the beam of light on the wall had disappeared and a dull twilight was visible above the central courtyard. It seemed absurd that after the preparation of weeks we should all of us be gathered tamely on the mat in my hall instead of bustling about in the temple. What a difference between the picture of the situation as I had visualized it and as it turned out to be! I said with a sigh, "All of us should be there at the temple."

"There is nothing very much to do at the moment," said the journalist. "This is a sort of intermission. The main worship is over—the poems have been read and dedicated."

"I missed it," I said ruefully.

The poet said, "You didn't miss much. I felt too nervous, and I don't think anyone understood anything."

"It was quite good," said Sen encouragingly. "Some people came round to ask where they could get copies."

"Probably they expect free copies."

"Free or otherwise, the world will have to wait until I am ready to print," I said.

Muthu said, "Please give me also a copy."

I said, "Yes," although I was not sure if he read anything.

The poet was by nature silent and retiring, and beyond sniggering a little he said nothing. The journalist had him in complete charge. "Oh, I am sending review copies to thirty newspapers first thing tomorrow, and a special copy to Sahitya Akademi at Delhi. They are wasting funds giving an award to every Tom, Dick and Harry. This is the first time they have had a chance to recognize real literature. Our Government has no lack of funds, but they don't know how to spend properly, that's what is the matter with them. I am going to show them a way to redeem themselves. I put this into the Chairman's speech, pretty strongly, and he just recited it as I wrote it, although he is a Congressman." He laughed at the memory of his trick.

Night fell. Lights were switched on. My wife began her work in the kitchen. I could hear the clinking of vessels. I said, all my responsibilities coming back into my mind one by one, "Did the flower supplies, did the . . ." I fretted until they assured me that everything was going well. And then one by one they came round to asking what really had upset me. I had to tell them about Vasu's plans. They were incensed.

"Who is this upstart to come and disturb us? We will get the police to seize his gun." "We'll throw him out of the town." "I'll knock him down with a hammer, if it comes to that."

I suggested, "Why not change the route of the procession?"

"Why should we? We will change nothing for the sake of this man! We will twist his neck so that he faces the other way."

"It's not possible. The route has been fixed and the licence taken for it. It's impossible to change anything."

"Why not drop the procession altogether?"

"Thousands of persons to be frustrated because of this fool, is that it?" "No—never. We'll deal with him. We have been too tolerant."

"Or why not leave the elephant out?"

"Impossible. What's a procession without an elephant. You know how much we've spent on the elephant."

"I'll be with Kumar myself, and let's see what happens. He is more sound in mind than any human being in this town."

"No, no, let's change nothing," Sen said. He swore, and the others agreed, "We'll route the procession as arranged. Nothing shall be changed. Let us see what happens."

Muthu became extremely nervous about his elephant. He lowered his voice and said, "I knew something had been going on. It started long ago. Do you remember that tailor? He is a friend of Vasu, fancies himself a part owner of the elephant. And I heard he has already received money from Vasu and has given him a document transferring to him his share of the elephant. I heard also a rumour that it was Vasu who tried to poison Kumar."

"Aha," said the doctor. "I suspected something like it."

They sallied out in a great rage, determined to tackle Vasu in a body. I could not stop them.

They were a determined lot. In their numbers they felt strong. First, led by the journalist, they started out to find the District Superintendent of Police at his home in Lawley Extension, for which purpose they hired Gaffur's taxi at the fountain. They found that he had just returned from a long journey, had put up a reclining chair and was resting on the terrace with a paper in his hand. Sen was his friend. He went straight to the terrace and spoke to him.

He listened to their complaint and said, "How do you know that he is going to create a disturbance? How do you know that he will employ his gun in the manner you suggest? He has an arms licence, hasn't he?"

"So any man with an arms licence can shoot at anything, is that it? A wonderful law!"

The D.S.P. was annoyed at the contemptuous reference to the law, and retorted, "That depends; we cannot simply snatch away a licensed weapon because someone thinks it will be fired."

"So you want to wait until the damage is done?"

"We cannot take action unless there is concrete evidence or a consequence."

"Can't you do something to prevent possible damage to life and property?"

"That only a magistrate can do, but even he cannot bind anyone over without a proper cause."

The Superintendent was a police officer, seasoned in jargon and technicalities. He refused to accompany them to Vasu's room, but telephoned to the Town Inspector, "Have you made proper arrangements for this evening's procession? Have enough men to handle the crowd along the route. There must be no trouble or complaints anywhere. I've some people here who apprehend a breach of the peace. I want you to go with them and tackle a man who is threatening to create a disturbance. Meet them at the market fountain in five minutes."

At the fountain, a police officer in uniform was there to receive them. They jumped out of the taxi, and surrounded the officer and gave an account of the impending trouble. He was a tall, lean man, with a lot of belts and cross-belts, a very serious-looking man with lines on his forehead. One look at him, and they were satisfied that here was a man who would stand no nonsense from anyone, a grim, determined man.

He simply repeated the doubts that the Superintendent himself had mentioned. "If the man possesses a licence, he can keep his weapon wherever he likes. Who can question him?"

"But can he shoot from the window?"

"Why should he do that? What's your basis for saying it?" They had no answer to give and he said, "All right, we'll see what we can do."

The Inspector stayed downstairs. Led by Sen, supported by the veterinary doctor, the pink-coated poet bringing up the rear, they boldly went up the staircase and knocked on Vasu's door. They were considerably emboldened by the fact that a real live Inspector of Police was down below, waiting to appear at the lightest summons. The door opened, and Vasu's head appeared with its dark halo of hair, set off by the light from his room. "You people want to see me now?"

"Yes," said the journalist. "Rather urgently."

Vasu raised his brow. "Urgent! All of you to see me?" And then he counted, "One, two, three, four people to call on me! I don't want to see anyone now. So try again tomorrow." With that he turned back and tried to shut the door in the face of his visitors. Since the door opened outwards, the journalist seized the knob and held it back. Vasu looked amused. "Do you know, I could easily pick up all four of you and toss you downstairs? When I plainly say I don't care to talk, how can you persist? All right. I will give you each a minute. Be brief. What is it?" He was not disposed to admit them. He blocked the doorway, and they were ranged on the landing.

The journalist stated point-blank, "We have a report that there is likely to be a disturbance while the procession passes down this road."

"If you know that, why don't you take the procession around somewhere else?"

"That's not your concern. We will not tolerate any disturbance."

"Oh, iron-willed men! Very good. I agree with you. Don't tolerate any disturbance."

"That elephant belongs to no one but the Goddess on the hill road. If anyone tries to harm it . . . ," began Muthu and Vasu cut in, "Why don't you mind your tea-shop and keep off the flies, and leave these issues to others? Don't try to speak for any elephant."

"We know what you have been trying to do, and we aren't going to stand any nonsense," the veterinary doctor said. "I have examined Kumar and know him inside out. He is in perfect health, more sober than any human being here."

"So what?" asked Vasu.

"If anyone wishes to drive him crazy, he'll not succeed, that's what I wish to say."

"Doctor, you may have an American degree, but you know

nothing about animals. Do they have elephants in America? Try to get into a government department, count your thirty days and draw your sinecure's allowance. Why do you bother about these matters? Poet, say something in your monosyllables. Why are you silent? Don't be smug and let others fight your cause. Sell me a copy of your poem as soon as it is read. That's all? Now be off, all of you."

The journalist warned him, "We are not bothered about you. We'll leave you alone. You leave our procession alone. This is a sacred function. People are out there to be with their God. . . ."

"If God is everywhere, why follow Him only in a procession?"

The journalist ignored this remark and said, "Hundreds of men and women and children with the chariot . . ."

"What's this special point about women and children? You are all practising chivalry, are you? If men are to be caught in a stampede, why not women and children also? What's the point in saving women and children alone? What will they do after their men are stamped out? If you are a real philosopher and believe in reincarnation, you should not really mind what happens. If one is destroyed now, one will be reborn within a moment, with a brand-new body. Anyway, do you know why we have so many *melas* in our country? So that the population may be kept within manageable limits. Have you not observed it? At *Kumb Mela*, thousands and thousands gather; less than the original number go back home—cholera, or smallpox, or they just get trampled. How many temple chariots have run over the onlookers at every festival gathering? Have you ever paused to think why it's arranged thus?"

Vasu's philosophical discourse could not proceed further as the Police Inspector showed himself at this moment. He pushed the others aside and accosted Vasu.

The Inspector asked, "You have a gun?"

"I have two," replied Vasu.

"I want to see your licence."

Vasu opened a cupboard, produced a brown envelope and tossed it at the Inspector. The Inspector went through it and

304 R. K. NARAYAN

asked, "Where are your arms?" Vasu pointed to his rifle on the chair, and his revolver on the table. The Inspector went over, picked them up, and examined them. "Are they loaded?" he asked.

asked, "Where are your arms?" Vasu pointed to his rifle on the chair, and his revolver on the table. The Inspector went over, picked them up, and examined them. "Are they loaded?" he asked.

"Of course they are loaded. They are not toys."

"Where is your ammunition statement?"

"In that envelope."

"When did you discharge your last shot?"

"Shut up, Inspector, and get out. I don't have to answer your questions. What's your authority for coming and questioning me?"

"Our D.S.P.'s order."

"It's my order that you clear out, with this bunch of men who have no business here."

The journalist protested. Muthu jumped up and down in rage. Vasu said, "Inspector, you are trespassing in my house. Where is your warrant to enter private premises? Come on, produce a warrant. Otherwise I will complain against you for trespass and these men will be my witnesses. I'll wire to the Inspector-General and the Home Minister. You think you can fool me as you fool all these wretched bullock-cart drivers and cobblers and ragamuffins whom you order about. Whom do you think you are talking to?"

"Be calm, be calm. I came here only as your friend."

"Nonsense. You my friend! I have never seen you."

"I came to ask something of you, that's all."

"What is it? Be brief."

"I just want to suggest, why not let me hold your weapons for you in our Market Station. You may take them back tomorrow."

Vasu said, "I see that you are still toying with that gun of mine. Put it down where you took it from. Come on. Don't play with it."

"I'll arrest you for disorderly behaviour and lock you up for the night or for any length of time under the Public Safety Act." He took out his whistle, and was about to blow it and call the men who were patrolling the road below. Before anyone could realize what was happening, Vasu plucked the whistle out of the Inspector's mouth and flung it away. It sailed over the landing and fell with a clatter down below amid the pythons and all the other stuffed creatures. The Inspector was enraged. He raised his arm and tried to slap Vasu's face. Vasu reared his head back, shielding his face with his hand, then gave a sweep with the back of his hand and brought it down with a slicing movement on the Inspector's wrist and dislocated it. The Inspector screamed and recoiled as if he had touched fire. He still held the gun in the other hand.

"I told you to put that gun back where you took it from. Will you do it or not?"

"You are trying to order me," cried the Inspector. Tears welled up in his eyes through pain. Vasu took him by the shoulder and propelled him to the cot, then pushed him down, saying, "Take a rest, you poor fish. You should not venture to do things without knowing what's what." He snatched the gun from his hand and put it away. The police officer wriggled with pain. Vasu looked at him for a while, and said with cynical laughter. "You have hurt yourself. I did nothing. I never hit anyone. Years ago I made that vow. If I had hit you with my hand—do you want to see what would have happened?" He brought his palm flat down on the iron frame of the cot and cracked it. The Inspector watched him mutely. Sen asked, "Do you know what the penalty is for assaulting a police officer in uniform?"

"Do you know what the consequences could be for trespass? Anyway my lawyer will deal with it. Now all of you leave me. I do not want to hit anyone, you now know why. Inspector, you should not have hurt yourself like that!" He mocked the man in pain.

The veterinarian approached the Inspector and said, "Let's get this dressed immediately. Come along, we'll go to the hospital." They were all for leaving. Sen said, "If anything happens to the people or the procession . . ." Muthu said, "We know what you are trying to do with that elephant. If anything happens . . ." which only provoked Vasu's mirth. The Inspector got to his feet, glared at Vasu and said, "I'll get you for this . . ." The poet alone tried to sneak downstairs without a word. Vasu just held him by the scruff, turned him round and asked, "Where is your patron saint? Send him up next. He's the one who has sent you all up on this fool's errand, I know."

While all this was happening (as narrated to me by Sen later), at home my wife was arguing with me to stay put on my mat. I had got a passing notion that I ought to visit the temple and take charge of the procession. My wife was aghast at the idea. She repeated several times, "The doctor has said you must not . . ."

"What doctor! He is only an animal doctor!" I said. "We can't pay serious attention to what he says."

But she was adamant and pleaded with me, "Can't you stay in at least one day in a year!" She had prepared a feast for me. She knew all my preferences: potato and onion mash, rice patties fried in oil, chutney ground with green chili, sauce with brinjal and grated coconut, cucumber sliced, peppered and salted. She was so full of enthusiasm that I had to prevent her by my rude remarks from exceeding ten courses. Our house was fragrant with the frying in the kitchen. All this felicity was meant to be a compensation to me for missing the magnificent flower decorations, the music, the lights and the crowd. My son came home with his schoolteacher and was full of descriptions of what he had seen. He said, "The chariot is made of jasmine buds, and they have fitted small electric bulbs all over it. Father, Father, I bought a sugar cane for the elephant. He snatched it from my hand, and you know how quickly he ate it! I bought him another one, and that left me with only six annas. I bought this whistle." He produced from his pocket a reed whistle and blew shrilly. "The mahout has promised to give me a ride on the elephant's back. My friend Ramu says that the elephant is borrowed and that it'll go away tomorrow. Is it a fact, Father? Let us have our own elephant for this temple. The mahout has taught him how to take a garland from a basket and present it to the God. He is very intelligent. Father, Father, please let me go and watch the procession." His mother added from inside, "If our neighbours are going and if you promise to stay in and rest, I would like to go and see the start of the procession and come back immediately. The child will love it. We can't say when we may have another chance."

"All right, why not let me take you both?"

"No, no, in that case I don't want to go," she said. "It's not so important." I enjoyed the status of being more important than the procession. To be fussed over like this came only once in a decade when one fell ill or down a ladder; it was a nice change from protecting and guiding others and running the household as its head.

I lay back on the mat, picked up a picture book and read Babu a story, much against his will as he only wanted to talk about the elephant and the procession. But we had exhausted the topic of the procession. He had been talking of nothing else; whom he met, who fell off the steps leading to the tower of the temple, why the drummer suddenly ceased in the middle of an enraptured performance because he found a grasshopper crawling down his spine—Babu knew who had perpetrated the joke because he had assisted him in tracking and trapping the grasshopper; how he and another friend snatched away from under the nose of the chief priest the plantains which had been kept on a plate for offering to the God, and to this minute no one could guess what had happened to the fruit. He looked at me triumphantly in appreciation of his own exploits. He narrated how he and his gang had devised a game of hide and seek between the legs of the devotees assembled in the hall and how, as they all stood in prayer with eyes shut, his friends had crawled between their legs and roused them by tickling their calf-muscles. I realized how he must have multiplied the task of those men who had been busy since morning chasing the urchins out. Then he went on to tell me how one of his friends was waiting for a chance to poke a needle into the elephant's side. At this I remonstrated, "Never do that. An elephant will always mark such a fellow down and . . ." I thought I might turn his ideas from these dangerous paths and picked up one of his picture books and tried to read him a story. "Once upon a time . . . ," I began, but he was not interested. The activities of the temple were so immediate and real that the images of fiction were uninteresting. He got up and ran to the kitchen on the plea that he felt hungry.

Presently my wife called me in to dinner. She had spread out

a large plantain leaf and had served my food on it as if I were a
rare guest come to the house. She had placed a plank for me to
sit on. She watched me with satisfaction as I made preparations
to eat with relish. I suggested, "Why don't you also put a leaf
for yourself and let us serve ourselves?" She turned down my
suggestion. She had decided to play the hostess and serve me
ceremoniously. Nothing I suggested was going to be accepted
today.

I enjoyed my dinner, and kept paying her compliments on
her excellence as a cook. There was a knock on the door. Babu,
who had finished his dinner, ran out to open it. He came back
to say, "A *mami* has come."

"*Mami!*" cried my wife. She was busy serving me. "It must
be our neighbour come to see if I'm ready for the procession.
Tell her to come in and take a seat. I'll see her in a moment."

The boy said coldly, "She is not asking for you. She is asking
for Father."

"What! Who is she?" asked my wife with a sudden scowl on
her face.

I trembled within myself and muttered with a feeble, feigned
surprise, "Asking for me. Ha! Ha! It must be a mistake!"

My wife set the vessel down and went out of the room, saying under her breath, "Let me see."

The boy tried to follow her. I called him back. "Boy, fetch me
that water-jug." When he came close to me with the jug, I asked
in a whisper, "Who is she? What is she like?"

"I don't know. She was in the temple dancing."

I knew now. My worst fears were confirmed. All the fine moments of the evening, the taste of exquisite food, everything
was turning to gall on my tongue. I knew my wife. Although I
had had no occasion to test it, I knew she could be fiercely jealous. Before I had time to decide what to say or how to say it,
she stood before me.

She said, "That woman wants to see you. What's your connection with her?"

"What woman?" I asked with affected innocence. I got up
from my dinner, went out to rinse my hand and wipe it on a
towel, and came back to the hall. "Bring the betel leaf and nut."

I put on a deliberate look of unhurrying indifference, though all the time I knew that Rangi was waiting at the door. I chewed the betel leaves and went back to the kitchen. My wife had settled down to her dinner, serving herself. She did not look up. I said, "Have you any food left, or have I eaten everything up? If there is nothing left, it's your own fault, you should not have excelled yourself in that way!"

She tried to smile; my praise, very sincere of course, had its effect. She was transferring food from the dining leaf to her mouth with her head lowered. Now she looked up to say, "I have asked her to wait in the passage. I didn't want the neighbours to see her at our door." She had to lower her voice in order not to be heard by the woman concerned.

I whispered back, "You did right, you did right," and then, "You could have asked her why she had come."

"Why should I? If it's your business, it's your business, that's all. I am not interested."

I made a noise of vexation, and said, "What a nuisance! It must be something connected with the temple. Can't I rest even for a day?" So muttering, I made my way towards the dark passage. There she was standing in the passage. She had taken off her gaudy dance ornaments and costume and was dressed in a plain sari; even in the dark I could see the emphatic curves of her body. I stood away from her, at a safe distance, right by the inner doorway, and asked rather loudly, "What is the matter?" I did not want to carry on a whispered dialogue with her.

But she replied in a whisper, "I wanted to know how you were, master?"

I was touched by her solicitude. "Oh, I'm all right. Nothing was really the matter."

"I saw everything, but could not come over because I was on duty before the God."

"Oh," I said, feeling rather pleased. "Are your duties finished for the day? What about the procession?"

"It's at nine o'clock. I shall have to get back."

"Oh," I said.

"Won't you go with the procession, sir?" she asked.

My son, who had stood around uneasily, feeling rather shy in the presence of a dancing woman, went away and hid himself in the kitchen. Rangi assumed an even softer and hoarser whisper to say, "He came to my house in the afternoon when I was at the temple, and left orders that I should see him."

I grew apprehensive. "Don't go. Get back to the temple. Be with the crowd."

"He may come to my house again and set fire to it. Only my old mother is there—deaf and blind."

"Why should he set fire to your house?"

"He is wild with me and wants to talk to me!" she said with a sigh.

"Talk to you! He will probably murder you!" I said. She brooded over my words. I told her, "Why don't you tell the police?"

She shook her head. "He won't be afraid of the police. He is afraid of nothing. The police will laugh at me. What can they do? He is not afraid of anything or anybody. That's how he is."

"Don't go to him," I implored her.

My wife had finished her dinner and was passing up and down on various minor errands, casting sly, sidelong looks at the two of us in the dark passage. Rangi was sobbing at the prospect before her. "I don't know what he will do to me! He has summoned me. He confided in me. I betrayed his trust. I had to . . . I hope, hope, you have taken precautions."

"Oh, surely," I said with a grand show of confidence and aggressiveness. "We won't let a fellow like that get away with his ideas."

"You don't know him well enough. He is afraid of nothing on earth or in heaven or hell."

"We have our own methods for dealing with such fellows. We are a match for him," I said.

"He is so strong and obstinate. If he thinks of something, he has to do it; no one on earth can change his mind."

The woman seemed obsessed with the grandeur and invincibility of the man. I was not going to tolerate it. "Rangi, don't be carried away by the notions you have of him. He is just an ordinary common bully. We know how to tackle him."

"Now, what shall I do, sir? I have come to you because I don't know what to do. I thought of going to him to see if I could get him into a good mood to listen to my words. I have cooked his favourite *pulav* and have it here." She indicated a hamper of food she had brought along.

"But you said yourself that it's impossible to make him change his mind."

She whispered seductively, "I'll try. A woman in my position has her ways."

I didn't know what she meant, but it sounded mysterious. I said, "He may not let you go back to the procession. Don't go to him. Go home."

"If I don't obey his summons he may set fire to my house, with my blind mother not knowing what is happening."

"I'll arrange for people to guard your house. Don't let him blackmail you into visiting him. He'll hold you back. He may even tie you up hand and foot. I'll send the proper people to guard your house." I spoke grandiosely, without the shred of a notion how I was going to arrange it. She brought her palms together in a salute and left me, and vanished down the moon-lit street.

I went back to my wife. I found her tidying herself up in the dark ante-room, before a mirror. I said expansively, "You know what's the matter with that woman?"

"Why should it interest me?" she asked. I was struck by the cold, indifferent tone in which she spoke. "I don't know who she is, and I don't care." She readjusted her sari and called, "Babu!" In a moment he was at her side. "Coming to the temple?"

"Yes, of course." He had already gone ahead, to the outer door.

I asked her, "Are you going to the temple?"

"Yes," she said monosyllabically.

"But you said you would not go!" I said.

"Now I say I'm going, that's all there is to it." I could see even by the dim light that her ears were red.

"I wanted to speak to you. I thought you might rest here and talk over things."

She turned a deaf ear to what I was saying. I followed her

mumbling, "You wanted me to stay at home, now you are going!" I sounded pathetic.

"Stay or go, it's all the same to me," she said and was gone
down the steps. She went on down the road, with Babu pranc-
ing beside her. She had not given me a chance even to pick a
quarrel with her.

I didn't like to go in. I sat on the *pyol*, looking in the direction in which she had gone. What was the use? There was a
silly little hope that she would repent her brusqueness and
come back to make amends. My only other companion for the
night was a street-dog curled up in the gutter. All the other living creatures of that area had gone to the temple. Not a soul
remained at home—except the asthmatic in the sixth house,
whom I could hear cough and expectorate. Sitting there and
brooding, I had time to take stock. The trouble with me was
that I was not able to say "no" to anyone and that got me into
complications with everyone, from a temple prostitute to a
taxidermist. I repeated to myself all the stinging rejoinders I
should have hurled at my wife. I should have behaved like one
of my ancestors (the story was often told by my great-aunt),
who used to bring home his concubine and have her dinner
served by his wife. So when my wife asked, "What is your business with her?" I should have instantly said, "I want to seduce
Rangi or be seduced by her." If my wife had said, "Of all
women!" I should have replied, "Yes, of course, you are blinded
by jealousy. No doubt she chews tobacco and looks rugged, but
she has it, it comes through even when she whispers to you.
How can any man resist her? I'm sorry for you. You should
take more trouble to keep me in good humour. It's no good losing your temper or sulking or snapping a reply. If I followed the
same procedure, you'd not be able to stand it for a second. As
a man I have strength no doubt to stand all your nonsense. But
you should not strain it too much. That's all now, don't do it
again."

The moon came over the roof-tiles of the opposite row of
houses, full and brilliant. I could hear the hubbub of voices
from the temple half a mile away. It saddened me to be detached from all this activity. I felt like a man isolated by an in-

fection. I almost formed, as a sort of revenge on my wife, a plan to appear at the temple precincts and take a hand in the conduct of the procession. Without creating a panic, I would gently navigate the chariot into a different route. That is, of course, if I rushed around a bit, met the D.S.P. and changed the permit for another route. There was not a single person in that whole throng who could organize and guide a procession as I could. I swelled with pride. I was the one man who could still achieve results.

But then I remembered I was an outcast. I felt nervous of appearing before the crowd again. I was not certain what I would do. Under the pressure of the crowd, if I let out a cry again, that would be the end of me. It might have the desirable effect of making my wife regret her petulance, but it was also likely to have me bundled off to the Madras Mental Hospital by the next train. I remembered a boy, a brilliant fellow, who had strode up and down Kabir Street singing all Tyagaraja's compositions for three days and nights continuously and had covered most of the compositions of that inspired saint. If he had been left alone for another day, he would have completed the repertory, but they seized and bundled him off by the five o'clock express to Madras. He came back a year later with a shaven head, but sober and quiet in all other respects. He was a friend of mine in my school-days, and he confessed that he had sung Tyagaraja's compositions only because he was keen on letting the public get an idea of the versatility of that great composer, but now he was afraid even to hum the tunes in his bath. Our Kabir Street citizens had exacting standards of sanity. I didn't want to be seized and put into the Madras train. Even if I didn't create a scene, the crowd would look at me as if I had recovered from a fit of epilepsy. They would not let me go with the procession.

All my old anxieties, which had been falsely lulled, suddenly rose to the surface. I took stock of the situation. What cause had I for smugness? I had done nothing to divert the procession, I had done nothing to disarm or dissuade Vasu; God knew what trick he might have up his sleeve. He might do nothing more than fling a firecracker from his window or bribe one of the torch-bearers to hold the torch close to the leg of the elephant. All evening we had done nothing but discuss the various methods of maddening an elephant—a needle stuck into a co-conut or banana and given it to swallow, an ant dropped in its ear, or a grain of sand in its eyes; it would be the easiest thing to drive an elephant mad. If people were lucky they might get out of its range or if they weren't a few might be caught and trampled to death, particularly if there was a stampede at that narrow bend in the Market Road, with the broad storm-drain on one side and the small mountain of road-metal heaped on the other (it was meant for the improvement of Market Road, but had remained untouched since 1945). People would thank anyone who shot the elephant at that moment. That poor ele-phant! He was enjoying all the fun today, decorated, happy, playing with the children, starting the day so well. Somehow he must return to the Goddess on the mountain road and graze in the forests on the blue hills and continue to delight the children in all those villages. Muthu hoped by hiring out the elephant for processions to earn enough money to build a tower for the temple of the Goddess, which would be visible for fifty miles around. It was impossible to conceive of Kumar stuffed and dissected and serving as an umbrella-stand or waste-basket in some fashionable home in the Eastern or Western world.

I had to do something. My wife had gone out, expecting me to act as the watchman of the house. It would be good to aban-don the house and let her discover that after all she could not presume on my goodness. A better plan still would be to lock the door and take the key away so that when she came back af-ter midnight she would wonder how to get to her bed. It was nearing ten, and the procession should be starting any minute now. No one could judge when it would arrive at the fountain. While on the road, the piper might start a big *alapana*, and until he attained certain flights and heights in a particular mel-ody and returned to earth the procession would not move, even if it took an hour. So by stages it might take hours to cover the distance between the temple and the fountain.

There was no sign of the music yet. Only the hubbub of voices indicated that the crowd was still waiting for the proces-sion to start. If it had started, I'd have heard the voices and music moving nearer, and above all my wife would have come back home. However temperamental she might be, I knew she would not go with the procession along with that crowd. She had enough sense to return home in time.

I felt angry at being chained to the house. I would go into the outer fringes of the crowd unrecognized and study the situation. I shut the door behind me and stepped down. I walked to the end of the street. Two men were coming in my direction. I stopped them to ask, "Has the procession started?"

"No they are waiting for ornaments for the elephant. Someone has gone to fetch them from the Talapur temple, head-ornaments of real gold."

Ten miles up and ten miles down, and perhaps an hour getting the ornaments out of the temple vaults. No chance of the procession starting before two a.m. What madness! Did it mean that my wife was going to stay at the temple till two? With the boy? I was in a measure relieved; every hour's delay seemed to me an hour's reprieve. I went back home; if the procession was starting late, then there was no purpose in my loitering at the temple gate. I went back home and laid myself down on the *pyol*. If I was to be a watchman, I'd better be one thoroughly, not a haphazard one! I didn't want the house to be looted; this was just the chance thieves waited for, when every householder would have gone out to the festival.

Lying on the mat on the *pyol*, as I kept gazing on the moonlit street, I fell asleep. I woke up hours later as I heard drums and pipe music approaching—I knew that the procession was in Market Road, parallel to our house. I grew worried about my wife and son, thinking that they were still out. On second thoughts I went in. I saw her asleep in her bed, with the child also asleep. I must have been soundly asleep indeed not to have known when she arrived. She must have come in long ago and gone to sleep. She ought to have wakened me, but she had preferred to go on practising her coldness towards me. In order to mete out to her the same treatment, I went back to my mat on the *pyol*.

I lay tossing on my mat. Far off the piper's music came from the procession. I followed it, visualizing all the stages of its progress. Now it must be passing the elementary school con-

ducted on the top storey of the Chairman's sweetmart, a rickety
terrace which would come down any day, but no one could
prevent it being there because it was the Chairman's building
and was certified to be safe. Some day when it fell it was going
to imperil the lives of a hundred schoolchildren and six or eight
teachers. But so far it had lived up to the optimistic estimate of
the municipal authorities and most of its ex-pupils were now
adults working and earning a living in various walks of life all
over India; I preferred to send Babu to another school, however. The drummer made enough noise to shatter the founda-
tions of this precarious building, but it was a matter of courtesy
for the procession to stop there, and the piper had saved his
breath for his masterpiece—"Bhairavi." He was beginning an
elaborate, intricate rendering of this melody, and that means
the crowd would gather round him, the God would repose in
his chariot, the elephant would stand ahead of the procession
with the mahout asleep on his back. People would crowd around
the piper and behave as if they had no further way to go.

It was much better that the procession halted here than at the
fountain. The time was around midnight now, and it would
take at least an hour for the procession to approach the market
fountain. I had plans to join the procession and mix with the
crowd an hour hence, and till then there was no harm in sleeping. "Bhairavi" could be heard as well here half asleep as anywhere, and so I allowed myself to be lulled by it, my favourite
melody in any case. It brought to my mind my childhood, when
visiting musicians used to come as our guests; there was a room
in our house known as the musician's room, for we always had
some musician or other staying with us, as my father was very
proud of his familiarity with all the musicians in South India
and organized their recitals in our town. (One of the charges
levelled against him by the opposing lawyer was that he had
squandered the family funds in entertaining musicians.) This
room was also used as a storing space for old bottles. The great
joke in those days was to answer, when anyone questioned why
old bottles were kept so safely, that if my uncles sued for them,
they could be given their due share. The room contained too
about seventy philosophical works; the entire philosophical li-

brary collected by my father or someone before him in Sanskrit and Tamil, along with bronze images used for worship. They had been willed to the third uncle, but they were left in our custody as my uncle was in the railway department and never stayed in the same place for more than three months. He was never known to have opened a book in his life after leaving school, but still he occasionally sent us a postcard to inquire if the volumes of philosophy were safe. Whenever my mother got into an argumentative mood, she would arraign my father for being a custodian of other people's property, and demand to know why he did not throw the articles out and get rid of all the responsibility. But my father was fond of his brothers, whatever they might do, and told her not to peep into that room as there was sufficient space in the rest of the house for her to mind.

I must have fallen asleep. When I woke up "Bhairavi" was no longer being played but some other tune, and the music was coming from close quarters across the row of buildings on Market Road. If my judgement was right the procession must now be near the silkware house. The next stop would be the fountain. I was seized with anxiety. The procession was nearing the range of Vasu's window. What reason had I for my inactivity? What right had I to presume that Muthu and the rest would have succeeded in restraining Vasu? Suppose they had done nothing, and a torch-bearer scalded the toe of the elephant and drove it mad? My duty now was clear. I must go and divert the procession away from the fountain and turn it into a side-street. But this might itself start a panic, and if Vasu really meant no mischief I should become responsible for a lot of panic and confusion.

There was no use lying here and cogitating while every minute a vast assembly was moving towards its doom. I had to do something about it. I got up briskly. I could hear my wife stirring, awakened by the pipe and band; she would probably come out to watch from the end of Kabir Lane, in which case I did not want to meet her. I walked across the road, opened the back door of my press and shut the door behind me. I was going to make a last-minute attempt to stop Vasu. He was not such a bad fellow after all. He would listen to me. He was considerably mellower than he used to be. I looked up at the attic. There was no light in it. Of course he would put out all lights. He was the prince of darkness, and in darkness his activities were to be conducted.

Suddenly I was inspired by all sorts of wonderful and effective plans. They were not shaped very clearly in my mind yet, but I was positive that all would be well. If you had asked me to see a blueprint, I would perhaps have fumbled, but deep within me the plans were ready, I felt sure. I would first steal up to his room, walk softly to his side; he was sure to be watching the window. Why not stun him from behind and save everyone all the worry and trouble of argument? Not practicable. One might talk of finishing off a cobra with a staff of bamboo, but it was always more likely that the cobra would prove smarter. Vasu might after all not be facing the window, but facing the door. Non-violence would be the safest policy with him. Mahatma Gandhi was right in asking people to carry on their fight with the weapon of non-violence; the chances of getting hurt were much less.

I had to squeeze myself through a little fence between my press and the staircase; the jeep was there all right. He was undoubtedly upstairs. It might be a good idea to set its petrol tank on fire. That would keep him busy until the procession passed. Of course he might make pulp of me if he discovered me doing it, but why not? No one was going to miss me. My wife was separated from me, there was none to bemoan my loss; true, Babu was likely to miss me for a few days, but children adapted themselves to new circumstances with surprising ease. It was pleasing to reflect that my wife would after all learn a lesson, that sulking did not pay. When Rangi spoke to me on an important matter, the thing for a rational being to do was to ask what exactly it was all about and approach things in a scientific frame of mind . . . No wonder Vasu was bitter against the whole world for its lack of scientific approach. If people were scientific-minded they would not jump to conclusions when a man spoke to Rangi in a half-dark passage.

I was at the foot of the staircase. The hyena was still there but pushed away to the side; it must have been a wasted labour for Vasu. It was surrounded by a few other odds and ends of dead creatures, nothing outstanding among them, but a miscellany of small game, such as a wild squirrel, a fox, a jungle dog, a small cheetah, and several reptiles. Vasu seemed to have turned his attention to small things in keeping with our Government's zeal for small industries. The smell of hide and packing-cases overwhelmed me.

I climbed the stairs. I had presumed all along that the door would be open. What if it should be shut? I would knock on it and allow events to develop. I was going to stop him from disturbing the procession; that was certain, but how was a question I still could not answer. I was going to depend upon my intuition. I was prepared to lose my life in the process.

I found the door open. I gave it a gentle push and peeped in. There he was as I had visualized him, beside the window, on a long easy chair. The lights, the Kitson vapour lamps and the torches of the procession were already illuminating the walls of the room, and there were moving shadows on them. The band and the pipe and the shouts of the men pulling the chariot could be heard from below. I could see his silhouette at the window, where he seemed to have made himself comfortable, with a pillow under his head. He had stretched his leg on a stool, he had his timepiece on another small table, and his gun lay on the floor within his reach. I could see so much by the flares flickering along the wall through the narrow window. Other silhouettes, of the small tiger cub and a few animals, stood out in the semi-darkness. He didn't move. That was a good sign. He had probably fallen asleep waiting for the procession to come along. All the drumming (they could at least have had the sense to pass the spot noiselessly, as a precaution) had apparently made no impression on him. He was obviously a sound sleeper, thank God.

My decision was swift; I would make a dash for his gun and seize it. My heart palpitated and my breath came and went like a bellows as I crawled towards the gun. If he woke up before I reached it, that would be the end of me. I started crawling like one of those panthers of the Mempi jungle, the distance between me and the gun being only a dozen feet; I covered half of it, the other half seemed interminable. My knees were sore, but

I felt that it was for a good cause that I was skinning them. He was still asleep. As my fingers reached the cold butt of his gun, I could have swooned with excitement. I had never touched a gun before and felt scared. I rose to my feet and covered him with the gun. Below the window the procession was passing rather quickly, as I thought. I wished I could go up and take a look at it, but he was between me and the window, and if he slept through it that would be the best arrangement possible. If he woke up, well, I had the gun with me at point-blank range. I would follow the method they used in films and command him not to stir until the procession passed. If he made the slightest movement, I would pull the trigger. My finger was on it already. Although I had had no practice with guns, I knew if I fiddled with the trigger the shot was bound to go off. I held the muzzle directly at his head, keeping it away, just out of his reach, in case he attempted to snatch it from my hand. I would hold him until the procession passed our road . . . and then how was our encounter to conclude? I couldn't say. I felt rather worried about it, although I was triumphant at my success thus far. I couldn't keep my eyes off him, although I was curious to watch the procession. From my place I could see the flower-decked top of the chariot and the little bulbs sparkling on it, the head of the elephant brilliant with the gold plates from Talapur, and the hunched form of the mahout. While passing he cast a look through our window. I supposed he had been advised to drive fast. In a moment he was out of view, and soon the procession itself was gone. The reflections on the walls vanished and the drums and pipes sounded far away, leaving a faint aroma of jasmine and roses in their wake. Just at this moment I was startled by the alarm bell of the clock going off. I gave a jump, the gun dropped from my hand, and I made a dash for the landing out of Vasu's reach.

CHAPTER ELEVEN

Life resumed its normal pace on the Market Road next morning, although the day started late. It was as if our town were waking up from a fantasy full of colour, glitter, crowd, and song. After this, it was difficult to wake to a dull workaday world. The Market Road was covered with litter, banana peels, coconut shells, leaves, and flowers. Municipal sweepers were busy. Sastri came only at nine o'clock and went straight to the type-board; he seemed determined to complete K.J.'s labels today. Muthu and the rest had left by an early bus for their respective homes. I sat at my desk and placed a pad and a pencil in position in order to make a note of payments to be made, cash in hand and cash promised. My head was still very unclear about the practical aspects of everything.

Our postman, Thanappa, whom we had known as children, old enough to have retired twice over but somehow still in service, was my first visitor for the day. I remembered seeing him in the days when postmen were given a red turban and a shining belt, a leather bag and khaki uniform. He had passed from that to the latest stage of donning a forage cap—a portly old man who not only knew the address of every citizen in the town but also the ups and downs of their fortunes. He was a timeless being. At his favourite corners, he spread out his letters and bags and packets and sat down to a full discussion of family and social matters; he served as a live link between several families, carrying information from house to house. All this took time, but nobody could hustle him, and we accepted our letters when they came. He was welcome everywhere. His habit when he came to my press was to stand in the doorway, rest his shoulder on the doorpost, and spend at least half an hour exchanging information with me. Only before leaving would he remember to give me the letter or book-packet. Today he stood on my door-step and looked serious, blinking through his inch-thick glasses. There was a frown on his face, and he breathed hard with excitement. He held up a letter without a word. I said, "Come in, Thanappa," and asked, "How did you like the procession last night?" He mumbled something and moved in as if he were in a trance. He placed the letter on my desk. "This receipt has to be signed."

I saw it was addressed to Vasu. "This is for him, Thanappa. Take it upstairs."

"I went up, but, but," he wetted his lips with his tongue, "he is dead." He spoke softly, he looked scared. "I usually take his mail to his bed, though I hate to go to his room. I thought he was sleeping in his chair. I went up with the letter. I almost touched him," he said with a shudder. The man looked desperate with the disgust he felt at the memory of that icy contact.

I said, "Thanappa, go and deliver those letters and try to get this thing out of your mind. Don't speak about this to anyone. I will go up and see things for myself and come back."

Thanappa hesitated for a second and decided to follow my advice. He asked, "So this registered letter goes back? Has no one else authorization to sign for him?" He picked up his bag and stepped out.

I went down the steps, around the side street and through the yard, and stood for a moment at the foot of the stairs, with the hyena shoved aside and mouldering in a corner, its glassy stare fixing me at the foot of the steps. I hesitated for a moment in the desperate hope that I might hear the stirrings of feet above. But there was the unmistakable silence of death. I reluctantly took myself up.

There he was as I had seen him last night on his canvas chair, with his arm dangling at his side. I went near and peered closer to see if he was really dead. For the moment I was not bothered with the mystery of his death but only with the fact. He had accustomed us so much to a still-life view that he seemed logically to be a part and parcel of his own way of life. The alarm-clock which had screeched in the dark on the previous night was now ticking away modestly. Its pale pink face must have watched the process of Vasu's death. I looked around. The frame of his bed was smashed; that was probably the reason why he could not sleep there but only on the easy chair. Somehow at that moment I took it very casually and felt no bother about how he might have met his end. I folded my arms across my chest, remembering that I had better not touch anything and leave a fingerprint. Anyway, Thanappa's fingerprints were bound to be there, so why add mine to the confusion and complicate the work of the police? My desire to search for Vasu's purse and read the blue letter in it was really great, but I didn't want the police to conclude that I had killed him and taken his purse. I peered closer to see if there was any injury. His black halo of hair was rumpled and dry. His eyes were closed. I could see no trace of injury. "Where is all your bragging," I thought, "now, and all your pushing and pulling and argument? Are you in heaven or hell? Wherever you are, are you still ordering people around?" I noticed on a low stool the jute bag containing food which I had seen in Rangi's hand on the previous night at my house. I wanted to see if he had eaten it, but the lid of the brass vessel was covered tight and I did not like to give it my thumb impression. His clothes lay, as usual, scattered on his cot and on every available space. The lid of his trunk was half open, revealing his familiar clothes, particularly the red check bush-shirt and the field-grey jacket he affected when he went out on his depredations. I stood over his trunk and kept looking in; if I could have rummaged in it without touching anything I would have done so. I wished I had gloves on, but this was not a part of the world where gloves were known. Not all my precautions to leave things alone could keep me from giving a jump when I saw the green folder peeping from within the folds of his clothes. What an amount of trouble he had given us over it! He had said, "An orang-utan has carried it up a tree and gone back to the jungle. If I see it again, I shall ask it to return it to the rightful owner, namely Mr. Nataraj. I know he will oblige us, he is a very reasonable orang . . . ," and laughed at our desperation. All I had been able to muster was, "We didn't know orang-utans

existed in India." "You want to teach me wild life?" he had
asked aggressively. That was before our last break, after which
he walked out of my office and I never saw him again until I
swallowed my pride and went up to the attic to plead with him
for the elephant. The green folder peeped out of a linen bush-
coat and a striped Singapore *lungi*. I brooded for a moment
about how to extract it without disturbing the arrangement. I
went out to the terrace to see if I could find some handy stick
with which to grasp it and pull it out. I became desperate, as I
realized that I must hurry now. The voices of people in the
street frightened me. I was afraid that Sastri might suddenly
come up and scream for the police. It was essential that I should
take charge of the green folder before anyone else saw it here. I
fervently hoped that Thanappa had the sense to keep his mouth
shut. The alum solution, moulds and various odds and ends
and nails were there, but not a cleft stick with which I could
pry the green folder out. I thrust my hand under my shirt,
worked my fingers through the end of my shirt, and gently
tugged the folder from his clothes. A couple of angry mosquitoes buzzed around my ears, but I could not wave them away
as my hands were engaged. I now had the folder in my hand.
This would solve, more than the mystery of his death, the mystery of the festival accounts. I could give the poet details of the
moneys collected on his behalf, though perhaps not the cash. I
hurriedly opened the folder and looked in; the papers were intact, the printed appeal and a list of the donors and the receipt
book; but cash? Not much to be seen, except a bundle of one-
rupee currency notes. I tucked it under my arm and was leaving
when I caught sight of the tiger cub on the small table, covered
over with a handkerchief. He had valued it at two thousand
rupees. I seized it with the covering and quietly went down,
leaving the door ajar. I passed into the side street; the cub, his
masterpiece, was small enough to be hidden under my arms
along with the files. A couple of pedestrians were passing along.
I walked bravely with my articles, dreading lest someone should
be in my office waiting for me. Luckily there was no one. I
quickly opened the roll-top desk, pushed the tiger cub and the
file in, and locked it.

My office became an extension of the Town Police Station. The District Superintendent of Police set himself up in the Queen Anne chair. They had found the grille I had put up between the treadle and the staircase irksome, as it made them go round every time by the side street. It was unlocked and the place was thrown open for the entire city to walk about in. All kinds of people were passing in and out, going upstairs and coming downstairs. It became so crowded that I found it impossible to do any work in the press, and Sastri had no space to stand and set his types. The sanctity of the blue curtain was destroyed, gone for ever. Anyone could push it aside and go up; I dared not ask who he was; he might be a plainclothes police officer, the Coroner's Committee man (there was a body of five to find out and declare the cause of Vasu's death), a newspaper correspondent; a hanger-on, or the thin-legged policemen sent up for sentry duty on the attic landing to watch that no one tampered with evidence. Vasu dead proved a greater nuisance than Vasu alive. Anyone who had had anything to do with him for the past six weeks was summoned to my press by the police. Muthu was there, away from his tea-shop, the poet was there, the journalist was, of course, there, and the elephant doctor and the tailor (who was bewailing all along that he had promised clothes for a wedding and ought to be back at his sewing machine). A police van had gone and brought them all.

Sastri proved to be the shrewdest. The minute he heard of the corpse upstairs he planned his retreat. He hesitated for a moment, smiled to himself and remarked, "I knew he would come to some such end; these people cannot die normally." He had been preparing to work on the fruit-juice labels. He just put his work away, wiped his hand on a rag, and took off his apron; I watched him silently. He went through his process of retreat methodically. He said, "These things happen only in the expected manner. Only I didn't think it would happen so soon and here. What a worry now! Our press has had such an untarnished reputation all through." He sighed and remained silent as if I had been responsible. Confirming this hint, he said broadly, for the hundredth time within the last few months, "On the very first day he came here you should have turned him out. You didn't."

I asked, "What's your plan now?"

"I am going home and then I am catching the afternoon train for Karaikudi. I have to attend my wife's niece's marriage."

"You never told me about it!" I said in surprised anger.

"I'm telling you now," said the imperturbable Sastri. "You were so busy the whole of yesterday that I couldn't get a word with you." He pulled out a yellow wedding invitation and showed it to me as evidence.

"When will you be back?" I asked.

"Well, as soon as the marriage is over," he said and prepared to go. "Our train leaves at one o'clock."

"The police may want you here," I said viciously.

"I have nothing to do with Vasu or the police," he said with a clarity of logic rare under the stress of the present circumstances. It was true. He had resolutely kept away from contacts with Vasu. While all of us were running around him, Sastri alone had maintained a haughty aloofness. No one could ever associate Vasu with Sastri. I had no authority over Sastri. I could not stop him. He went out by the back door to Kabir Street. At the doorway he paused to say, "Anyway, what is the use of my staying here? There is no space for doing any work here." With that he was off.

As I said all my friends were there as if we were assembled for a group photo. Rangi . . . oh, I have forgotten Rangi. After the night's endless gesticulations before the God, she looked jaded in a dull sari, with unkempt hair, and stood in a corner. She would not sit down before so many. The lean man, the Town Inspector, was among those who had to be provided with a seat. The D.S.P. from his seat of honour kept glancing around at us. He had demanded a table and I had to request my neighbour with the Heidelberg to spare me one from his office. He was only too willing to do anything. He looked overawed by the whole business—a murder at such close quarters. He gave me a teak table which the burly D.S.P. heaped with a lot of brown papers and drew up before the Queen Anne chair. To this day I do not understand why he held the inquiry in my office rather than at the police station. Perhaps they wanted to hold us until the body was removed to the mortuary, which was a small tin shed at a corner of the compound of the District Hospital. Under this hot tin roof, there was a long stone table on which Vasu would be laid. I was depressed to think that a man who had twisted iron rods and burst three-inch panel doors with his fist was going to do nothing more than lie still and wait for the doctor to cut him and examine his insides to find out what had caused his death.

At the mortuary, the wise men, five in number, had stood around the stone-topped table, read the report of the pathologist, and declared, "Mr. Vasu of Junagadh died of a concussion received on the right temple on the frontal bone delivered by a blunt instrument. Although there is no visible external injury to the part, the inner skull-covering is severely injured and has resulted in the fatality." In addition to this they had also taken out his stomach contents and sent them for examination to Madras Institute, there to be examined for poisoning. The wise men reserved their final verdict until they should have the report from Madras. Meanwhile they ordered the burial of the body according to Hindu rites in order to facilitate exhumation at a later stage if necessary. At this one of the five demurred, "How can we be sure that the deceased would not have preferred to be cremated?" At this they looked at each other, and since there was no way of ascertaining the wishes of the person concerned, they hesitated for a moment until the foreman said, as if on a sudden revelation, "We shall have no objection to a final disposal of the body in the form of cremation; the present step is only an interim arrangement until we are able to ascertain the causes of the death of aforesaid Vasu with certainty." Everyone grabbed this sentence as a way out.

Assembled at my press, they desperately tried to discover the origin of the brass food-container found in Vasu's room. They kept looking round and asking, "Can anyone throw light on who brought this vessel? Can anyone say to whom it belongs?" They turned the vessel round in their hands, closely looking at it for any signature of ownership. They failed. I could see Rangi squirming in her corner, twisting and untwisting the end of her sari around her finger. She kept throwing anxious glances in my direction and fidgeting; if the police officer had not been so hectically busy writing, bent over his papers, he might have easily declared, "I charge you with being the owner of this brass utensil," and led her off to the lock-up. When I opened my mouth to say something she almost swooned with suspense. But I merely remarked from my seat on the edge of my desk, "I often noticed his food coming to him in that vessel."

"Where was he getting his food from?" An excellent chance to confuse things by making the nearest restaurant busy defending their innocence. I thought over the name of restaurants I might mention. What about the Royal Hindu Restaurant? The owner used to be my customer and had walked out after creating a scene over a slight delay in the delivery of his printed stationery. I dismissed the thought as unworthy, and said, "I've really no idea. The deceased must have been getting his food from various quarters." I spoke breezily. The Superintendent looked up coldly as if to say, "Don't talk more than necessary." But I was in my own place and no one had the right to ask me to shut up. I added, "It doesn't seem as if its lid has been opened." The Superintendent made a note of this also, and handed the vessel around for inspection to the Committee. They all examined it and said, "Yes, the lid does not seem to have been opened." The Superintendent made a note of this again, and then asked, "Shall we open this to see if it has been touched?" "Yes," "Yes," "Yes," "Yes," "Yes." He took a statement from the five to say that the lid had been opened in their presence. They watched with anxious concentration as the lid was prised off. It was placed on the table. The smell of stale food hit the ceiling. A strong-smelling, overspiced, chicken *pulav,* brown and unattractive, was stuffed up to the lid. Everyone peered in, holding his nose. "It has not been touched." The verdict was unanimous. "Shall a sample be sent to Madras?" "No." "Shall we throw this food away?" "No." "What shall be done with it?" "Keep it till the report from Madras is received. If there is suspected poisoning, the food can be analysed."

The Superintendent wrote this down and took their signatures. He passed the container to be sealed in his presence to an orderly, and then the five men appended their initials on the brown paper wrapped around it. The D.S.P. worked like an impersonal machine. He did not want to assume any personal responsibility for any step and he did not want to omit any possible line of investigation, always laying the responsibility on the five wise men chosen for the purpose. If they had said, "Put this Nataraj in a sack and seal him up; we may need him in that state for further investigation," he would have unhesitatingly obeyed. Sealing up was the order of the day. Vasu's room was sealed, the food-container was sealed, and every conceivable article around had been sealed.

The Superintendent's writing went on far into the night; he must have written several thousand words. Each one assembled there had to say when he saw Vasu last, why, and what were that worthy man's last words. While Rangi totally denied having seen him last evening, the others were not in such a lucky position, the whole lot of them having gone there in a body after seeing the Superintendent. They gave a sustained account of what he had said to them. It was computed that he must have died at about eleven at night, and where was I at eleven?—at home sleeping on the *pyol* after seeing my wife off to the temple. My wife was brought in by the back door to corroborate me, my son too. Fortunately no one knew of my last visit to the attic. I bore in mind our adjournment lawyer's dictum, "Don't say more than you are asked for."

The only satisfaction I felt was that our Town Inspector was treated as one of us, made to sit in our group and answer questions before the Committee. Normally they would have let him handle the investigation, but the situation was no different; he was also one of us, an aggrieved party. His hand was in a sling and his finger was encased in a plaster cast, having suffered a slight fracture. He had to clear himself first—a most awkward thing. When his turn came to make a statement, he began bombastically, "I was ordered to supervise the peace and security arrangements on the Market Road on ____ at ____ when I had a call at the control room from our District Superintendent of Police ordering me further to investigate a complaint of threat to the safety of the crowd from one Mr. Vasu of Junagadh. When I went up to question the said person and take charge of his licensed weapon, he assumed a threatening attitude and actually assaulted the officer on duty, causing a grave injury." He held up the bandaged part of himself as an exhibit. And then, according to him, he went away to take all reasonable precautions for the peaceful conduct of the procession. He intended to file a complaint as soon as they were free in the morning, and proceed against the same person officially for assaulting an officer on duty. He failed to mention that he had told Vasu before leaving, "I will get you for it."

I and Muthu discussed it later, when the incident was officially closed. If anyone had breathed a word then, it might have complicated the Inspector's version and placed him definitely on the defensive. But everyone was considerate. Still, the Inspector had to prove where he was at the time of Vasu's death, which occurred two hours after he had been visited by the Inspector. He explained that he had left the security arrangements in the hands of his assistant while he had gone in the police car to the District Superintendent's residence to report to him, and then to the District Headquarters Hospital to secure medical attention. He could cite both the District Superintendent of Police and the medical officer on duty at the casualty section as witnesses. But still Muthu felt, as he confessed later, "What prevented the man from sending someone to do the job? A number of them might have gone and overpowered the man. I don't say it is wrong, but they might have done it, and hit his skull with a blunt instrument."

During the following days the air became thick with suspicion. Each confided to the other when the third was out of earshot. Sen, who walked down the road with me for a breath of fresh air after the police left us, said, "That tea-shop man Muthu . . . I have my own doubts. People in rural areas are habitually vindictive and might do anything. How many murders are committed in those areas! I won't say in this instance it was wrong. Someone has actually done a public service. I wouldn't blame anyone."

"What would be Muthu's interest in murdering Vasu?"

"Don't forget that the elephant was his and that he was anxious to save its life at any cost. He could have just sneaked up. Where was he at eleven o'clock?" He cast his mind back to remember if Muthu had by any chance slipped away from the procession. He gave it up, as they had been too much engrossed in the procession to note each other's movements.

The poet came to me three days later all alone. "I was with Sen this afternoon in his house in New Extension, and, do you know, I noticed in a corner of his room, amidst a lot of old paper, a blunt thing—a long iron bolt which they use on railway sleepers. He looked embarrassed when I asked why he had it. Easiest thing for him to have slipped upstairs, gone up from behind . . . I don't blame him. He had stood enough insults from that man. I knew that Sen would do something terrible sooner or later . . . I wouldn't blame him."

I knew that they were all unanimous in suspecting me when I was not there. I could almost hear what they were saying about me. "Never knew he could go so far, but, poor fellow, he had stood enough from him, having made the original blunder of showing him hospitality. Whether he took him in as a tenant or just as a friend, who can say? Who will let his house free of rent to another nowadays? Whatever it may be, it is none of our business why he gave him his attic. But how that man tortured poor Nataraj! Poor man, his patience was strained. Deft work, eh? What do you say? Smashed the vital nerve in his brain without drawing a drop of blood! Never knew Nataraj could employ his hand so effectively! Hee, hee!"

My wife said the same thing to me that night when I went home. Our friendly relations were resumed the moment she heard that there was a dead body in the press and that the police had assembled in my office. Since the Rangi episode, the first words uttered between us had been my urgent invitation to her to come and say where she had seen me at eleven o'clock on the previous night. She hesitated, wrung her hands in fear and despair. "Oh, why should you have got mixed up in all this affair? Couldn't you have minded your own business like a hundred others?" I was very humbled now, and very pleased that at least over Vasu's dead body we were shaking hands again. I had been gnawed by a secret fear that we might never resume friendly relations and that all was over between us. She rubbed it in now. "That woman, and all sorts of people—what was your business with them really?"

I had no satisfactory answer for her, and so said, "I have no time to explain all that now; the D.S.P. is waiting; you will have to come and say where I was last night at eleven o'clock."

"How could I know?" she asked. "I will tell him that I didn't see you."

"Yes, say that and see me hanged, and then you will proba-bly be able to collect a handsome insurance on my life." She screamed and covered her ears. "You could also describe how you deserted me on the *pyol* to guard the house and went out. It will do you good to speak the truth. And if you remember your visit to the temple, you will probably also remember hav-ing seen Rangi there, so that you will not be tempted to say I had gone out with her."

"I didn't see her at the temple," said my wife simply. She had got out of her suspicious mood of yesterday but had not de-cided to let go of it fully.

I said, "While we are bantering here, the police . . ."

"Why should they believe what I say? Won't they think you have tutored me?"

"Oh, it is only a formality, they are not analysing evidence of any sort. They will record whatever you say or I say or anyone says, and that is all that they want at this stage, so you had bet-ter come along." She was very nervous at coming before the Superintendent, but she would not hear of the public recording her statement at home. She said, "After all these years of hon-est and reputable living, we don't want the police marching in and out. Even in the worst days when the property was parti-tioned no one dreamt of asking the police to come. We don't want to do that now." She preferred to walk across the street when the neighbours were not looking and slip into my press by the back door and face the police.

That night I went home at eleven o'clock. Babu had gone to sleep. My wife said, "Hush, speak gently. Babu wouldn't sleep. He was too excited about everything. I managed to send him to sleep by saying that it is all false and so forth. But he is terribly excited about everything . . . and, and, feels proud that you killed a *rakshasa* single-handed! At least you have Babu to admire you."

"For God's sake don't let him spread that sort of talk. The noose may be put around my neck."

She sighed deeply and said, "A lot of people are saying that. After that rent control case . . ."

"Oh, shut up," I cried impatiently. "What nonsense is this!"

"You may close the mouth of an oven, but how can you close the mouth of a town?" she said, quoting a proverb.

I saw myself as others saw me, and was revolted by the picture.

CHAPTER TWELVE

At first I resented the idea of being thought of as a murderer. Gradually it began to look not so improbable. Why not? It had been an evening of strange lapses. I could remember nothing of what I had said or done to cause the fuss around me that evening at the temple hall. Later was it quite impossible that I had battered someone's skull and remembered nothing? Going over my own actions step by step, I remembered I had gone up the staircase stealthily, opened the door on the landing. So far all was clear. The procession was passing in the street below. Vasu lay in a long chair beside the window. I had crawled towards his gun and run out when the alarm-clock screamed. Between my entrance and exit I remembered holding the gun at Vasu's head until the lights of the procession vanished. Perhaps while he slept I had rammed the butt of the gun into his skull. Who could say? But what about the time of his death? The doctor had declared that the man must have died at eleven, long before I had sneaked up the attic stairs. But the doctor might have hazarded a guess; it was one more item in a long list of conjectures!

I had clung to the hope that Rangi had poisoned Vasu and then smashed his head, but the chemical examiner at Madras reported, "No trace of poisoning." With that the last trace of hope for myself was also gone. While I sat in my press all alone I caught myself reconstructing again and again that midnight visit to the attic, trying to gain a clear picture of the whole scene, but each time I found it more confounding. When people passed along Market Road and looked at me, I averted my head. I knew what they were saying, "There he sits. He ought really to be hanged for murder." My friends of Mempi village never came near me again. They had had enough trouble with the police as the result of knowing me and visiting my press. "That press! Lord Shiva! An accursed spot! Keep away from it!"

There was not a soul with whom I could discuss the question. Sen avoided me. The poet was not to be seen. He took another route nowadays to the Municipal School. During my morning trip to the river and back no one stopped to have a word with me. The adjournment lawyer and the others hurried on when they saw me in the distance. All the same one morning I accosted the adjournment lawyer at the bend of the street where the barber's house abutted. He pretended not to see me and tried to pass. "Sir," I cried, stepping in front of him.

He was flurried, "Ah, Nataraj! Didn't notice . . . I was thinking of something . . ."

"I want to ask you . . . ," I began.

"What about? What about?" he asked feverishly. "You see I am out of touch with criminal practice. You should really consult . . ."

"Consult? For what purpose?" I asked. "I have no problem."

"Oh, yes, yes, I know," he cried, fidgeting uneasily. "I remember that they left an open verdict, nothing was imputed or proved. After all who can be sure?"

"Oh, forget it," I said with the casual ease of a seasoned homicide. "It is not that. I am more worried about the collection of dues from my customers. When did you celebrate your daughter's marriage? Months ago! Why don't you pay my charges for printing those invitation cards? What are you waiting for?"

"Oh, yes, by all means," he said, edging away.

"I have no one in the press to help me. Even Sastri has left me. You had better send the cash along instead of waiting for me to send someone to collect it." A touch of aggression was creeping into my speech nowadays. My line of thinking was, "So be it. If I have rid the world of Vasu, I have achieved something. If people want to be squeamish, they are welcome to be so, but let no one expect me to be apologetic for what I have done." I hardened myself with such reflections, and suffered at the same time. The press was silent. I kept my office open at the usual hours. Visitors were few. I spent my time attempting to read Tolstoy's *War and Peace* (discovered among the seventy philosophical volumes in the family lumber room) and diverting myself by following the complex fortunes of Russian nobility on the battlefields of ancient Europe.

I caught sight of the poet one morning beyond the fountain. Before he could avoid me and take another route to his school I ran forward and blocked his way. I implored him to come into the press and seated him in the Queen Anne chair.

"What has happened to you all?" I asked.

"They have given me eight more hours of work a week, with so many teachers absent!"

"Ah, innocent poet!" I thought. "What clumsy guile you have cultivated within these last weeks!" I asked aloud, "What about Sen?"

"I don't know, he was expecting a call from a Madras Paper."

"Don't lie!" I cried, suddenly losing my temper. "Haven't I seen him sneaking in next door to get some work done on the Heidelberg? You people are avoiding me. You think I am a murderer." He remained silent. I checked myself when I noticed the terror in his eyes. He glanced anxiously over his shoulder at the doorway, interpreting the glint in my eyes as maniacal. I wanted to speak to him about the accounts entombed in the green folder, about the moneys collected on his behalf and spent by Vasu, and to explain to him about the tiger cub I had seized; but all I could produce was a shout of abuse at the world in general. I realized that I was frightening the poet. I modified my tone to a soft whisper, smiled, and patted his back. I said, "I want to give you a present out of the money collected for your benefit. Something in kind, something salvaged." I fixed him with a look lest he should try to escape, flicked open the roll-top desk, and brought out the stuffed tiger cub. I pulled off the kerchief covering and held it to him. He looked transfixed.

"A tiger! What for?"

"It is yours, take it," I said. "He valued it at two thousand. Something at least . . ."

He gazed back at me as if noticing in my eyes for the first time unplumbed depths of lunacy. He pleaded desperately, "No, I don't want it. I don't need it. I do not want anything. Thanks." He suddenly shot out of the Queen Anne chair, dashed out, and was soon lost in the crowd on Market Road.

"Poet! Poet!" I cried feebly. In addition to thinking me a murderer, perhaps he thought I had embezzled his funds and was now playing a prank on him. This was the greatest act of destruction that the Man-eater had performed; he had destroyed my name, my friendships, and my world. The thought was too much for me. Hugging the tiger cub, I burst into tears.

While I was in this state Sastri parted the curtain and entered. "I came by the back door," he explained briefly.

"Ah, Sastri!" I cried in sheer joy. "I thought you would never come back."

He was business-like, and turned a blind eye on my emotional condition. "After the marriage at Karaikudi, my wife insisted on going on a pilgrimage to Rameshwaram, and to a dozen other places. A couple of children fell ill on the way. I was fretting all along to get back, but you know how our women are! Sickness or not, my wife insisted on visiting every holy place she had heard of in her life. After all, we get a chance to travel only once in a while . . ."

"You could have dropped me a postcard from somewhere."

"True," he said, "but when one is travelling it is impossible to sit down and compose a letter, and the idea gets postponed." He took out of his pocket a tiny packet containing a pinch of sacred ash and vermilion and held it out to me, saying, "Offerings from all the temples mixed together." I daubed the holy dust on my forehead.

He noticed the tiger cub on my lap and exclaimed, "Ah, what a tiny tiger!" as if humouring a child. His silver-rimmed spectacles wobbled and his face was slightly flushed. I knew he was shuddering at the sight of the stuffed animal, but still he pretended to be interested in it and stretched out his hand as if to touch it. He was trying to please me. He said, "It must have been a pretty baby in the forest, but what a monster it would have become when it grew up! Did *he* give it to you?" he asked after a pause. I couldn't explain that I had stolen it from the dead man, and so I remained silent.

"I meant to give it to the poet," I said, "but he spurned it and went away." I was on the point of breaking down at the thought. "He may not come again."

"It is natural that a poet should feel scared of a tiger. In any case what could he do with it?"

"He may never come this way again."

"So much the better for us. Anyone who refuses to come here and waste our time must be viewed as a well-wisher. K.J. is our customer, and you may be sure he will always come to us."

"Naturally. Where else can he get the magenta, even if he wants to leave us?"

"People who have business with us will always come and keep coming."

"Everyone thinks that this is a murderer's press," I said gloomily.

He gently laughed at the notion and said, "They are fools who think so, but sooner or later even they will know the truth."

"What truth?" I asked.

"Rangi was with him when he died. You know I am on the temple committee," began Sastri, "and she came to see me on business last evening. I had a feeling all along that she was hiding some information. I refused to listen to her problem unless she told me the truth. Much against my principles, I called her inside the house, seated her on a mat, gave her coffee and betel leaves to chew, and induced her to speak. My wife understood why I was asking this woman in and treated her handsomely on the whole."

"What did Rangi say?" I asked impatiently.

"It seems that evening she carried a hamper of food to him. He refused to eat the food, being in a rage over many things. Rangi had perhaps mixed some sleeping drug with the food, and had hoped that he would be in a stupor when the procession passed under his window. That was her ruse for saving the elephant that night. But the man would not touch the food!"

"He might not have felt hungry," I said, remembering the eatables that I had plied him with earlier that day.

"It may have been so, but it embarrassed the woman because she had duties at the temple that night. She was really bothered as to how she was going to get out of the place. When he understood that the procession might start late, he set the alarm-clock and sat himself in his easy chair. He drew another chair beside his, and commanded the woman to sit down with a fan in hand and keep the mosquitoes off him. He hated mosquitoes, from what the woman tells me. He cursed the police for their intrusion, which had made him break his cot-frame to show off his strength and now compelled him to stretch himself in an easy chair instead of sleeping in his cot protected by a mosquito-net. Armed with the fan, the woman kept away the mosquitoes. He dozed off. After a little time she dozed off too, having had a fatiguing day, as you know, and the fanning must have ceased; during this pause the mosquitoes returned in a battalion for a fresh attack. Rangi was awakened by the man yelling, 'Damn these mosquitoes!' She saw him flourish his arms like a madman, fighting them off as they buzzed about his ears to suck his blood. Next minute she heard a sharp noise like a thunder-clap. The man had evidently trapped a couple of mosquitoes which had settled on his forehead by bringing the flat of his palm with all his might on top of them. The woman switched on the light and saw two mosquitoes plastered on his brow. It was also the end of Vasu," concluded Sastri, and added, "That fist was meant to batter thick panels of teak and iron . . ."

"He had one virtue, he never hit anyone with his hand, whatever the provocation," I said, remembering his voice.

"Because," said Sastri puckishly, "he had to conserve all that might for his own destruction. Every demon appears in the world with a special boon of indestructibility. Yet the universe has survived all the *rakshasas* that were ever born. Every demon carries within him, unknown to himself, a tiny seed of self-destruction, and goes up in thin air at the most unexpected moment. Otherwise what is to happen to humanity?" He nar-

rated again for my benefit the story of Bhasmasura the uncon-
querable, who scorched everything he touched, and finally
reduced himself to ashes by placing the tips of his fingers on his
own head. Sastri stood brooding for a moment and turned to
go. He held an edge of the curtain, but before vanishing behind
it he said, "We must deliver K.J.'s labels this week. I will set up
everything. If you will print the first colour . . ."

"When you are gone for lunch it will be drying, and ready
for second printing when you return. Yes, Sastri, I am at your
service," I said.

NOW AVAILABLE FROM PENGUIN CLASSICS

The Guide
A Novel

Formerly India's most corrupt tourist guide, Raju—just released from prison—seeks refuge in an abandoned temple. Mistaken for a holy man, he plays the part and succeeds so well that God himself intervenes to put Raju's newfound sanctity to the test. R. K. Narayan's most celebrated novel, *The Guide* won him the award of the Sahitya Akademi, India's National Academy of Letters, his country's highest literary honor.

ISBN 978-0-14-303964-8

PENGUIN
BOOKS

NOW AVAILABLE FROM PENGUIN CLASSICS

Malgudi Days

Introducing this collection of stories, R. K. Narayan describes how in India "the writer has only to look out of the window to pick up a character and thereby a story." Powerful, magical portraits of all kinds of people, and comprising stories written over almost forty years, *Malgudi Days* presents Narayan's imaginary city in full color, revealing the essence of India and of human experience.

ISBN 978-0-14-303965-5

PENGUIN
BOOKS

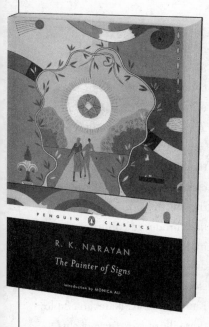

NOW AVAILABLE FROM PENGUIN CLASSICS

The Ramayana
A Shortened Modern Prose Version of the Indian Epic

ISBN 978-0-14-303967-9

A sweeping tale of abduction, battle, and courtship played out in a universe of deities and demons, *The Ramayana* is familiar to virtually every Indian. Although the Sanskrit original was composed by Valmiki around the fourth century BC, poets have produced countless versions in different languages. Here, drawing on the work of an eleventh-century poet called Kamban, R. K. Narayan employs the skills of a master novelist to re-create the excitement he found in the original.

PENGUIN
BOOKS